CRITICAL AC̲
HOWEY'S HIS̲

"*Sheik's Glory* is a story full of spirit, one that will capture your heart!"
—Diane Hager, Bestselling Author Of
Courtesan

"Carole Howey weaves magic with words....*Touched By Moonlight* is a delight, a beautifully written book that sparkles with wit, wisdom, and plain good fun. A wonderful love story not to be missed."
—Katherine Kingsley, Bestselling Author Of
No Greater Love

"*Sweet Chance* is a delightful, well-paced, and charming Western romance!"
—*Romantic Times*

"With its witty dialogue and intriguing love-hate relationship, *Sheik's Promise* demands your attention from beginning to end."
—*Romantic Times*

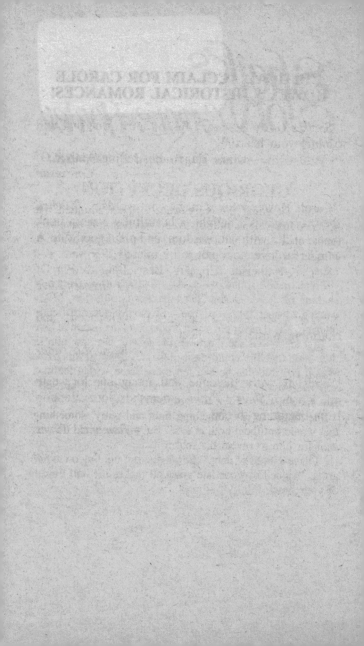

Sheik's Glory CAROLE HOWEY

Bestselling Author Of _Touched By Moonlight_

GLORIOUS DECEPTION

"I'm not doing this very well," Flynn admitted. He sounded more than a little awkward, which might have been an act on his part, but it nevertheless made Missy warm to him all the more. "It's been a very long time since I—I mean—"

Flynn made a sound of disgust and turned away from her, shaking his head. Despite her terror and confusion, Missy wanted to hear the words he was having such difficulty uttering. She'd never put much credence in the notion of love at first sight, but she'd known the instant she saw him in the stable that she could easily lose her heart to this man. Was it possible that he had felt those same strong feelings and was even now struggling to understand them himself? Her mouth went dry at the possibility.

She longed to say something light and witty, something that would put them both at ease. But all she could do was wait for him to reveal his soul to her.

"I have a letter of debt," he whispered, holding on to her arms, "signed by your late uncle. It makes me half owner of your ranch."

Other *Leisure* and *Love Spell* Books by
Carole Howey:
TOUCHED BY MOONLIGHT
SWEET CHANCE
SHEIK'S PROMISE

CAROLE HOWEY

Sheik's Glory

LEISURE BOOKS **NEW YORK CITY**

For Linda, who made me not the youngest and not the only girl.

A LEISURE BOOK®

February 1996

Published by

Dorchester Publishing Co., Inc.
276 Fifth Avenue
New York, NY 10001

If you purchased this book without a cover you should be aware that this book is stolen property. It was reported as "unsold and destroyed" to the publisher and neither the author nor the publisher has received any payment for this "stripped book."

Copyright © 1996 by Carole Mrak Howey

All rights reserved. No part of this book may be reproduced or transmitted in any form or by any electronic or mechanical means, including photocopying, recording or by any information storage and retrieval system, without the written permission of the Publisher, except where permitted by law.

The name "Leisure Books" and the stylized "L" with design are trademarks of Dorchester Publishing Co., Inc.

Printed in the United States of America.

ACKNOWLEDGMENTS

My deepest gratitude to my family, especially Bob, Techno-mage and Spouse Extraordinaire. Thanks also to (in alphabetical order): Rose Bengardino, Joyce Cantor, Judy DiCanio, Eve Homan, Kate Howell, and Victoria Roza, for the laughs, the love, and the editorial input; to Laura Lee Lemmon and Ted Nation (my own personal four-wheel cowboy), for horse sense; to M. Phyllis Lose, D.V.M., and her wonderful book for broodmare information; to Bobby Lee Whitmire, for being the perennial, jaundiced, right-wing curmudgeon offering tea, sympathy, and the occasional (if overly enthusiastic) well-aimed boot to the rear; and to the loyal Ladies and Knights of The Keep, most notably Missy's "Auntie Dora."

Sheik's Glory

Part One

Sic Transit Gloria

Chapter One

February, 1892

Missy Cannon's first mistake was wearing gloves to the Louisville breeders' auction. Thanks to her inclination to touch everything, they were already stained and wilted, and she'd only been out for two hours. Her second mistake was slipping away from Joshua Manners and Mr. and Mrs. Foster, who had escorted her. She wondered, as she entered the busy stable behind the auction arena, if she was about to embark on her third error of the young day.

She was sure of it.

A nearby gray yearling lifted its black, broomlike tail and released an avalanche of excrement. Missy was not quick enough to react, and the droppings exploded on the cobblestone floor, spattering fresh manure onto the ribboned hem of her last clean dress, formerly a suitable

13

shade of navy blue. She eyed the damage sadly. Allyn
had scolded her that very morning before they'd left for
the auction about the further destruction of her wardrobe.

"Hey! Gangway!"

Missy started at the harsh order. A surly groom
pushed by her leading a reluctant gelding, not seeming
to notice, or care, that she was a lady.

"'Scuse me." His mutter seemed more a taunt than
a courtesy. The horse, adding injury to insult, stepped
on her toe as he moved forward. She smothered a mild
curse at the familiar pain. Her black velvet pumps were
ruined now, of course. Another casualty of her folly. Her
toe throbbed besides, but that, she knew, was not why
she felt like crying.

"Bugger off!"

Missy jerked her head up at the crude sentiment and
glared at the groom. "I beg your pardon!" she exclaimed with a haughty disdain learned from Allyn.
"How dare you!"

"Bugger off, I tell ya!"

The fellow she'd addressed looked abashed at her rebuke, but clearly it had not been he who had made the
vulgar remark, for the second time she heard it, she saw
that his lips did not move. Moreover, the words had
obviously been uttered by someone far younger than he.
A boy. The man before her glanced over his shoulder at
the stall on the far side, then shrugged his sloped shoulders before moving along without another word to her.
Huffing with sudden humiliation, Missy hurried away
from him. Since he went forward, she moved along
back, deeper into the cavernous stable.

"Wet behind the ears?" A man's voice rasped an
ugly chuckle. "More like he's still wettin' his drawers,
wouldn't you say, Hike? How old are you, boy?"

Missy stood beside the closed door of the stall from

which both the coarse language and the rough voice had come. Inside, a horse nickered nervously. Missy felt a knot form in her stomach, although she was not sure why.

"Never you mind how old I am!" It was a young voice that answered the rough one. Painfully young. Too young. "I'm here, and I'm lookin' after this horse. Why don't you mind your own damn business?"

Missy winced at the swear word uttered by the otherwise sweet, if youthful, voice. The boy who used it could not know how ugly he sounded. Whatever would his mother think?

"Well, you look after her good, 'cos she's headed for the glue factory," another older voice remarked, taking unmistakable glee in reporting his news. "I got a order right here, says we're to take her at the close of business if she ain't sold. This'll be her third day on the block, and no one's come close to an opening bid."

"She'll sell." There was more bravado than confidence in the youth's retort.

"Ain't sold yet," the first voice pointed out.

"They put 'er up at the end of the day," the boy complained. "When everybody's gone home for supper."

"Everybody but you." There was contempt in the older man's observation. "I guess you live with this here nag, don't you, boy? You sure smell like it."

"I could do plenty worse."

Missy could not help smiling at the lad's cheeky implication, even as she questioned his good sense in baiting the men.

"Well, I guess you better find yourself someplace else to bed down after today." The laughter of the two men was cruel. Missy winced at the grating sound, unable to deny a stab of pity for the boy, and for the animal he defended.

15

"She'll sell." There was even less conviction in the quaking young voice this time.

"She won't hold to service, and she shows a lot of daylight," sneered one of the mare's detractors. "Buyers ain't blind."

The boy apparently had no answer for that. Missy ruminated: a mare with overly long legs, especially one who couldn't carry a foal, was next to useless in thoroughbred breeding. She started to edge away from the stall as quietly as she could.

"You brush and curry her good, so she'll be all pretty for the glue wagon," the second man advised. "We'll be back for her at four."

Missy stopped and shuddered, not from the February chill, although it was cold and drafty in the bustling stable. She hated to think of a creature as noble as a horse ending its life in so mean a fashion, even a leggy, barren mare.

"Glue wagon, hell!" The boy's voice was hostile and shaking. Missy understood; she almost felt like crying herself. "She'll sell. You'll see. She'll draw an opening bid, and then some, and I'll jam your words down your throat, you sorry-assed sons of bitches!"

My, but the lad had a mouth on him!

"Why, you—"

The stable door beside her thumped and rattled. The boy's groan of pain exactly harmonized with the small cry in Missy's heart.

Don't go in there. Allyn might have been beside her, urging prudence. *This isn't your concern.*

"Give 'im one for me, Hike," the other man crowed. "Wiry little bugger. Hold him for me while I break his smart-assed little jaw."

Missy threw her shoulder against the door and it slid back so quickly that she fell face first into the stall.

Mistake number four.

16

"What the—"

"Get out of here!" she gasped, trying to rise, struggling to regain the breath that had been knocked out of her. "Leave this boy al—"

"Leggo, dammit!"

Missy looked up and saw the small figure in ragged clothing twist away from his captors who, unfortunately, were neither as old nor as inconsequential as they had sounded from the other side of the door. The boy sent a spirited kick into the shin of the man who would have rearranged his facial features before he scampered behind the mare, back by the stall window.

What was wrong with that boy? she thought, irritated. Why hadn't he run out, as he should have?

"Who's this bitch?" Hike growled, and Missy felt a pair of strong hands lift her roughly from the straw and shake her like a rag doll. She could not take in enough breath to give him a sharp answer, much as she longed to. She struggled weakly against him, but he only laughed at her efforts.

"Well, I'll be! A hellcat! And dressed like a queen, to boot. Who is she, boy? Your whorin' ma?"

"I'm not a *whore*!" Missy's breath returned in time for her to shout the final word with authority. Hike, no doubt as surprised as she, released her. Her knees buckled, but she kept on her feet, swaying.

"Look, and she's drunk, besides." His companion laughed. "Would you do me for a nickel, sweetheart? A penny?"

Her arm was wrenched from behind, and a man's face pressed close to her cheek, his foul breath a cloud of gray mist in the cold stall.

"Naw, two bits, at least. Can't you see how fine she's dressed?" Hike laughed. It was a sound that would peel paint. Missy scraped her heel down her captor's shin.

"Eeyowwww!" The hands released her as if she'd

17

suddenly become red-hot. Encouraged by her success, she spun about until she faced both men, her back to the increasingly anxious mare. She fixed a grim look on her face, hoping to mask her fear with it.

"Get out!" she bellowed at the two men, exercising a commanding tone that not even the most recalcitrant yearling ever resisted. "And don't come—"

"Hie! Hie!"

It was the boy, and he sounded frantic. She turned to look, but something knocked her shoulder from behind, hard, forcing her down onto the used straw on the floor. The strength of the blow numbed her for an instant before the hot bolt of pain surged through her.

Realization was slow to take hold as she lay there in pain, but she'd trained enough horses to know that the mare behind her had, in its sudden panic, reared and struck her.

"Glory! Down!" Through her swimming consciousness and the red glare of fresh pain, Missy heard the boy try frantically to calm the animal. He wasn't having much success, apparently, for the floor thundered at her ear as the horse's hooves landed close to her head, over and over. Must roll away, she thought. She tried to move. She could not command her limbs. At any moment those pummeling hooves would strike her, and she'd be dead where she lay.

"Damn fools!"

Before she could catalog the new voice, except to recognize it as male, she was seized by the shoulders. She hurt too much even to cry out against the treatment. She was dragged a good distance across the fouled straw, then dropped unceremoniously like a sack of grain.

She struggled against her cumbersome skirt to sit up, hoping to breathe, hoping to live past the pain, and cursing silently at the foolish bustle that hampered her efforts. It had shifted to the side, where it had no business being. She hated the infernal things, anyway. Back home in Dakota, she never wore them except maybe to church on Sundays. When she'd been a lady's maid to Allyn Cameron back in Philadelphia, she'd never had need for one. Truth to tell, she didn't know why she needed one now, except as tribute to the gods of fashion. It was more troublesome than it was attractive in any case, especially just now.

Why on earth was she thinking about bustles? Here she was in a stinking stall with her shoulder on fire. Gingerly she sank back against a small pile of straw. Ordinarily she found the various smells of horses to be, on the whole, rather pleasing, but combined with the unrelenting waves of pain, they made her want to retch.

"Calm that horse, boy, or it'll be the worse for both of you." The new voice was deep and clear, like a rain-filled quarry. It was also more than a little annoyed. Missy wished she could crawl away without being noticed, but figured her chances of that were slim, at best. Her shoulder throbbed so from the mare's kick that she saw stars dance in the darkness around her.

Missy closed her eyes again and swallowed hard to keep from being sick from the pain. The sounds of a hasty retreat brushed past her ear, and she knew the men who had baited the boy were gone. Good riddance. She'd wanted to take a stick to them for what they'd done, but she would have to satisfy herself that they'd been scared off. She tried to get up.

"Oh!"

She hadn't meant to cry out loud, but the burning pain in her shoulder squeezed the sound from her lips.

"Trying to kill yourself? Don't move. It's dislocated."

Missy knew it was so. She'd known it before she heard the words. She wanted to retort to the terse, dispassionate voice, but she was afraid she'd cry out again

19

if she opened her mouth. Instead she tried to open her eyes.

She was sure she hadn't succeeded, for all she saw before her, like an illusion born of pain, was the face of an angel. An angry angel, but an angel nonetheless. She might have believed she'd died and gone to heaven but for the stern, censuring expression on the angel's face, the unremitting stench all around her, and the constant, tearing ache in her shoulder.

She remembered a picture from her childhood which had always held a morbid fascination for her, from the old family Bible, the only memento she had of her deceased Georgia kin. The bookplate was a fanciful rendering of the angel whom God had expelled from heaven. She could not recall his name, but that seemed unimportant. What was important was that the angel had had an ascetic, yet oddly sensual, sculpted face: hollow cheeks, a perfect cleft chin, a high, noble brow ridge, and intense, deeply set eyes. His hair had been fair and curly, piling perfection on top of perfection.

But had his eyes been the lush, endless blue of the replica before her?

How could they have? she chided herself. It was a print, not a painting.

The angel spoke.

"What kind of a damn fool are you, ma'am? That horse could have killed you. And those men . . ."

His reprimand trailed off, as if he figured she needed no enlightenment as to their intentions. Missy's delusion was effectively shattered. Her shoulder ached again, and she felt sick, besides.

"Let—let me up."

"Best lie still till I fix you. That shoulder's bad."

Flynn Muldaur knelt beside the woman and pressed her backward with a slight pressure against her breastbone. She was smaller than she'd seemed moments ago when she'd turned on those two fools in the stall. And weaker. His hand went gentle, to his surprise, when he touched her. Weak? This woman? Not likely.

So this is Melissa J. Cannon, he thought, cautiously feeling around her injured shoulder for the damage. Orphaned at a young age by the War between the States. Trainer of horses, specialty thoroughbred stock. Former owner, with Allyn Cameron, now Allyn Cameron Manners, of the stallion Sheik, who'd won the Triple Crown and the Travers in '89, and races since too numerous to count. Current owner of the C-Bar-C ranch, just outside of Rapid City, South Dakota.

For now.

Melissa Cannon held her breath. She squeezed her eyes and her mouth shut tight. She was scared, he guessed, with a twinge of pity. But she looked as if she'd rather die of the pain than admit it.

She was prettier than he'd expected, thank God, even with her face all puckered like a dried piece of fruit. She looked smaller, too; he'd been told that Melissa J. Cannon was quite an armful of woman. So far, though, she'd lived up to her reputation in every other regard: blunt, outrageous, unpredictable. He'd followed her when she left the auction area, for no better reason than to discover where she might be going, and he was chagrined but not overly surprised to see her make for the stable. What had surprised him was to find her in a stall defending a foulmouthed urchin against two boorish ruffians.

Flynn felt a smile test the muscles of his face as he surveyed the wreckage that was Miss Melissa Cannon. She was wearing a bonnet that had once, no doubt, been a stylish trig, but it was sadly smashed and sat at a queer angle on her dark mass of hair. Her face was the golden brown of one who spent much time in the sun without benefit of either hat or parasol, but the hue of her skin was both becoming and strangely fitting. Her clothing was in ruins.

She was certainly no lady. Not in the accepted sense, in any event. Flynn could not envision her, for example, participating in such time-honored feminine rites as afternoon tea with the minister's wife, or presiding over mindless chatter in a drawing room. Not like Madeleine . . .

So much the better, he thought, shutting that door in his mind. It would make his task much easier. His tasks.

"This is going to hurt," he informed her, aware that the fact caused him an unexpected, even an unwelcome, regret. "But I can set it back."

"No!" In sudden panic, she grabbed his lapel with her left hand, and her gray eyes grew wide and wet. They reminded Flynn of the silvery iridescence of abalone. She was afraid. Well, she had a right to be. He'd seen men who'd fainted, heard men who'd roared bloody blasphemy when their shoulders were wrenched by unholy force back into their sockets. Her look of terror, and his own recollections, so disturbed him that he looked away.

"Trust me." God, had he really said that to her? Him, Flynn Muldaur?

With but another small whimper of weak protest, she released his coat and closed her eyes. She was resigned, it seemed. Against his will, Flynn felt a surge of admiration for her. He took a deep breath himself and positioned his hands on her arm and shoulder.

"Ready?" He forced a light tone to mask his emotions.

She gave a single, hesitant nod, and it was the last thing he saw before he blacked out.

Chapter Two

Missy did not see the blow that cast her angel down hard on the straw, but with the boy standing over her, brandishing a wooden bucket, she quickly deduced what had happened.

"He hurt you, miss?" His lower lip was set and quivering.

From the floor of the stable, the child looked like a spindly giant. His thin legs were splayed like a reckless buccaneer's and he clutched his unlikely weapon in one hand as if wielding a mace. She realized, staring at him, that he was much smaller than he at first had looked. And probably a good deal younger.

"He was—he was helping me," she managed to gasp. She could not be angry with her gallant young cavalier, who no doubt thought he'd rescued her from the man's evil designs.

"Helping you?" The boy's features clouded with dismay. "But I thought—"

"He was about to slip my shoulder back into place, until you clouted him. Help him. I—I can't move."

The boy's look became guarded. "Where're those other fellows?"

"They ran off." Missy tried to control her urge to cry out in pain. "This one came to help. See—see if you can bring him around. If you didn't kill him, that is."

"Oh, gol . . ." The boy tossed his bucket aside as if it, and not he, had given offense, and he knelt in the straw beside the angel. His clothing, Missy noticed, was threadbare, besides looking as though it belonged to someone far smaller than he.

"Hey!" He shook him. "Wake up, mister! It ain't but a knot, miss. See?"

Missy craned her neck, afraid to move more than that. There was a knot on the angel's head, all right. Missy had seen full skeins of tangled wool yarn that weren't as big. Or as bloody.

"Dear lord," she muttered, feeling light-headed at the sight.

"Derlord?" the boy echoed, with a frown on his dirty face. "That his name?"

"N-No." Missy stiffened against another surge of pain and prayed for patience. "His name is—is—oh, I don't know what his name is. Wake him, please, uh . . ." She realized, annoyed, that she did not know the boy's name either. She'd gotten herself injured and had ruined an otherwise perfectly good dress over a boy she did not even know and a horse who'd kicked her for thanks. She wanted to laugh at her foolishness, but the relentless, burning ache in her shoulder reminded her that she had little to laugh about.

"Gideon," the boy supplied, sounding glad that at last

24

he'd been given a task within his means. "My name's Gideon."

"Gideon what?"

"Just Gideon."

"Well, 'Just Gideon,' " Missy breathed, feeling as if her shoulder were packed in embers. "I suggest you revive our angel over here, and quickly. I do believe— I do believe I'm going to faint, myself."

Missy had never fainted in her life, and she felt foolish doing it now when she so needed her wits about her, but she had no say in it. Blackness overcame her like a silent storm.

"Hold her, now."

Something, someone, had a grip on her arm. Something else, an irresistible weight, pinned her down in the straw. Her shoulder still ached, and it felt as if it had swelled up like an India rubber balloon. It took but a breath for her to realize she'd revived just in time to fully experience the spectacle of her shoulder being wrenched back into its proper position.

"Ready?" a familiar voice asked.

No! she wanted to shout, but she sensed that the voice was not addressing her. Moreover, her tongue was still asleep in her mouth. Wouldn't Allyn laugh at that, when she heard?

In the next moment, laughter was the farthest thing from Missy's mind. She was pulled. A bolt, a fiery lance of dizzying pain shot through her shoulder from front to back. Humming. Grinding. Screaming.

"Good thing she was unconscious already, or that would have knocked her out for sure." She recognized the voice of her angel, panting as she'd never have believed an angel might.

I *am* conscious! she wanted to scream at him. She opened her mouth to say so, and was promptly sick.

She sobbed.

"Bleeding Jesus," he growled. "This is too much, Manners. I came in here to help out a la—a woman, I get knocked on the head by a crazed child—"

"My name's Gideon, and I ain't a child!"

"Shut up." The angel's testy voice silenced Gideon's petulant contradiction. "And for icing on the cake, I get to wear the contents of the woman's stomach on my best coat!"

"When was the last time you went anywhere without there being some profit involved, Muldaur?"

Missy felt a shudder of relief at the sound of Joshua's voice, despite the fact that there was no drollery whatever in his address. His baritone was, in fact, cold with skepticism, making his words a scathing insult to her angel.

"We got her shoulder put to rights," Joshua went on flatly. "Now why don't you just get the hell out of here?"

Oh, yes, she thought, squeezing her eyes shut tight. Go. Please. The notion of facing the angel after she'd vomited all over him was more than she could bear.

"I thought I'd earned a civilized introduction for my gallantry, but as it is, I suppose retreat is the wisest course." Muldaur's humor was acid. "Maybe we'll meet at Filson's tonight."

Dear God, she hoped not. How could she ever look the man in the eye again, having thrown up all over him? And them not even properly introduced?

"The lady is a friend of mine. Like a sister of my wife." Joshua's reply was no warmer than his previous words. "I suggest you stay away from her."

"Do you?" Muldaur sounded amused. Dangerously so. Excitingly so. "Advice is cheap, Manners. Cheaper still when it comes from you. But I'll be seeing her. Count on it."

"Only a fool counts on you, Muldaur."

There was a tense, electric silence after Joshua's drawling taunt. Not even the mare seemed to breathe.

"Nevertheless, I will be seeing her. And you too, I suppose, since you appear to be her watchdog. Until then."

She neither saw nor heard the angel go, but she knew he'd left the cramped stall as surely as if he'd kissed her hand before his departure. Something about Mr. Muldaur's drawling words evoked in Missy a troubling memory, but it slipped through a renewed wave of pain like a mischievous child playing hide-and-seek in a dark forest. . . .

"She's comin' around." Gideon's whispered remark chased it away entirely.

"Missy?"

Missy opened her eyes at Joshua's gentle command, but her vision was clouded with unshed tears.

"Gideon here told me what happened," he said, wearing a sympathetic, if rueful, grin on his wide mouth, displaying none of the antagonism he'd shown to her angel. "I left the Fosters inside to come look for you. You're a sight. Allyn's going to flay us both alive for this. You realize that, don't you?"

Missy could only nod in fresh anguish. Of all the misery she had endured this afternoon, she most dreaded Allyn's reaction.

"Who's Allyn?"

"Never you mind, Gideon. I have the feeling you'll find out soon enough." Joshua glanced at the boy, who stood just at his left shoulder; then he scrutinized Missy again. "How's that shoulder? Hurting much?"

"It's been dislocated before. I'll be fine."

If Joshua noticed that she'd avoided a direct answer to his query, he gave no indication.

"I have to get you back to the hotel, preferably without anyone seeing,'' he mused, looking about as if for assistance in this endeavor.

"I want to purchase this mare," Missy told him, hoping she sounded more sturdy than she felt. Out of the corner of her eye, she saw the boy, Gideon, straighten his slim shoulders.

"We can discuss that later," Joshua replied briskly. He rose. "Can you walk?"

"We can't discuss it later. They said she's to be taken away at the close of today's sale if she's not sold. There's no time." Missy got to her feet with Joshua's help. She closed her eyes again until the stall stopped reeling.

"Do you know the animal?" Joshua challenged her.

She shook her head. Joshua made a sound Missy recognized as masculine impatience for feminine whimsy.

"She's a steady walker," Gideon piped up eagerly. "Has a nice high gait, but mild enough to take a lady's sidesaddle—"

He was interrupted by Joshua's laughter.

"He doesn't know you, that's certain," he said to Missy, sounding more regretful than lofty. "She's looking for a breeder." He addressed Gideon again in a nononsense tone. "Miss Melissa Cannon's a trainer and breeder of top thoroughbreds, Gideon, and she's in the market for a dam for a very special sire. You'll pardon my saying so, but this mare doesn't look quite up to the C-Bar-C's usual standards."

"Joshua, I want this horse."

Joshua closed his eyes as if praying for patience.

"All right. All right. It's your money. Just keep your voice down. If the owner's about, he's liable to bid against us just to drive up the price. Or Gideon here may go running to tell him."

Joshua sent a critical glare in the boy's direction, and Missy perceived his meaning exactly.

"Gideon won't be doing any such thing, will you, Gideon?"

Missy detected not a trace of artifice in the boy's vehement shake of his shaggy, scruffy head. "No, ma'am. Miss. Miss Cannon."

"I'm sure." Joshua was laconic, and doubtful. "By the look of him, he scarcely knows soap and water, let alone the owner of a thoroughbred mare. Am I right, Gideon?"

Gideon glowered, but did not meet Joshua's gaze.

"What are you doing here, son?" Joshua prodded in a softer tone. "This horse isn't anything to you, is she? Is your pa a handler here?"

"I'm not your son," Gideon asserted in a voice cold with youthful anger that scarcely cloaked hurt. "And I don't have a pa. Nor a ma. All I have is Glory."

"Glory?" Missy was confused.

Gideon thrust his hand into his coat and withdrew a haphazardly folded paper. He punched it out toward her, his lower lip sucked firmly under the upper.

Joshua took it for her and smoothed it open. He held it up to the pale light from the window.

"*Sic Transit Gloria*,'" he muttered, frowning. "What an unfortunate name."

"Sick?" Missy grew alarmed. "She doesn't look sick! Is she—"

"No, that's just her name, apparently," Joshua assured her, showing her the faced, crumpled document. "*Sic Transit Gloria*. It's Latin."

"I just call her Glory." Gideon sounded as if he dared not express so much as a hope.

"Just as well," Joshua observed, not smiling as he looked at the now quiet animal.

Missy scanned the paper Joshua had handed her. On it she found the name of Stockton Farm, a stable with which she was unfamiliar. Below that, in rich, enviable, flourished script, the animal's name: *Sic Transit Gloria*. She traced the beautiful letters with the tip of her gloved finger. She left a dirt smudge between the *Sic* and the *Transit*, but that did not concern her: by the close of business today, the document—and the mare—would be hers.

"I think it's a lovely name," she murmured, sidling closer to the mare, who flicked her long, inky tail in greeting. "Latin, you say? It sounds very noble and exotic. Inspiring. What does it mean?"

"Oh, it's noble, all right, but hardly inspiring," Joshua agreed dryly. "It means, roughly, 'fame is fleeting.' "

"I call her Glory," Gideon ventured again. "She likes that."

"I imagine she would," Joshua mused, examining the mare. "Missy, she's showing a lot of daylight. Did you notice that? And she looks a bit short in front."

"But she has open elbows." Missy found herself defending the creature, not even sure why. She had no use for the kind of brood mare Joshua was describing. There could be no question of it. But somehow she knew she wanted this horse. And, thank heaven and the C-Bar-C's late profitability, she was in a position to indulge herself with a speculative venture now and again.

"And look here, Joshua." She pointed to the lineage. "*Sic Semper Tyrannis* out of *Gloria In Excelsis*." She struggled over the last word, but got it out intact. "Call it intuition, but I think this mare has potential. The blood's here. Blood will out. And besides," she felt compelled to add, unable to withhold a grin, "I can't credit that the Lord would put me through so much on this animal's account if I wasn't meant to have her."

"Since when have the Lord and intuition anything to do with one another?" Joshua pressed his lips together as he regarded Missy.

Missy liked Joshua very much. She theorized that his steady, powerful self-assurance was a perfect complement to his wife's brash, playful nature, and the three years of Allyn and Joshua's marriage had borne out her hypothesis. Even though they had not seen one another very often in that time, Missy had grown close to Joshua through Allyn's frequent correspondence. She had come to admire and respect him for many things, but above all for his good sense in having fallen in love with her best friend, Allyn Cameron.

Joshua, it seemed to her, was a man who knew what he wanted. Moreover, he was a man who possessed remarkably keen instincts as to what might be good for other people. Coupled with this was his extraordinary ability to guide them, painlessly and without their having the slightest hint of outside interference, to an appropriate course of action. It was for this reason that he had become an effective and respected congressman in his home state of Maryland. It was also for this reason that Missy suddenly did not want to look at him anymore, or hear anything else he might have to say to her regarding her fresh—and probably unwise—preoccupation with the unknown mare and her devoted young steward.

"I see you're set on it," Joshua observed, sounding as if he wished it might be otherwise. "Although I suspect that your interest may be as much on the young man's behalf as on the horse's."

Missy said nothing. Gideon was, indeed, of more than passing concern to her. He seemed to have no one else to champion him, and in that regard he reminded her more than a little of herself as a child. In any case, she'd suffered insults, the ruin of her clothing, and a dislocated shoulder on his account; she had more than a little invested in the boy's welfare already. Joshua's intuitiveness, though, was uncanny, and more than a little troubling.

"I'll handle the details of the purchase," Joshua went on in a brisk, businesslike way. "But we'd best get you back to the hotel before anything else happens to you. We can't have you parading about inside, smelling and looking like a stablehand. The Fosters and the others are understanding of what they see as your eccentricities, but even they have their limits. Now how am I going to get you safely home, and finish up your business for you here at the same time?"

"Perhaps Mr. Muldaur could escort me."

Missy covered her mouth with her dirty, gloved hand as soon as the words left her lips. She was stunned, mortified, that she'd even thought of the angel accompanying her back to the hotel, let alone that she'd said the words aloud. She did not even know Mr. Muldaur formally, nor he her. Goodness, she did not even know the man's first name. She recalled the terse exchange between him and Joshua when they'd thought her unconscious: Joshua, at least, seemed to want to keep it that way. She could not help wondering why, but watching as he stroked his dimpled chin, she dared not ask.

"So you met him," he remarked with an appraising nod and grimace. Missy, neither wishing to lie nor to admit the truth—that she'd only heard Joshua call the man by name when they'd both thought her unconscious—did not reply. Her face, however, grew uncomfortably warm under Joshua's long, steady, proprietary gaze.

"Think of the most dangerously unreliable person— man, woman, or child—that you've ever known, and multiply that by about four," he went on, pinning her with a look that brooked no dissembling. "That's Flynn Muldaur. Through and through."

Gideon stood still as a fence post, hoping neither adult

would look in his direction. He had not lived to be nearly 12 years old with neither father nor mother, and managed to stay out of an orphanage since he was eight, without having learned a thing or two. He was a mite small for his age, he knew, but he'd quickly learned that his size could as often work to his advantage as not. Especially when it came to slipping through tight places such as improperly closed stable doors or out of the hammy grasp of a policeman hoping to collar a nimble young thief.

He'd also learned to keep his mouth shut, for the most part, except when it came to bullies like the two men who'd tried to needle him about his Glory. That was why he just stood there in the stall with his mouth pressed tight as a new-corked bottle when he heard the name Flynn Muldaur. Especially since he recognized the name of Melissa Cannon in connection with something he'd heard only a few hours before.

Chapter Three

Gideon stuffed himself into a corner of the cab as if there weren't all the room in the world in there, with just Miss Cannon as his companion. She gave him a funny look as the driver helped her in, but she didn't say anything. She just sat in the corner opposite and lay back against the leather seat with a broken-up sigh, as if her breath were climbing a rickety old ladder and having a hard go of it. If she or anyone else dared to think, let alone say out loud, that he was acting scared, his fists were bunched, ready to straighten them out.

But Miss Cannon didn't seem inclined to tease him. She closed her eyes—they were pretty eyes, he allowed, kind of a soft gray, like the fur of the kitten that sometimes visited Glory's stall—and she winced a little and bit her lip when her shoulder hit the back of the seat. But only a little. Had he blinked or looked away for an instant, he'd have missed the unguarded look of pain. He got the feeling, looking at her sideways so she wouldn't think he was staring or interested or anything, that she was in a lot more discomfort than she was willing to let on.

A flush of heat in his face made him look down at his old, cracked shoes: he was responsible for that pain. He and Glory.

Well, dammit, he'd only been trying to help her, he reasoned, fidgeting. He'd figured if Glory reared and made a fuss, she'd chase those fellows right out of the stall without a backward look. How was he to know that Miss Cannon would put herself between them? After all, there'd never been anyone in all of his life who'd put themselves between him and harm.

He stole another look at Miss Cannon. Her eyes were still closed, but she wasn't grimacing anymore. Her mouth, though, was tight, as if she were thinking about something that made her feel bad. . . .

Gideon felt sort of choked, all of a sudden: he hoped he hadn't brought that feeling on her. He owed her. She'd saved him, after all. Him and Glory.

"We'll get you a good hot meal and some decent clothes." Miss Cannon's soft voice interrupted the creaking of the cab and the rumbling of the wheels, and Gideon thought it would be okay to look at her. She hadn't opened her eyes, though, he noticed, both relieved and saddened. He didn't answer her. He guessed maybe she was thinking out loud more than talking to him. People didn't talk to him much. Grown-up people, anyway. Other boys did, but they didn't count. They were just street orphans, like him, with nothing real important to say except maybe to tell you where the pickings were good, or where there was a dry, safe corner you could curl up in for the night.

"I suppose you'd better tell me about yourself." She surprised him by speaking again, and she sounded stronger this time. "Allyn—Mrs. Manners, that is—is sure to ask, and I'll feel even more foolish than I already do if I can't answer her."

She opened her eyes and aimed a look straight at him across the cab. Even though her look wasn't mean or angry, he had to fight an urge to squirm. He reminded himself that, for once, he wasn't in any trouble. He took a couple of gulping breaths and figured he'd best come up with some sort of answer for her. His instinct was to lie, and he knew he was good at it. He'd had to be.

"Well, my name's Gideon," he began tentatively. It was always easier to begin a lie with a little bit of truth.

"That much I know. How old are you?"

"Fourteen." He'd been telling that small lie for months, but this was the first time it stung.

"Hmm. Tell me about yourself."

Miss Cannon had a pretty voice. Like soft, buttered honey. Real gentle. Well, the tall fellow who was with her said she trained horses; Gideon guessed she knew how to use her voice on people, too.

"I'm not from around here." He felt his way, as if he were in a lightless room.

Miss Cannon waited. Her silence was a weight around Gideon's neck, forcing his head down. And his gaze.

"My pa's a handler," he invented, although the new lie felt, strangely, like a prickly pear on his tongue. "He drinks some. He left me in charge of Glory when we got to Louisville, and I ain't seen him since. Guess he went on a bender. But he said I was to stay with Glory, no matter what, no matter where she went. He'd find me when he could. And he'd beat me fierce if he found I'd disobeyed him."

Gideon had to stop himself from piling on more. He'd never had to lie to a lady before, at least not one who'd done him so many favors. He was unnerved to discover that it made him feel sort of sick inside, as if he'd forced himself to eat a plateful of tainted, underdone meat. Maybe even his own liver.

"You told Joshua—Mr. Manners—that you had no ma or pa."

Damn, he'd forgotten. But she hadn't. Gideon considered flipping the latch on the cab and bolting out, escaping from her and from his lies, but the cab was in traffic, and going along at a pretty good clip. Besides, to vamoose on Miss Cannon would mean he'd have to forsake Glory as well. He knew for sure the mare would be in good hands, but it was a sacrifice he was unwilling to make. He swallowed his agitation.

"I don't have no ma," he allowed, fixing his gaze on the ever-changing view from his window. "And I might as well not have no pa, most times."

Outside, a policeman's whistle brought the cab to a rocking halt. The sudden absence of movement made Miss Cannon's silence all the more unsettling. Gideon didn't realize he was holding his breath until the cab jolted forward again and forced a gasp from his lungs.

"Well, now, which is it, Gideon?" she asked, with a soft gentleness in her voice that coaxed an unwanted swelling behind his eyes. "I've told one or two lies in my life when I thought I had to, but eventually I found out that telling the truth was always better. Always made me feel better, anyway. Not sick and uncomfortable. Imagine how you'll feel looking at the nice dinner I'm going to order up for you at the hotel, and feeling like you can't eat a bite of it."

Gideon envisioned such a meal—maybe chicken and biscuits and plenty of gravy, and a nice, big slice of pie for dessert—and he winced before he could stop himself, thinking about not being able to look at it, much less do it justice, for his afflicted conscience. His stomach whined in protest.

"I ain't nothin' to you," he growled, trying to cover the commotion of his insides, and trying not to sound as hungry as his invention made him feel. "Why are you going to order me a dinner?"

"Because you're hungry."

Gideon fell in love with Missy Cannon at that very instant.

Of course, she hadn't mentioned the requisite bath yet.

"Flynn Muldaur?" Allyn Cameron Manners frowned as she pulled Missy's shift over her head. "Joshua's never spoken of anyone by that name, but I—lord, Missy, this thing stinks like everything else!—I imagine he knows many more people than I've heard about in the past three years, especially from his days with the Secret Service. Get into the bath before you freeze."

It was chilly in the small lavatory in Missy's hotel room. She slipped gratefully into warm water that smelled of roses.

"Well, he knows him. And he didn't seem to particularly like him," she murmured, favoring her shoulder as she sat back against the cool enamel of the cast-iron tub. "Although except for calling me a damn fool, which I was, Mr. Muldaur treated me in a very kindly manner."

Missy so relished the soothing bath that she did not immediately notice Allyn's silence. When she became aware of the quiet in the room, she opened her eyes to find Allyn searching her face with a speculative look that made her feel as if she wanted to cover herself with a towel.

"Well, I must say, Missy, this is an encouraging development," Allyn said at last, although Missy did not care one bit for the prim, faintly teasing note in her friend's voice. "I wish I'd been there to witness the whole thing. I don't recall ever having seen you blush

38

when discussing a man. Come to think of it, I don't recall you ever discussing a man when you might be discussing a horse. I must hear more about him.''

Missy cringed at the thought of reviewing the mysterious and intriguing Flynn Muldaur further with her alarmingly astute companion.

''But the children—''

''Albertine's still napping,'' Allyn argued, referring to her and Joshua's two-year-old daughter. ''And your young Gideon will probably be in his bath for at least half an hour, if Phyllis has anything to say about it.''

Phyllis would no doubt have a great deal to say about it. Phyllis Hammond was Albertine's devoted nursemaid, and a veritable martinet in her standards of both discipline and cleanliness. Missy suspected that Gideon would have a devil of a time talking the woman into—or out of—anything, especially the thorough pumice scrubbing he so desperately needed.

''There isn't anything more to tell,'' Missy protested, working the soft, rose-scented soap into a lather with her washcloth. ''I opened my eyes, and there he was. Then he and Joshua yanked my shoulder back into place. Then I got—'' Missy stopped herself, her face heating at the memory.

''You got what?'' Allyn prodded, releasing Missy's hair with painless, effective jerks of the hairpins.

''Nothing.''

''Nothing!'' Allyn echoed in disbelief.

''Ouch!''

Allyn had yanked her hair, not at all painlessly.

''Then I got . . . ?'' Allyn prompted sweetly, by way of reminding Missy of her earlier, unfinished remark.

''Oh, very well.'' Missy relented with a huff. ''I got sick on him. All over his shirtfront. I thought I'd die of shame. I didn't dare look at him after that, but luckily

Joshua bade him go, rather sternly—Allyn, stop laughing! It isn't funny!''

Missy half turned in the tub to see Allyn sink to the stool, weak and shaking with mirth. It was only her consideration for Allyn's pregnancy that prevented Missy from hurling a wet washcloth in her direction. Her cheeks burned.

"Not funny?" Allyn gasped. "Oh, Missy, only you could place yourself in such a predicament! And where was Joshua during this, uh, event?"

"Right behind me." Missy had no shame left to feel, and the warm, fragrant bathwater was already soothing her temper as well as her muscles. "He held me while Mr. Muldaur wrenched my shoulder back into place."

"Humph! That shoulder of yours has come apart and been put back together again so many times, I wonder you couldn't have done it yourself. Look here; it's not even swollen, although I expect it's still tender."

"A little, although it's not bad. I mean to go to Filson's tonight, you know."

Allyn sighed. "Of course you do," she muttered, balling Missy's soiled, discarded clothing. "Well, the dressmaker is coming at three to fit you, so you'd best hurry." She sniffed the air and made a face. "And wash your hair, too. It stinks. Shall I stay and help you?"

Missy rolled her shoulder to test it. "No, I think I can manage."

"Good, because I believe I hear Albertine bellowing, and I'm sure Phyllis is still busy with your Gideon. What do you mean to do with the boy, Miss? It's obvious he thinks you've purchased him right along with his mare, and it's equally obvious that he's delighted with the arrangement."

Allyn's green eyes had grown serious as she held Missy's soiled laundry against her stomach. Missy sighed.

"He says he's an orphan," she murmured, laying her head back against the rim of the tub. "I considered taking him to an orphanage, but . . ." She trailed off, unwilling to finish. Allyn, she knew, would have an opinion on the matter, very likely a strong one. And Missy was not up to a lecture. Especially not an Allyn Cameron Manners lecture. Allyn had lived a life of privilege as a child, until she chose to orphan herself by moving west with Missy nearly ten years earlier. On the other hand, she, Missy, had been orphaned as an infant by the war, and had never known a real home or family until the Camerons of Philadelphia had made her a part of theirs.

"This could very possibly be the best thing in the world for both of you," Allyn mused with a slow nod. "You've been alone too long on that spread. And don't bother to tell me that the hired help is any company for you; I know you too well, remember. You've been working yourself to an early grave at that ranch ever since we lost Bert. You've needed someone, something more than those four-footed animals upon which to bestow all of your motherly attentions; God only knows what you've been doing with them since I left. Gideon seems a decent enough boy who's had less than his fair share of good fortune. And unless I'm much mistaken, that fortune is about to change."

Missy considered her friend, unable to conceal her astonishment: she had anticipated a litany of advice from Allyn regarding the boy, culminating with strong exhortations to deposit him at the nearest home for indigent orphans. Even though Missy knew she would not have followed such well-intentioned guidance, she felt, along with her relief, a queer disappointment that she'd been denied the opportunity to gainsay Allyn.

*   *   *

When the dressmaker was through, all Missy wanted was to climb into bed. Fittings, alterations, and hairdressing were more tiring to her than a vigorous day of breaking two-year-olds, probably due to her impatience with the comparatively tedious activity.

Still, the results, she was forced to admit, were almost worth the agony. In the end, she was sheathed in a regal purple velvet that she could not help but admire as she examined her reflection in the full-length mirror. The color seemed a perfect complement to her changeable eyes, rendering them an amethyst hue. The gown featured sumptuous leg-of-mutton sleeves and yards and yards of material draping from her waist to the floor. She should have been warm in such a creation, she thought, but the neckline left her so exposed, down to the very tops of her breasts, that instead she felt chilled. She wondered if Flynn Muldaur might notice an otherwise ordinary Missy Cannon at Filson's while she was wearing such an exceptional dress.

Perhaps it would be enough to make him forget her disgraceful exhibition this afternoon. . . .

"Missy, you said you were cold, but your cheeks are as pert and pink as if you'd just returned from a brisk walk," Allyn observed, fluffing out a sleeve with a few expert plucks.

Missy felt her blush deepen, and she looked away from the mirror, not wanting to witness the reflected result of her friend's innocent comment.

"Well, anyway, you look exquisite." Allyn seemed as pleased as if she'd effected the transformation all by herself, like some all-powerful Merlin.

"I can't move."

"Yes, you can. Don't be absurd. You just can't stride about as you do in your work clothes. Remember to take smaller steps and you'll be fine. Oh, and here."

Allyn selected, from her own accessory box, a hair-

42

piece of black and purple ostrich plumes joined by a
diamond hairpin. She scanned Missy's upswept hair as
if about to stake a claim. Then, with a lightning-quick
jab that was not to be argued with, she sent the ornament
to its place amid Missy's glossy, flawlessly placed dark
curls.

"There," Allyn pronounced with a satisfied grin.
"Perfect."

"It wouldn't dare not be," Missy commented dryly,
although she doubted that perfection, particularly in the
area of couture, was a word anyone might ever employ
in the same breath as her own name.

Allyn gave her a wilting look. She herself was wearing an elegant, emerald green creation styled in a manner
that made her pregnancy scarcely noticeable. Allyn
seemed to own the color green the way some women
possessed priceless family heirlooms. It was, in Missy's
opinion, unarguably Allyn's color, and anyone else who
dared wear it when in the same vicinity as Mrs. Manners
inevitably looked like a mountebank. Or at least like a
piece of old, green cheese.

"Missy, you look stunning," Allyn pronounced, as if
daring contradiction. "Ravishing. Like a grand, fashion-
able lady."

"Like an overdone old maid," Missy muttered, but
she could not help nursing a secret delight at the result
of her numerous dressers' efforts.

"Oh, nonsense. Just for heaven's sake, please don't
forget yourself and use any stable language. Joshua
thinks he managed to contain speculation about what
happened this morning at the auction, and if Mr. Muldaur is any kind of gentleman, no one will even know
of the incident. You have nothing to worry about."

Except encountering Mr. Flynn Muldaur at Filson's,
Missy thought gloomily. How, she wondered, following
Allyn out of the dressing room, did one gracefully apol-

ogize for having emptied the contents of one's stomach upon a gentleman's shirtfront? Although perhaps he would not even give her the opportunity.

I'll be seeing her, Muldaur had said. *Count on it.*

Trembling with unfamiliar, maidenly excitement, Missy found herself hoping she might do just that.

Chapter Four

Missy wondered, staring around the fabulous ballroom at Filson's, how a roomful of richly attired women and men could be more intimidating to her than a corral of restless, unbroken stallions. These were society's elite, not only from Louisville, but from all over the country. The women seemed to wear their clothing like weapons. She stayed as close to a large potted palm in an alcove as she could without risking the impression that she was actually hiding.

Off to her right, she spied Allyn. Mrs. Joshua Manners chatted in an easy way with four women, each of whom wore satin gowns that looked like blue steel bayonets. The women had sharp, appraising looks on their otherwise lovely faces. Nearby, Joshua carried on a serious but spirited conversation with another gentleman and a lady Missy took to be the man's wife. She was wearing an exquisite, boldly striped gown of black and gold, giv-

ing her the appearance of a predatory jungle creature.
And not far away, but attracting an almost vulgar
amount of male attention, was a young woman clad in
a velvet dream the exact shade of the burgundy wine
Joshua had bade her sip for fortification before they'd
left for Filson's.

The woman in red was young. She possessed the face
of a lovely child, with a complexion that put fresh cream
to shame. A fair-haired Persephone she was, and her
azure eyes sparkled with youth and spirit. Missy was
sure every man present felt her reckless power. The
woman's smile was constant yet ever changing. She addressed each gentleman attending her as if he were a
secret lover with whom she shared a most intimate confidence, a promise her womanly form appeared more
than capable of delivering.

Missy had heard the expression "holding court"
somewhere, although she could not recall the association. Watching the breathtaking, unapologetically sensual woman cast her net about a wide sea of admirers,
Missy realized at last what the phrase meant, for that
was exactly what was happening before her eyes. She
respected the woman's ability to command attention
even as she felt a spasm of envy. Never in her life had
she herself attracted those kinds of looks, even from so
much as a single man, and here was this woman, little
more than a child by the look of her, reigning over half
a roomful of them.

Missy forced her chin up an inch: the goddess in wine
red velvet probably did not know a Morgan from a mus-
tang. She was about to turn away from the spectacle
when the crowd of men suddenly parted, as if Moses
stood upon the far bank with his staff held high. It was
then that she saw there was a man on the woman's arm.

Flynn Muldaur.

His wheat-colored curls were trained back, giving her

a clear view of the stark lines of his face. She remembered him as an angel, but he looked more like a suave Satan this evening, particularly with the young goddess on his arm. He was smiling, but Missy sensed a guarded quality about his expression, as if he knew he could not afford to unleash the fullness of his pleasure or pain. His elegant evening clothes were starched and flawless. They fit him as if his tall, lean form had been created by God for no other purpose than to show them off. Staring at him, Missy was certain that he would appear elegant even in rags.

He looked like the kind of man mothers warned their daughters about. The kind who never gave women like Missy Cannon a second look, unless possibly for amusement.

She shuddered.

A painful eternity passed in an instant. Flynn Muldaur's gaze met hers, and she saw in it a gleam of recognition that called to mind every shameful event of the afternoon in excruciating detail. Missy was helpless to do anything but watch as Muldaur murmured something to the paragon of feminine perfection on his arm, all the while keeping his gaze fixed on Missy as if he meant to hold a nail steady for hammering.

Muldaur's companion nodded without so much as a suggestion of petulance and withdrew her arm from his in a graceful, fluid motion, leaving him alone. A scant ten feet away, Muldaur took two steps toward her, obviously intent on exchanging words with her.

Missy panicked. Her legs played her false, and retreat was impossible. Desperate, she searched the room, hoping to attract either Allyn's or Joshua's attention so she would not be left to confront the devilish angel unprotected, or so her tongue would not make a further shambles of what her deportment had already wrecked.

But it was too late.

"Miss Cannon."

Her name sounded like celestial music in his deep, lilting baritone. . . . God, she was about to make a public spectacle of herself over a man she did not even know, a man who no doubt already thought her quite the fool. She gathered her wits and forced her stare upward from his stiff collar to his hopelessly wonderful eyes. Her voice caught in her throat. He offered a slight, but not teasing, smile that hinted he was aware of her discomfiture.

"We were not formally introduced this afternoon," Muldaur continued, his tone smooth as a lazy river on a sultry summer afternoon. "But I expect we were both too, ah, indisposed for that to be of importance at the time. My name is Flynn Muldaur. Is your shoulder better?"

Missy's heart felt as if Muldaur had strapped tight metal restraints around it that prevented it from beating as it should. A spear of heat pierced her neck, and she realized that she was looking at his cummerbund. She did not even try to speak.

I suggest you stay away from her. Joshua's icy warning echoed in her memory.

"What a stupid question." Flynn Muldaur snapped his gloved fingers as if incensed at his own idiocy. "Of course it's better, or you would not be here this evening."

Flynn moved closer to Missy to accommodate a lady who was attempting to pass behind him. His cologne was simple, yet seductively spicy. She could not identify it, except to know that it was nothing at all like the scent Joshua sometimes wore. It wrapped itself around her like the warmth of a down comforter . . . or the deadly gossamer of a spider's web.

"Well, I had intended to ask you to dance, but perhaps your shoulder is not up to such an endeavor. Indeed, I'm amazed to find you here at all, after the injury you suffered.''

He called you a damn fool at the time, and he was right. Now he's going to smile, nod, say ''good evening,'' and return to his lady in red, Missy thought. And you will never see him again. Tears of disappointment threaded her eyelashes.

She had to speak to him, or she knew she would regret it for the rest of her life. Which might not be that long if, as she half expected, she expired from mortification right here in front of him.

''I might not be here at all, had you not come to my aid.''

That had not been nearly so difficult as she'd imagined. Encouraged, even emboldened, she dared to continue. ''As I recall, you yourself suffered an injury on my behalf. How is your head?''

She had the perfect excuse to look at his face again, and was able to keep her blush at bay by telling herself she was merely inspecting the wound for which she was indirectly responsible. Flynn Muldaur pressed his lips together in a rueful but pleasant expression and glanced about the crowded ballroom.

''Oh, it's fine,'' he told her, seeming reluctant to elaborate. ''There's but a small bump. Just—here.'' He caught her fingers and began to raise them to his head.

''Oh, but of course you're wearing gloves. You'll never even feel it. Here.''

As if it were the most natural thing in the world, Flynn Muldaur proceeded to strip Missy of the glove on her right hand by tugging ever so gently on the ends of the fingers. Missy felt the soft kid slide away from her hand and her arm. *Oh dear, my calluses!* She remembered the state of her work-worn hands with renewed horror. But he did not seem to notice. In any case, the wonder of being touched by Flynn Muldaur quickly seduced her into a dreamy, bewitched condition, as if it were not her glove he was stripping from her, but her shift.

Skin brushed skin. He took hold of her bared fingers with his and Missy watched in mesmerized silence as Flynn Muldaur raised her hand until the pads of her fingertips grazed a swelling at his hairline, above his left ear. "Feel it?"

She swallowed hard. She felt it. His honey-colored hair was soft as a baby's, and she found she wanted to play in it, to explore it more fully with her fingers and her hands.

"Flynn, cheri, you are making a spectacle." The girl-woman's voice was not so much annoyed as it was play-ful. Without turning around, Missy knew it was the gorgeous creature in the red velvet extravaganza. In-stantly she felt dowdy and awkward. She pulled her hand away from Muldaur's and fumbled to cram her fingers back into her glove.

"But I enjoy making a spectacle, Antoinette; you know that." Muldaur was convivial. Missy envied him and his escort their poise. She began to wish again for Allyn or Joshua, or both, to arrive and save her from this increasingly uncomfortable situation.

"Miss Cannon, may I present my niece, Miss Antoi-nette Deauville? Her mother has charged me with her care here in Louisville, and I fear I am not the most scrupulous chaperon, as witnessed by the scores of gentlemen at her feet."

His niece? Missy frowned. Accepting Miss Deau-ville's gloved fingertips in her own in a perfunctory, ladylike gesture Allyn had taught her, Missy murmured a greeting. She found herself searching the younger woman's face for a family resemblance to the tall, hand-some Muldaur. She surprised herself by finding two ob-vious similarities, and several more subtle ones.

Antoinette Deauville's luxuriant hair was the identical

hue of sun-ripened wheat as Muldaur's, and her almond-shaped eyes were a like shade of blue, more topaz than sapphire. But that glimmer they sported, as if the world were but a trinket for their amusement, was entirely a Muldaur trait, Missy guessed. She felt more awkward by the moment.

"Ah . . . Antoinette, will you excuse us for a short while, please?" Flynn's tone became serious, although still pleasant, but he offered no further comment or explanation to his niece. Antoinette did not ask for either. She bestowed a smile on them both, and Missy noted with amazement that the expression was devoid of any condescension when it touched her.

Indeed, it was devoid of anything. As if she were made of glass.

Flynn Muldaur captured her elbow and gently guided her to one of several sets of mirrored doors that lined the vast room.

Oh. Oh dear. He's taking me aside, apart from the party, she thought, assailed by a sweet but gut-gripping panic. She knew what occurred between a man and a woman who purposely isolated themselves from the mainstream of activity; Allyn had seen to it that she was schooled on all matters politic between gentlemen and ladies at such affairs. What she could not credit was that a man, especially one so attractive as Flynn Muldaur, seemed actually to be propelling her toward just such an assignation. Thinking she should offer some protest, however halfhearted, Missy tugged away from him.

"Mr. Muldaur, we scarcely know one another. I don't think—"

"That is precisely what I intend to correct," Muldaur whispered at her ear, eradicating more than a little of her doubt and nearly all of her fear as he took hold of her elbow once more. "I have studied you, Miss Can-

51

non. I learned a lot about you, and I intend that I shall learn still more.''

They were the words of a man with a mission. A lover, perhaps? Missy felt her face charge with heat. I'm 27 years old, she reminded herself, sternly, even as her slippered feet followed Muldaur's guidance. I'm an incurably romantic old maid, and my imagination is making far more over this than reality warrants.

Missy found herself in a deserted, vaulted corridor, where crystal chandeliers burned a low gas flame. There was enough light to see, and to transform everything into the burnished gold of a hidden hoard of treasure. Flynn Muldaur pulled the doors closed behind him, and the levers clicked the bolt into place with a surprisingly cold sound, like the engaging of the trigger of a gun.

''Here we are,'' he announced breathlessly, wearing a smile she found most devastating.

Why, oh why did she think then of a predatory beast that separates its prey from the herd before closing for the kill?

She pulled herself together, no easy task, and clasped her arms about her for protection.

''Yes, here we are,'' she parroted. She was painfully aware of the quiet that surrounded them. She desperately wanted to fill it with something. Anything. Even idiotic babble.

''I'm sorry I—I mean, I'm sure I ruined your shirt this afternoon. I'd be happy to compensate you for the cost of replacing it, or for laundering. . . . ''

Muldaur waved his hand, and she thought he grimaced at her blundering suggestion, but she could not maintain her gaze long enough to be certain. She fell silent, waiting for the next thing to happen, having no idea what it might be.

Muldaur did not speak right away. He stood but three feet in front of her, close enough for Missy to feel his heat, yet far enough that she sensed an even greater, invisible distance between them. As if he were guarding a guilty secret.

Silly, romantic fool! she scolded herself with a chiding laugh.

"I beg your pardon?"

"What? Oh, I—Nothing. I said nothing."

Allyn was right: she had spent far too much time alone. At home, on the ranch, she often carried on conversations with herself, sometimes even lively debates, and she never had need to concern herself about who might overhear her monologues. Missy gripped her arms until her shoulder ached again.

"Miss Cannon—may I call you Melissa?" His whisper was the intimate plea of a hopeful lover.

Oh, dear. Missy felt herself falling. She clutched her arms about her, as if by so doing she could keep her heart where it belonged.

"Missy," she murmured, knowing she shouldn't.

"Missy," he echoed on a breath, sounding, to her amazement, suddenly, appealingly uncertain of himself. "And you must call me Flynn."

She dared a look at him, only to discover that he quickly looked away. Her heart did a clumsy but enthusiastic dance.

"You have a successful and very promising stud farm and ranch outside of Rapid City, South Dakota," he recited, as if telling a child a favorite bedtime tale. "And you live alone, training all of the horses yourself. You work your spread with adequate help, but you keep yourself apart, even from the people in town. It's a lonely life you've chosen, Missy Cannon. Although I sometimes wonder if perhaps it was the life that chose you."

Missy said nothing. It troubled her that this man, this stranger, no matter how attractive, had taken the time to learn such intimate details about her life, even if only through hearsay. Even more troubling, though, was the way his plain remarks had reduced her existence to a few basic facts that, in and of themselves, were about as interesting and as colorful as old bread.

She wanted to protest his assessment. She wanted to leave him. She waited for him to say more, half dreading what painful new truths his words might reveal.

She didn't know what she wanted.

"You've been mostly alone there for three years," he told her, and in the plaintive sound of his rich baritone she felt every day of them like the turn of an old grinding wheel. "You're an attractive woman—no, don't look away!—and you have a lot to offer. Don't you ever wish for more out of your life?"

Her breath caught with a small sound like a hiccup. She took a step backward in response to a nameless terror that gripped her.

"Missy, I don't know what you may have heard about me," he said in a surer tone, pursing his mouth as he clasped his hands behind him and gazed at the carpet. "But not many people truly know me. I've heard it said that I'm a womanizer, that I can't be trusted, that I've made and lost more fortunes than three men could make in a lifetime. While I can't say for certain if any of that's true, I do know that I've had my share of luck, bad and good, in my life. And you know from experience, I'm sure, that talk is, more often than not, just talk.

"As you can see, I'm not a—a young man. I'm not old, either, but I'm sure I have a good deal more experience than you, in a lot of things. A lot of ways. Ways you would perhaps blush to think of."

Missy's panic redoubled. This was sounding more and more like a seduction, and she was utterly out of her element. Why, she'd never so much as been kissed! Yet here was handsome, appealingly earnest Flynn Muldaur, whom she'd never seen before this afternoon, about to declare himself to her. And all she'd done was throw up on his shirt!

"I'm not doing this very well," he admitted. He sounded more than a little awkward, which might have been an act on his part, but it nevertheless made her warm to him all the more. "It's been a very long time since I—I mean—"

Flynn made a sound of disgust and turned away from her, shaking his head. Despite her terror and her confusion, Missy wanted to hear the words he was having such difficulty uttering. She'd never put much credence in the notion of love at first sight, but she'd known the instant she saw him in the stable, when he'd called her a damn fool, that she could easily lose her heart to this man. Could he—was it possible that he had felt those same strong feelings and was even now struggling to understand them himself? An experienced man of the world like Flynn Muldaur? She dared not hope so much, yet her mouth went dry at the possibility.

"What, Flynn?" She found her voice at the bottom of some deep place where it had been hiding. There was a distant roaring in her ears, as if they knew the words Flynn Muldaur was about to utter and they ached to hear them. She dared to touch his sleeve.

He faced her with a fierceness on his stark features that was lionlike. Magnificent. His eyes, aquamarine in the golden light, sent waves of sweet anticipation washing through her, cleansing her, it seemed, of every doubt and insecurity she'd ever had about her ability to captivate such a man. She longed to say something light and witty, something that would put them both at ease, but she knew she was not the sophisticate that Flynn's lovely young niece was. All she could do was hold her heart in her hands and her breath in her throat and wait for him to reveal his soul to her.

"I have a letter of debt," he whispered, holding on to her arms, "signed by your late uncle. It makes me half owner of your ranch."

Chapter Five

Missy, who had never before this day fainted in her life, did so for the second time.

"Damn it all to hell!"

Flynn caught her as she slumped forward, and discovered that Missy Cannon was quite a bit more woman than he was prepared for. The weight of her ample figure made his knees buckle and he needed all of his will to prevent himself from falling, or from dropping her. Part of him wanted to laugh at the absurdity he had visited upon himself by his blunt revelation: it was as if an armload of purple velvet and the woman it clothed went along with the piece of paper in his pocket, its implications and responsibilities. And he most certainly did not want any of them.

"Missy!"

A woman in green swept through the door Flynn had lately secured. She hurried to Missy Cannon's side and helped him lower her, gently, to a nearby horsehair settee. The woman treated him to an appraising green-eyed glance that made him feel inadequate in a way no one else ever had.

"May I assume that you are Flynn Muldaur?" she inquired of him coolly, patting Missy's pale cheeks with gentle urgency.

"Y-yes," he stammered, to his own annoyance. He knelt by Missy's side and held her arm to prevent her from falling off the seat. "And you are . . . ?"

"Outraged that you would presume to subject a respectable lady to the kind of gossip that is sure to ensue after your having pointedly removed her from the company," the woman retorted, pushing his hand away from Missy's arm with a deliberate, proprietary gesture. "This is a most reprehensible demonstration. You are not a gentleman, Mr. Muldaur, and you have already lived down to everything my husband has told me about you."

This had to be Allyn Cameron Manners, Missy Cannon's outspoken counterpart. Annoyance pushed embarrassment aside and Flynn made shift to answer her.

"I assure you, Mrs. Manners, this is not at all what it seems. I had business of the most urgent sort to discuss with Miss Cannon, having to do with her . . . uh, the ranch, and this was the first opportunity to present itself."

"Business meetings can be arranged," she told him frostily, with another pointed look that was no doubt intended to put him in his place, "in situations far more appropriate than a deserted hallway behind a crowded ballroom. Or was it your 'business' to ruin Miss Cannon's reputation?"

"She seems more than capable of doing that without my help." Flynn could not resist the retort. This woman defending Missy Cannon had more sharpness to her wit than a case of new silver carving knives, and he found himself wishing Joshua Manners joy of her. "Did she or your husband trouble to tell you the circumstances under which we—"

"She did," Mrs. Manners interrupted in a low, dangerous tone, although except for the fire in her eyes she looked anything but dangerous. "Miss Cannon, if you ever have the good fortune to discover, is a woman of irreproachable integrity. And as you obviously know my husband, I'm sure I have no need to certify his honesty to you."

"Oh, I assure you, madam, I am well acquainted with your husband. And while I've been at odds with him on many subjects, I have never contested his character. Have you no smelling salts for her?" Flynn was disconcerted that Missy was still indisposed.

Mrs. Manners glared at him down the bridge of her patrician nose.

"I do not carry smelling salts, Mr. Muldaur, having never had need for them. Perhaps you have a feather, or a cigar, or a bit of paper we might burn to revive her with the smoke?"

Flynn looked down and saw the paper in his hand, the clerk's copy of the letter of debt he had shown to Missy. He envisioned the hornet's nest he'd surely disturb by sharing it with Missy's bosom friend. He slipped it into his pocket, where he found a matchbox.

"Here; let's try one of these."

"I'll do it." She took the object from his hand with authority and extracted a wooden matchstick. "You go and fetch her a glass of water, or punch. But no champagne. And try not to look as if the world has ended," she added, giving him a queer look, almost a smile, that made him feel strangely clumsy. "She has only fainted. It won't do to alarm the rest of the party with so grim

59

a countenance. And if you see my husband, please send him to me.''

A new thought alarmed him, and he could not prevent himself from looking at her slightly rounded abdomen.

''Are you—are you well?''

''Of course I am,'' she replied, looking so amused at the question that he found himself blushing, to his annoyance. ''Go.''

What a tangle, he thought gloomily, wearing an empty smile as he edged through the crowd in the ballroom to find a punchbowl. How could he have so misread Missy Cannon's constitution as to believe such news about her ranch would not shock her to the point of fainting? Of course, the mere fact that she was present at the party despite her injury gave testament to her fortitude, if not her good sense. Still, it was not his way to misread women. Not since Madeleine, at any event.

''Have you told her?''

The voice at his ear might have been Satan tempting him.

''Stay out of my affairs, Antoinette,'' he seethed through his unwavering smile. ''You'll find I work far more effectively on my own.''

''Effectively, perhaps,'' Antoinette conceded in a murmur full of doubt, tucking her hand into the crook of his arm. ''But not nearly swiftly enough for Grand-mere or Mama. Or me. Tell me, *uncle*, has it always been thus?''

Flynn closed his eyes and struggled mightily against the urge to administer to Antoinette the spanking she so desperately needed, the one her mother had probably never even considered. Hell, Madeleine would have raised the girl to be just like her, and Madeleine, thanks to her own mother, had been indulged in every way possible. Probably even in a few ways no one else had thought of yet.

"Don't think you can manage me," he warned, keeping his voice low, not looking at her. "Your mother has always gotten what she wanted from me, one way or the other. She knows that. But on my time. Surely she's told you."

"Mama told me very little about you. Except for what she deemed important."

"Like where the money for the bills came from?" Flynn could not keep a note of bitterness from his voice, and he was angry that she had provoked him to revealing that much of himself.

"Don't be disagreeable. You are furrowing your brow. People will wonder why."

"You are your mother's daughter, Antoinette," he muttered.

"Thank you for the compliment."

"It was intended as an insult."

"I know." She laughed, and the sound was like the tinkle of a thousand tiny crystal teardrops on a chandelier swaying in a light breeze. "Oh, she did tell me something about you." She added that last as if it were an afterthought.

"I'm almost afraid to ask what."

"She said you are tediously predictable. Just like your brother."

Flynn wanted to shake the condescending little brat until her teeth rattled in her pretty little head. He clenched his fists and slowly counted to ten. He felt a cold shudder of wind, as if a ghost had been let into the room, and he knew Antoinette was gone from his side. The little bitch! If she had made one more insulting remark about Seamus, he would have made her regret it.

You are tediously predictable, she had said, in Madeleine's own voice. So of course she would have known the emptiness of any threat he might have tendered. Whatever her faults, and they were epic, Madeleine had always known him and Seamus, through and through. She had always known just how to play the Muldaur brothers. And apparently she had schooled her only daughter well in the art.

"Beg pardon, suh."

A waiter bearing a tray of full glasses of punch knocked into his shoulder, reminding him of his mission.

". . . can't believe she fainted. Missy never faints."

Allyn's voice sounded as if it were coming from the other side of the world. Missy floated toward the sound.

"She did a passable imitation of it this morning at the stable." Joshua was laconic, but not unkind.

"Oh, lord. Here comes Mrs. Foster. Try to get rid of her, Joshua. You know what a gossip she is. If she sees Missy like this and knows that Muldaur left the room with her . . ."

Muldaur. The name brought Missy to nauseating awareness. A moan of pain wove its way into the fabric of noises about her, and she felt the full weight of her consciousness.

"Oh, thank heaven. You've come around." Allyn's whispered relief was measurable. "Do try to sit up, Missy. Tell me what happened. Quickly. Joshua will be back at any second. And Muldaur, as well."

Missy tried to speak, but she heard herself moan again. She felt the warmth of Allyn's hand gentle against her cheek.

"Oh, Missy, do try," Allyn coaxed with quiet urgency. "We haven't much time to avert a scandal. Apparently more than one person saw you come here with Muldaur. What is it? What did he say? What did he do?"

Muldaur again. Missy struggled to open her eyes. It was such a comfort to lie there and listen to Allyn's voice; she wanted to wish herself back at the hotel as if this evening had never been. She was hurt. Wounded. Flynn Muldaur had set her on the summit of a gleaming pedestal; then he had willfully knocked it from beneath her with one smart, well-placed blow.

She tried to tell Allyn the story, but only one word came forth, softly, from her sluggish lips.

"Ranch."

"Ranch? Whose ranch? The C-Bar-C?"

Missy nodded twice. Her head felt heavy, but she struggled to hold it up.

"That's it," Allyn encouraged, supporting Missy's back with her hand. "Sit up, if you can. And try to open your eyes. Now what about the C-Bar-C?"

Missy obeyed Allyn's request. The golden light, which had seemed so pale and seductive before, was bright as polished brass, as if to highlight her folly. After several fluttering attempts, Missy managed to focus on Allyn's face in time to see the latter smile with relief.

"That's better. And I see Joshua has headed off the Fosters. Good. Now if only Muldaur would return with that punch, I'm sure we could have you perky again in no time."

If only it were that simple! Missy groaned, and once again her eyelids became too heavy for her will alone to support them.

"It's the ranch, Allyn," she breathed. "He—I thought he—"

No. As dear a friend as Allyn was, Missy could not bring herself to confess her shame, that she had misinterpreted Flynn Muldaur's actions as being inspired by a romantic motivation.

"He has a paper. He claims it makes him half-owner of the—my ranch."

"I assure you it's quite legal, Mrs. Manners."

Missy closed her eyes, not trusting herself to look upon the man who had thrust such shame upon her. Her fists balled themselves, and she longed to pummel him.

"That may be, Mr Muldaur," Allyn replied, in what Missy recognized as a falsely sweet tone that always prefaced trouble. "Nevertheless, your timing in this matter has been deplorable. I thank you for bringing the punch. Now you really must go, or there'll be a scandal."

"But what about Miss Cannon?" Muldaur, to his credit, sounded contrite. Missy squeezed her eyes shut, hoping to hold back tears. "Will she be—"

"Miss Cannon will fare much better when you are far away," Allyn interrupted him tartly, her pitch and volume rising. "Call upon us at our hotel tomorrow, if you must. I'm sure you know where we're staying."

With a rush of velvet, Allyn got to her feet and placed herself between Missy and Muldaur like a barricade.

"With all due respect, Mrs. Manners, the business between Miss Cannon and myself is not your concern, and you would be well advised to stay out of it."

"Indeed." Allyn was arch.

"How kind of you to be so solicitous of my welfare, Mr. Muldaur," Allyn purred, and Missy was able to imagine the look of challenge on her face, having seen it before on many occasions. "Sadly for you, however, I am utterly incapable of taking such advice seriously, particularly when tendered by a stranger whose motives, if not his methods, are highly suspect. It is now I who advise you to withdraw."

"Be very careful, Mrs. Manners," Muldaur warned, his voice a notch lower. "I'm not afraid of you, or your husband."

"Nor should you be." Allyn's apparent concurrence sounded more like a warning. "We are not at all menacing. Are we, Missy?"

Missy got to her feet slowly, pushing aside her own shame and fear. Allyn's words and tone alarmed her.

While she knew her friend wanted to protect her from the scandal of being the center of a deplorable spectacle, Missy also was certain that Allyn had no compunction whatever about landing herself in such a position. She could all too easily envision Allyn, who was infamous for dousing her adversaries with various foods and beverages, bestowing such a dubious baptism upon the sartorially splendid but blithely ignorant Flynn Muldaur. . . .

Actually, the thought rather amused her. Still, she could not allow Allyn to create such a diversion just to spare her from further embarrassment. She avoided Muldaur's speculative gaze.

"Allyn, perhaps I should talk with Mr. Muldaur alone."

"You've had a bad fright, Missy, and you're by no means strong enough. I'm sure Mr. Muldaur does not expect you to strain yourself on his behalf. Do you, Mr. Muldaur?"

Muldaur felt like an idiot standing there with each hand wrapped about a prissy little cup of ruby red punch. How had he gotten himself into such a predicament? Two women stood before him: one glaring and ready, he guessed, to disembowel him for a perceived crime, the other, fragile, agonizingly polite, utterly crestfallen, on the verge of tears. Both made him feel deficient in manners, sensitivity, and, yes, fortitude. He wanted to escape, to reevaluate his rapidly failing strategy, but he was trapped by the glasses of punch he held out as surely as if he were restrained by a pair of handcuffs and leg shackles.

Meeting the gaze of each woman in turn, he knew, with a sense of dread heretofore unknown in his vast experience with the female of the species, that neither of them intended to release the locks.

*   *   *

Gideon awoke from a troubling dream with a start, and sat up on his cot. He was shaking, and the clean nightshirt he'd put on after his long bath—well, it had been more like a swim—was soaked with his sweat. He felt bad. Sick, as if he'd eaten far too much of the heavenly supper he'd wolfed down under the disapproving eye of that old nursemaid, Miss Hammond. Yet he felt hungry again, too.

The dream was forgotten. He sucked in a shuddering breath.

Damn, this place was too quiet. The baby and the nursemaid slept like the dead in the far corner of the room, both of them on beds, both quiet as corpses. Gideon had lain awake earlier and listened to the sounds of their falling asleep. He was amazed at how quickly they'd done it, and how thoroughly. He'd seldom slept long in one place. He'd never felt safe enough for such a luxury.

But he was safe, here in this fancy hotel room. He was surrounded by pure, white sheets and a down comforter, besides. The feather pillow let his head sink like a stone, and he didn't know which he liked more, the warmth, the softness, or the smell, a smell like fresh air and soap and the inside of a cedar closet.

He crossed his legs and scratched his head, figuring: he'd had a scrubbing, a hot meal—hell, as much food as he could eat—and a clean, quiet, safe place to sleep that was almost a bed. More like a bed, in fact, than anything he could ever remember sleeping on. The fact that he was sharing the room with a woman and a baby didn't fret him much. The woman, Miss Hammond, looked at him as if he might steal something, and the baby was a pest, but asleep they weren't any bother. He'd shared quarters with lots noisier and dirtier folks, that was sure.

So why couldn't he sleep?

Glory.

The name formed in his head as if someone had spoken it aloud to him in the dark, quiet room. For the past two months, since he'd broken into that stable and found Glory, he hadn't left her side. He'd gotten to know all of her smells and humors and he'd even gotten used to her snoring.

Hell, he missed her.

What if she missed him, too? She probably did. After all, who was it who changed her straw? Drew her fresh water? Who was it who saw to it she got her feed all proper? Who was it who curried her, and knew just what spot along her flank she liked having special attention paid to?

And who was it who left her quicker than a bee after honey at the thought of a hot meal and a good bed?

His feet hit the floor with a guilty thud.

He looked at the bed on the other side of the small room, half expecting Miss Hammond to leap out of it and demand to know why he was up. She didn't. He let out the breath he'd been holding, and slowly, stealthily, Gideon got to his feet.

Chapter Six

"I thought you were going to spill your punch on him," Missy whispered to Allyn after Joshua had alighted from the cab.

"So did I," Allyn muttered back. "I think Muldaur thought so, too. Did you see the expression on his face when I took the punch glasses from him? He looked as if his eyes were going to fall out of his head, one into each cup."

The notion was amusing, but Missy could not muster a laugh.

"It's a good thing he excused himself when he did." Allyn smoothed her seal muff. "Joshua is furious as it is."

"He must be. He hasn't spoken since we left Filson's."

"We'll make this right, Missy," Allyn declared, patting her hand. "Joshua will see to it. Surely this document, this letter of debt, that Muldaur claims to have is a forgery of some sort. It must be.''

A letter of debt. The more Missy thought about it, the more frighteningly plausible it sounded.

"My uncle was something of a wastrel," she ventured. "I remember my pa saying, more than once, that his brother was fond of gaming—"

"None of that, Missy," Allyn interrupted her firmly. "Muldaur must first prove his claim beyond a shadow of a doubt, and I suspect he'll find that difficult to accomplish. You mustn't allow him to think, even for a moment, that you believe his nonsense. In the meantime, we will simply behave as if nothing were amiss. You know, Flynn's brother Seamus is a congressman from Ohio."

"A congressman?" Missy wondered just what that might have to do with her, or with Flynn's claim.

"Yes. Joshua knows—well, knows of him. He may be able to give us a clue as to what this Flynn is up to."

This Flynn, Allyn said. As if Muldaur were not a man, but some sort of blight or vermin.

Missy's heart ached. Well, wasn't he? How different was he from the bloodsucking parasite carpetbaggers who had run the Cannons off their place in Virginia back in '68? And where had Muldaur been with his so-called letter of debt back in the early days, in '84, when she and Allyn had struggled alone at the C-Bar-C to make tax payments and keep a roof over their heads? Why had he waited until the ranch was not only solvent but thriving before bringing this document and its significance to light?

Missy knew the answer. The man was a fortune hunter, or a confidence man, or both. A sob knifed her. She should have known better than to think that a man, especially one as charming and as attractive as Flynn Muldaur, might actually be interested in her for herself.

Joshua had said something to her a year ago that she'd let pass, something about her being an easy mark. Being vulnerable. Being prey to ruthless con men. Feeling strong and self-confident at the time, she had dismissed his concerns.

But that had been when she was willing to believe she was meant to go through life alone. Before she'd been rescued by a fallen angel who had tugged her shoulder right side up and her heart upside down.

"Oh, I'm quite the prize fool, I am," she mourned, and it was not until Joshua appeared at the door of the coach wearing a consoling look that she realized she'd spoken the opinion aloud.

"Don't be so hard on yourself," he reproved, helping her out of the coach. "This isn't the fiasco you imagine it to be. We averted a scandal at Filson's, although for a time"—he sent a severe look in his wife's direction, which she ignored—"I feared we would not. And I'm nowhere near satisfied that this claim of Muldaur's is genuine."

"I was just telling her that," Allyn declared, stepping down with Joshua's assistance. "Rest assured, Missy, we will—"

"*We* will do nothing." Joshua contradicted his wife with a meaningful shake of his head. "*I* will start an investigation. On my own." The emphasis Joshua placed on the final three words was aimed at Allyn, and it was unmistakable. To Missy, at least. Allyn, she knew, might conveniently choose to disregard it.

"First thing in the morning," Allyn asserted.

"Actually, I was planning to start right now," he corrected her, holding on to her hand. "I'll see you both inside first, but I've asked the driver to wait for me. There were some people at Filson's who might be of some help. I've no time to go into details now, though."

"But it's so late!" Missy felt deeply indebted to both

Joshua and Allyn already, and she hated the notion of either of them fretting so over her crisis.

"It's not even midnight," he soothed. "And we can't afford to lose any time. Go along, both of you. And don't wait up for me."

"Don't order me about, Joshua Manners," Allyn huffed, tugging Joshua's lapel playfully. "I have a daughter for that purpose."

Joshua kissed her. "I'll be back soon."

"See to it that you are."

It was obvious as ever to Missy that he adored Allyn, and she him. Stifling a sigh rife with painful longing, Missy looked away from the lovers, wondering if a man would ever look thus at her.

Every lamp in the suite was lit. Albertine's nurse, Phyllis Hammond, met Missy and Allyn at the door. She was wearing a flannel dressing gown on her tall, dead-tree frame, a whiny, fractious Albertine on her hip and a distracted look on her lined face.

"It's the molars," she explained as Allyn reached out to take her daughter in her arms. "She woke up half an hour ago, crying for you."

"My, my!" Allyn cooed in a high, placating voice to the mewling toddler. Albertine's sweet little face was distorted with sleepy irritation, and her finger was rooting about inside her pretty pink mouth. In no time at all, there was a spot of drool staining the breast of Allyn's emerald green silk. Allyn either did not notice or did not care. Missy suspected the latter.

"Does our mouth hurt?" Allyn bounced the little girl lightly in her arms, touching the tip of her finger to Albertine's round cheek. "Poor precious. So much noise for one little girl!"

Missy concurred. She could scarcely hear Allyn's

71

voice over Albertine's caterwauling, and Allyn was by no means softspoken.

"I'm surprised she didn't wake Gideon up," she commented, undoing her cloak with Phyllis's assistance.

"She didn't wake him up because she couldn't," the nurse informed her. "He was up and gone before she even started to fret."

"What!" Missy's face drained of color.

"When I turned up the lamp, I noticed his bed was empty," Phyllis reported sourly. "It was cold, too, so he'd been gone a while."

"My God!" Missy felt faint for the third time that day, and she found herself a chair in which to collapse. Gideon, alone late at night in Louisville . . . She remembered the two men at the stable, and how they had nearly beaten the child—for that was what he was, despite his air of fierce independence—and her heart faltered.

"Did he leave a note explaining where he might have gone?"

Albertine laid her head down and chewed on Allyn's shoulder. The room was filled with a tense quiet, as if it might explode with noise again at any moment.

"I doubt he can read," Phyllis replied, tugging on her thick, graying braid. "And I'm sure in any case that he doesn't write."

Phyllis, Missy guessed, was brusque because she keenly felt her own failure in this new crisis. Missy understood the feeling precisely.

"This isn't your fault," she muttered, wanting to reassure the conscientious nurse. "It's mine. I had no business leaving you an extra responsibility for the evening. After all, I'm the one who brought Gideon here. I should have stayed behind myself to see to him."

That way I might have avoided making a fool of myself and learning Flynn Muldaur's nasty surprise as well, she thought, but could not bring herself to add. It was a naive assumption, she knew. In reality, she would only have postponed the inevitable.

Her decision was made before she drew another breath.

"Help me change out of this thing," she told Phyllis tersely, striding toward her room as fast as she could in the cumbersome hobble skirt. "I'm going out to look for Gideon."

"But Missy, you shouldn't!" Allyn whirled around so quickly that she startled her young daughter, who began to howl again. "You can't! It's late. It's unthinkable. And—and you don't even know where he might have gone!"

"On the contrary," Missy heard herself say in a firm, sure tone that both surprised and pleased her. "I know exactly where he's gone."

She changed into her comfortable old riding habit, closing her ears to Allyn's strong and, she knew, wise arguments.

Curses paraded through Missy's mind as she stalked her way through the long, dark stable. She should not be here now, alone. She hadn't needed Allyn's admonitions, or the cabdriver's disapproving looks, or the night watchman's surliness to tell her so. She needed only her good common sense which, like a fickle lover, deserted her at the thought of Gideon in danger.

The night watchman, who hadn't seen anyone fitting Gideon's description and acted as if he doubted her story, followed her like a suspicious, sniffing hound. Missy was glad—not for the company, which was taciturn at best, but for the safety it represented: the few stablehands who idled about looked more than passingly interested in the presence of a female, otherwise unescorted, in the stable at night. More than one lewd remark stalked her down the darkened corridor, but she ignored them. She felt at ease in her familiar working habit, in complete command of herself and her surroundings. Words and gestures that might make her uncomfortable in a dress scarcely affected her at all in her working clothes. They were a form of armor for her, she realized. And she was glad of even that flimsy defense in this dark and hostile place.

She assumed her bold, no-nonsense stride and made straight for Glory's stall, less certain than hopeful of what she would find there. Tacked outside on the stall door was a tag marked *Sold* that bore her name, Glory's, the mare's mark, and the name of Missy's ranch. Glory was hers. Feeling nowhere near the elation she usually felt over a new acquisition, she tried the door with a tentative left hand.

It was unlocked. She'd half expected it to be stopped somehow from the inside. Had she guessed wrong about Gideon? A dark shadow of dread stilled her heart: if the boy wasn't here, he might be anywhere. She might never see him again.

She commanded herself. He was here. He was devoted to Glory, just as she herself had been, and was, devoted to Allyn. Where else would he be but by the mare's side?

She pulled the door back and slipped inside with her new mare.

"Gideon?" she called softly.

There was no reply, except for a patient snort from the huge, dark shape that was Glory.

"You'll be all right here, miss?" The night watchman was impatient. "I got rounds to make."

Rounds. Most likely with a jug, Missy mused grimly. She remembered her painful accident of this afternoon, and the crude stablehands who had marked her arrival tonight. She thought of the dubious protection this watchman represented to her and decided she could do

74

better herself. She bit her lip.

"Can you leave me the lantern?" she asked.

There was a rich sigh of untold suffering.

"I suppose."

The lamp was as stingy with its light as the watchman was with its loan. He looped its handle over a hook above the door. It cast a dull, dirty glow in the stall that extended only about four or five feet from its sooty glass chimney. The watchman scarcely met Missy's gaze, and she sensed the man's personal embarrassment that he was leaving her alone.

Good, she thought, glaring at him as he skulked out of the stall. He ought to be ashamed to leave her alone, under the circumstances. Gideon would be a far more stalwart champion. And he was here. She could feel it. The watchman was guilty of downright laziness, if nothing else. Missy could not abide sloth. Without a further word of farewell or dismissal to the man, she turned her attention to the mare.

In the dim light, Glory looked black from forelock to tail. She possessed a narrow face that sported no distinguishing marks of any kind save a pair of bright, alert eyes. Missy's gaze traveled downward to the animal's right foreleg, the limb that had no doubt been responsible for her dislocated shoulder. Amid the mare's glossy, healthy black coat, Missy detected but one hint of contrast, a coronet of white about her right forehoof. Like a wedding band, she thought with a wistful pang.

She immediately felt foolish for her musing and reminded herself of the real purpose behind her mission.

"Gideon, I wish you'd come out of hiding," she pleaded softly, looking into the shadows. "You've no idea how idiotic I feel, standing here talking to myself."

Glory nudged her arm with her muzzle, and Missy caught her bridle.

"Trying to apologize to me, are you?" she scolded

the mare, stroking her throat. "Hoping I'll forgive you for knocking me about earlier? I have a long memory, my girl. And if you're thinking I might have brought you a treat for your bad behavior, you're sadly mistaken."

There was a squeaking noise behind Glory, a distinctly unhorsey sound from the direction of the closed feedbox. Relieved and amused, Missy started toward it.

After only two steps, she stopped. Gideon was a child, she reminded herself. A lonely child, for all his independent bluster. A frightened child who, when he felt pangs of insecurity or doubt, turned to an animal with whom he had forged a special bond. Missy understood such feelings. She'd had them herself.

But she needed to find a way to earn some of that trust, and quickly. Glory was hers now, and her home was the C-Bar-C. If Gideon still meant to be a part of the mare's life, he would have to take a chance on trusting Missy. And the way to gain Gideon's trust, Missy was certain, lay in that elusive, unspoken covenant between boy and horse.

She drew a line down Glory's face with her finger from poll to muzzle.

"Gideon talks to you, Glory, doesn't he?" she began in a conversational tone.

Missy spoke to all of her horses, but this occasion felt a little odd. Glory did not feel like her horse. She was Gideon's, no matter what the papers of ownership might decree. And Gideon, she was certain, shared private dialogues, and private feelings, with the mare. Glory was not likely to impart these secrets, but the mare might help her make Gideon understand that she meant him no harm, and that he might trust her as he had never trusted another human being.

The importance of what she was about to undertake made her tremble. She prayed swiftly for guidance. She felt as if she were confined in a room and shown several closed doors, behind only one of which lay deliverance.

She had no alternative but to choose one and go on.

"Gideon has taken good care of you," Missy said to the horse. "He's a fine groom, isn't he? Your coat is clean and silky. You're healthy and strong. And look— why, there isn't a tangle at all in your mane or tail."

Glory snorted softly and pushed her muzzle into Missy's open palm. Missy took the gesture as a sign of encouragement.

"You want to take care of Gideon, too, don't you, girl?" Missy made herself keep her voice strong, although her inclination was to speak in a whisper. "He needs you, I think. Just as you need him. And you're going all the way to Dakota with me."

Glory nickered. She smelled warm and sweet, and Missy sensed she'd made a friend. She prayed she'd make two.

"I have a ranch there, with acres and acres of the finest grazing you've ever seen," she went on, feeling a twinge of homesickness combine with her yearning to coax Gideon from his hiding place, wherever that might be. "And lots of horses. There'll be plenty of companions for you and for the colts and fillies you'll have. Dakota's a wonderful place for horses. For boys, too. Tell me, do you think—do you think Gideon would like Dakota?"

It would still be hard winter in Rapid City, Missy guessed, but by the time she made her way home with Glory and her other acquisitions it would be spring. April. The foreman, Micah, and the other ranch hands she'd left behind to run the place would be hard at work on their spring chores. The ranch house, which she'd expanded only last year to a comparatively lavish bungalow with two bedrooms, kitchen, greatroom, and sitting room, would be waiting for her to plant her gardens.

The stock would have foaled and calved; every creature on the place would have something to look after and to show off.

And what, or who, would she have?

"I love it there, but sometimes I'm so lonely, Glory," she murmured, keeping a tremor from her voice by force of will alone. "I feel as if I put myself out there, between heaven and earth, and I don't really belong in either place. And there's no one to tell me any different. I need someone. God, I've needed someone for a very long time, and I never even knew it. Do you think he'll come with us, Glory?"

Missy had to stop. She had said far more than she'd intended. Far more than she should have. Things that she'd felt, vaguely, but had never been able to put a name to until this moment. She had Gideon to thank for that, she knew. And Glory.

And Flynn Muldaur.

She was near tears, and she shook with a confusion of emotions she'd tried to hold back all evening. She took several swallows as she listened to the stillness and tried to keep herself together for one last effort.

"I do hope Gideon comes with us," she managed in a heavy, choked voice, her cheek pressed against Glory's. "I suspect you'll miss him dreadfully if he doesn't. And—and so will I."

A soft rain began to tap on the roof above their heads, but there was no other sound in the stall. Missy wanted to say something else, to talk forever if she had to, but there was nothing left to say. It was just as well, for her throat had closed up so she could scarcely breathe, let alone speak.

She allowed some time to pass, then a little more. She sighed brokenly. If Gideon was there, by his silence he'd refused to have any part in the picture she'd tried to paint. If he was not, she'd merely poured out her heart in vain.

Either way, she had lost him. And she had lost a part of herself, as well.

A single tear strained through her eyelashes and slid partway down her cheek before she brushed it away. How could a waif so quickly and easily have found his way into the complicated maze of her heart? She sighed, straightening her shoulders, shrugging in her habit. Her armor had never felt so oppressive.

"Well, then." She cleared her throat. "Good night, Glory. If you see Gideon again, tell him we'll miss him."

Her feet felt as if they were made of lead as she trudged to the stall door.

"I heard tell some about Dakota."

It was Gideon's voice behind her. It sounded small. Raw. Young. Missy could not see for the water that suddenly flooded her eyes. She put a hand on the wall to steady herself.

"That you, Gideon?" She tried to sound nonchalant.

From behind Glory, there was a shushing of straw. Missy turned around to see him shuffle into the light. His cap was fixed low over his brow, shading his eyes, and his hands were jammed into the pockets of his old, too-short coat. Missy suspected, guarding a smile, that his fists were balled. She resisted a mighty urge to hug him.

"You really mean it? You'll take me to Dakota, too?" he asked gruffly, keeping his head bowed.

Missy would have promised him far more than that, had he asked.

"You'll have to do something for me in exchange," she told him, keeping her voice light out of fear that it would betray her joy.

"Take care of Glory? You know I'll do that." He

sounded defensive again. Surly. A smile tugged the corners of her mouth even as the youthful defiance in his reply tugged at her heart.

"More than that, my lad," she told him, trying to sound severe. "The C-Bar-C is a working ranch, and we all pull our weight. You'll have your chores, of course, but the most important thing will be for you to go to school. To better yourself. I take my responsibilities as seriously as you do, and one of them will be seeing to it that you grow up just as fine as I can manage."

Gideon looked up unexpectedly and met her gaze with a direct, probing look.

"Why do you want to do that?"

Missy had not expected so candid a question from him, and she was obliged to look away. Honesty, she told herself. The boy has had so little of it in his lifetime, and if you mean to set an example, you must start with yourself. But how could she be completely honest when she wasn't sure herself that she understood her motivations? She swallowed and met his gaze again.

"I think we need each other, Gideon, just as you need—as Glory needs you," she answered at last, folding her hands before her. "God put us in one another's paths for a reason."

"Hmph. God never did me no favors."

Missy bit her lip.

"He found Glory for you, didn't He?"

"Found her myself," he retorted. "When I broke in here two months ag—Shit." Gideon, abashed, hung his head. Obviously he had not intended to reveal such a detail to her.

We'll work on your language, too, Missy thought, hiding her smile.

"Seems to me we have a choice, here." She smoothed over his gaffe and kept her distance, despite her desire to take off his filthy cap and ruffle his hair with her fingers. "Both of us. Your choice is whether or not you want to come with us, Glory and me. Mine is whether or not I want to take you. I already made mine. Now it's up to you to make yours."

Gideon buried the toe of his shoe under the straw and looked up. He wanted to go with Glory. He would be lost without her. He sure liked Missy Cannon enough, too, although he couldn't bring himself to tell her that just yet. Dakota and the C-Bar-C sounded like heaven, if anything did. And while he didn't know about God and such things, he had a funny, prickly feeling that Missy was right about there being some reason why the three of them, he, Glory, and Missy, had met up.

He had another thought.

"That Muldaur fella. Is he comin', too?"

Even in the dim light of the small lantern, he could see Missy's face go beet red.

"Why ever would you ask a question like that?" Her voice was funny all of a sudden. Like she'd swallowed a bug. "I hardly know the man."

Gideon shrugged, watching her with wonder.

"I didn't say nothin' before," he remarked, "but I'd seen him around here a couple of times before today. This morning, too, in fact. Talkin' to some of the grooms and owners and such, askin' questions about the C-Bar-C. And about Melissa Cannon. That's you, right?"

Missy nodded twice. She looked as if she were strangling. Her expression made him want to laugh, although he thought she might not appreciate that.

"He was makin' noises like he was interested in buyin' the place, was what I thought."

Missy's eyelids fluttered like the wings of a butterfly.

"He say anything to you about it yet?" Gideon prodded.

"What?" She jerked her head up. "He—I—We—I mean, I—No. Well—"

81

Gideon could not help laughing.

"You ought to see your face," he told her. "You're red as the inside of a watermelon!"

Missy's flustered agitation quickly became a scowl, and Gideon stopped laughing at once.

"It's far past your proper bedtime," she grumbled, sending him a glare that didn't frighten or fool him in the least. "And I won't have you meddling in my business. Please keep that in mind in the future."

"Yes, ma'am." He tried to sound meek, but it was difficult. The beginning of an idea was forming in his head, and he sort of liked the way it looked.

Chapter Seven

"Ironclad?" Missy echoed Joshua's grim declaration weakly.

"The judge's very words," Joshua confirmed, slamming himself into the wing chair that faced the suite's fireplace. He'd spent most of the past week meeting with a succession of legal counselors and exchanging telegraph messages with a number of correspondents, all over the issue of Muldaur's claim. He looked and sounded as if he'd reached the end of not only his tether but his hope, as well. "That letter's properly witnessed and registered. It wasn't made out to Muldaur, of course, but the fact that he apparently won it in a poker game doesn't make it any less binding, in the eyes of the law."

Missy digested this with a hard swallow.

"What about Congressman Seamus Muldaur, Flynn's brother?"

Missy was glad that Allyn had asked the question, for

she doubted her own ability to sound calm.

"Muldaur's brother claims he knows nothing about it. I have his reply right here."

In agitation, Joshua fished in his inside breast pocket and withdrew a small, neatly folded scrap of paper. He extended it to Missy. She waved it away. She did not even want to touch it.

"Apparently the brotherhood of congressmen is not as loyal as the brotherhood of siblings." Allyn turned away, wearing a thoughtful look. "Isn't there anything else we can do?"

Joshua laid his head back and closed his eyes with a weary sigh. An intense, scrupulous man, he did not take such a defeat well, Missy realized.

"If there were, I'd have done it," he said on a breath. "I'm sorry, Miss. It looks as if we'll have to meet with Muldaur after all and deal with this thing face-to-face."

Flynn Muldaur had been trying to see Missy all week, since the fiasco at Filson's. She'd refused, partly at the urging of Joshua and Allyn, who had been hopeful that his claim would be proven false by their efforts. But only partly. More than anything else, she dreaded the thought of facing him after she had so horribly and embarrassingly misconstrued his motives at Filson's. That part of her never wanted to lay eyes on him again.

"Excuse me." Phyllis Hammond slipped into the sitting room from the nursery next door. "The bellboy just brought this up. He's waiting outside for a reply. Shall I just send him away again?"

Missy accepted the calling card from the frowning nursemaid. On it was printed the name she most dreaded: Flynn Muldaur.

"Muldaur again!" Allyn snapped. "Tell him—"

"No." Missy's reply was crisp. "I suppose I'd best speak with him and find out what his intention is regarding his share of the ranch."

"But Missy, you need time to think about this!" Allyn said, taking her by the shoulders with a little shake. "Suppose he—"

"I've had all week to think about it, Allyn." Missy surprised herself by feeling as calm as she sounded. "I've decided that Mr. Muldaur really has only three choices. Since there's nothing in the document that states a dollar amount, he must either sell his half-interest to me, sell it to someone else, or buy my half. There's no question of me selling him my half, of course. I haven't the ready capital to purchase his half from him at the current market value—"

"Of course we could loan you the money!" Allyn interjected firmly.

"Unthinkable," Missy told her. "I would never consent to such a loan. So that leaves him only one alternative."

"Two," Allyn corrected, giving her a direct and unsettling look. "As unlikely as it seems, he might actually be of a mind to move to the ranch and behave as a full partner."

Missy found herself staring at the rug. She had thought of that, but she'd dismissed it as an impossibility, based on Joshua's assessment of the man. She was dismayed to discover that the thought of Flynn Muldaur choosing to live at the C-Bar-C was as intriguing as it was disturbing. It made her insides feel most peculiar.

"I doubt that." Joshua looked disdainful. "Oh, he might move in, but if he did it would only be with the intention of driving Missy out."

He sounded so cold that Missy felt impelled to voice what had been on her mind for the past week.

"You told me when I first met him he isn't to be trusted," she ventured, risking a glance at Allyn's unusually stern husband. "But you never said why. You never told me how you knew it to be so. Since he was evidently telling the truth about this document of his, I would like to know what prompted you to say that. In any event it would be helpful for me to know, if I am to have any sort of dealings with him.''

Joshua glanced at her, then at Allyn, then back again, reluctance printed plainly all over his serious, angular face.

"You don't have to deal with him at all," Joshua insisted, planting his elbow in the armrest and hooking his thumb about his chin. "I could take care of—"

"The C-Bar-C is my responsibility," she interrupted him pleasantly but firmly. "You and Allyn have done far more than you needed to on my behalf. You have your own burdens. I know you wanted to go back to Annapolis three days ago, but you stayed here to help me in this—this emergency. I appreciate it. But it's time I took over and handled this matter as best I may, on my own.''

Allyn paled. "Missy, you can't mean that you intend to—"

"I can, and I do," she said as reasonably as she could through the turmoil of uncertainty in her stomach. "I have relied on you both for far too long. I made my decision years ago to keep the C-Bar-C and to maintain it myself. I've had good years and lean ones, mostly good, of course, since Sheik. This is nothing more than a new challenge for me. And you both understand me well enough, I think, to know that I have no intention of losing everything I've worked so hard for. What would be helpful, though, is to know as much about the man as I possibly can, so I can enter into whatever arrangement I may with my eyes open, so to speak.''

"Actually, I should like to know, too," Allyn remarked, her grudging tone proclaiming her surrender to Missy's resolution.

Joshua granted them both a whimsical smile with his

mouth, but not his eyes. "Knowledge is power, eh?" He addressed his comment to Missy. "You're right. The least I can do is tell you what I know of Flynn Muldaur. But I warn you: You won't much care for what I have to say."

Missy nodded swiftly. She did not like it already, and so far Joshua had not said a word. She directed Phyllis to convey the message that Mr. Muldaur was to come up to the suite in ten minutes' time. Then she sat in the little Queen Anne chair facing Joshua's and folded her hands in her lap.

"I'm ready," she said.

Joshua shifted in his chair as if hoping to make an uncomfortable subject more comfortable for both of them.

"Flynn was an agent under me in the Secret Service," he began, stroking his cheek with an idle, telling finger. "He was a good one. A little brash, a little hotheaded sometimes. The kind to act before he thought . . . Hmm. Come to think of it, he sounds a little bit like—"

"Joshua!" Allyn's warning was a low growl.

"As I was saying, he was, unlike anyone we know, somewhat precipitous. But he was dependable and honest. At least until one disastrous case. It involved a smuggling ring out of New Orleans, operated through a very exclusive, ah, bordello. We'd worked for months undercover—"

"I wager you did your part for God and country," Allyn interrupted, her features a thundercloud.

"Be still, Allyn. This is serious," Joshua scolded.

Allyn said nothing more, but looked as if she were mentally preparing a lengthy and passionate oratory for later.

"As I was saying, we worked undercover to be sure that the net, when we finally cast it, would be tight. No one involved could be allowed to slip through. It would compromise the entire effort. Muldaur volunteered to spearhead the final phase of the operation, and because he'd been undercover the longest, it was natural that he should.

"When the hour came, Muldaur just flat out wasn't where he said he'd be. The net failed because of it; more than half of those involved got away, including the ringleader, the madam, and several crooked high-ranking government officials. Those who were caught eventually were let off with light sentences, because the evidence had been severely compromised. It was a disaster. And the worst of it was, when we discovered that Flynn wasn't where he should have been, we assumed something had happened to him. Two men lost their lives in the trouble that followed. Another lost his sight." Joshua let out a long sigh and shook his head, as if he still could not credit his own stupidity in having trusted Muldaur.

"Flynn turned up a little while later, after the dust had settled. We were surprised. We thought he'd been fed to the sharks in the Gulf. He offered no excuse for his behavior. At first he was believed to have acted as an accomplice to the smugglers, but in the end nothing could be proven. He was charged with dereliction of duty, but he opted to resign rather than to be dismissed from service.

"It came out during the hearing that he'd gotten involved with the daughter of the madam, a la—a woman by the name of Madeleine Deauville. The adjutant accused him of having betrayed his colleagues for the charms of this woman, and so costing two men their lives. He never denied it."

"Deauville?" Missy could not prevent herself from echoing the name aloud.

Joshua arched an eyebrow. "You've heard of her?"

She did not answer right away. Her mind was racing

right along with her heart. Deauville was the name of the "niece" Muldaur had been squiring at Filson's last week. Antoinette. Could Muldaur be, in reality, the girl's father? But she was far older than this story, certainly. Joshua, she knew, was 36 years old; Muldaur could not be much older than that. Antoinette Deauville was no younger than 16, probably closer to 18. That would have made Flynn no older than 20 at her birth, far too young to have been a Secret Service operative at the time. The mathematics of it were all wrong. Unless . . .

Unless Muldaur had known the woman in question for a much longer time than he'd admitted to his superiors. Unless he was even less principled than Joshua's story implied.

Unless there was another explanation entirely for the events Joshua had outlined to her, and the very existence of the lovely Miss Deauville.

"After that"—Joshua had gone on, and Missy strove to catch up—"he helped his brother campaign for Congress, but with his connection to that scandal, he proved a greater liability than an asset and he was asked to resign. He's been notably successful in a number of speculative ventures over the past ten years, some land deals, involvement in a professional baseball team, and, I believe, once even a partnership in a thoroughbred stable. But his profits always seem to dry up or vanish. His associates come out all right, which is a wonder, considering his peculiar record of building, then quickly and mysteriously losing, his fortunes. But he ends up as broke as he started. Some say he lives under an unlucky cloud. I think he makes his own bad luck."

Missy pondered Joshua's words in silence. She'd wanted to believe that Flynn Muldaur represented no great threat to her, to the ranch, or to her peace of mind. She'd longed to hear something in his words that would give her hope that she could, indeed, manage Muldaur and this distressing turn of events that made him her legal partner, but Joshua's story produced the exact opposite effect.

He'd been involved with a woman. With illegal activities. With scandal. Missy had no stomach for scandal, and no taste for intrigue. And she had no desire to risk the C-Bar-C, and all she'd worked for during the past ten years, to fall victim to Muldaur's scams, ill luck, or whatever it was that resulted in catastrophe for him. His partners had so far escaped sharing his bad fortune, but she was all too aware that that, too, could change. Nothing was certain about Flynn Muldaur, it seemed, but uncertainty.

The clock ticked loudly on the mantelpiece and a burning log collapsed, with a spray of sparks and ash, into the embers in the fireplace.

"Shall I arrange for some tea to be sent up for this meeting, or don't you intend to refresh your guest?" Allyn broke the silence with her quiet question.

Missy looked up, striving to keep her features composed. Both Allyn's and Joshua's expressions were probing and unreadable. Missy got up from her chair and turned toward the window. It was snowing outside, a heavy, wet snow that melted at once into still, slushy puddles in the street.

"I'd prefer coffee, I think," she replied, keeping her voice even and light. "And I cannot concern myself as to Mr. Muldaur's fancy."

Missy thought it best that Allyn and Joshua withdraw when she heard the knock upon the door of the suite moments later. Their presence at the meeting would, she knew, only serve as a distraction, given Joshua's and Flynn's open animosity toward one another. And she had need of every shred of her ability to concentrate if she and the C-Bar-C were to survive this crisis. Joshua and Allyn withdrew, offering assurances that they were as near as the next room should any unexpected trouble arise. Missy closed the door behind them and leaned on it for a moment, gathering her strength before she responded to the knock.

Composing her features into a cordial but not overly welcoming expression, she swung the door wide.

"Mr. Mul—"

But it was not he.

"Gideon, what in blue blazes are you doing out here in the hallway?" she exclaimed, seizing the lad by his bony shoulders and pulling him inside. "You were told to wait with Miss Hammond and Albertine in the nursery. And look at your new clothes!" She groaned.

Gideon was apparently as efficient at ruining his wardrobe as she was. He was covered with mud and filth, from the soles of his new shoes to the crown of his recently trimmed sable hair. His cap and bow tie were missing entirely.

He looked contrite, to his credit, although not sufficiently abashed to persuade Missy that his remorse was genuine.

"I ain't seen Glory in two days," he explained, as if that should excuse any and all transgressions. "She was missin' me. I could tell. Hey, I saw that Muldaur feller downstairs again. He's come to see you again, I bet. You gonna talk to him this time?"

Missy stared hard at her new ward. She had the feeling that his knowledge was not as innocent as he tried to make it sound, that he'd waited outside the door listening to the conversation of the adults. The open expression on his young face gave her no clue.

"None of your business, young man. I'll have to save my lecture on the evils of snooping, and the dangers of running off, for a later time," she scolded him, attempting to brush the smudges of dirt from his freckled cheeks

91

and his wool tweed coat. "Not that any of them seem to have made an impression so far. Get off with you next door. Miss Hammond is probably frantic."

"Oh, she never even knew I went," he boasted proudly. "I skipped out the window."

They were five floors above the street.

"You *what*?"

Another knock interrupted her dismay, and she glanced at the door. Flynn this time, no doubt.

"Scoot next door," she told him, her voice low and swift. "Now. I have business to attend to."

"With Muldaur?" he asked, his dark eyes lighting up as if in anticipation of some great, dangerous adventure. "Let me stay! I can help."

"I doubt it. Anyway, this is private. I—"

The knock sounded again, a trifle louder.

"Miss Cannon?"

Flynn Muldaur's honey baritone was all business, edged with a hint of impatience. She'd made him wait for this meeting all week; it seemed he didn't want to wait another moment. Missy put her right hand on her stomach, hoping to still its mad fluttering. She turned Gideon toward the other door with her left hand.

"Go."

Gideon pivoted and looked her dead in the eye.

"No." He pronounced the word succinctly.

"Gideon!" She was exasperated.

"Miss Hammond will scold me again, and so will Mr. and Mrs. Manners," he told her, perching on the window seat like a curious young bird. "I'd as soon wait here and get my scolding from you. I won't make no noise. I promise."

"Miss Cannon?" Another brisk knock.

"Well, it's either that or having you listening at the keyhole again," Missy grumbled, trying to hide an unexpected relief that she would not face Muldaur alone

92

after all. "But not a word, now." She shook a finger at him and tried to look stern. "Remember, you promised."

Gideon nodded with such enthusiasm Missy thought his head was going to come off. He clambered onto the window seat and crossed one knickered leg up beneath him, allowing the other to dangle. Then he fixed his gaze on the door as if he could burn holes in it with his stare alone. Missy turned her head to hide her smile at the thought of such a gallant, if inconsequential, knight standing to her defense.

When she opened the door, her smile retreated behind a wave of astonishment.

"Good afternoon, Miss Cannon." Flynn Muldaur, handsome as ever, elegant in a dark gray pinstripe suit, held out a small but breathtaking bouquet of red hothouse roses, sprinkled with baby's breath. She must have looked as stunned as she felt, because he tendered a rueful grin along with a self-conscious glance at the flowers. "We started off badly on both previous occasions, and it's time to rectify that. May I come in?"

Unable to speak for shock, Missy accepted his lovely floral offering. She would have been far more at ease had Mr. Muldaur come in full of anger at having been made to wait all week to see her. His conciliatory manner, combined with her own natural attraction to him, made her feel as if she had ventured onto thin ice in a thick fog.

Some time passed before Missy realized he was still standing at the door.

"Y-yes," she stammered, looking away quickly, lest he perceive her heated blush. "Please. Come in. I'm sorry to have made you wait."

She took several quick steps into the room ahead of him, amazed that she did not trip over her skirt in her awkward haste. There was a noise in the corner. She looked up to see Gideon eyeing them both. He sat very still, but he fingered his throat as if he'd just cleared it. Somehow the sight heartened her. She deposited the bunch of roses on the settee with a careless gesture, and she collected her wits sufficiently to invite Flynn Muldaur to be seated.

Muldaur moved with the grace and efficiency of a cat. His clothing was tailored to a perfection not found every day, for it complemented him like a second skin. Missy found herself wondering at the body shielded beneath the expensive suit, and that wonder was enough to renew her blush.

He placed his crisp gray derby on the small table beside the wing chair lately occupied by Joshua; she had forgotten to take it from him. Another social gaffe. She swallowed and glanced once more at Gideon for fortification. He grinned at her. Muldaur looked over his shoulder, then commanded Missy's gaze once again.

"So the boy is yours," he remarked with an oblique look that might have meant anything, and nothing complimentary. "Or at least a part of your, ah, entourage?"

Missy shook her head, fighting a blush.

"No, he's—his name is Gideon, and he takes care of Glory. The horse. The one in the—the one where I—" She gave up on that course as being both unwise and impossible. "I've recently, er, hired him." She did battle with a compelling urge to explain everything to Flynn Muldaur, and won.

Muldaur allowed several meaningful seconds to pass before he nodded twice. Missy could almost see him cataloging her: takes in strays, he would note in his mental ledger.

"I had thought we would converse in private," he remarked with politeness that sounded ever-so-slightly forced, a quizzical look in his steel blue eyes.

Missy held her back erect and dared a bold smile.

"We are as private as we need be," she assured him, enjoying Gideon's ensuing wink beyond Muldaur's broad shoulder.

It was Muldaur's turn to appear ill at ease. Missy felt a surge of confidence. She folded her hands in her lap, determined not to justify Gideon's presence any further. Muldaur drew a long breath in concession.

"I take it by your agreement to meet with me that you are satisfied as to the validity of my claim." His tone was formal.

"For the present." She nodded once.

Flynn Muldaur had, aside from the most handsome face she'd ever seen, the most interesting one as well. He seemed capable of expressing a subtle nuance of mood. His mouth, although not full, was sensuous, especially when it twitched once at the corner and curved slightly downward, as it was doing now. It was a pale reflection of a smile. Missy felt she could pass an eternity exploring that look and believe her time to have been well spent.

Flynn was intrigued by the softened set of Missy Cannon's pleasant features, for Missy, according to his admittedly limited experience, was not by nature a flirtatious woman. He wondered what it could mean, for surely it meant something. She was not a woman who wasted anything about herself, whether a word, a look, or a thought. He'd come here with a mission in mind, but something in her eyes, a pearly amethyst hue on this gray afternoon, made him rethink his straightforward agenda. He felt intriguingly out of his element with this unusual woman.

He reined himself in: he could not afford the luxury of exploring her ever more interesting attributes. And even if he could, he had sworn never to relinquish his common sense to an imprudent dalliance again.

"Miss Cannon, we both know that the more time

passes, the less likely it is that my claim will be proven false." It helped to stick to business. "I happen to know you've wasted some time here in Louisville on that fool's errand, and you wish to be away to put your new mares to stud. As it happens, our desires at the moment are very much the same."

"I doubt that, Mr. Muldaur." Her voice was low and pretty like a seasoned musical instrument. A French horn, perhaps. Or a cello. It sent a curious tingle along his spine, low into his back, as if she'd played him with a horsehair bow.

"Oh, I believe you'll find that they are," he assured her, leaning forward in his chair. Now, why in heaven's name should a simple remark like that make her blush? he wondered, although he had to admit she did so more becomingly than he might have expected.

Was that roses he smelled? Surely not the flowers he had brought; they were too far away. Missy's own fragrance, then. And something spicy, besides. A scent that he, who knew every perfume a lady might wear, should know. The fact that he could not put a name to it distracted him, and for a moment he forgot what he'd been about to say to her.

"I believe you'll find that they are," he repeated, hoping to regain his train of thought. "And I believe you'll be very amenable to my proposal."

"Oh . . . Oh?"

Her response was so bizarre that he stared at her. Her round cheeks blazed a fiery crimson hue and she looked away, her bosom rising and falling rapidly with each brittle, panting breath.

Proposal, he'd said.

Why don't you marry her, Flynn? Antoinette had asked him half-facetiously three days earlier. *Then you can get your hands on the whole fortune instead of only half.*

Chapter Eight

Damn Madeleine, her grasping, covetous mother, and her avaricious offspring! He had even started to think like them!

Thoroughly disgusted with himself, he got up and strode to the fireplace. He felt as if he were contaminating the place. He wedged his elbow against the mantelpiece and tried to order his thoughts.

"I want to apologize to you, Miss Cannon," he said swiftly, fearing he would lose his nerve if he paused to think about what he was saying. "This whole damned business has come out back end first. You have a reputation for honesty; I can't be anything less than honest with you."

He regretted his dangerous course of action as soon as he uttered the words, but it was too late to recall them.

"Anything less than honesty is not what I wish to hear from you, or from anyone."

Flynn bit his lip. Josh Manners had no doubt told Missy Cannon exactly what the word *honesty* meant, when uttered by Flynn Muldaur. That would be, according to his former superior, precisely nothing.

Which meant, he supposed, that he had nothing to lose.

"When this letter of debt came into my possession—"

"When you won it in a poker game, you mean," she interrupted him with cool politeness.

"Poker isn't a crime, you know, and winning at it—honestly—is even less of one." Lord, was she one of those fire-and-brimstoners who believed a man should never have any fun?

"Of course not," she murmured, her self-rebuke not ringing quite true. "Pray, continue. You were speaking of being honest, I think."

A noise in the corner drew Flynn's attention. He looked up to see the boy again, shifting in his seat, eyeing him with a look that made him feel as if he'd been pronounced guilty and sentenced to hang. Gideon, Missy had called him. Flynn had almost forgotten that he was there.

He ground his teeth. He wanted to lay his cards down before Missy Cannon but, damn it, having the boy there as a silent witness unnerved him.

He purposely fixed his stare on Missy again.

"I thought at first I'd sell my interest in the ranch to someone else," he said. "Turn over a quick profit, and move on."

"That sounds like something you might do, from what I've heard."

Muldaur ignored her courteous insult.

"That wasn't as easy as it sounded, and in the process of trying to find a buyer, I learned that the C-Bar-C was a fairly thriving concern."

"I've enjoyed good fortune recently," Missy conceded with a wary look. "Although it wasn't always so, as anyone can tell you."

He'd heard about the years of hardship. The story of the C-Bar-C's rise to prominence was pretty much a legend on the circuit. A fairy tale. Flynn had never believed in fairy tales. The older he got, in fact, the less he believed in anything.

"When I found out the owner was a woman, I—"

No, that didn't sound right. Damn it, why hadn't he just stayed with his original plan? He'd have been in and out of here in five minutes with everything he'd wanted in his pocket. But no, he'd had to go and let himself be moved by her. He straightened and shrugged his coat into place. Honesty, he reminded himself. As much as he—and Seamus—could afford.

"You thought you'd what, Mr. Muldaur?"

Had the room gone chilly? Muldaur cursed under his breath at his blundering stupidity. That a simple, forthright woman should reduce him to a stammering fool just when he most required his celebrated smooth address was an alarming occurrence. He sucked in a much-needed breath.

"I don't wish to complicate your life any further than I already have, Miss Cannon," he managed to say lightly, turning toward her again. "I'm willing to sell you my half-ownership in the C-Bar-C for a reasonable price. I assume you're interested in clearing the title."

Missy smoothed the gathers of her gray silk morning dress. It was a plain affair, hardly as flattering as the regal purple velvet she'd worn to Filson's. Yet she imbued the simple gown with presence and dignity. And something else . . . He couldn't quite name it.

Flynn found himself, to his chagrin, staring at the floor between them, waiting for her answer like a penitent child awaiting punishment.

"My interest is academic, Mr. Muldaur," she intoned

dryly. ''Unless the 'reasonable price' to which you refer is the fair market value of the property when your letter of debt was issued. That would make the buyout somewhere in the vicinity of seventy-five dollars, given the probable condition of the place at the time. Somehow I expect you had a slightly higher figure in mind?''

She was being facetious. Or was she? He chuckled, hoping for the best.

''Slightly.''

Missy leaned against the back of her chair, rested her elbow on the cushioned arm, and crossed her slippered feet at the ankles. It was a pose that a man might have assumed under the circumstances, Flynn realized, staring. He was unnerved by it.

''How much higher?'' Her gray eyes were appraising. Direct.

Integrity. That had been the word he'd sought earlier. He forced himself to maintain her gaze, and to answer her without blinking.

''Fifty thousand dollars.''

Even Madeleine would be satisfied with that windfall, he reflected bitterly. For a time, anyway.

Missy betrayed her shock by a lift of one tapered eyebrow.

''You can't be serious.'' Her voice was faint.

''I've made inquiries.'' He tried to remain nonchalant while monitoring her face and ignoring her posture. ''It isn't the property which commands such a price, you realize, although its value has certainly increased, thanks to the improvements you've made in the past several years. As a piece of ground in that area of the country, I daresay the whole place isn't worth more than half that amount.''

Missy's toe bobbed rapidly in the air, and she bounced the tips of her fingers off her thumbs as her hands hung from the front of the armrests.

"If that's so, then why are you asking for such an exorbitant amount?" she inquired in an admirably calm voice, despite her nervous display. "If the property isn't worth a hundred thousand dollars, how can you in good conscience expect me to give you fifty for your scrap of paper?"

Muldaur pressed his lips together. For an instant, he considered handing the document over to the distraught woman before him, or balling it and feeding it to the fireplace. He wanted to, as he'd never wanted anything before in his life. As he wanted to take the shadow of fear from Missy Cannon's face. As he wanted to see what that moist, quivering lower lip of hers tasted like . . .

Then he thought of Madeleine. And Antoinette.

And his brother.

Damning them all, Missy included, with one unspoken curse, he turned away again.

"I said the property itself wasn't worth that much," he went on, forcing a cool, businesslike tone despite his mounting agitation. "But the letter specifically states 'the property known as the C-Bar-C.' That means not only the ranch—the land, the buildings, the paddocks, the fences—it means the name as well. It's the name that's contributed the most to the value of the place in the past few years." The name that Missy, not her kind but improvident uncle, had built to such prominence. The irony of it sickened him.

"I'm afraid I don't understand." Her voice was very small. Distant. He sighed, a trifle louder than he would have liked.

"Look at it this way. If the situation were reversed— that is, if I were offering to buy out your half—I would stipulate expressly that the name 'C-Bar-C' be retained by me. Why? Because it's the name people in the business have come to recognize, and to associate with excellence. With performance. If such a stipulation were

101

not made in our agreement, there would be nothing to prevent you from taking the name and using it else-where, creating at least confusion and certainly competition for my interests.''

''But it's just a name,'' she argued. ''My uncle named it for himself and out of love for my father. When Allyn and I took it over, we didn't change it because the two C's were still appropriate—Cannon and Cameron.''

''Think of it this way.'' He faced her again, crossing his arms before him and pressing one finger against his lips as he strove for an analogy. ''You're familiar with patents and with copyrights, aren't you?''

''Vaguely.'' She looked confused.

The mechanics of business and corporate law had always held a fascination for Muldaur, and he found himself warming to the explanation upon which he was about to embark.

''There's a fellow in England by the name of Conan Doyle who writes stories, a serial, for a magazine. His leading character is a fellow by the name of Sherlock Holmes. This magazine has a contract with Doyle for stories featuring Holmes, which means Doyle must write these exclusively for them. He may not write them for any other publication.''

''But—''

''Let me finish.'' He sat down again but stayed on the edge of his seat, his knees wide apart. ''Doyle's contract with the magazine, however, does not grant the publishers the right to print stories by other authors using the character of Sherlock Holmes, which Doyle created. This would constitute an infringement, a violation of their covenant with Doyle. It would unfairly allow someone else to profit from Doyle's creation. Just as a patent is issued to prevent people from profiting from someone else's invention.''

''Unless the writer, or the inventor, specifically gave

up that right in their contract.''

"Exactly.'' She was no fool. His regard for her rose.

"Then what you are saying is that you're really selling me back my own good name. Is that right, Mr. Muldaur?''

Her assessment took him aback.

"Well—''

"And suppose I am not interested in buying?'' she wondered aloud, pressing her hands together as if in prayer. Her pretty gray eyes narrowed in a most dismaying, if attractive, manner. "In essence, that means that we each, technically, own all of the name, but only half of the ranch itself. Am I correct in that assumption?''

"I suppose, if you—''

"And the tax bill,'' she went on, gaining alarming momentum. "The one that's due this April. You are responsible for half of the payment? As well as half of the payroll and other expenses?'' She sounded positively delighted.

How had he lost control of this interview? And when? "Miss Cannon, I think you've missed the—''

"Oh, no, I haven't missed the point at all, Mr. Muldaur.'' She interrupted him with a quick, pixie smile completely incongruous with her womanly aspect. "You have taught me too well, I think, for your own good. I have exactly what I want from the C-Bar-C, and that is my good name and my reputation. Having you as a partner does nothing, as far as I can see, to compromise that. And since you now have a half-interest in the C-Bar-C, I'll wager that you won't do anything to undermine its continued success.''

"Good lord,'' he muttered.

"Beg pardon?''

He colored. "Nothing. I—Does this mean you're not interested in buying out my share?''

"I am very interested in buying out your share, Mr. Muldaur,'' she corrected him, maintaining his gaze with an uncompromising look which took him aback. "But I am unable to consider it. For now, at least. My resources are stretched to the limit, and all of my capital is in my stock. The mares I've purchased here, for example. I'll begin entertaining bids for the foals sired by Sheik as soon as I'm sure the dams will hold to service. There is no chance that I'll have anywhere near the kind of resources you expect before this time next year, at the earliest. Of course, you could try the bank. But I doubt they'd consider the equity in the name to be of anywhere near the value you estimate."

Flynn could only stare at the lady with the melodious voice, whose hint of a Southern accent was long buried in the Black Hills. Obviously she was an accomplished businesswoman as well as a respected breeder and trainer of horses. And he'd sat there like a prize fool, explaining a basic business tenet she'd probably cut her teeth on! He felt his defeat so acutely that he could not speak.

Missy stood up. She felt grand. She'd groped her way along throughout the interview, as if trying to find her way out of a maze in the dark, and when she'd least expected it, Muldaur himself had handed her a torch. She wanted to leap from her seat and do a little jig about the room, possibly even sing a gay ditty. She commanded herself, doing her best to suppress a grin at Flynn Muldaur's obvious vexation.

She stole a glance at Gideon who, as good as his word, had remained silent throughout. To her surprise, he wore a pensive frown. She thought perhaps he did not understand that she had won the round, and quite possibly the match. Well, she would explain it to him later. She stood up.

"I guess Mr. Muldaur could run the ranch with you," Gideon, in his corner, mused aloud.

Missy felt a draft on her tongue. She realized her

mouth was hanging open, and she shut it. Muldaur sat straight up and half turned in his chair, as if Gideon's reckless remark had imbued him with a fresh, if alarming, notion.

"Mr. Muldaur's interest is obviously a quick profit," she said hastily. "And a quick profit is not what one gains by going into the business of raising horses. It is a slow process which requires patience, an investment of time, money, and energy. Not to mention a basic knowledge of husbandry, stud value . . ."

While Missy enumerated on trembling fingers, Muldaur saw a bright, emancipating light: Madeleine demanded her pound of flesh with tedious regularity. He was only 37 years old, but was already running out of ways to satisfy her voracious appetite for money. What Gideon was suggesting represented a solution not only for this week or the next, but quite possibly, if he played it right and if she could be even a little patient, for year after year of steady and even increasing income. Tribute.

Flynn detested the sound and the deeper meaning of that word, but tribute, he knew, was what it amounted to. Or blackmail. And like it or not, he was tied to it for life, or at least as long as Seamus lived. Perhaps it was time he considered a long-term solution to the problem.

Even if he did not like it.

He concentrated on Missy again. She looked as if she'd just bitten into a cow pie. Against his better judgment, he grinned.

"I think Gideon may have hit upon the ideal compromise for us both," he said, enjoying the irony of his comment; it was obvious that Missy thought it a far from perfect resolution.

"But you can't—I mean, I don't think I could work with a partner."

Flynn's grin widened. Missy was most fetching when she babbled.

"You worked with Allyn Cameron," he reminded her, laying a finger beside his cheek. "My back's somewhat stronger, I'd guess. And I wouldn't have the distraction of trying to run a saloon at the same time, as she did."

Flynn tried to decide exactly which shade of red best described Missy's face. He settled on carmine.

"Unthinkable!" she pronounced firmly, closing her pretty mouth abruptly.

"More than thinkable, I'm afraid," he corrected, folding his hands behind his head. "Inevitable."

If nothing else, he thought, this unexpected development might make her reconsider her available resources and prompt her to at least make him an offer of financial settlement, just to be rid of him. But Gideon had planted the seed and it was taking root. Flynn was intrigued by the idea of moving in on Missy Cannon's well-ordered life. He doubted his new plan could be confounded, even by a full-price offer. He decided he must remember to thank Gideon for his interference.

"But you can't mean to—I—Think of the scandal! Where will you stay?" She spoke in a heated whisper, as if her nosy, disapproving neighbors up north in Rapid City, South Dakota, might hear her all the way down here in Louisville, Kentucky.

"By rights, the house is half mine. I expect you have more than one furnished bedroom?"

Flynn thought she might faint at that, for she went pale as a bleached bedsheet. He braced himself to leap up and catch her.

Gideon remained planted in his window seat, watching the grown-ups. He wasn't at all sure he'd done the right thing, butting in the way he had. He knew for sure Missy wasn't going to thank him for it. Hell, she'd looked as if she'd like to kill him when he'd handed up that idea to Muldaur about him partnering with her. And

106

he wasn't exactly easy in his mind about Muldaur, except he could tell that Missy, for all her show, had taken to him like a kitten to cream. She could deny it all she wanted; he, Gideon, could tell she was sweet on the guy.

Missy meant to take him back to Dakota with her, he knew. She'd make a fine ma, he guessed, but he wouldn't mind having a pa, and she had no husband to make that happen.

Yet.

Gideon heard Muldaur say something more to Missy about the C-Bar-C and setting himself up there to partner her, but he didn't bother to listen any further. He had his own problems to work out, namely how to get these two mule-headed people together, when neither one of them seemed ready to admit that they even liked each other.

As Missy retorted to Flynn's comment, Gideon remembered something he'd heard in the last orphanage he'd gotten out of, something the matrons never seemed to get tired of telling everybody, whether it was about the swill they fed them or the regular whippings: You don't believe it now, they used to say, but it's for your own good. You'll understand when you grow up.

Observing the uproar he'd brought about, he wondered when, or whether, he would know he was growing up. He wondered if anybody ever did. But he knew one thing for sure: It was going to be real interesting watching Missy Cannon and Flynn Muldaur try to do it. Fun, too. He found himself enjoying it already. And anyway, he reasoned, watching them square off like a couple of contentious birds in a chicken coop, it was for their own good.

Part Two

Fructus Ventris Tu

Chapter Nine

May, 1892

"End of the line, ma'am."

Missy awoke from a troubling dream with a jolt.

End of the line. Rapid City.

Home.

Gideon, on the seat beside her, was still asleep. She shook his shoulder gently.

"We're home," she whispered as the train slowed. "Wake up, son."

It was a habit she'd fallen into, calling Gideon *son*. She only did it while he was sleeping, or when she was otherwise certain he could not hear her. It was not a good or wise habit, she knew: Gideon did not react kindly when strangers, meaning only to be familiar, applied the term to him. In the past three months, she had reached a fragile pact with the boy, a treaty of sorts for which none of the provisos were written down or even spoken aloud. One of the conditions they had tacitly agreed upon was that their relationship was intentionally vague.

Allyn had had an expression for it: she referred to Gideon as Missy's "ward." Which meant, Missy decided, tongue in cheek, that the boy was more than a piece of luggage and less than a blood relative.

Gideon stretched, one fist shooting heavenward, the other flush against his thigh. "Are we there yet?" He yawned.

Missy glanced out the picture window against which Gideon's tousled head had recently rested. She saw a lot of mud and wagons beyond the unfinished station house, and several brick edifices interrupting rows of clapboard structures.

"Yes."

She ached to see the ranch, and the changes effected by the winter months. She'd been homesick the last few weeks in Annapolis while Sheik had serviced her new mares and she waited to see if they'd hold. She'd hoped for three out of four, but the stallion had served all four ladies well, including Glory, to Missy's surprise. One had slipped during the long journey to the far side of South Dakota, but Missy was hopeful for the remaining three.

And now she was home.

Gideon plowed his fists into his eyes and yawned once more before he sat up straight and focused his sleepy stare on her.

"You suppose Flynn Muldaur's here, too?"

The train jerked to an abrupt but dignified halt, like an old widower bumping into a spinster at church. Missy looked at the carpetbag beneath her seat.

"We haven't heard a word from Mr. Muldaur since we left Louisville," she reminded him, nursing a combination of relief and regret that she hoped to keep secret from the alarmingly perceptive boy. "I'm sure he had second thoughts about partnering with me in the C-Bar-C and wisely thought better of attempting it. In any event, I'm sure we would have heard from him if he'd decided to exercise that unlikely option. Men like Flynn Muldaur, it seems to me, resist anything that smacks of hard work or putting down roots. Let that be a lesson to you."

"I bet you he's here," Gideon grumbled, yanking at his suspenders and straightening his knickers as he shuffled to his feet. "I know he is."

"And just why is that so important to you?" Missy could not help inquiring.

Gideon gave a careless shrug. "It ain't." He slammed his cap on his head.

Missy sighed. Gideon, she'd discovered over the past three months, could be talkative or taciturn, usually alternating between the two without warning. His moods convinced her that he did far more thinking than speaking, which was an admirable yet distressing quality in a companion. She'd have liked to have paddled him when, back in February, he'd very vocally pointed out to Flynn Muldaur his option of assuming a co-ownership role at the ranch.

The truth was, though, that a part of her wished Gideon had convinced Muldaur. Time had softened her memory as well as her opinion of the man Joshua Manners had called untrustworthy. She hadn't heard Flynn's side of the story, after all. It wasn't that she did not believe Joshua Manners: the integrity of Allyn's husband was beyond reproach. It was just that she'd learned during her 27 years that things were not always what they seemed, and there were at least two sides to every story. She never thought of Flynn Muldaur anymore without remembering his mesmerizing blue eyes, his engaging smile, and the way the two had worked together to make her heart do some splendid acrobatics.

And her heart, over the past three months, had gotten quite used to the exercise.

"Come along," she said, anxious to change the subject. "I've wired ahead; someone will be waiting to take us out to the ranch. And you do want to see Glory first, I assume."

Glory, Missy had quickly discovered, was the best way to redirect Gideon's thoughts, no matter what odd or embarrassing topic he fixed himself on. She found herself mentioning the mare frequently to deflect the boy's unnerving curiosity about everything, most especially her private affairs: Gideon could not credit that she was unmarried and he questioned her endlessly about her situation, much to her chagrin. Missy had always thought herself a patient person, but within a few days of their association she theorized, wearily, that God had put Gideon in her path to demonstrate to her that she had not previously known what the word patience meant.

Gideon raced down the platform to the livestock car to find Glory, his coattails flapping in the light spring breeze like the wings of a young bird. Missy followed at a more sedate pace. She paused to present their baggage claims to the porter and was stopped by a familiar voice.

"Miz Cannon."

Micah Watts, the C-Bar-C foreman for the past two years, approached her in his usual respectful manner, one hand on the brim of his dusty gray Stetson, the other shoved into the back pocket of his ancient jeans. He wore a tentative smile on his bristled, weathered features that put Missy on the alert at once.

"Mi!" she exclaimed, shading her eyes. "I never ex-

pected you'd come yourself to fetch us! You could have
sent one of the hands.''

Mi was not old, but long years of hard work outdoors
made him—and his clothing—look that way. The lines
about his eyes, however, gave him an anxious look that
she suspected had little to do with either age or wear.

''No, ma'am, I couldn't.'' His thin smile faded like
his pants.

Missy's mouth went dry.

''There's—there's nothing wrong at home, is there?''
Her mind instantly invented every sort of catastrophe
that might have befallen the C-Bar-C, its stock, and its
personnel during her absence. Fire, flood, tornado, epi-
demic, or any combination spelled disaster. She held her
breath and braced herself for the very worst.

''N-no.'' Micah looked around and scratched the back
of his neck, making the knot of his bandanna bob at his
throat. ''Leastways nothin' like, uh . . .'' He trailed off.

It was not like Mi to be evasive. Missy's dread
swelled in her breast.

''Mi?''

''What I mean is—'' He broke off and made a sound
she took for annoyance at his own ineptitude. Missy's
worry became impatience. Was he planning to ask for a
raise in pay, or might he be considering asking her to
marry him? In either case, the answer would be an em-
phatic no.

''Micah, is there something wrong or not?'' She was
abrupt.

A shy man, Micah flinched under her direct scrutiny.

''Well, no, not exactly. That is, not accordin' to Mr.
Muldaur. You see—''

''Who?'' Missy thought she might strangle on the
word.

Micah grimaced as if he expected her to rain blows
on him.

"Oh, damn," he muttered, shuffling his big, booted feet on the dusty planks. "I knew I shouldn't—but then when he brought the sheriff around with that paper a' his . . ."

"Flynn Muldaur?" Missy pronounced the name very carefully, although she felt such a storm of conflicting emotions she thought she might burst on the spot. "Am I to understand that—that a Mr. Flynn Muldaur has presented himself at the C-Bar-C, and is—"

"—livin' there now; yes, ma'am," Mi finished for her. He looked relieved that Missy had guessed. He'd been spared most of the onerous task of actually telling her.

Missy remained very still, not trusting her legs to support her if she tried to move. Why couldn't it have been a mere flood or a fire? she wondered miserably. There was no calamity she could envision that would have been worse than this.

"Miz Cannon?"

Micah Watts might have been prodding a dead coyote with a stick.

"Glory's just fine." Gideon came skipping up, happy as a pig in mud. "She looks a bit hollow around the eyes like as if she needs to take on water, but I think she's glad to be—What's wrong, Miss? You look spooked!"

The fact that Gideon laughed did nothing to ease Missy's peace of mind, such as it was.

"When did he arrive?" She addressed her question to Micah.

"Who?"

"Gideon, be still a moment."

Micah looked at Gideon, then back to Missy with one eyebrow a full inch higher than the other.

"I'll explain this in a minute," she said tersely, working very hard to keep her temper in check. "Tell me about Mr. Muldaur."

"Muldaur's here?" Gideon interrupted gleefully. "See, I told you—"

"Gideon, go wait with the horses. *Now*."

Gideon only looked at her for a second before he stalked off down the platform again.

"Tell me everything," she ordered the foreman, pinching the bridge of her nose with her thumb and forefinger. She meant to ward off a headache. Screaming would have worked better, she thought, but on a busy train platform in the middle of Rapid City she did not have that luxury.

Micah's wide, wiry shoulders relaxed. Missy guessed he was glad the weight of his news was off of them.

"Well, it's sort of a long story," he warned her. "Maybe I ought to tell it on the way."

A long story? Missy's stomach sank. By how much had Muldaur beaten her back to Rapid City?

"Tell me here and tell me now," she said through clenched teeth. "I don't care if it takes until midnight."

"Well, I doubt it'll take that long," he mumbled, looking downcast as a whipped puppy. "He showed up about three weeks ago. Came right up to the house with Sheriff Garlock; guess he knowed we'd give him a hard time, else. Anyways, Eldon said the paper Muldaur had was all legal right enough. He even showed us a telegraph message from some judge or some such. We was to let him stay, at least until you came home to straighten it all out. At first we thought he was just some flimflammer, but Eldon, he made us set down with him and talk. Muldaur was real straight with us. Said we wasn't to change nothin' about what we was doin', just to keep on doin' it until you came back. The way he spoke, we—we kinda thought he was—that he and you were—" Micah broke off his explanation as if he suddenly realized he'd waded into a hidden patch of quicksand.

Missy felt her color rise.

"You thought what?" It was best she knew exactly what speculation the hired hands had put forth, because whatever theories they'd arrived at, they'd no doubt expounded on them at length on Saturday nights in the saloon. Which meant her neighbors and the whole town had surely learned of the interesting development out at the C-Bar-C by now.

Micah half turned away from her and muttered something unintelligible.

"What was that?"

"We thought he mighta married you."

Sweet, holy mother of God.

Missy did not want to hear any more.

"Let's go," she said tersely, shouldering her carpetbag. "Gideon!"

"But I ain't fin—"

"I'll hear the rest later." She cut Micah off without looking at him. "Gideon! We're going. Micah, see to the luggage and hitch those mares up in back. Mind you, they're in foal. I have to send a telegraph; it won't take me but a minute."

The short walk to the telegraph office was not sufficient to cool her simmering anger. Old Dick Wyman, the operator, looked up from under his visor as she entered. The little bells he kept on the jamb jingled as she slammed the door, a preposterously lighthearted accompaniment to her foul humor.

"How do, Miz Cannon," called the dried-up husk of a man, who usually called her Missy. "Welcome back. Understand congratulations is in order."

Was it her imagination, or did Dick Wyman regard her with disapproving appraisal in his hawk eyes? She felt a rush of heat seep upward from beneath the stiff, starched collar of her shirtwaist.

"Mr. Muldaur is a temporary state of aff—business I will very shortly take care of," she huffed, compelled, by her mortification, to look away. "He—We—"

"I was talkin' about them fine mares you brung back," was the operator's amused, unruffled interruption. "Heard they was in foal."

"Oh." Missy swallowed her fresh humiliation. "Yes. They are. Three of them, anyway. Th-thank you." She placed her gloved hands on the polished counter hoping to still their trembling and found the courage to look Wyman in the face.

"I'd like to send a tele—"

" 'Course, since you mentioned that Muldaur feller, I guess I can tell you there's been some speculation hereabou—"

"There is no truth to any scurrilous rumor about my being—being involved with Mr. Muldaur in an unseemly way!" she snapped. She stared hard at him, hoping to shame him. She'd seen Allyn give people just such a look on more than one occasion, and it had never failed to make them rue their incautious words.

Dick Wyman, however, wrinkled up his mouth like an old prune and crossed his arms, with their white, gartered sleeves, in front of his chest.

"Speculation," he went on without so much as a blink, "that you might be thinkin' about sellin' the C-Bar-C."

Patience, Missy recalled Allyn saying often, had never been her chiefest virtue. Never did she more regret that flaw than under the speculative scrutiny of the calm telegraph operator in front of her. She found herself looking at the gapped seams in the plank floor.

"Oh." She managed a muffled tone. "No. I'm not. I won't. I expect to square things with Mr. Muldaur and send him on his way in short order."

She wanted to escape the office, and Mr. Wyman's stare, as quickly as possible; the telegraph to Allyn and Joshua could wait for another time. She got her hand on the door lever before Wyman spoke again.

"It's none a' my business, a' course," he remarked. "But I expect Bill Boland'll be happy to know that."

Not only did the bells jingle mockingly as she slammed the door behind her, but the four panes of glass in the door rattled as well.

Bill Boland was a neighbor and a good friend who, over time, had made no secret of the fact that he wished to be more to her than that. A widower, he'd courted Allyn years back until she married Joshua. Missy preferred to continue to treat the older man as a friend and colleague, although she knew he'd been steering their relationship in another direction since then. She had not thought of him much since she'd left Rapid City four months before. She found it unnerving that Dick Wyman had chosen that moment to remind her of him.

What had Bill made of Muldaur's arrival?

She found that his opinion of the event mattered to her. And that fact bothered her more than the event itself.

"Micah says to tell you we're ready, Miss." Gideon, quiet as a cat, had come up behind her.

Missy's stomach squirmed: Gideon's presence was another event sure to provoke speculation among her neighbors and the townspeople. She suddenly wished she could fold the boy up into her carpetbag until they reached the C-Bar-C. Both he and her neighbors in town were a little too curious for her peace of mind.

"All aboard!" the conductor called out as the engine let off a hiss and a belch of steam. The train was east-bound again, back to the stability and sanity she'd left behind with Allyn and Joshua. For a wild moment,

120

Missy considered stepping up to the car and climbing back on.

Bill Boland, besides being the nearest neighbor to the C-Bar-C, was the biggest, hardest-looking son of a bitch Flynn had ever met. And he'd met him the very first day he'd moved in. Boland was old, too. Near 50, Flynn guessed. Said he'd buried a wife ten years back. He sat a horse as if he were born to it, and it was clear to Flynn that the man took a very proprietary interest in Missy Cannon and her welfare.

Boland "dropped by" the C-Bar-C every afternoon; it would have taken an idiot to miss the fact.

"Them six-penny nails'd do the job to last," the widower commented from atop his sorrel gelding.

The hammer came down on Flynn's thumb instead of the head of the four-penny nail he was using to secure the birch shingle. He swore.

"It's only a privy roof," he retorted. "Anyway, it only has to last the winter. I plan to put in a water closet next year."

"Oh," Boland replied, as if he meant to add, "If you're still here next year."

Flynn had hoped Boland would see he was busy and leave. He'd been unprepared for the man's regular visits at first, but as soon as it became obvious that Boland intended to come every afternoon, ostensibly to see if Missy had returned home yet, he'd tried to find something of compelling importance to do just before Boland was expected. Sometimes Boland took the hint and stayed only long enough to exchange a few terse words of courtesy, as if he were counting out every syllable against some invisible ledger of debit. More often than not, though, the widower remained, content, it appeared to Flynn, to watch him in whatever task he'd undertaken and to find fault, most politely, with his execution thereof.

It hadn't taken more than three or four visits for Flynn to come to despise him.

"Heard from Miss Cannon yet?"

Flynn placed another birch shingle without looking at the older man. That was another thing about Boland that annoyed him: Boland called her Missy until he, Flynn, referred to her by the same name. Then Boland, without fail, started calling her Miss Cannon with a chilly edge to his voice.

Who the blue hell did the man think he was?

He had half a mind not to tell Boland what he knew, but nevertheless he did so, grudgingly.

"Micah got a wire from her last night," he allowed, then plied a few steady whacks to a nail, wishing it was Boland's head beneath his hammer. "Her train's due in this afternoon. He's in town now picking her up."

Boland seemed to ponder this, adjusting the brim of his sandy white Stetson and shifting his lean, muscular form in his saddle. The leather squealed. Flynn bent to his work again.

"Guess she'll be glad to see her privy's in good repair."

Flynn looked up to try to determine if Boland meant to be insulting, but the rancher had reined off without a word of farewell.

Good riddance, he thought, biting his lower lip as he surveyed the dust cloud Boland's gelding kicked up. He tried to imagine Missy Cannon as a wife to the taciturn mountain that was Bill Boland and found himself grinning at the unlikely picture: the irresistible force—that was Missy—meeting with the immovable object.

Unwittingly, he remembered his encounters with the dauntless woman who ran the C-Bar-C. He recalled the determined set to her round chin, the kaleidoscopic variability of her bright eyes, and the hourglass armful of her robust figure. He remembered the bewitching gleam of her dark curls and the delicious, unfamiliar aroma of her perfume.

He pictured her standing on the train platform in Rapid City as Bill Boland rode up high, wide, and handsome to greet her.

He nearly fell off the privy roof in his haste to climb down, and he hollered for a horse.

Chapter Ten

Missy's fondest ambition was to depart Rapid City without either encountering or creating a scene, and she got as far as the center of town before her hopes were crushed.

Rapid City was hardly a booming metropolis of the stature of Annapolis or Louisville, but it was a good-sized settlement with a wide, paved main street that the railroad had put in when they'd finished the spur line the previous year. Wagons and buckboards lined the thoroughfare as Micah guided their conveyance away from the station, and Missy could not help but notice that pedestrians on the boardwalk were staring down the road in the opposite direction as if anticipating a parade.

She heard the thunder that had captured their collective attention before she saw the reason for it, and she looked up ahead even as more curious spectators peered out of shop doors and second-floor windows. The rumbling grew louder. Just as she was about to caution Micah to pull off to the side of the road, she saw two horses and riders round the bend a quarter of a mile away amid enthusiastic shouts and cheers and an impressive storm of dust.

She shook her head in disgust. "Fools," she muttered. "Racing good animals on these stones! They ought to be horsewhi—"

Astonishment and mortification took the rest of her denunciation away from her.

Bill Boland got the better of the contest by about half a length, and he doffed his hat with a big gesture.

"Howdy, Miss," he panted, a triumphant smile creasing his handsome, dusty face. "Welcome home!"

"Good afternoon, Miss Cannon." Flynn Muldaur's urbane baritone was every bit as rich as she remembered it, but there was a heated rasp to it that hinted at the exertion to which he'd just subjected himself and his horse. "I trust you had a pleasant trip."

She stared in amazement from one man to the next. Bill Boland, nearest to her on her right, was as breathless as if he'd run the distance without benefit of a horse. He put his hat back on to shade his eyes against the late sun and surveyed her with hopeful cobalt eyes. Despite the cool spring breeze, a seam of sweat darkened the front of his blue shirt right down the lapel to the belt buckle at his trim waist. His big hands, in stained leather work gloves, gripped the reins and pommel of his lathered mount, betraying a tension only hinted at in his bluff address.

Flynn Muldaur seemed scarcely able to keep a scowl from his features. He appeared, in addition, to be attempting to rivet her with his gaze while glaring openly at the man who'd bested him in their contest, an undertaking she might have found comical were she not so furious. He wore work clothing she'd never seen on him before, including a dark red shirt with lacings at the throat rather than buttons, and a leather vest in the same shade of brown as his hat. Flynn, though, was coated with dust to his curly blond hair, evidence that he'd trailed Boland for a good part of the contest, maybe all of it.

And he was riding one of her best mares, besides.

She had more than enough displeasure to spare for both of them.

"I don't know which of you is the bigger fool, racing these animals that way on a paved street!"

Both men's expressions, different as they'd been from one another to start, blended to a single representation of openmouthed shock.

Micah seemed to shrink in the seat beside her. Curious onlookers emerged from nearby shops, but Missy no longer cared about creating a scene: Bill Boland and Flynn Muldaur had already accomplished that with no help whatever from her. Before she realized what she was doing, she was on her feet before the seat of the wagon, clenching her gloved hands in rage as she stared down at the two nonplussed competitors.

"What can you have been thinking of, Bill Boland, to risk a calamity?" She exploded the full force of her fury on the stunned rancher to her right, whose square jaw hung open like a broken old door. "I thought you had more sense than that, or at least a greater respect for your horses. And you!" Trembling with rage, she turned on Flynn Muldaur, whose deep-set blue eyes looked like twin thunderheads. "How dare you appropriate my stock for such a dangerous and foolhardy exhibition! She might have been lamed on these stones. Or worse! A pair of rare idiots, the both of you! Now get out of my way. I am going home, and I don't wish to see or to speak to either one of you until hell freezes, or until you gain a little common sense. Something tells me the former will occur long before the latter. Drive on at once, please, Micah.''

Missy expected that would be the end of it and she sat down as Micah chucked to the team. Flynn, however, with a look of fury in his eyes, leaned over and set the brake of the wagon.

''Get down, Micah. I'm driving.'' He addressed the foreman at the rein, but he looked straight into Missy's soul as he spoke. His tone was cold and hard as steel.

''Don't you move, Micah!'' Missy's voice trembled, just like the rest of her. How dared this upstart profiteer challenge her will on a public street in her own town? How dared he behave as if he were half-owner of the C-Bar-C, and, worst of all, how dared he be so perilously appealing, besides?

Micah looked as if he wished he were under the wagon instead of in it. His uncertain, petitioning gaze incited a renewed wave of anger in Missy.

''Who signs your pay voucher, Micah Watts?'' she demanded, growing hot in the face.

''You,'' the foreman mumbled. ''Except''—he half rose from his seat—''Mr. Muldaur, he did sign the last one.''

Muldaur seemed eager to take advantage of the foreman's hesitation. He spoke up again quickly.

''This is a matter between me and Missy,'' he told the man, shooting him a conspiratorial, sympathetic expression that Missy found infuriating. It as much as said aloud, ''Women don't understand these things like we men.''

She was on her feet again.

''There is nothing between us, Mr. Muldaur.'' She pronounced each word with furious deliberation. ''Not this matter or any other. I don't know by what manner you have insinuated yourself into my home and my business, but you may rest assured that it is a temporary state of affairs at best."

Muldaur seemed unfazed by her heated remarks, except to raise one blond eyebrow in sardonic amusement.

"I beg to differ, Miss Cannon. I have been resting assured, and in fact resting quite comfortably, on your best mattress at the C-Bar-C for the last three weeks. Would you like to learn what else I've been doing? I mean to tell you, so it's entirely up to you whether you want me to do so here on a public street in front of a score of witnesses or in the more private setting of the ride back to the ranch. So which is it to be?"

"Want me to take care of this for you, Missy?" Bill Boland's growl was annoyingly patronizing.

"I can take care of myself, thank you!" she retorted, turning to the widower. "If you really want to be of help, you may just leave. Both of you."

There was quite a throng of interested spectators lining the walk nearby, and all traffic had come to a standstill in the street. Missy avoided the eyes of people she'd known for ten years, people who surely wondered why Missy Cannon, who had never attracted more than the polite interest of any man in the area, suddenly had not one but two attractive and by all accounts eligible bachelors literally racing through the streets to her side and vying for her attention. Wild speculation would no doubt ensue about the event for weeks.

She wanted to die.

"Anybody care to tell me what in Sam Hill is goin' on here?"

The gathering crowd parted for Sheriff Eldon Garlock. He was an unprepossessing man of medium height, age, and build, utterly unremarkable except for his inexplicable and uncanny ability to command attention and respect, but not fear, with a direct look and a few well-chosen words. This occasion proved no different.

Not without an obvious, collective disappointment, the onlookers began to disperse. Eldon eyed Flynn, Missy, and Bill with silent appraisal and a curled lower lip.

"I figgered this to happen," he said by way of greeting. " 'Cept I was hopin' it wouldn't happen in the middle a' the day in the center a' town. It's a fine 'welcome home' for you, I guess, Miz Cannon, but it looks like you'll have to make the best of it for now." He nodded in Flynn's direction once. "Anyways, you can't hash it all out right here in the middle of a public street. You're holdin' up traffic. So move it along, please, or I'll hafta fine all of you for creatin' a public nuisance. And I hope I don't hafta tell you two again"—he aimed an acid glare at both Flynn and Bill—"that horseplay's a misdemeanor, punishable by a fine and a week in jail. So no more showin' off. I expect you're both a sight too old for that kind a' tomfoolery, anyway. Now you all got"—he withdrew a gold watch from the pocket of his leather vest and studied it—"thirty seconds to remove yourselves, else I start handin' out citations. And I get mite grumpy when I hafta waste my time with that when I got more important business on my mind." He spread his stern gaze out over the crowd, as if making sure they all understood they were included in his blanket admonition. Accordingly, they edged away.

"But Sheriff—" Missy tried.

"Twenty-five seconds."

She huffed in annoyance. "You don't—"

"Twenty seconds."

"Micah, get out of the wagon," Flynn ordered swiftly, dismounting. "Take the mare, unhitch the ladies you have in back, and lead them home."

"Don't you dare get—"

Garlock sighed. "Fifteen seconds."

"Move, Micah!"

Micah moved. In moments Flynn was parked in the

driver's seat. He gripped Missy's wrist with a firm hand and pulled her down beside him. Bill Boland uttered a sound that was half disgust, half resignation and reined his gelding away.

"Ten seconds."

Flynn touched the brim of his hat to the sheriff, released the brake with a soft grunt, and flicked the reins of the team.

"H'yah!"

The wagon started through the diminishing crowd with a quick jerk that made Missy put a hand to her hat. They were up to speed and heading out of town in no time. Missy stiffened her back.

"I have never been so publicly humiliated in all of my life, Mr. Muldaur," she said icily. "And if you ever do such a thing again—"

"—you'll probably thank me for it," he finished for her with a hard sigh of disgust.

"An unlikely occurrence." She sniffed.

"It didn't have to play out like that, you know."

The back of Missy's neck prickled.

"No, I suppose it didn't, as long as I was willing to go along with you peacefully." She employed her most sarcastic tone.

"Are you always so hard to get along with?" His gloved hands tightened on the reins.

"Only when people try to order me about to suit their whims," she retorted, stung. She held herself to the far edge of the seat to avoid contact with any part of Flynn Muldaur's long, lean form.

"Yeah? Well, when your whims don't make any damned sense, expect me to override them."

"Don't take that condescending tone with me, Mr. Muldaur."

"It's Flynn," he corrected her, sounding pleased to be contradictory. "No need to stand on some stupid convention, Missy. We're partners. Equal partners.''

"We'll see about that.''

"But you already have seen,'' he pointed out to her. "Face it. You wasted a lot of time in Louisville trying to prove otherwise, and you failed. It's a fact we both have to learn to live with, so we might as well get used to it.''

"I'll never accept you living at my house, calling half of my ranch yours,'' she declared, keeping her gaze on the road ahead of them. "And of course, now that I'm home, you'll be moving out of the ranch house.''

"Like hell I will!''

Missy made a show of wincing. "Guard your tongue, Mr. Muldaur. There's a child in the back of the wagon.''

"What!''

"I ain't no child.'' Gideon spoke up at last, grumbling. No doubt he'd enjoyed the performance in town tremendously, Missy thought, and was probably sorry he'd been noticed just as things were getting even more interesting.

"Sweet mother of God, what's he doing here?'' Flynn demanded, turning to her at last with his wheat-colored brows in deeply plowed furrows.

Missy felt a shimmer of wicked delight. So Gideon's presence surprised and annoyed him. Good, she thought, trying to keep her triumphant smile to herself.

"Gideon is my ward,'' she said, determined not to look at Flynn, although she felt his piercing stare on her like needles. "He's been with me and Glory since Louisville, that day when you—when we met in the stable. He's agreed to let me be his guardian for the time being, and he will live at the ranch. In the house. In the spare bedroom.''

The room that had been Allyn's, when she'd lived at the C-Bar-C. If that was where Flynn had ensconced himself, she thought, he could damn well pack up and

132

move elsewhere. Out to the bunkhouse, for instance. Or to perdition, it was all the same to her. In fact, the farther away the better.

"He's welcome to the spare bedroom," Flynn remarked with an edge of amused sarcasm. "I moved into the other room, which I guess is yours. But don't worry. I only take up half the bed."

Muldaur's remark evoked a quick, vivid image in Missy's mind that made her dizzy and short of breath. This time she was thankful when Gideon spoke up.

"Miss Cannon's a lady," he said in as menacing a tone as an adolescent boy could manage. "It ain't right, you talkin' to her that way, and you know it. I thought you was a gentleman, Flynn."

Flynn didn't know whether he was more annoyed or embarrassed by such a dressing-down at the hands of a mere boy, but then neither did he know how he'd allowed himself to get so flip with Missy, when he'd meant all along to be nice. The whole day had been shot to hell, he decided gloomily, from the time Bill Boland rode up to the privy.

"You'd best call me Mr. Muldaur, son," he growled, because he'd rather do that than apologize to the stern, stiff woman beside him.

There was a sound from the back of the wagon that Flynn took for an expression of disdain.

"I call Miss Cannon Missy," Gideon drawled. "Guess you ain't no better'n her. Flynn'll do for you. And you can call me Gideon when you call me anything, because I sure as hell ain't your son."

"Language, please, Gideon," Missy murmured, her gentle rebuke to the boy several shades softer than her previous declarations. "Thank you for standing up for me that way. At least there's one gentleman in this wagon."

"Flynn can bunk with me in the spare room." Gideon

133

went right on as if he'd been hired to mediate for the two of them. Moreover, he sounded, to Flynn's chagrin, as if he were making the concession grudgingly. "And I'll make sure he don't bother you, Miss."

"I said the bunkhouse!" Missy sputtered and hissed as if she were a hot piece of metal dunked in a water barrel. "Don't think you're going to interfere with the management of my ranch, Gideon, just because you're—"

"*Our* ranch," Muldaur cut in, glad that at least the boy seemed to be on his side in one respect. "And frankly, *Missy*, as long as Gideon's there to play chaperon, I don't think you need concern yourself about your reputation."

Missy drew away from him and stiffened as if she'd overstarched her drawers. Damn, he hadn't meant that to come out sounding so cold and unfeeling, as if to declare he had no interest in her as a woman, but it was too late. The words were spoken. Missy's silence answered any question he might have raised as to how she'd taken his incautious comment.

The wagon hit a rut, and he smothered a curse. He'd meant to impress Missy with all he'd done at the ranch in the past three weeks, but as he thought about it, those things—nailing a few shingles on the privy roof, for instance—seemed less and less noteworthy. Absurd, even. A part of him had wanted to find the place hanging by a thread, waiting for a competent man to take over. But the truth of it was the C-Bar-C was already a thriving concern, worked by people who obviously cared a great deal about the place, and about the owner. The more he thought about it, the more he realized Micah and the hands had all just humored him until Missy returned. Hell, they were probably glad he'd found things to do that made him think he was helping and kept him out of their way.

Maybe they were even laughing behind their hands

and calling him the new janitor.

Muldaur restrained a compelling urge to spit a bitter taste out of his mouth over the side of the wagon.

Damn.

Gideon yanked his cap down over his eyes to keep out the sun. He settled against the sack of flour at his back. After the long, boring train ride, he'd sure enjoyed the excitement in the middle of town. The wagon jolted along the dirt road, though, and the town faded behind them. Except for the creak of the wheels and the constant clopping of the horses, it was quiet. A kind of tense quiet, like the stillness before a thunderstorm.

Things were even better than he'd hoped. What a piece of luck that Flynn Muldaur had actually heeded his suggestion in Louisville and come to the C-Bar-C! Missy, he'd learned during the past few months, was apt to point to some pretty farfetched coincidences and say they were the work of God. Maybe God had played a hand in this, too. Never mind that the two of them together were as prickly as a briar patch. At least they were together. That part of the problem was solved.

It was nice to think that maybe God and he were on the same side, for once. It seemed to him that if there was a God, he, Gideon, had spent most of his life on His wrong side. Well, maybe that was about to change. Maybe it had changed already. He smiled at the idea and shifted onto his side.

Doing so, his gaze came to rest on a nearby jug. He guessed it was molasses, at least he hoped it was. He was partial to sweets. He stared a while longer at the jug, wishing he could read what was marked on the outside of it, but he'd only learned his letters so far, not how to sound them out or put them together.

But there were things he *could* put together. And, he thought, glancing over his shoulder at the straight backs of Flynn Muldaur and Missy Cannon, maybe God

135

wouldn't mind a little bit of help doing His work, either. . . .

In spite of her agitation, Missy felt a thrill of pride when she set her eyes on the C-Bar-C again after nearly five months away. From a distance, it appeared that the house and the buildings had weathered the winter well, and the paddock, alive with yearlings, was a sight that made her heart glad, despite her latest problem. New life had a way of bringing out her best, of making her feel as if even impossible situations might turn out all right. Allyn often called her an optimist, and she said it in a way that made Missy think her friend envied her the quality. She wasn't sure exactly what that meant, but if it meant she could always find something good even when things seemed at their worst, then an optimist she was.

"It's a nice place."

"What?" It had been an eternity since either of them had spoken, and she wasn't sure she'd heard Muldaur correctly. It seemed as though he was reading her thoughts.

He cleared his throat and continued to look straight ahead at the road before them.

"I said it's a nice place," he remarked a little louder, as if he begrudged her the words. "The C-Bar-C, I mean. You should be proud of it."

"Well, thank you," she murmured, aware that his compliment, however reluctant, warmed her. "It is nice, and I am proud. I'm surprised you didn't choke on such pleasant words."

"Me?" He sounded as if he were choking as he turned toward her wearing an incredulous look. "I've tried to be pleasant about this from the very beginning. If you'd been willing to listen—"

"If you'd behaved like a gentleman—"

A low moan from the back of the wagon cut them

off. Missy turned about quickly. To her dismay, Gideon was doubled over on the floor of the wagon clutching his knees. Beside him, uncorked and on its side, was a bottle of molasses. Dear lord, she had been so distraught over this business with Flynn Muldaur that she'd all but forgotten about Gideon. It wasn't hard for her to put together what had happened.

Chapter Eleven

"Can you move, Gideon? If not, we'll have to carry you."

Missy had gone from a sharp-tongued shrew to a paragon of maternal concern quicker than Muldaur could blink, and for about 30 seconds the change in her rendered him mute and paralyzed. She was out of the wagon and beside the boy before he'd even set the brake.

The answer Gideon gave was another mournful groan.

"Take the supplies and Miss Cannon's things inside," he ordered the hands who'd come out front to bid Missy welcome home. "Micah's behind us with those new mares. Are the stalls ready?"

"You bet, Mr. Muldaur."

Missy's eyes flashed at him like twin steel sabers, as much as to say, Don't you interfere with my routines!

"Plenty of clover and alfalfa hay on hand?" she challenged the men, looking capable of inflicting bodily harm if they answered incorrectly. "And salt blocks? I have three foaling thoroughbreds, gentlemen, and I intend to have three live, healthy births come January."

The hands looked at one another, apparently puzzled by her brusqueness.

"Well, sure, everything's ready," Rich Hamper, the self-styled leader of the delegation of two, spoke up. "Just like you like it, Miss. Why wouldn't it be?"

Missy, mollified, blushed prettily to the roots of her hair and managed only a brief glance at Muldaur that he took for apology.

"Well, I thought maybe Mr. Muldaur might have instructed you otherwise in my absence."

Hamper grinned at her, revealing crooked, tobacco-stained teeth.

"Him? Naw. He said to just keep on doin' like we was doin' till you got back, so we just kep' on doin'. He didn't bother us none. Good to have you back, though, Miz Cannon."

He didn't bother us none. As if he, Muldaur, were nothing more than an insect, or a pesky child. Muldaur masked a scowl, but he realized his jaw and his fists were clenched nonetheless. He avoided looking at Missy, sure that he'd be unable to endure her patronizing, perhaps even smug, look.

Gideon gave another low, piteous moan. All attention focused once again on the boy, for which Muldaur silently blessed him. He did not wait for instruction or a request. He simply scooped the groaning boy into his arms and carried him into the house.

Missy always loved homecomings, especially after prolonged absences. The ranch house had its own distinctive smell as all houses did, a blend of smoke, people, and good cooking. She breathed deeply as she entered her home and received an unexpected, but not wholly unwelcome, surprise: woven among the texture of aromas was a trace of something new, like a rich strand of fine, fancy red wool in a plain bolt of gray. Following Muldaur's purposeful stride through the small greatroom to the stairs, she realized what it was.

Long ago, it seemed to her, Flynn Muldaur had touched her at Filson's and put a spell upon her heart. That spell was a secret, devastating blend of his heat, his voice, his merry blue eyes, and his beguiling, spicy scent. It was that aroma she smelled, hopelessly entangled with the smells she'd always recognized as home. Flynn had already become a part of them, she realized, changing them ever so slightly, but irreversibly altering them nonetheless. She could not help but notice that his own scent had undergone a slight but indisputable change as well, no doubt as a result of his having lived there among her home scents for the past three weeks.

The C-Bar-C had become, in that short time, home to him as well.

"He feels a little warm, but his color's fine," Flynn remarked as he carried Gideon into the clean, bright room that was once Allyn's bedroom. "He'll be good as new as soon as the effects of all that molasses wear off. Maybe he'll take a lesson from that: Gluttony carries its own penalty." He laid the boy down on the bed on top of the wedding ring quilt with the kind of care a father might exhibit.

Missy found herself smiling as Gideon uncurled himself on the bed.

"You sound like a fire-and-brimstone preacher, Mr. Muldaur, but your gentle actions belie your true feelings. I would never have expected it of you."

Muldaur straightened and faced her, hooking his thumbs into his belt. She realized there were but three feet separating them. His blue eyes surveyed her with somberness that quickly gave way to amusement.

"Do that again."

"What?" She was confused and alarmed; she thought she'd somehow committed another embarrassing, if not unforgivable, error.

"Smile," he told her, his own grin widening. "You look real pretty when you do."

She opened her mouth to retort, but discovered that in the face of his unexpected, gentle teasing no crushing, scathing remark occurred to her. Utterly stymied, she brushed by him, pretending to be more concerned about Gideon than about Muldaur's partiality to her smile.

"I'll have a cot brought up here from the bunkhouse, Mr. Muldaur," she managed in a muffled tone as she loosened Gideon's crooked collar with trembling fingers.

"I'll go see to it." His tone was cool again behind her. She heard him walk toward the door.

Gideon gave a piteous moan and writhed on the bed.

"Here, let me help you with him first."

Muldaur was beside her again and he sat on the edge of the bed by Gideon. "Let me get your shoes off, son. You'll be more comfortable that way." He began unlacing Gideon's boots.

"I ain't your—"

"I know, I know," Flynn soothed him wryly. "You're not my son. But that doesn't mean I can't slip once in a while and call you that, does it? You ever make a mistake? Say, like dipping once too often into the molasses jar?"

Missy stifled a giggle, but not too successfully, for Flynn glanced up at her with a reproving look. Gideon, she noticed, said nothing. Silence gives assent, she reflected, helping the boy slip his arms from his coat sleeves.

"Have you helped many men undress?"

"No." She answered Muldaur's breezy inquiry before

it occurred to her that he was teasing. When she glared at him, he grinned.

"Mr. Muldaur, we're going to be sharing close quarters for a time, it seems, much as I would rather things were different. I must therefore ask that you refrain from—that you don't—"

"Tease you?" he supplied, arching an eyebrow in wonder. "But that's my nature. I tease people, especially women, the way some people breathe. I don't even think about it. I just do it."

"Well, just *don't* do it!" she snapped. "Or find someone else to tease. I can assure you, the habit finds no favor with me!"

She went about turning Gideon's coat sleeves right side out, and she hung the garment on a chair. She wondered if she sounded as much like a fussy little old maid to Muldaur as she did to herself.

"Funny," Muldaur, behind her, mused, as though it were anything but. "When other women say that, I get the feeling they mean just the opposite. With you, though, I'm betting it's true. Might be that's one reason why I like to—Well, Lucy doesn't seem to mind it. Guess I'll stick to teasing her."

"Who's Lucy?" Missy could have bitten her tongue off for the abrupt question, and having asked it, she could not even pretend to be busy brushing Gideon's coat.

"She's the cook I hired." Did Muldaur never sound anything but amused? "Didn't you wonder where those heavenly smells were coming from when you came in?"

Missy wondered if the walls of the small room had inched inward, or if she was simply losing her mind. Neither prospect pleased her.

"I do the cooking for the C-Bar-C." She turned to him with what she hoped was a look of icy disdain. "Since you hired the woman, you may tell her we no longer need her services. And her pay will come out of your half of the expenses.''

Why had she not remembered how tall and imposing Muldaur was? He straightened before her, shifting his weight so that his left leg was crooked at the knee and his right hip jutted out slightly. He exaggerated the pose by sliding his right hand into his back pocket. His left arm hung at his side, limp but ready. For what? she wondered.

''You're a hard-nosed case,'' he said slowly, appraising her with a long, unsmiling look. ''Anybody ever tell you that? Lucy stays. This is my decision.''

Missy drew herself up. ''How dare you—''

Gideon made a sound on the bed that was half groan, half whine, effectively cutting off their argument. Muldaur looked beyond her to the boy, his features changing to reluctant concern.

''Do you need a bucket?'' He addressed Gideon in a softer but cautious tone. ''Or maybe a trip to the privy? Where does it hurt?'' Gideon, Missy knew, had a way of making people tread lightly around him, especially when they'd already been stung once by one of his defensive retorts. Muldaur sank to the bed at the boy's side, tentatively reaching for Gideon's belly.

Gideon rocked on his side and uncurled a bit. His face was still screwed up in agony, his eyes were scrunched closed, and he had his arms clutched across his middle as if they were strapped there.

''Maybe he's really hungry,'' Missy fretted, sitting opposite Muldaur on the other side of the small bed. ''It's nearly dinnertime after all, and we didn't have but a small luncheon on the train.''

She rubbed Gideon's back through the soft linen of his shirt. After three months of good, regular meals, she was surprised that she was still able to feel his ribs. His shoulder blades, too, jutted out like promontories. It was hard to remember, sometimes, that Gideon was nothing more than a boy. This kind of contact served as a sharp reminder.

Muldaur pressed his lips together in a doubtful look. "Try lying on your belly," he suggested to the boy.

To Missy's surprise, Gideon rolled over, giving only a small grunt as proof of his continued discomfort. She and Muldaur watched him for another minute. He neither moved nor made further noise.

A minute crept by. Missy began to feel a renewed wave of uneasiness sharing the bed with Muldaur, even with the prone, unusually silent Gideon between them. She stood up again, wanting distance. He was too close. Too dangerous. He scared her.

"I'll get you a cup of tea, Gideon," she murmured, loosening the uppermost buttons of her peplum. Goodness, but it was warm in this room. Why had she not noticed it before?

"I'll open a window," she heard Muldaur mutter. Oh, so he felt it, too. Then it was not just her imagination. What a relief.

"I hate tea," Gideon groaned. "I won't drink it."

"Missy can't just let you lie here and suffer," Muldaur said. "Tea's not so bad. As long as you don't smell it first."

Unexpectedly, Gideon chuckled. The merry sound brought a sigh forth from Missy, a sigh she hadn't realized she'd been hoarding.

"I guess you're not feeling too bad, if you can laugh." Was the relief in Muldaur's voice real, or had Missy only invented it? "Let Missy get you some tea, like she said. Never turn down a pretty lady when she offers to serve you; it'll happen seldom enough in your life, I can tell you. I'll stick around and help you get into bed."

Gideon sat up slow as a slug. His hair stayed just as

it had been on the pillow. She watched Flynn smooth it back with a tender hand, and something inside her melted like chocolate in a pot.

"I'll get into bed," Gideon groused, although his eyes had lost some of their typically hostile look. "But I can do it myself. And I ain't takin' no tea." He said that last for her benefit, and he sent her what he no doubt thought was a fierce scowl to back it up. She smiled.

"All right; no tea," she promised as solemnly as she could. "But"—she glanced at Flynn, who was drawing the quilt back on the bed so Gideon, still wearing his clothes, could climb between the covers—"I'll see if Lucy can fix you up some broth. Nice hot soup is the best thing for you, with a tummyache. Don't you agree, Mr. Muldaur?"

"It's Flynn."

"Beg pardon?"

"Flynn," he repeated, standing up. "That's my name. Gideon here intends to use it. I hope you do, too."

Overwhelmed by sudden confusion, she looked away.

"Well, I—"

"Look at me, Missy." His hand closed about her arm, warm, but not rough.

She would rather have been snatched baldheaded by a buzzard than to obey his mild command, but she followed his tug and found herself gazing into his eyes once again.

Such beautiful eyes, she thought, wishing she could stare into them forever.

"Why are you blushing?"

"I'm not blushing!" Her face heated.

"If you say so." He shrugged, and she knew his concession to be one of expediency rather than acceptance. "I just wanted to tell you that except for hiring Lucy, I haven't changed anything in the three weeks I've been here. I wanted you to know that. I would have told you

145

before, on the ride home from town, but we couldn't seem to get more than five words out at a time without it turning into an argument. And—'' he seemed to anticipate her retort, and he released her arm to raise both of his hands in a pacifying gesture—''I guess I'm as much to blame for that as anybody.''

Missy found herself staring at the floor between them.

''I had a hand in it, too,'' she conceded by way of apology.

''We both have a lot to learn about partnering a business like this,'' Flynn went on. ''And a lot to learn about each other. Sort of like a marriage, I guess. And we sure won't learn it all at once. My brother has a favorite saying: 'Rome wasn't built in a day.' ''

''Your brother, the congressman?'' She found that she enjoyed talking with him in an uncontentious way and she wanted to prolong the experience.

Flynn's brow furrowed, and his eyes darkened to the stormy indigo of a blue northern. Missy drew back in alarm. The storm subsided. Flynn quickly recovered, although not quickly enough to make Missy forget that it was her mention of his brother that had brought such a look of menace, however fleeting, to his handsome features.

''What I was getting at,'' he went on as if she had not said anything, ''is that we should start trusting each other at least enough to call each other by our first names. If we go around saying 'Mr. Muldaur' and 'Miss Cannon' and looking like every other minute we want to kill each other, it's bound to be bad for morale. Our own as well as everyone else's. And as you said, we have three foaling mares, and we want three live, healthy births. My understanding of mares is they get testy and fractious when they're foaling, and they do best when they're surrounded by peace and tranquillity. So maybe we could agree to use our first names, and to keep our argu—debates within the walls of the house. For everyone's sake.''

Missy forced herself to meet his gaze again. *He might move in,* she remembered Joshua saying that day in Louisville when she'd learned the chilling truth about Flynn Muldaur. *But if he did so, it would only be with the intention of driving Missy out.* Gazing at the man before her, who had so tenderly cared for Gideon in his distress, she realized she was finding it harder and harder to credit such a nefarious scheme.

Quite possibly, that was exactly what Flynn Muldaur intended.

She drew in and released several breaths while she tried to decide what her next remark should be. For whatever she said, it was sure to set the tone for their relationship here at the ranch. It would be all too easy, she sensed, to acquiesce to his deceptively sincere blue eyes and his quiet, abnormally respectful address. He no doubt realized that, too. Still, she wanted to trust him. She longed to. If she was being truthful with herself, she longed for far more than that from Flynn Muldaur.

The most dangerously unreliable person . . .

Those had been Joshua Manners's very words. And she would be a fool to forget them if she wanted to hold on to the ranch she'd struggled so hard for during the past eight years.

She swallowed hard and maintained his gaze.

''Since Gideon intends to call us by our first names, I suppose it would be rather stupid for us to do otherwise,'' she said, monitoring him for any sign that he took her response for a victory of some sort. He betrayed none, by not so much as a lowering of his eyelids. She felt only a slight relief at the fact, and plunged ahead, lest he mistake her concession for something more than it was.

''But I think I'll reserve further articles of surrender

until I've seen whether or not I can trust you. After all, I've been managing quite nicely on my own for a long time. You cannot begrudge me prudence, Mr.—Flynn.''

How nice it felt to say his name aloud! She wanted to say it over and over again like a chant, or a song. What a lovely name it was. And oh, what a dangerous feeling it engendered within her.

''That's fine, Missy,'' he said, so softly that the words scarcely bridged the narrow gap between them. ''I can accept that, for now. And I intend to prove myself to you. That'll be a lot easier to do if you at least seem to trust me, too.''

Perhaps too easy, a naughty voice inside her scolded. Probably her common sense.

Flynn glanced at Gideon again on the bed.

''I think he's asleep,'' he whispered. ''Why don't you stay here with him and I'll get Lucy to rustle him up some broth? You look like you could use some rest, too. Then when I come up, you can go, uh, freshen up for dinner, if you like. It's nice not to have to think about making it yourself, isn't it?''

Missy could only nod. She felt as if she were strangling on a host of raw emotions. She found herself wondering about this Lucy. She didn't know anyone named Lucy in the area. She wondered if Flynn Muldaur had imported the woman from somewhere and hired her strictly for her culinary skills. Lucy liked to be teased, he'd said earlier, when they were still contending with one another. Staring at Flynn, she saw a line of tears form along her eyelashes. She dared not blink, lest they fall from her eyes and betray her feelings to him.

What had she allowed him to do to her?

What had she done to herself?

She waited until Flynn closed the door behind him before she blinked away her tears. It was too late to cry. The damage was already done.

* * *

Damn it, women just didn't blush anymore. Not the women he knew. Not like Missy Cannon did.

Flynn descended the stairs slowly, afraid he might fall ass over teakettle if he tried to take them at his usual brisk pace. He was shaking, and he knew why, and both facts bothered the hell out of him. He'd wanted to be in complete control of that interview. He'd needed to be. Hell, he *had* been. Then Missy Cannon had looked up at him and blushed like a schoolgirl. . . .

Flynn shook his head as he gained the first floor. Nothing had gone right the whole blessed afternoon, from the time Bill Boland had ridden up on his sharp, fast gelding. Then the scene—multiple scenes, really— with Missy. And finding out she'd taken in that stray, Gideon, who'd knocked him on the head with a bucket in Louisville.

Not that he had anything against orphans; far from it. He wasn't much more than one himself, him and Seamus. But except for their own foster mother, who had died far too young, he could not recall another woman in his experience who so gamely took on challenges like the Missys of the world. Or of running a ranch.

Or of making wary pacts with devils like Flynn Muldaur.

Hell and damn, he should have tried harder to sell his half of the ranch when he'd had the chance. He should have guessed he'd be too softhearted, when push came to shove, to use a woman like Missy the way he—and Seamus—needed to. But how could he have known such a thing? he demanded of himself, massaging his chin. After all, the only women he'd known as an adult male were women like Madeleine and her viperous mother.

And her daughter.

Damn them. Damn them all!

God, he'd come down here to do something. What

149

was it? If he couldn't remember, Missy would surely think him an idiot, which, he knew, would not be the worst she must think of him at the moment.

But how she longed to trust him! It was so obvious in her eyes. Her eyes longed for so many things. And Flynn found himself, to his alarm, wanting to be the one to give her those things, and more, in abundant measure.

Dusty, breathing hard, Micah Watts slipped into the small foyer, dragging his gray hat from his head as he did so. Flynn bit off an urge to chew the foreman out for coming in the front door, but Micah wasn't to blame for his sudden foul humor. It wasn't fair to take it out on him.

"Oh! Uh, howdy, Mr. Flynn." Micah always called him that, and it always annoyed Flynn. "I wuz just—uh, them mares is here. The fellas took 'em on out back. I come in to ask Lucy for a cuppa coffee from a fresh pot. That trail has me parched."

Lucy. The broth for Gideon. Thank you, Micah, Flynn thought, stifling a sigh of relief.

"Well, go on, then." He waved the foreman ahead.

Micah stood there scratching his head of thinning, dull hair. He looked like a confused prairie dog. Flynn wanted to laugh.

"Is there something else?" he inquired with forced patience.

"Well, I followed the wagon, and I noticed from about a mile back there was a trail, like as if somethin' was leakin' from the wagon," Micah mused, as if to himself. "I had to stop once to check a shoe, and them mares found it right tasty. Seems it was molasses."

Flynn frowned. Molasses? But Gideon . . . The stomachache . . .

He didn't know whether to laugh or to box the boy's ears. What was that scamp up to?

"Oh, there's somethin' else." Micah struck each of

his various pockets as if he were killing lice. Finally one crackled. He pulled out a folded piece of paper with his thumb and two fingers. "A telegraph message come for you. From New Orleans. Dick Wyman said it came in just this mornin', or he'd have had it brought out here straightaway."

Chapter Twelve

A telegraph message from New Orleans could not be good news. Flynn's heart, which had felt oddly swollen and tight in his chest moments before, suddenly plunged to some area below his belt. He eyed the paper in Micah's fingers, wishing he could use it to light a cigar and blow away the ashes.

Seamus, he reminded himself, straightening. The "good" Muldaur brother. The one Ma and Pa would have been proud of. For Seamus, he took the paper from Micah and unfolded it.

Micah shifted his weight to one foot. Flynn arched an eyebrow at him.

"Weren't you going to get some coffee?"

"Yeah. Oh. Yessir." Micah bobbed his head and ambled by him, back toward the kitchen.

"Tell Lucy I need some kind of broth, or something to cosset a sick stomach," Flynn called after him, remembering Gideon again. By God, if the boy was going to pull stunts like spilling molasses out of wagons and pretending to be sick from having overindulged for God alone knew what reason, he, Flynn, would quickly teach him the folly of his ways. He hoped Lucy could rustle up something suitably awful for the little liar.

Micah made a sound of acknowledgment as he ambled off. Flynn took his telegraph message and went into the parlor, sliding the oaken door shut behind him. He carried the paper over to the window and squinted at Dick Wyman's neat but cramped handwriting.

Deauville asks five thousand, he read. *Says you are greatly in arrears.*

It was signed S. Muldaur.

What the hell was Seamus doing in New Orleans? Flynn fumed inwardly, crumpling the paper in his fist. And why was he telegraphing him? They had agreed from the very beginning that it was best for Seamus and his career that he have no direct contact with his younger, more reckless brother, Flynn. Why had Seamus broken that pledge now, after nearly a dozen years of silence? Surely he knew what a calamity he was inviting by doing so!

Flynn drew in several steadying breaths and tried to think. Seamus, a Harvard graduate, was not an idiot. A fool at times, perhaps, but what man was not, particularly when a beautiful woman was involved? Seamus had been impetuous in his youth—Madeleine and her daughter were proof enough of that—but never stupid. Not even when he'd fallen in with that nest of smugglers in his early days as a congressman. He'd been desperately in debt and in need of funds. Besides, he'd been in love then, not stupid.

But maybe the two were not so very far removed from one another.

Flynn, filled with anger he could not unleash, expelled

a hard breath. Seamus had not sent that telegram, he realized suddenly. It had come from Madeleine herself. It was her not-too-subtle way of telling him that she had waited long enough for promised funds, and that she had precisely the correct wedge to shove beneath his wheels if he thought he was going to escape her clutches. Damn her!

This was doing no one any good, he reflected, jamming the note into his vest pocket with two forceful fingers.

"You were going to bring up some broth." Missy's voice, behind him, was accusing. "What happened?"

"And you were going to rest." He congratulated himself on the ease of his reply despite her ambush. "Why have you come down?" He faced her, hoping to see her blush again. He was pleased to see that she obliged him, even if she did look quickly away.

"As weary as I get from travel, I always seem to revive when I return home," she answered. There was a snow globe on the table before her. She picked it up with surprisingly graceful fingers, shook it, then watched the white flakes slowly descend on the tiny house, tree, and horse-drawn sleigh inside. Flynn was sure she did it only to avoid looking at him. The thought made him feel sad in a way he did not fully understand.

"I've never had a home I felt that way about," he heard himself say softly. "You're very lucky."

How was it, he wondered, watching her, that Missy had such a way of making the harsh world vanish for him? It was as if her sphere existed in one of those glass bubbles, untouched by the wicked realities of day-to-day living that made a hell on earth for other people.

A shudder went through him. Whether she knew it or not, and he very much doubted she did, he had brought those ugly realities to Missy Cannon's doorstep. How long, he wondered, swallowing a bitter mass in his throat, until they forced their way inside?

Missy put down the globe as if she'd made a momentous decision about something. He wondered what that decision might be, and how it might affect him. Trailing her fingers along the lace table skirt, she turned to him. Her pale, silvery eyes pierced him with their innocent, frankly hopeful expression.

"Perhaps," she ventured, in a voice as soft as the late-afternoon sunlight warming the room, "you have found such a home right here. As disturbing as this—all of this—is to me, I can only think it would be a good thing for—for a man of your type."

Flynn closed his eyes against the emotions her words, and her tone, inspired within him. As guileless as Missy was, even she would surely find him out if he allowed her to look. He could not afford the luxury of sharing himself with anyone, least of all Missy Cannon.

Or was she truly as guileless as she seemed?

He opened one eye.

"A man of my type?" he inquired, opening the other eye. "I'm not sure I know what you mean."

The blush that flooded her face told him she had no wish to be any more specific.

"And you'll forgive my skepticism," Flynn went on, feeling an anger which was not her fault, "but that seems an odd sentiment from someone who'd just as soon see me gone from the C-Bar-C."

Missy looked stricken.

"You would like to see me gone, wouldn't you, Missy?" he prodded, unable to stop the anger he was aiming at her as if it were Madeleine Deauville standing before him instead of Missy Cannon. "At least, that's what you've been telling me all along."

"I . . ."

She was silent after that one strangled word. Flynn's hands fell to his sides. There wasn't much distance between them, but he closed that, stalking her until the lapels of his vest brushed the snow-white front of her shirtwaist. Her eyes grew wide with fright, and Flynn relished that fright even as he loathed himself for having caused it.

"Well?" he demanded, taking hold of her arms. "It's the truth, isn't it? You'd rather I just packed up and left, wouldn't you? Why stand here with me now and pretend I'm another helpless, homeless stray, like the conniving little brat in the bed upstairs? Why pretend you want to mother me as you will him, and like you do your stock, because you haven't a husband or any real children of your own to shower your affections on?"

Her iridescent eyes blinked once, and the blink washed away the surprise and hurt he'd first seen in them, leaving only cold steel fury in their wake. She's going to strike me, he thought, with an odd sense of detachment. And I deserve it.

"Take your hands off me, Mr. Muldaur." There was a January blizzard in the room despite the warm May sunshine from the windows. "At once."

But he did not want to take his hands off her. The flesh of her arms yielded enticingly to his grip and he knew he wasn't hurting her. Not physically, in any event. Missy Cannon was a hardy woman, more than capable of dealing him a blow that would at least smart, and at worst send him to the floor, unconscious. He was certain of it. Staring into her cold platinum gaze, though, he saw that his verbal blow had struck much deeper than mere physical hurt. And he thoroughly hated himself for it.

He hated himself so much that he suddenly wanted to kiss her to take the hurt away.

She was panting. Each outraged breath she drew pressed her breasts against the soft calfskin of his vest. He wondered if she could feel his own heart hammering in his chest even as he felt the soft heat of her womanliness before him.

Damn, he wanted her.

He leaned forward, intending to capture her lips with his own. Her breasts pressed against the pocket of his vest with a resulting crackling sound as the note inside was crushed. The noise brought him abruptly to his senses.

"I'm sorry," he growled, releasing her at last, turning away lest she perceive the heat in his face. "Christ, I'm sorry, Missy. I'm . . ."

He flexed his hands, longing to punch something. How could he explain to her, without compromising either himself or Seamus, the reason for his behavior, which must seem odd to her in the extreme? The answer was devastatingly simple: He couldn't. Not now. Probably not ever.

And why would Missy care, anyway? The Deauvilles were his problem, his and his brother's. Long ago he had made a pact with Seamus, then already a promising freshman congressman, before his own life had any sort of shape or definition beyond government Secret Service. It had seemed perfectly logical at the time, even though he'd liked his somewhat unconventional job and was good at it. But of the two of them, Seamus was the one with more education and a far better chance at succeeding in the world, thanks to the friendships he'd cultivated at the university. Little had Flynn dreamed then that he might someday meet a woman who would make him question everything he thought he knew of the sex.

A woman with just enough sass to make him wonder if her lower lip might taste like lemons . . .

His legs weakened treacherously.

"I'm sorry," he said again, although this time his tone, he knew, was flat. He felt as if he'd been sucker-punched and had the breath knocked out of him. He could only imagine what his cruel words had done to her.

"You mustn't be sorry." Her voice was tight. Caustic as lye. "At last I know what you truly think of me. It's actually a relief to have it out in the open, to have no more uncertainty about it. I've always thought of myself as a plainspoken woman, I guess I can hardly take offense when someone speaks so plainly to me in turn. Perhaps I should even thank you for it, although I expect you'll forgive me if I don't."

"Jesus, Missy—"

"I will, however, thank you not to blaspheme in my—in the house." She cut him off as if she wielded a well-honed knife. "I'm trying to teach Gideon better manners and language and though I may not be his mother, as you and he have both so kindly pointed out to me in your own charming ways, I do have a responsibility, as his guardian, for his moral upbringing."

Wiping all emotion from his face, Flynn forced himself to look at her again. Missy's features were equally composed, although she looked pale as a corpse. She was putting a barrier between them, as surely as if she were drawing a line or building a wall. As bad as that made him feel, he could not deny a sense of relief that she was doing it, for he knew it had to be done, and he possessed neither the strength nor the wisdom to do it himself.

Still, in order to make her do it, he had hurt her. And for that he would never forgive himself.

One more sin to the epic tally of Flynn Muldaur, he told himself. He opened his mouth to try to defend himself, but he was spared by the opening of the parlor door.

"Broth don't cure what rotgut causes!" A cheerful feminine voice preceded the ripe young form of Lucy Battle into the room. Bearing a bowl on a tray, the cook took three steps forward before she looked up, spied

Missy, and stopped as if she'd been shot. Muldaur heard a hammering sound in the distance. He dismissed it, deciding it was probably nothing more than the final nail in his coffin.

Faced with the merry young cook, Missy could no longer deceive herself as to the reasons for Muldaur's hiring of her. As reality crushed her, she tried to speak in a normal tone of voice.

"You must be Lucy." She sounded almost too normal. She cleared her throat. "I'm Missy—Miss Cannon. Surely Fl—Mr. Muldaur told you about me."

But what, exactly, has he told you? she wondered, with a renewed sense of chagrin.

"Y-yes, ma'am."

Lucy moistened her lips, obviously aware that she'd committed a breach of decorum with her unceremonious entrance. Missy took that moment to observe her, and she realized in a glance that the girl was at least five years younger than she and, with her fine blond hair and liquid blue eyes, certainly a good deal prettier.

Moreover, she was very obviously several months gone with child.

Missy had never been a covetous woman, not even when she'd thought that Antoinette Deauville was the object of Flynn's amorous attention in Louisville. But looking at Lucy, then glancing at Flynn—who looked like a fox caught in a henhouse—and back to Lucy again, she was aware of a screaming bolt of jealousy that made her want to claw the girl's fair face and pull out her silky golden hair in great clumps.

Missy welded her feet to the floor to prevent herself from running from the room. This was her house, after all, and if anyone was going to leave, it was going to be Flynn Muldaur's pregnant trollop.

"What is your last name, Lucy?" She was amazed at the even quality of her voice.

Lucy, to her credit, looked down at her burgeoning middle.

"It's Battle, ma'am. Mrs."

"Of course. And Mr. Battle?"

Lucy bit her lip. "I'm a widow."

A widow. That's what every whore says of herself when she gets into an interesting condition and is forced to move on. Missy hated herself for the mean things she was thinking and feeling for the girl before her.

"I see. But you can cook?"

Lucy's eager nod was genuine.

"I cooked for the commander and his wife at Fort Pierre," she offered. "Col. and Mrs. Pettigrew. Then my husband, who was sergeant at arms, was killed when a powder magazine blew up." The blue eyes filled with tears. "That was three months ago. We'd only been married a year. After that, the army didn't have no use for me and I was let go." If Lucy was acting, she was doing a mighty credible job of it. She even sent a grateful look Flynn's way that Missy found painful to behold.

"I met up with Mr. Muldaur here when he first come to Rapid City," she said, blushing. "He—"

Lucy Battle did not seem able to go on. She looked down at the steaming bowl of aromatic broth on her tray and sniffled.

"There's a boy upstairs in the front bedroom." It was Flynn who broke the uncomfortable stillness in the parlor. "The broth's for him, not for me. I hope it's not too tasty; he needs to be taught a lesson. Although if it tastes as good as it smells, I expect the lesson will have to wait for another time."

For all her pregnant girth, Lucy grinned becomingly at the compliment.

"Can you—that is, are you quite all right to climb the stairs?" Missy could have bitten off her tongue for so solicitous a question.

"Oh, sure." The girl smiled again, her brief melancholy apparently forgotten. "I feel wonderful. Haven't been sick a day. I like being busy, and I like your place. When I started, the hands told me I had pretty big shoes to fill since you were such a good cook yourself. But soon they allowed I was almost as good as you. There're fine people here at the C-Bar-C, Miss Cannon. Especially Mr. Muldaur. I owe him a lot."

Yes, she was sure Lucy did, although Missy was uncertain of precisely how much the cook owed him.

"It isn't what you think, Missy." Demonstrating uncharacteristic tact, Flynn waited until Lucy had excused herself and closed the door behind her before he made his quiet declaration.

Missy felt as if she'd spent an entire afternoon plowing without benefit of a draft animal. She wanted to take a hot, soothing bath, then sleep for a week and awake to find that this dreadful afternoon had never happened.

And she did not want to exchange further words with Flynn Muldaur.

"Oh?" she breathed, still staring at the closed door of the parlor. "And what, exactly, do I think?"

Flynn's sigh was the perfect mirror of her own exhaustion.

"Lucy's a fine cook, and the hands all like her. They've taken a personal interest in her and her baby, and I expect you'd find a lot of them would take it hard if you were to let her go now. Give her a chance. If not for my sake, then for hers, and for the sake of the men's feelings. I think Micah especially has taken quite a shine to her."

Micah only? she wondered. She said nothing.

"I really am sorry about what I said earlier," he went on, scarcely above a whisper.

So am I, she thought, silently damning him as tears pricked the backs of her eyes. She heard the sound of

161

movement as he walked toward the door. She turned the opposite way as he passed her so she did not have to look at him.

"I'll get my things out of your room and have a cot brought up from the bunkhouse."

The casters of the sliding door creaked. Missy, remembering something Flynn had said to Lucy, composed herself.

"What did you mean when you told Lucy that Gideon needed to be taught a lesson?"

"Oh." Flynn laughed, but it was a hollow, forced sound. "Micah said he and the mares followed a trail of molasses home behind the wagon. So that means—"

"Gideon pretended to have eaten all of it, and is feigning his stomachache," she finished for him. "But why?" she asked, turning to face him.

He was looking at her with a blessedly blank expression; she could not have tolerated a look of remorse or contrition. He shrugged and shook his head.

"He's a kid; who knows how he thinks?" he dismissed; then with a nod he left the room.

Missy was not so sure. It seemed to her that Flynn actually knew a great deal about how a young boy thought. Certainly more than she did.

Missy lay on her back and stared up at the ceiling. She missed her own bed most of all when she traveled, and she always enjoyed a blissful, unbroken night's slumber on the first night of her return. But not on this occasion. Accustomed to solitude, she was all too aware of the new people breathing in the house, both across the hall and in a room downstairs off the kitchen. Besides, despite the fact that her body had long since resigned itself to a need for rest, her mind still hummed like a hive of bees.

Despite her having known him now for months, she

discovered that Gideon was still capable of astonishing her. She'd challenged him about the molasses incident, gently, as one might prod a sleeping partner to ease over in the dead of night. He'd looked her in the eye, as he was wont to do, and denied it. She'd known he was lying at once, but something stopped her from accusing him outright; such a confrontation, she knew from experience, would only lead to an argument and would solve nothing. As his guardian, she knew she had her work laid out for her. Gideon, after all, was as accustomed to lying as ordinary people were to breathing.

What kind of example, she found herself wondering as she stared at the ceiling in the darkness, would Flynn Muldaur make for such a youth?

She flopped over onto her stomach, sinking her face into the freshly aired feather pillow. She did not even want to think about Flynn Muldaur, his opinions, his behavior, or his cook. But she found, as the hours dragged by, hours she should have spent sleeping, that she was unable to think of anything else. Like, for example, the fact that the man had slept in this very bed for the past three weeks . . .

She inhaled deeply, trying to catch some trace of his familiar, spicy scent in the pillow. What she found was that she couldn't breathe at all with her face buried in the pillow that way. Disgusted with herself, she turned on her side and instead hugged one pillow to her breast.

As if it were a willing lover.

Outside in the distance, a coyote howled. It sounded just enough like laughter to make her face grow warm. *You haven't any husband, or real children, to shower your affections on,* Flynn had callously reminded her only that afternoon. He hadn't added *And you never will,* but she'd heard the words nonetheless as if they'd been shouted. She heard them because in her heart she had always suspected it was so. Still, she could have lived a long time without having someone point it out to her so coldly. Especially when that someone was a man for whom she entertained outlandishly fanciful romantic notions. Then the pretty, very pregnant young Lucy whom he had hired to cook for him had appeared, cheerful as only a contented woman could be.

Missy might as well have been a bug, and Flynn might as well have stepped on her.

She seized the pillow and was about to pull it over her head when she heard a floorboard creak in the hallway.

She listened hard, not breathing, not moving. She heard nothing more for what seemed a long time. Then there was another protest of wood, this one nearer to her door.

Mice? She was doubtful. Mice scampered and skittered, scratching on the floor with their tiny claws. Mice didn't make floorboards groan. And mice didn't carry lamps that made a dull yellow glow on the floor at the seam beneath the door.

Another board reported. This one was right outside her door. The pale light flickered.

Missy clutched the bedsheet in a knot just under her chin and strained her eyes. Should she call out? Suppose it was Flynn? But what would he want? No, more likely it was Gideon, unable to sleep in a strange place. But that was absurd. Gideon, thanks to his vagabond orphan existence, had no doubt slept in far less hospitable environs than the spare bedroom at the C-Bar-C. She knew him to be capable of falling asleep even in the most adverse conditions.

Whoever it was seemed to stop right outside her door, for she heard no more noises of advance or retreat and the light did not subside. She waited, expecting next to hear a knock or a soft voice call to her from the other side of the door. She heard neither.

Then she had a dreadful thought.

Was it Lucy, come to her regular nightly assignation with Flynn Muldaur?

Missy had not mentioned the change of rooms to the girl, and neither, to her knowledge or recollection, had Flynn. Dinner had been a noisy affair with everyone, including Micah and the two other hired hands, sitting down at the table right along with Missy, Flynn, and Gideon. Missy did not recall seeing Flynn exchange any words with Lucy then. After dinner, he'd stepped out back to have a smoke with the hands, and then they'd all repaired to the bunkhouse to play cards. Flynn might have paid Lucy a call in the cook's small compartment behind the kitchen when he came in, but Missy suspected that he would prefer his liaisons in more spacious surroundings, such as those that could be had here in this very room where he had slept for the past three weeks.

Missy's mouth went dry at the thought. If Lucy were, indeed, outside her door looking for Flynn, then she, Missy, would be well within her rights to discharge the girl on the spot, pregnant, popular, or not.

Missy slid out from beneath the covers as quietly as she could. She found herself desperately wanting it not to be Lucy. She didn't know whether she wanted it more because she wanted not to believe that Lucy and Flynn were lovers, or because she genuinely liked and pitied the unfortunate girl. Moreover if it was not Lucy, Missy did not know whether to be afraid or hopeful that it might, instead, be Flynn Muldaur.

Did he wear a nightshirt? she wondered, then chided herself for her foolish whimsy.

Missy crossed her own carpeted floor in silence. She couldn't swear to it, but she thought she heard short, nervous breaths on the other side of her door. A child's? A guilty lover's? She placed one hand over her stomach,

165

where a tight, painful knot had formed; she would soon find out which.

She closed her fingers about the lever. Drawing a deep, steadying breath, she turned it and pulled the door wide.

Lucy Battle gasped and drew back, meeting Missy's gaze with a wide-eyed stare.

Chapter Thirteen

There could, Missy realized with detached logic, be any number of reasons why her young, pregnant cook might be wandering the hallway barefoot in her nightdress and wrapper. But she could think of only one.

"Mr. Muldaur is not here," she heard herself say in a cool whisper. "He's sleeping in the smaller bedroom across the hall with Gideon."

Lucy's pretty features took on a tight expression by the light of the lamp, and Missy perceived that the girl was insulted.

"I wasn't looking for him," she replied, her words low and deliberate. "I couldn't sleep for wanting to talk to you about something, so I came up here on the chance you might still be awake. When I saw there wasn't a light under your door, I guessed I'd go on back downstairs."

Lucy did not back down from her gaze. Missy pressed

her lips together, shamed by the assumption she'd made.

"Well, I'm awake now," she murmured, stepping aside and opening the door wider. "If you have something to say to me, I expect we might as well have it out."

Lucy followed her in and closed the door quietly behind her. Missy didn't want to invite the woman to sit down, but Lucy's condition compelled her to be charitable. Lucy turned up the lamp, set it on the nightstand, and settled into the small armchair Missy used for dressing. Missy realized she herself was still standing in the middle of the room clad only in her nightdress, but she had no wish to sit down with her guest just yet.

"What was it you felt you needed to tell me?" Although she dreaded hearing Lucy's disclosure, Missy was pleased by the casual tone she effected.

Lucy folded her hands beneath her belly in what remained of her lap, accentuating her pregnant bulk. Her blue eyes looked dark and hooded. Missy realized she might have felt compassion for her, if she were not so dreading what the girl was going to confess to her.

"When I said today that I met up with Mr. Muldaur when he came to Rapid City, it wasn't altogether true."

Missy wished she had been sitting down. As it was, it required all of her composure to muster a steady, dignified walk to the bed, where she sat at last.

"I thought it might not be," she said lightly, tracing the spindled footboard with an idle finger so she would not have to look directly at the girl. "Where did you meet him?"

"Oh, I met him in town," Lucy hastened to assure her. "But it was when I first came to town, not him. You see—" She stopped, expelling her breath. "I'm not altogether proud of—I mean, this isn't easy for me to—"

"I daresay," Missy murmured faintly. Why didn't Lucy just get on with it and crush her completely? Flynn had already done a journeyman's job of it this afternoon; why should his lover not finish the task now, in the dead (oh, what a fitting label!) of night?

Lucy took in a swallow of air, and Missy could not help noticing that the breath shuddered at the end. Obviously Lucy was upset. Well, why wouldn't she be? Missy reasoned, gripping the footboard so that her hand ached. She was about to confess to something that would likely result in her dismissal.

"What I mean is—" Lucy drew in another sharp breath, and Missy felt the stabbing pain of it deep within her own breast. No, she wanted to beg the other woman. *Please don't tell me. If I don't hear it, I might still believe it isn't so.*

"I've always found that complete honesty is the best way to ensure a good night's sleep, Lucy," was what she said, staring at the girl's tightly interlocked fingers. "We must be able to live with our own secrets, however unpleasant." *Like loving a man who has the power to devastate you, both emotionally and financially?* her conscience taunted her. She fell silent, waiting for Lucy's response. Lucy sighed heavily.

"You're right," she admitted, sounding miserable, a fact from which Missy took no consolation whatever. "What I didn't tell you today was that Mr. Muldaur came up to me on the street in Rapid City as I was standing outside of Lettie's," she said, naming the town's most notorious brothel. "I was trying to get up the courage to go in and ask for a job. A job as a cook," she hastened to add, with a proud look. "See, I hadn't had but a few jobs here and there since I'd had to leave Fort Pierre; seems no one wanted to take me on, being as I'll have the baby and all. But you see, I had to eat. I have to live. I have Jed's—that is, Mr. Battle's—baby to think of. And it got to where I couldn't afford to worry that decent people wouldn't look at me. I mean, they could look at my starved corpse, sure, but I'm not much interested in dying of starvation or anything else, and I'd have stolen before it came to that, believe me."

Lucy placed a protective hand over her swollen abdomen. Her narrative was coming easier now, as if the floodgates of a dam had been opened. Indeed, the roar in Missy's ears could be likened to that of rushing water.

"Anyway, Mr. Muldaur, he—he rode up on a fine-looking bay; he must have seen me from quite a ways off, 'cause he wasn't anywhere around when I'd first got there. I could tell right off he was a gentleman, like my Jed. He tipped his hat to me and asked if he could be of service. Well, Miss Cannon, it had been so long since anybody had even sounded like they cared about me, and I guess I was so ashamed that I'd been about to take Jed's baby into a—into a—one of *those* places, that I admit, I up and cried on him right there in the street."

Lucy sniffled and dragged the back of her wrist across both eyes. Missy felt water back up behind her own eyes, but she pictured Flynn Muldaur standing in a public street with his arms full of a weeping, very pregnant woman and very quickly brought herself under control.

"And then he brought you here?" Missy felt as light as if she had no body at all.

"Well, no, not right off," Lucy explained, shifting in her seat. "He's a gentleman, but you know he's not stupid. He quick sent a wire to Pierre to check on me. He apologized for that, but said he knew I understood that he couldn't have anybody with questionable character working out here at the C-Bar-C. Wouldn't be fitting, you being a maiden lady and all. Besides, he wanted to check with Micah—I mean, Mr. Watts—to see if he thought it'd be all right with you, my coming out here to cook. Meanwhile, he gave me enough money for dinner and a decent room for the night while he waited for his answers. The answer was, Mi—Mr. Watts came out the next morning in a buckboard to bring me here.''

The silence in the room was tranquil, not at all like the tense stillness that had preceded Lucy's revelation. Missy wanted to laugh, she felt so joyful. To discover that not only was Flynn not a shameless philanderer, but that he was actually a thoughtful and compassionate gentleman raised her spirits enormously.

''I felt it best that I come clean with you about all of this, because I guessed you'd be wondering, and I can imagine what you must have thought, coming home to a cook in the family way,'' Lucy was saying. Missy forced herself to concentrate on the words, and to meet the girl's gaze. She hoped her relief and her delight were not as obvious as she felt they surely must be. When Lucy said nothing else, Missy blushed, for she knew she must say something, even though the notion of forming a sensible comment seemed impossible to her.

Moreover, what could she say? That she had been thinking the worst? Worse, possibly, than even Lucy herself might have imagined? Missy felt a renewed wash of shame at her jealous assumptions. She thought of her earlier remark to the girl, about honesty being the best way to ensure a good night's sleep. Well, she'd forgo a night's sleep, she guessed ruefully, at the expense of her pride. And consider it well worth the price.

''You're a very lucky woman, Miss Cannon,'' Lucy ventured shyly.

''Me?'' Missy was startled by the artless declaration. The truth was she didn't feel particularly lucky at the moment, just relieved. And a little ashamed. And very stupid.

''I mean . . .'' Lucy hesitated, and if Missy had been forced to guess, she'd have said the girl was blushing, although of course it was impossible to tell by the light of the lamp. ''You care about Mr. Muldaur a great deal.

171

I could see that right off today, in the parlor. And that's what makes it so nice, you see, because I can tell he cares for you, too. I expect you're—that is, if you don't mind my asking, are you two engaged to be married? He never said anything about it, but then men seldom do, if you know what I mean. Take my Jed, for instance. He was—''

''No, Lucy, Mr. Muldaur and I are not engaged to be married.'' Missy tried to sound casual with her interruption, but the sharp look of astonishment Lucy gave her convinced her she'd failed. Miserably. She had no choice but to look away. The brief silence that followed was torture as she felt Lucy's speculative gaze on her.

''Oh.'' The syllable was rich with layers of meaning. ''I'm sorry.'' Lucy was kind, but testing. ''Is it Mr. Boland, then?''

Missy did not know whether to be offended or amused. Lucy, after all, reminded her strikingly of another young woman in a position of service who had never known when to keep her mouth shut, either. She suspected that she and Lucy were going to become friends.

''No, not Mr. Boland either,'' she said, trying to keep a smile from her lips as she sent Lucy a chiding look. ''Not that it's any of your business, but I expect to die an old maid, married only to my ranch and my horses. I learned a long time ago that horses are much less complicated and much easier to please than men. In any case, when you know me a bit better, you'll see that I'm far too independent for any man to find me attractive as a marriage partner, particularly one set in his ways like Bill Boland.''

''What about one like Flynn Muldaur?''

Missy bit her lip to hold in a rude retort. Lucy must have noticed, for she quickly stood up, taking her lamp as she went.

"I'm sorry. Jed was forever telling me my big mouth would get me in trouble someday and I should mind my own business. Looks like he was right. Bless him, but how I wish he was here to tell me so himself." She sighed and waddled to the door. "Good night, Miss Cannon. I'm pleased you let me get this off my chest and I hope you don't think the worse of me for it. I'm mighty glad to be here, and you can bet I'll do my best to make sure you have no cause to ask me to leave."

Missy guessed that meant from here out, Lucy would try to keep her speculations to herself. At least, she hoped it did.

"When is the baby due, Lucy?"

Lucy turned and patted her stomach fondly. "July," she replied with a smile, and Missy could only envy her serenity. "Good night, miss."

"Good night, Lucy." Missy followed her guest to the door and watched her waddle down the short hallway past Flynn and Gideon's room. The steps creaked under Lucy's weight and the light of her lamp soon faded down the stairs.

The house would be home to another soul in a few months, Missy reflected, quietly closing her door. And it already had at least one more than it needed. She wondered, as she climbed back into bed, how the C-Bar-C had been transformed from a hermitage to a hostel. She wasn't sure the change was for the worse.

Gideon woke up while it was still dark, but he had a feeling dawn wasn't far off. His stomach told him so. He listened to its familiar noises, remembering, as he always did of late, a time when its needs had not been so easily met. Stomachs were peskier than babies, he decided. No matter that they just had a gutful of supper the night before; they always wanted more attention come morning. Spoiled brats, that's what they were. Just

Carole Howey

like the rich kids he used to see in the streets of Louisville, riding in their carriages while he tried to dodge
the wheels.

Flynn snored, he'd discovered during the night. He
wondered if Missy knew that.

Damn, there'd been a time the day before when he'd
thought they'd never leave off wrangling with one another! Made his head ache just to think of it. Good thing
he'd faked that stomachache and kept their minds on
him instead of how much they hated each other's guts.

Well, they didn't exactly hate each other's guts, Gideon amended, although he wasn't sure either of them
realized that yet. Anyway, he knew for sure that he liked
them both. He wasn't sure why he liked Flynn; after all,
he didn't know him near as well as he knew Missy. But
he'd been mighty impressed by the way Flynn had gal-
loped into town hell-for-leather with that other fella who
was sure too old for Missy anyway. And he liked the
way Flynn had talked to him when he was sick, or pretended to be. He was a right enough guy.

And if Gideon was any judge at all, he was sure Missy
thought so too, in spite of all her carrying on.

Funny, he mused in the darkness. In Annapolis at the
Mannerses' place, he'd watched the big stallion Sheik
mate with Glory. They hadn't seemed to like each other
much, biting and rearing, snorting and backing off, but
in the end they'd come together the way horses do. Gideon thought it was pretty mean of the handlers to stay
with them while they'd done it, but Missy, who'd
dragged him away as soon as she'd realized he'd hidden
himself there to watch, told him it was for the horses'
own good. They were expensive animals, she'd said, and
high-strung. They might hurt themselves or each other
if they weren't watched real close.

The cot creaked as Flynn shifted on it, and soon he
was snoring again, making quiet, snuffling kinds of

noises. Gideon decided he wouldn't mention that habit of Flynn's to Missy; she might not cotton to the notion of a husband who snored.

He crooked his arms beneath his head and wondered what the new day in a new place held in store for him. Missy had talked at dinner about school; he knew he didn't want that. She'd told him that most boys his age already knew how to read and that he had some catching up to do. The last thing he wanted was to sit in some dumb schoolhouse all day and make a damned fool of himself because he couldn't read and write. The other kids would sure laugh at him, and he didn't need that. No, sir. Anyway, he just wanted to hang around the ranch. Tend to Glory. Get to know the place a little better. He already knew he liked the C-Bar-C, but there was still plenty about the place he didn't know, such as where the best hiding places were. Where a body could catch a smoke if he needed it or just get out of some chore or something even more unpleasant, like a bath, or going to church or to school.

Or a place where he could plot and plan how to get Flynn Muldaur and Missy Cannon together.

He wondered how close they'd have to be watched so they wouldn't end up hurting each other.

Gideon sat up in the bed and yanked his nightshirt over his head. He had plenty to do, he realized. And the day was already wasting.

Missy overslept, something she hardly ever did. It never failed to exasperate her when it happened, mostly because it happened at the most inconvenient times. She'd intended to take Gideon to the schoolhouse by nine. It was already nearly half past ten. She dashed down the stairs working the last of the buttons on her blouson. She was ravenously hungry for breakfast, but breakfast would have to wait.

"Where's Gideon?"

She burst into the kitchen to find Lucy in the midst of baking bread. The place smelled agreeably of yeast, and Lucy was placidly kneading a lovely white mound of dough. Three other loaves had already been set aside to rise, Missy noticed, and there were several more waiting their turn. The sight and the smell reminded Missy of how much she herself loved that task and, unfortunately, of how hungry she was.

"Oh, good morning, miss," Lucy sang out, so cheerfully that Missy, despite the fact that she'd decided she liked the girl, wanted to strangle her. "I guess it was so nice to be back in your own bed that you decided to sleep in. Everyone else is up and gone; Gideon slipped out while I was just starting the stove for breakfast. There's a bowl of oatmeal mush for you under a tea towel in the dining room, and there's a fresh pot of coffee—"

"No time," Missy interrupted through her teeth. "I expect Gideon's out with Glory. I'll find him. But if he should come through here—"

"I have a sweet roll and a glass of buttermilk that ought to hold him," Lucy assured airily as Missy went out the back door.

The sun was warm, but the midmorning May breeze was cool. Missy wished she'd grabbed her old coat from the peg by the door before she'd run out; her habit, with its mustard brown blouson, coffee-colored pantskirt, and matching vest, was comfortable and easy to work in, but it provided little protection against cold. She'd not need such protection when she worked, of course, but now even her energetic stride was not enough to warm her. She hunched up her shoulders and folded her arms about her to hold in what warmth she could.

Gideon was not in the stable, but then neither was Glory. Hamper was, though, raking down new hay from the loft. He paused in his labors to talk to her, resting the palm of one hand on the end of the rake handle and planting his stubbled chin on his gloved knuckles.

"That boy musta asked me about a thousand questions, I guess, from how cold is the water in the cistern to do I know how to read and write," Hamper told her wearily, pushing his hat back with the other hand. "I swan, Miss, he'd like to drive me loco. He's real good with that Glory you brung home, though. Jim had a hell of a time last night with her, but this mornin' Gideon was right here takin' care of her like he was her mama. She was right good-natured about it, too, which is more'n I'd'a been with that boy yakkin' my ears off."

Missy smiled. Rich Hamper was no slouch when it came to talking, himself.

"Did he take her out to pasture?"

"Sure did." Hamper applied his back to his work once again. "Wouldn't surprise me if he means to be a daddy to her foal. That'd be all right with me; the bi— I mean, she took a nip outta my arm last night." Missy noticed that Hamper softened the word he'd started to use. She didn't mind a few hells and damns, in fact she often used those expressions herself, but there were worse ones she avoided, and the hands seemed to try not to use them in her presence. She hoped the men would extend their prudence to Gideon now that he was here, and she was sure she did not have to school them in their behavior around Lucy. Flynn said they liked her. Come to think of it, where was he this morning?

"She looks real peaceful-like," Hamper was continuing, referring, she knew, to Glory. "But then she turns on you all mean for no reason."

"Just like a foaling mare," Missy reminded him with a chuckle. She debated her next question. "Has Flynn been about?"

Hamper shrugged, but otherwise did not break the

rhythm of his work. "Not as I've seen. Saw him at breakfast, a'course. But not since. You'll be workin' with them yearlings today, I expect? Micah said to take 'em to the paddock near the ring."

"That's fine," she told him, realizing that she was not as interested currently in her prized yearlings as she was in the whereabouts of her partner. "I'll look in on them when I can, but I may not get to them for a few days."

Hamper nodded his acknowledgment, and Missy started to go.

"Oh, Rich?"

"Miss?"

"Do you know how to read and write?"

Hamper grinned his gap-toothed smile. "Hell, no! Why?"

Missy smiled ruefully. "Just wondering. Thank you."

Gideon had certainly filled out since she'd first seen him in Louisville, Missy realized, watching the boy tempt Glory in the pasture with a wild barley stalk. But he still looked small and wiry beside the mare. She didn't know any other 12-year-old-boys—although Gideon still professed to be 14—so she had no way of knowing whether or not he was undersize for his age. She did know, however, that while she still had a long way to go before she could claim to understand him, she had already begun to love him. She only wished she knew better how to show him that she did.

"You were supposed to go to school today, young man!"

Gideon, still 20 or more yards from her on the other side of the fence, looked up. His relaxed, playful expression was immediately guarded.

"Ain't goin' to no school."

"You most certainly are."

"Am not."

Gideon ambled through the new grass to the fence where Missy waited. Glory followed for a few steps, then discovered something interesting to nibble on. Gideon concentrated on an old termite tunnel, poking at it with his fingernail.

"Rich can't read or write," he told her, as if that settled the matter. "Neither can Jim. Don't guess they need to, workin' a place like this."

"Working a place like this for *me*." Missy corrected him, resting her arms on the fence rail that came to his forehead. He sent her a glance.

"For you and Flynn, you mean."

"The point is, Gideon, they work for the C-Bar-C. If they had more education, they might be running a place of their own, or they might have a different sort of job altogether, using their brains instead of their backs. Here, they work under Mi. Mi's the foreman; he makes more money than the others. One reason is because he can read and write. I can entrust him with other responsibilities because of it."

"Yeah? Like what?" Gideon was skeptical. He picked a winged termite out of the splintered top rail and held it up to the sunlight with two fingers, examining it. Not fond of insects, Missy mastered a shudder.

"Lots of things."

"Name one."

"Oh, Gideon, really!"

Gideon flicked the termite away on a breeze and climbed up on the middle rail, giving her a speculative look.

"Can you read?"

"Of course."

"Can Flynn?"

Missy felt obliged to look away from Gideon's too-probing gaze.

"You always get red in the face when I talk about

179

him, you know that?'' Gideon chuckled.

''I do not!'' Missy was mortified.

''Yeah, you do,'' Gideon assured her, rocking back, catching himself on the top rail with his hands each time. ''Well, can he?''

''Can he what?''

''Read!'' Gideon laughed once more. ''See, you're all red again!''

''I am not!'' She pressed her fingers to her face. Her cheeks were warm.

''Are too!''

''Am not!'' She reached over and tried to knock the cap from his head.

He drew back from her attempt, slapped her outstretched arm lightly, and laughed. ''Touched you last!'' And he was off.

Missy ducked between the fence rails and was after him.

He was quick and cunning, no doubt from experience dodging policemen and such, but he was also laughing, which made one weaker and less cautious than usual. Besides, he didn't seem to be trying very hard to elude her. She tackled him by midfield, and they both fell, giggling, to the new grass. Inspired, Missy started tickling his side. Gideon tried to roll away from her but she held him fast, and in moments he was laughing so hard she thought he might suffocate.

''Leave off! Leave off!'' he gasped to the sky. ''I give!''

Missy collapsed beside him, but she did not take her arms from about him. To her delight, he did not try to pull away from her. She moistened her parched lips with her tongue and listened to the sounds of their panting breaths as they recovered from the run. Out of the corner of her eye, she watched an inchworm measure a short blade of grass.

Gideon was very still in her arms.

"Now I know you're ticklish," she teased him, daring to ruffle his hair as she'd wanted to do since she'd first set eyes on him. "If you want me to keep it a secret, you'll have to behave yourself."

Gideon rolled over onto his belly but still did not try to escape her closeness. Missy felt as if a butterfly had landed on the back of her hand. She didn't dare move, lest it be frightened into flight.

"Oh, I know a few secrets myself," he told her with a knowing look, pulling up a handful of grass and showering it on her blouse.

He was baiting her, and she was up to the game. She looked at him doubtfully.

"What about?"

He looked very pleased that he'd piqued her interest.

"About Flynn," he remarked, eyeing her with disconcerting steadiness.

If he saw the redness creep back into her cheeks from her heated blush, he made no comment. She pretended to busy herself brushing the grass from her shirtfront.

"What kind of secrets might he have that I could possibly be interested in?" She hoped he couldn't hear her heart proclaiming the lie.

He gave her a look far too wise for his tender years.

"A big one," he assured her in a voice hushed with mystery. "About you."

Chapter Fourteen

"About me?"

Missy was glad she was lying down, perfectly still, or she might have fallen. She tried to rid herself of a sudden fuzzy thickness in her throat but gave up after the second swallow.

"Uh-huh." Gideon's nod was so sage that it bordered on comical. But Missy no longer felt like laughing.

"What?" She could not curb her curiosity. "What did he say?"

Gideon shrugged with a drop of his eyelids and picked a sprig of new sagebrush.

"I thought you didn't care." He twirled the blue seedling between his thumb and forefinger.

Previously Missy had thought that men learned, over a period of time and with tutelage and practice, how to goad women, but she decided right then that they must instead be born with the ability. At least this one seemed to be. And he was as yet but 12 years old. She spared a fleeting moment of pity for whatever woman might be in Gideon's future.

"I don't care what he said about me," she made herself say, closing her eyes as if by so doing she might close the subject.

"Suit yourself." She pictured Gideon's careless shrug.

"I don't care," she repeated slowly, opening her eyes again to deliver a reproving look. "But I suppose I should know. After all, until I can figure out a way around it, he and I are partners. I'd be a fool if I didn't try to learn everything I could about the man, especially what he thinks of me."

Gideon's grin let her know just how much her rationale fooled him. He rolled onto his back and played with the sagebrush as if it were a feather.

"Oh, he thinks of you," he said in an expansive way. "He thinks of you plenty. I come right out and asked him last night—after we'd talked, y'know, man to man for a spell—what he thought of you."

"And?" Missy was certain Gideon's pause was merely for effect. She had to admit, it did have an effect. A most unsettling one, at that.

Gideon rolled the sage sprig between his flattened palms, and the clean scent of bruised sagebrush surrounded them.

"What's this stuff called?" he asked.

"Sagebrush," she answered automatically. She was used to Gideon's childlike habit of changing a subject without warning. She started to spell the word, as she did for him whenever he asked about such things. "S-a-g-e—"

"Say, I have an idea!" Gideon sat up fast as thought and crossed his knickered legs, a gleam in his dark eyes.

"I'm half afraid to ask," Missy grumbled, not liking

183

that mischievous gleam one bit. "But I suppose I'd better. What?"

"You can teach me how to read!"

She sat up and smoothed the folds of her habit in an effort to keep a rein on her patience. It was a struggle.

"Gideon, that's why we have a school."

His expression darkened at once, as if a thundercloud had passed before the sun.

"So you want me to go to some dumb school and make a jackass of myself in front of a schoolteacher and a bunch of sodbuster brats?" His voice was cold, but Missy felt the hurt hidden therein. Before she stopped to think about it, she reached for his face, brushing a rebellious dark forelock from his eyes.

"But Gideon, I have plenty of work already to keep me busy!" she argued gently.

He was not mollified.

"Flynn hired Lucy to cook, and you got him here now to do half the work you were doin' before." His dark brows met over his puck nose. "I'll learn fast. I promise. I ain't stupid. I bet I could learn before the summer's out. If you teach me. You and Flynn. You could both do it, you know."

Gideon, Missy had learned, had all the energy of a restless stallion when it came to getting his way. She sensed herself capitulating to his earnest entreaty, but she didn't want to appear to give in too easily.

"What about Flynn?" she countered, pressing the forefingers of her joined hands against her lips. "Have you already spoken to him about this?"

"Didn't have to," Gideon answered with a look of superiority. "He told me last night that it'd be all right with him, right before he told me he was in love with you."

"*What?*"

Gideon laughed. "That was the secret I told you

about!'' he said. ''Guess I forgot to tell you.''

''We—we got sidetracked by sagebrush,'' Missy managed despite the hollow rushing in her ears. ''Gideon, are you—are you quite sure that's what he said?''

She found his youthful, careless shrug maddening.

''Ain't likely I'd forget somethin' like that,'' he remarked in an offhand way. ''He said he'd take me fishin' sometime, too, if you'd let him. I like him, Miss. I like him a lot. I think you could do worse than to marry up with him.''

The absurdity of the conversation she was carrying on with the boy struck her, and she laughed nervously.

''Gideon, you have quite the imagination,'' she declared, shaking her head. ''I can't picture this conversation you had with Flynn, about learning to read, about going fishing, and—and about his being in love with me. Are you certain you didn't dream all of this up?''

Gideon got to his feet and planted his hands at his waist. His square chin stuck out like a warning.

''You don't believe me?''

''Oh, I believe you *think* he said these things,'' she hastened to assure him. ''I can even see why you'd find them agreeable, except for the part about his being in love with me. That I don't understand at all.''

''Why?'' he demanded, his features fixed in a scowl. ''Don't you think he could love you? Don't you want him to love you? Sure looks to me like you do!''

No, yes, and yes. Part of her wanted to answer Gideon with the same childish simplicity he'd exhibited to her. In reality, her feelings were very simple. It was everything else tangled up with them that made them so complex. Things she could not even hope to make Gideon, young as he was, understand. Things she knew she did not fully understand, herself.

She stood up and brushed her skirt free of the dirt and debris of the pasture.

"Well?"

"Flynn is a man with a purpose, Gideon," she said simply. "I don't know what that purpose is yet, but I do know that settling down on a ranch or a horse farm isn't a part of it."

"Oh." Gideon sounded wise. "You're afraid, then."

She could not prevent herself from delivering him a sharp look.

"There are precious few things I'm afraid of, my boy. And Flynn Muldaur isn't one of them."

"Okay." Gideon got to his feet, too, but he didn't seem to mind the bits of Dakota that still clung to his clothes. "That's fine. So you'll both teach me how to read and write, then?"

Missy gave up trying to follow Gideon's broken line of thought.

"I'll talk it over with him." She surrendered with a bow of her head.

"Well, come on, then!" Gideon took her hand and pulled her forward. "He's back at the house."

Missy stopped short. "At the house!" she echoed, confused. "But he wasn't there when I—" At least she hadn't thought he was. Where could he have been?

"He came out to the barn early this morning when I was cleaning out Glory's stall," Gideon informed her, pulling her again until her legs cooperated. "He talked to me some about this reading stuff, and—well, we talked about a lot of things." Gideon seemed to want to be evasive this time, but Missy did not pursue it. There'd be plenty of time to learn everything she wanted to know later, after she was able to catch her breath. She wondered, following Gideon's distressingly energetic lead, if she might accomplish that by Christmas.

Gideon used the walk back to the ranch house to think up another fib or two to tell Flynn. He hadn't been quite honest with Missy about his conversation with the man the night before, but he guessed he wasn't too far off the mark. Flynn hadn't exactly confessed to being in love with Missy, but neither had he denied it when asked. Love was a complicated and private business, Muldaur had said with a jaundiced look in his eye, and not one that men discussed in detail with folks they hardly knew. It was a gamble that Missy wouldn't call Flynn on it, but Gideon had learned how to gamble on people in Louisville and found out that he was pretty good at it.

Gideon surprised himself by liking Flynn more and more, in spite of the fact that Flynn had figured out his trick with the molasses and the stomachache. Flynn, he decided, was a sight smarter than a lot of people he'd dealt with in the past, and he'd have to be pretty clever about whatever he tried with him in the future. Missy was smart, too, he knew, but Missy, unlike Flynn and Gideon, trusted people too much. That was her weakness, if he cared to profit by it.

People in general, he'd learned quickly, believed in things they wanted to believe. That was why they were so easy to scam. He didn't particularly like the notion of scamming Missy as she'd been real good to him, but he told himself what he was doing was harmless. Nobody would be hurt by it if it worked, and if it didn't, well, there was always that Bill Boland fellow who had come tearing into town yesterday with Flynn hot on his heels. Because sure as hell, Missy needed a husband.

And he, Gideon, needed a father.

The house was quiet but filled with the mouthwatering smell of baking bread when Missy pushed open the back door to let them both inside. The kitchen was empty. Lucy was outside in the garden; she'd waved to them as she hoed. Lucy was all right, too, Gideon allowed. Hell, everybody at the C-Bar-C was fine. They treated him like a person instead of a bother, and they talked to him like he was somebody instead of just a hungry bunch of rags. This was the first real home he'd ever known, and he knew he'd lie, cheat, or steal to keep it if he had to. He just hoped he wouldn't have to.

Missy didn't particularly want to face Flynn Muldaur having learned what she had in the pasture, especially not under the too-watchful eye of Gideon. But she was neither a coward nor a quitter. And she was damned if she'd go walking on eggs about her own house for anybody, especially Flynn Muldaur. Even if what Gideon said about Muldaur's being in love with her were true.

Especially if it were true.

She thought about calling out to Flynn, but something held her back. It was not any wish that she appear in a more ladylike light to him, she knew. He'd seen her worst already yesterday and in Louisville; she doubted she could make him think any worse of her.

Particularly if what Gideon said was true.

Flynn is in love with you.

Oh, Gideon was a foolish, fanciful child, prone to imaginative untruths, she scolded herself. But nevertheless there was a part of her that wanted so very much to believe him this time. Maybe she would see something about Flynn that would tell her for certain whether Gideon's words were fact or fanciful invention.

She feared she would.

There was a room off the parlor where Missy kept her accounts and the ranch records. The place was a cluttered little hole, but she used it often enough that she kept the door open when she had no company to entertain. Flynn wasn't in the parlor, but she immediately became suspicious when she noticed the door to her small office was closed. With sickening dread, she ran to the door and opened it.

Flynn was inside, seated at her desk, an open ledger

188

book before him. He looked up at once, his features darkening.

"Don't you believe in knocking?" he demanded, making no effort to camouflage his activity.

"This is my house; I'll enter a room wherever and whenever I want!" she retorted, feeling her face fill with hot rage. "How dare you come in here and snoop about my business! These accounts are—"

"—my business, too," he interrupted her with infuriating equanimity. "We're partners, remember? I have every right to know what financial footing the ranch is on. And you can bet I'll be sure and remember your philosophy about closed doors."

"You might at least have asked me to see them!" she flared back at him, ignoring his sarcasm. "Instead of sneaking behind my back!"

Flynn stood up but did not close the ledger before him. He fixed his blue-eyed gaze on her in a way that made her tremble.

"You're right," he conceded with a nod, curling his lower lip. "I should have asked. Then we could have had this argument before instead of after. Gideon, what the he—heck are you doing here? Why aren't you in school?"

Missy recalled Gideon in the pasture, employing a similar technique to change the subject. She wondered who was the teacher and who was the student.

"Leave the child out of this," she said, keeping her voice low, although it was a great temptation to shout and throw things at him. "We'll discuss him presently. In the meantime—"

"I ain't a child," Gideon grumbled.

"Go wait outside, Gideon."

"But what about—"

Missy whirled on him.

"Go into the garden with Lucy, Gideon." She pronounced each word slowly and leveled him with a look that made him take two steps backward and swallow hard. "I must speak with Flynn alone. And if I find that you've disobeyed me and listened at the door . . ." She did not finish her remark but allowed her voice to trail off with as ominous a tone as she could muster. She was gratified to see him flee the room at a dead run.

"Don't think I've ever seen him listen so well."

Flynn's wry remark recalled her attention. She turned to him again with another hot remark, but his hands were up in conciliation.

"You're right, Missy, and I apologize," he told her, without a hint of mockery in his look or voice. In fact, to her astonishment he actually appeared contrite. "But the truth is, I came into the parlor, noticed this room, saw that the door was open, and—"

He stopped and averted his gaze.

"Damn it," he swore under his breath. "I can't do this anymore."

"Do what?" At his baffling words, she forgot her anger.

He glanced at her, but seemed to find the effort painful and looked away again.

"It's hot in here," he muttered, taking her by the arm. "Let's go into the parlor. I'll tell you. Everything."

Too stunned to protest, Missy followed his direction. He led her to a chair and she sat down without a word. Flynn remained standing, his splayed hands settled at his hips. He paced. *He's in love with you*, Gideon had said. Looking at him, though, she knew that his were not the words or actions of a man in love.

They were the actions of a man in a great deal of trouble.

She sat very still, waiting. Watching.

"Missy, I need five thousand dollars."

Missy said nothing. She sensed they were among the

truest words Flynn Muldaur had ever spoken to her, and she cherished them for exactly that. She drew in and released several slow, even breaths.

"What for?" She was amazed by the tranquillity in her address.

"I can't tell you that." He looked away from her.

"I thought you said you would tell me everything."

"Well, I meant everything I could," he answered testily, looking at the far wall.

She stood up.

"We're partners, according to that piece of paper you have," she reminded him saltily. "And until you trust me enough to tell me everything—"

"Damn it, Missy, I can't!" He spun on her with real distress on his features. "You see, it's not just about me. If it was, I'd be happy to tell you everything just to have it all out. My God, it's been like some yoke about my neck for just about half my life. But there's—there's someone else involved. Someone who would be hurt a great deal, probably even destroyed, if the truth ever came out. And I love that person too much to allow that to happen."

Missy fell back into her seat as if a lance had pinned her there right through her heart. This was worse than she thought. Far worse. She remembered the lovely Antoinette Deauville in Louisville, and remembered the woman Joshua had told her about: Madeleine.

Flynn's lover?

"Is it a woman?" She forced the question.

Flynn wanted to be sick. He clenched his hands and his teeth and made himself stare at Missy, who looked as if he'd just run her through. He knew, looking at her, what she wanted to hear from him. He found that he wanted to tell her, but he knew he never could. For Seamus's sake.

191

Carole Howey

"Yes," he said dully. He thought he'd choke on the lie.

Missy's lustrous gray eyes misted, but she pinched her mouth into a poker-straight line.

"You're lying, Flynn," she said softly. "Why?"

Flynn's chin fell to his chest, and he could no longer keep his eyes open. How did she know? Had he become that awful at spinning falsehoods? Was lying a skill that deteriorated with use? he wondered wearily. Or had he simply allowed Missy Cannon so far inside his defenses that he was no longer capable of deceiving her? Or himself?

He let out a small, bitter laugh.

"Christ, Missy Cannon, you're going to be the death of me," he muttered. "What do you want me to tell you?"

"The truth," she ventured in a small voice. "Would it be so very hard?"

"Harder than you know," he said, half to himself.

"Half your life," she mused in a voice so tender that it ripped through his breast like a jagged blade. "It's a long time to live with a lie. I'm surprised you're no more bitter than you are."

Did she mean to kill him with kindness now? Did she know how easy it would be?

"Don't do this to me, Missy," he breathed, turning away from her. "I'd rather have your outrage than your pity. I know how to deal with that. I don't deserve your sympathy, and I don't deserve your—your—" He could not summon the strength to utter the word he found suddenly on his tongue.

"My love?" Her question was a whisper.

Love. That was it. You remember love, Flynn? his conscience taunted him. *It's what you thought you felt for Madeleine. It's what keeps you protecting Seamus. And it's what's breaking your heart right now.* He stared

A Special Offer For
Leisure Romance Readers Only!

Get
FOUR
FREE
Romance
Novels
A $21.96 Value!

Travel to exotic worlds filled with passion
and adventure —without leaving your home!
Plus, you'll save $5.00 every time you buy!

Thrill to the most sensual, adventure-filled Historical Romances on the market today...

FROM ▙ LEISURE BOOKS

As a home subscriber to Leisure Romance Book Club, you'll enjoy the best in today's BRAND-NEW Historical Romance fiction. For over twenty-five years, Leisure Books has brought you the award-winning, high-quality authors you know and love to read. Each Leisure Historical Romance will sweep you away to a world of high adventure...and intimate romance. Discover for yourself all the passion and excitement millions of readers thrill to each and every month.

Save $5.00 Each Time You Buy!

Each month, the Leisure Romance Book Club brings you four brand-new titles from Leisure Books, America's foremost publisher of Historical Romances. EACH PACKAGE WILL SAVE YOU $5.00 FROM THE BOOKSTORE PRICE! And you'll never miss a new title with our convenient home delivery service.

Here's how we do it. Each package will carry a FREE 10-DAY EXAMINATION privilege. At the end of that time, if you decide to keep your books, simply pay the low invoice price of $16.96, no shipping or handling charges added. HOME DELIVERY IS ALWAYS FREE. With today's top Historical Romance novels selling for $5.99 and higher, our price SAVES YOU $5.00 with each shipment.

AND YOUR FIRST FOUR-BOOK SHIPMENT IS TOTALLY FREE!

IT'S A BARGAIN YOU CAN'T BEAT! A Super $21.96 Value!

▙ LEISURE BOOKS A Division of Dorchester Publishing Co., Inc.

GET YOUR 4 FREE BOOKS
NOW — A $21.96 Value!

*Mail the Free Book
Certificate
Today!*

4
FREE
BOOKS

A
$21.96
VALUE

Free Books
Certificate

YES! I want to subscribe to the Leisure Romance Book Club. Please send me my 4 FREE BOOKS. Then, each month I'll receive the four newest Leisure Historical Romance selections to Preview FREE for 10 days. If I decide to keep them, I will pay the Special Member's Only discounted price of just $4.24 each, a total of $16.96. This is a SAVINGS OF $5.00 off the bookstore price. There are no shipping, handling, or other charges. There is no minimum number of books I must buy and I may cancel the program at any time. In any case, the 4 FREE BOOKS are mine to keep — A BIG $21.96 Value!
Offer valid only in the U.S.A.

Name _____

Address _____

City _____

State _____ *Zip* _____

Telephone _____

Signature _____

If under 18, Parent or Guardian must sign. Terms, prices and conditions subject to change. Subscription subject to acceptance. Leisure Books reserves the right to reject any order or cancel any subscription.

A
$21.96
VALUE

4
FREE
BOOKS

Get Four Books Totally
FREE — A $21.96 Value

▼ Tear Here and Mail Your FREE Book Card Today! ▼

PLEASE RUSH
MY FOUR FREE
BOOKS TO ME
RIGHT AWAY!

Leisure Romance Book Club
65 Commerce Road
Stamford CT 06902-4563

AFFIX
STAMP
HERE

at Missy Cannon, who looked back at him with steady, sorrowful gray eyes.

"I do love you, you know," she said in a voice that was more air than sound.

My God, what had it cost her to say it? he wondered, shamed by her strength and sincerity, and by his own cowardice. He could only guess, and he knew his guess would fall far short of the reality.

He stiffened his spine and squared his shoulders. He could not afford such a sentiment. Neither of them could.

"Don't say it," he advised her coldly, turning toward the wall. "Don't even think it. I'm a part of something so ugly you'd hate me for it if you knew the truth. I could stand that, but it wouldn't be fair to you. I've already made you suffer enough for something you don't deserve. I wish to hell I could just walk away from here today as if that damned paper didn't exist. But the fact is right now that title is the only thing that's giving me a chance to claw my way out of a hole that I've been buried in for over twelve years, a hole I spent six years before that digging.

"I could love you, Missy," he confessed to her. "Easily. I wouldn't have thought so in February, or even a month ago, but I know it now. Oh, too well. But it would be wrong for both of us. Dead wrong."

"Why?"

He started. How had she moved directly behind him without his knowing it? This was not good. He was losing his mind or his good sense, and either would spell disaster for him and Seamus, and for Missy as well. He tried to move away, but the smell of her—fresh air and apples and cinnamon—held him fast.

"You don't understand," he managed to whisper. "And I pray you never do. You're so trusting and straightforward. I'm sorry as hell I had to be the one to show you artifice and deceit. That's as big a sin on my soul as all of the others combined. The only bigger one is that I can't let you go until I get my pound of flesh to satisfy—"

God, he'd almost told her.

"Who?" she urged him.

But he had control of himself again. That was close. Too close. Fixing a cold, blank look on his face, he forced himself to turn around, to look at her. The expression of tender concern on her face nearly made him look away again.

"I have a proposition for you," he said in a clinical tone, staring through her instead of at her. "Give me five thousand dollars today as the first payment of a buy-out of my half of the deed. As long as we operate in the black, you can give me five thousand every other month until next May. That's seven payments of five thousand dollars each; thirty-five thousand dollars total. If we keep making a profit, that is. By that time, I'll have bought myself an extra year to figure out what I'm going to do for money in the future, and you'll have your ranch back, free and clear. What do you say?"

"If I say no?" She laid a finger alongside her cheek.

He hoped his look was as uncompromising.

"I need that five thousand now," he told her. "If you don't give it to me, I'll have to get it some other way."

Missy considered him. His blue eyes were cold as a December sky and his features utterly blank. His words were such a revelation to her as to make Gideon's earlier remarks seem absurd and unimportant. Flynn loved her, as certainly as she loved him. But was it really love, if he could not trust her with his secret?

There, she sensed, was where it ended. He could not tell her his truth, whatever it was, and she could not live with his lie. He might as well not have loved her after all.

And she would never stop loving him, no matter where the future led her.

Along with an agreement worded the way Flynn had suggested, Missy wrote out a bank draft for five thousand dollars, not because she felt constrained to do so, but because she feared what Flynn would do for the money if she did not. Besides, it meant that in a year she would be free again. She was no longer certain, though, of what she was freeing herself from. Or if she wanted to be free of it.

"Gideon said you'd offered to help teach him to read," she said when she handed him the draft.

Flynn accepted the check with a grim look.

"I told him I'd help, if he minded his manners and did as he was told," he answered in a wooden voice. "That boy needs a strong hand, Missy."

She looked up. "What?"

"Can we at least be friends?" he asked, his voice hoarse, his eyes hooded. "I'd like that."

Missy nodded. She even managed to smile, although she would rather have put her face in her hands and cried in despair.

Part Three

*Preservantia
Wincit*

Chapter Fifteen

July, 1892

"Is Missy to home?"

Bill Boland stood there on the front porch in a summer suit with his hand on his white Stetson.

Damn it all to hell and back, Flynn thought, looking the aging rancher up and down. Was it Sunday afternoon again? Where had the week gone?

Bill Boland had taken to calling on Missy every Sunday afternoon since May with unfailing regularity, and Flynn had no choice but to put the best face on it. After all, he'd as much as told Missy that spring day that anything beyond friendship was out of the question for him. He'd felt a small relief at the time, getting it out in the open, but he'd found himself regretting it every day since, as he'd been obliged to watch Bill Boland, that smug, secure, self-righteous son of a bitch, come by every Sunday and make inroads into Missy's tender affections.

Damn it.

"Come in, Bill." Missy was right behind him, and her warm invitation was issued as if he, Flynn, were not even present. Boland brushed by him with no more regard than he might have tendered a coatrack.

"Gideon and I are going fishing." Flynn addressed his statement to Missy but he had a glare to spare for Bill's back.

Missy's look of disappointment was gratifying. That is, until she spoke.

"Oh, I was hoping he'd want to come along on a drive with us," she fretted, sending the rancher an apologetic glance. "Bill's driving his new surrey this afternoon, and he wanted to show it off to me. He had it at church this morning, too. Did you see it outside, Flynn?"

New surrey. Flynn scowled.

"Nope," he replied airily. "You can ask Gid, if you want." The invitation was a taunt and a challenge. Gideon loved fishing, and he was only allowed to do it if he'd successfully completed a week's worth of lessons. This past week, he'd proudly finished the third-grade primer and had written out the Lord's Prayer in a better hand than Flynn himself. Besides, Flynn knew that Gideon's role on the drive would be one of chaperon, and that Missy wouldn't go with Bill without one. If he, Flynn, could ruin the rancher's courting plans on a fine afternoon, he considered it a mark in the credit column.

Flynn tried whenever possible to be out of the house when the courting widower came to call of a Sunday afternoon. Seeing Boland took away his appetite for Lucy's fine Sunday suppers.

"I expect he's all ready to go fishing," Missy mourned, shooting Flynn a surreptitious, grateful look.

"Of course, you could go by yourself with Bill," Flynn suggested, purposely ignoring the look. "After all, it's not as if you two haven't known each other since the flood."

The flood was Bill's favorite metaphor, and Missy had confided to Flynn only that morning before church that despite their long courtship, she did not feel ready to be alone with Bill Boland yet. Flynn felt a moment of triumph goading both of them with one remark, but only a moment. For if Missy went out driving alone with Bill Boland, that would be a clear signal to the widower that Missy's favors were available. If Boland kissed her, Flynn would have to kill him.

Damn it twice.

Missy's gray eyes were wide as saucers; for a moment Flynn feared he'd spoken his curse aloud. Served her right, Flynn thought, grinning at her even as he felt like strangling her. Maybe it was about time she learned what was in store for her if she married Bill Boland.

Well, you're sure as hell not going to ask her to marry you, his conscience taunted him. *Who in the hell are you to stand in the way of someone who wants to make her happy?*

Missy had come to trust him in small ways in the past two months as they'd worked together with the ranch, and with Gideon. The results were that the ranch was thriving even more than it had under Missy's supervision, which was no mean accomplishment, and Gideon was coming along just fine in his manners and his lessons, losing the cautious look in his lively eyes and taming the wilder side of his nature. Flynn found that he genuinely liked the boy, even if he was a sight smarter than he needed to be.

Flynn had also shared many an intimate, if brief, conversation of an evening with Missy, and she had revealed a little of herself to him. He'd liked what he'd seen. Admired it, even. And found himself, against his will and better judgment, growing to love the woman more and more for her frank, gentle nature uncluttered by artifice and ulterior motives. So unlike most women in his experience. So unlike Madeleine and her ilk.

Missy's alarmed expression blended to one of reproach that Flynn was certain Boland could not see, and he remembered her immediate predicament. He pretended to ignore the look, though, as he pushed by the rancher in the foyer.

"I'll take a look upstairs and see if Gideon's ready for our fishing trip," he muttered to no one in particular. As he climbed the first step he heard Missy's pleasant, if desperate, soprano invite Bill into the parlor for some refreshment.

Flynn wasn't sure precisely when he decided that he—that is, that Gideon—had to save Missy from being alone with Bill on that surrey ride, but if he was pinned to it, he'd say it was right around the fourth or fifth step.

"I swear, Gideon, if you go driving with them, I'll take you fishing twice this week before Sunday." Flynn was out of breath.

Gideon looked up from lacing his boots, one eyebrow arched, one eye squinted. "You run all the way upstairs?"

He had, but he wasn't about to admit that to Gideon. Gideon was even sharper than Missy about some things, and far less charitable in his candid observations.

"What do you say?" He decided that ignoring the question was the best tack to take.

"Missy says I can't go fishin' until all my lessons are done." Gideon bent his head to his bootlacings.

"I'll make it all right with Missy," Flynn said swiftly, still panting. "Just get on down there right now and tell her you'll go. But don't make it look like you're doing her a favor, or she'll get suspicious."

Gideon glanced sideways at him, pausing.

"The favor's for you, isn't it?" he asked.

"Hurry up!" Christ, couldn't the boy move any quicker?

"Must be pretty important," Gideon commented, taking his time with his boots.

"Damn it, Gid!"

"Missy'd sure hang you out to dry if she heard you swearin' around me. You know how she is about that."

"Yeah, I know," Flynn growled. "Just get down there. Fast."

"Wait a minute. I didn't say I was gonna do it," Gideon reminded him with a cool look. "I was all set to go fishin', like you promised. I finished that dumb old primer, and—"

"Twice this week. Cross my heart." Flynn looked out the window anxiously. The surrey was still there in the drive, unattended. He thought it a garish affair, with a sissy fringe dancing about its canopy, but he guessed women—and very old men—went in for that sort of thing. So far Missy and Boland were nowhere in evidence. They must still be in the parlor. He allowed himself a quick breath of relief.

"I don't know." Gideon's youthful voice was heavy with doubt.

Flynn spun on him. "What do you mean, you don't kn—"

The look on Gideon's face cut him short. He realized at once that the boy was playing him, and that Gideon knew exactly how high the stakes were. He grimaced.

"All right, three times," he muttered, grudgingly admiring the boy's scheming intellect. "But we won't tell Missy a thing, all right? Just—"

Gideon shook his head slowly, not smiling, not taking his somber gaze from Flynn's. Flynn would have sworn the kid was the son of an undertaker, or a preacher, as serious as he looked.

"I don't know," he intoned again. "I don't like the notion of not tellin' Missy. You know what a store she sets by honesty. If she was to learn that I'd deceived her . . ." He trailed off, making a great show of looking troubled.

"Why, you little faker! You didn't have any trouble looking her in the eye last night when she asked where that last dish of slump went!"

Gideon looked offended.

"That was different."

"Like hell it was." Flynn peered through the gap in the curtains to check outside.

Damn it, Boland must have talked her into it after all! There they were, standing by the surrey. Missy seemed skittish as a colt. Boland had a look on his lined face that was smooth as whipped butter. Flynn clenched his hands, aching to whip something else.

"Three times, Gideon, and you can have my dessert for a whole week," he said through his teeth. "Now get down there quick! They're getting in!"

"My Sunday clothes are all put away just the way Missy likes, though, and I already got on my reg'lar clothes," Gideon fretted. Missy had been at him for days to put them in the laundry for Lucy to wash, Flynn knew, but the boy seemed to like the fact that they smelled like Glory.

Strongly.

Flynn grinned.

"All the better," he said swiftly. "Try to sit between them if you can. If you can't, sit right in the middle in the back, and be sure to sit forward if you think they're getting too cozy."

"I got a powerful lot of chores to do this week."

Damn it, the boy was worse than a wheeler-dealer politician.

"If you think I'm going to—"

Flynn's declaration was interrupted by the sound of a buggy whip cracking.

"I'll do them," he muttered swiftly. "Go, you little scoundrel! And if you don't catch up with them, all bets are off!"

But Gideon was gone before Flynn's codicil had left his lips. By the time Flynn got to the window to see what happened, Gideon was already yelling for the pair to stop. With no small sense of relief, Flynn watched the boy climb into the rear seat of the surrey behind the courting pair. He wished he could see Boland's look of disappointment, but the rancher's face was obscured by the broad brim of his hat.

"Thank you, Flynn."

It was dusk. The Black Hills glowed amber and rose with the setting sun behind them. The heat of the afternoon had relented to a comfortable warmth, enough to make the evening breeze pleasant on the front porch. Flynn did not look at Missy as she emerged from the house. He sank further into his seat, slid his booted feet up the porch pillar, and drew on the stub of a cigar clenched in his teeth.

"What are you talking about?"

"Don't pretend you didn't send Gideon down after me and Bill," she chided him. "His clothing smelled terrible. But still, it was sweet of you."

He was sweet now, was he? Flynn choked back a bitter retort.

"Don't be lettin' it get around," he growled instead, flicking his butt into the dirt beyond the porch.

"And don't be leaving your butts in sight," Missy admonished him in turn. "I've smelled tobacco on Gideon's breath a time or two, and he's far too young for that habit. I think he picks up your leavings, pinches some papers from Mi, and rolls his own cigarettes.''

Flynn chuckled ruefully. ''The little imp. Guess I'll have to carry the damned things around in my pocket from now on.'' He got up, stretched, and sighed. ''Want to sit down?'' He offered her the only chair on the porch, the one he'd lately vacated.

She shook her head, avoiding his eyes. She did that a lot. He knew why.

''No, thanks. Mi just told me Miss Mabel's been coughing, and she looks as if she might be shaping up,'' she explained, referring to one of the three dams serviced by Sheik. ''I'd better go have a look.''

Flynn frowned.

''But it's nowhere near her time!''

She met his gaze at last, and he saw that she was grim with worry. ''I know.''

''I'll come with you.''

A cough could be trouble, Flynn knew, especially if it was accompanied by a runny nose or an elevated body temperature. Such a condition in foaling mares often resulted in abortion, and worse, was contagious. The other two foaling mares were susceptible. Miss Mabel would have to be kept apart from the rest of the stock, particularly the remaining brood mares.

The mares weren't due to foal until January. One had slipped early, Flynn recalled, but Missy had been very diligent and careful with the other three, and she was optimistic about three live, healthy births. She'd pinned many hopes on Sheik's unborn progeny, Flynn knew. Not the least of them was her ability to buy out the remainder of his share of the ranch. Besides which Flynn had a feeling she'd take the loss as personally as she would one of her own, if the mare were to lose the foal.

After all, if anyone had been born to be a mother, it was Missy Cannon.

The strong scent of pine oil mingled with the smell of horse and clean hay in the stable. Rich was already scrubbing down the birthing stall, and Mi was with the mare. His usually bland face was grim. Apologetic.

"It don't look good, Miss," he greeted Missy in a low tone, as if Miss Mabel were a human patient who might understand him and become alarmed. "She's down. It don't look like she broke her water yet, so that's good, but she ain't et all day as I can see, and she looks to me like she's bagging up."

Flynn looked as Missy stooped to examine the mare. What he hadn't known about foaling before he came to the C-Bar-C, he'd read up on once he got here. By the light of the three lamps in the stall, it seemed to him that the mare's udder was, indeed, swollen, and that meant she was near foaling.

It meant disaster.

"Christ," he muttered, as much a prayer as an oath.

"Maybe just another spontaneous abortion, just like the other one," Missy said in a matter-of-fact, clinical manner, rising as she rolled up her sleeves. "Although I'd guess it's equine pneumonia. For now, we'll keep her apart. Otherwise, we'll just have to wait and see. It's going to be a long night, I guess."

"Yes, ma'am," Mi agreed heavily, getting to his feet. It was obvious to Flynn that the foreman didn't like this situation any better than Missy did. Flynn realized he didn't, either.

"Why don't you go on back to the house?" he suggested, touching her arm. "I'll stay with Mi. Gideon wants tucking in. Besides, you're not dressed for—for the kind of work we'll have here tonight."

Missy's gaze followed the trail his arm made until she was looking into his eyes. Her own eyes were shining

like wet pearls, and he knew the wetness was unshed
tears. He wished he could make them go away with a
touch of his hand, or an embrace, but he knew he did
not possess that kind of power, even if she still loved
him as she had said two months before.

"Thank you," she said softly. "I'll be back."

In less than an hour, she was. She'd put on trousers
that she sometimes, but not often, worked in, and a soft
flannel shirt. She brought with her blankets and pillows.
Lucy, immense with her late pregnancy, followed bearing a coffeepot and a small wicker hamper.

"Thought you might need some victuals," she offered, sounding far more subdued than usual. "I'll be
going to bed, myself, miss, if you don't mind. My back's
been botherin' me all afternoon."

With a nod, Lucy left them alone.

"I don't like the sound of that either," Missy fretted,
looking after the waddling girl. "Mi, I want you to go
for the doctor. I think Lucy and Miss Mabel both might
need one before this night is out."

Where Lucy's welfare was concerned, Mi didn't need
to be asked twice. In moments, Missy and Flynn were
alone in the stall except for the ailing mare. Silently
Missy handed Flynn one of the blankets and a pillow.

"Is Gideon asleep?" Flynn, accepting them, didn't
know what to say to her, but he needed to say
something.

She nodded, folding her own blanket and plunking it
on the straw like a cushion. "Like a baby," she remarked quietly. "I think he could sleep through an
earthquake." She tried to smile, but her effort did not
deceive him.

Arranging his blanket beside hers against the wall,
Flynn tried again. "Going to be a long night, I guess."

She did not answer.

He lowered himself to the straw beside her, wanting

to touch her, wanting to reach her. He wished to God he knew how.

"Did you at least have a nice ride this afternoon in Bill Boland's surrey?"

Now, why in blue hell had he asked that? he wondered, biting his lip in disgust. The widower was hardly his favorite topic of discussion, and worse, he had the feeling Missy knew that. He clenched his fists, steeling himself against a knowing chuckle.

It never came.

"You don't like Bill," she said instead, wonderingly. "I can't understand why."

Can't you? he wanted to ask her. He knew he couldn't. The knowledge choked him like a chicken bone stuck in his throat.

"Seems to me it's you who doesn't much like him," he retorted gruffly, picking bits of straw from his trousers because he needed to do something to keep from looking at her there beside him. "He's been coming around here 'since the flood,' and I don't guess you two are any closer to tying the knot than you were before I got here. Hell, I bet you've never even let him kiss you."

He felt reckless in the comparative darkness of the stall. Surely Missy, if she were looking, would not be able to see the redness he felt in his face. And much as he hated talking about the ardent rancher who courted her, he found that he was burning to learn if the man had ever known a pleasure from Missy more personal than, say, holding her hand. In fact, he felt he might scorch to a cinder if he didn't find out soon.

Two months earlier, Missy realized, she would have taken umbrage at such an invasive question from Flynn Muldaur. But that had been when she'd entertained a fevered crush for the man beside her. After he'd gently but firmly spelled out his feelings to her that afternoon in May, she'd managed to put aside those girlish fancies of hers. She felt as if she'd stuffed them in a little-used corner of her heart, as if they were cherished but fragile mementos to be hoarded in a box out of the light. Now, she told herself by rote, he was merely a business associate. An acquaintance. Sometimes even a friend, when she allowed herself to admit to that much feeling for him.

She'd missed having a friend such as he. She found herself liking it. And she'd found herself, despite the secret that kept a certain distance between them, confiding in him more and more.

"Flynn Muldaur, you're as nosy as any old widow," she declared, even managing a slight, if shaky, laugh. "And I can name half a dozen of them hereabouts who'd give their false teeth to know the answer to that question."

Flynn held his breath. Then, when she said nothing more for several seconds, he let it out again.

"Well?" he demanded softly.

A rush of heat filled her face, she wasn't sure why. No, she was sure why, and that was what scared her, suddenly.

"No," she answered at last in a muffled voice, watching the quiet mare. "I've never let him kiss me."

Flynn shifted in his seat, his shoulder jostling hers. His enormous sigh was baffling. "Why not?" he asked at the end of it.

Another rush of heat filled her face and she stared at his boot tops.

"You'll laugh."

"No, I won't."

"Yes, you will."

"Won't. I promise." He made an X across his chest with his finger, something she'd seen Gideon do many times. Against her will, she giggled. The sound echoed in the otherwise quiet stable, coming all around the high-beamed ceiling again to mock her. She risked a sideways look at him but could not maintain her gaze, because he was staring at her intently. Suddenly she felt his fingers lace with her own between them in the straw, loosely. His fingers were warm and strong. The feel of them in hers coaxed a lump to her throat.

"So tell me," he urged her in a whisper, shaking her hand once, gently. "Why hasn't Bill Boland ever been allowed to taste your lips?"

God, why had he put it that way? The very sound of his sugar-and-cream baritone sent a prickly sensation right down her neck, clear past her spine, and into some deep part of her that turned at once to hot, shimmering liquid. She didn't remember, for a moment, whether she'd been sitting down or if she had fallen down. Or whether she might still be falling.

Flynn was waiting for an answer. She tried to collect herself, but it was not easy between the activity of his fingers on hers, and that odd but utterly glorious feeling between her legs.

"Why he—I mean—" She moistened her lips, which had become dry as dust. Besides being distracted by his attentions, which might or might not have been innocent, she felt terribly embarrassed by what she was about to confess to him.

"No one's ever kissed me before," she blurted, because she knew that was the only way she'd be able to get it all out without falling over her pride. "I don't know how it's done. I was afraid to let him know that. In fact no one else knows that about me, not even Allyn."

Chapter Sixteen

Of all the things Missy might have told him, that was
the very last thing Flynn expected. It wasn't that he
didn't believe her, either.

It was that he did.

"You promised you wouldn't laugh." Missy's grum-
ble reminded him that he hadn't yet answered her.

Laughing was the farthest thing from his mind, unless
it was with relief.

"I'm not laughing," he defended himself, hoping he
sounded natural.

"No, but you want to."

"You don't know me, Missy," he told her. "You
think you do, but you don't know me at all."

That made him sad, all of a sudden. She didn't know
him, he realized. But that wasn't her fault.

Her fingers were soft and warm in his, and he felt
them close over his hand. Why had he gotten so close

to her? What good could possibly come of it? He wanted to pull away from her, yet at the same time he didn't. His confusion kept him riveted right where he was.

"What I was hoping," Missy continued, sounding surprisingly cool and matter-of-fact, "was that—Oh, but no. It's a foolish idea."

"What?" He looked at her profile. Her cheek was round as a half moon and her lips were pursed in a way he found tempting. She was staring hard at the mare in the straw as if she didn't dare look at him. He had to know what she was thinking.

"What, Miss?" he asked again, turning on his hip. "Come on. We're friends, aren't we? Tell me."

She stole a look at him but could not seem to sustain it beyond a glance. Suddenly she jerked her hand away from his and got up, as if she could no longer abide his nearness.

"No," she said firmly, wrapping her arms around herself. "I'm sorry I said anything. Forget it. I feel foolish enough as it is without—without—"

"You want me to show you how it's done."

The words came out of Flynn's mouth before his good sense could hold them back. He could only hope he didn't sound like a prize idiot. He sure felt like one for a variety of reasons, not the least of which was that he knew kissing Missy was something he should avoid. For both their sakes. He wished, staring at her back in the dim light of the stable, that he could gather up the words he'd uttered, like the glass marbles Gideon often played with on the parlor floor, and stuff them safely back in the small, dark pouch they had come from.

To Flynn's surprise, Missy let out a small, quavering laugh.

"No, that's quite absurd," she told him, although she did not sound entirely convinced of it. "We're friends, as you said. It wouldn't be . . . appropriate. And anyway, it certainly wouldn't be like—like kissing a—a—''

"A lover?" Flynn didn't know whether he was more amused that Missy, so chaste and circumspect that she'd never even allowed herself to be properly kissed by a man, could not even breathe the word *lover*, or whether he was more insulted that she didn't think him capable of behaving like one. He stood up and dusted the straw from his sleeves.

"I think you underestimate me." Damn it, he'd show her the way lovers kissed; see if he couldn't!

"No, Flynn, this is silly." She sounded composed and resolute this time, but he noticed she still did not look at him. She probably couldn't look at him. The notion inspired a tightness in his chest that was part want and part need.

"I expect when I'm ready to kiss Bill, I will," she continued stolidly. "How I do it doesn't really make any difference, I suppose. For all I know, Bill will like the fact that I've never done it before. Men seem to set a great store by being the first; heaven only knows why. I can't see any great advantage to it. I guess it'll just . . . happen. I'm not ready yet."

I'm not ready yet.

Missy, Flynn knew, if left to her own devices, would never consider herself ready for a man's kiss. Even now, she was pulling away from him like a wary, skittish mare. For some reason he didn't care to ponder, the thought made him even more eager than before to gentle her into sweet submission.

"Excuse me for asking this, but how will you know when you're ready?" he wondered aloud, taking two steps toward her.

"I think you ought to put an end to all your doubt and wondering and fear—and don't try to tell me the idea of kissing a man doesn't scare you, because I know you too well by now—and let me kiss you." He nearly choked on the word because his throat closed up on him unexpectedly, but to his amazement he made it through to the end of his casual remark without faltering.

Unexpectedly, she faced him. He was not prepared for the challenging look in her narrowed eyes, like polished pewter by the light of the lamps in the stall. There was fear behind that bravado, he knew, but Missy Cannon did not back down from a challenge. It just wasn't in her.

He knew further that she was not the only one of them who was afraid. He felt as if he were standing on the edge of a precipice. It remained to be seen whether he possessed the courage—or the stupidity—to step off the edge into the abyss.

"All right, Flynn," she allowed with a stiff nod. "What harm could there be in it?"

Her lower lip, glistening gold in the light, trembled, betraying her. Staring at the tempting vista, Flynn knew what harm lay in it for himself. But it was sure too late to worry about that now.

He steeled himself. It's a kiss, he told himself. Just a simple little kiss. Nothing more. Just wet your lips, and—

His mouth was dry as paper. He realized it was because his breaths were coming short and fast. She held him in her direct, bold gaze.

"Well?" she demanded softly, folding her hands at her stomach. "Is this going to take all night?"

If we're very, very lucky, a naughty voice in his head answered. He tried, in the face of her matter-of-factness, to smile.

"I'm trying to decide the best way to do this," he told her, testing the evening stubble on his chin with the fingers of his left hand as he considered her, two feet away.

"You mean there's more than one way?"

Sweet mother of God, there were a million ways. And how he wanted to show her all of them, slowly, slowly. . . .

"Stand very still," he ordered her, moving closer. "And don't move, unless you feel as if you absolutely have to."

With a suspicious look she took half a step backward, which took her nearly to the stable wall.

"You won't try to . . . ?"

He held up his hands and hoped she could not see them shaking.

"You can belt me one if I touch anything you don't want me to touch."

She blushed berry red. He could tell, even in the poor light. He would have grinned, but his heart was pounding too hard.

"Fine."

She pressed her mouth shut like the seam on a tight pair of trousers and closed her eyes.

Flynn laughed. Missy opened her eyes at once, glaring murderously.

"I'm sorry; I couldn't help it," he told her, still chuckling. "You looked as if you'd just eaten a persimmon. Where'd you get the idea that you were supposed to do that to your face?"

"Well, what should I do?" she demanded crossly, wedging her fists at her hips. "You're supposed to be the teacher! Why don't you tell me, if you're so all-fired—"

"You're right, you're right," he conceded. "I should have been more specific. Here. Just—" He pulled her hands away from her hips gently. They were ice cold and shaking. He placed her arms at her sides, electing not to comment. "There. Now—" With the tips of his fingers, he tilted her chin up slightly until her head was at the perfect angle for him to easily lower his lips onto hers. "Just—"

He realized with a swallow that she was looking into his eyes across a very narrow gulf. Her gray eyes were warm and fluid as quicksilver. He had been this near to her only a few other times, he recalled, and two of those times she'd fainted, either in shock or pain. He wondered if she'd faint now, and if she did, what sensation would be the cause of it.

He did not take his fingers from her chin. Instead he found himself stroking the smooth flesh with the pads of his fingers in small, circular motions.

"Oh," Missy murmured, as if she'd just had a remarkable revelation, or possibly a moving religious experience. Her tongue advanced from between her lips and retreated again quickly, leaving a fresh moistness behind that Flynn found himself aching to taste. Her trapped gaze made him feel as if he were the one in the snare.

On a soft breath, "What now?"

He shook his head slightly, drawing her full, warm, lush figure close in his arms.

"Nothing," he whispered. "Except—"

Nothing except roses and honey and fresh straw and Missy. And the feel of her gentle, untried mouth achingly soft and warm under his. And the bittersweet taste of her innocent longing on his tongue.

Joy and terror blended with the new and entirely unexpected feelings that Missy experienced at the first gentle touch of Flynn's mouth on hers. He tasted, to her amazement, like salt, as if he'd been crying, but also like something sweet and delicious. Something oddly familiar, yet something she'd never known before. She moved her tongue along the corner of his mouth to find more of that peculiar but exquisite delight. She found that she wanted to give the flavor a name, or perhaps it was that she knew its name but could not quite recall it. It was suddenly the most important thing in the world, and in order to accomplish it, she needed to sample more.

Her tongue seemed to tell Flynn what she wanted, for he then gave to her, in cautious, maddening little sips, tiny, fleeting bits of that essence as if he were jealously hoarding it. But she found that she wanted it too badly to be denied by a stingy nature.

"More," she heard herself murmur against his mouth, too enthralled by the wonder of it all to be embarrassed by her forward request.

He gave it. And she began to take.

Sweet, heavenly God. Flynn groaned inwardly as Missy's soft warmth melted against him. Her first kiss, and already she was teaching him things he'd never dreamed! He'd taken her for the motherly type; it had not previously occurred to him that the very fact of motherhood required a fiercely passionate nature. And discovering this, he had not thought that being the one to awaken that aspect of the deceptively complicated Missy Cannon would yield such thrilling results.

For she was deep. And thrilling. She slid her hands up the front of his shirt as if she were marking him with some invisible, bewitching brand, making him hers without asking his permission. He willingly gave his silent assent, aware that he would have given far more than that for the pleasure of exploring her kiss and whatever else, spiritual or physical, she would care to share with him.

He hoped it would be everything.

When her hands found his hair, she made a small, whimpering sound in her throat that made him want to devour her. Afraid of the power of the emotion she elicited from him, he dragged his mouth from hers and sought her ear instead.

"Good God, Missy, what have we done?" he whispered, for his voice, like his good sense, was in tatters.

Her first answer was a series of shallow, shuddering breaths against his neck that set his blood thrumming. Her next response made things even worse.

"It's—it's all right, Flynn," she assured him on a panting breath. "Really. Just hold me for—for another moment. Don't say another word. I understand. I won't ask for anything more than this. Ever."

What the hell was she saying?

He pulled back just far enough to look into her eyes. She put her hands on his shoulders firmly, but it was impossible to tell whether she meant to keep him from pulling her close again or to prevent him from retreating further. As he had no intention of doing the latter, the thought that she might mean to do the former both hurt and bewildered him. Her eyes were closed; they told him nothing. But her mouth, berry red and still swollen with his kiss, trembled. He brushed it again with his own because it seemed a shame not to.

"Flynn, don't." Her request was simple and devastating.

"What?" A spear of ice spiked him. He prayed he hadn't heard her correctly. "What do you mean?"

Her fingers tightened on his shoulders like claws. Madeleine, he recalled vaguely, had held him once thus. But Madeleine, shrewd and calculating, had meant to mark him and hold him to her for life. Missy, he knew instinctively, meant to do quite the opposite. She ducked her head, unwilling—or unable—to meet his gaze.

"It was wrong of me to suggest this," he heard her say in a subdued but steady voice.

He started to remind her that she had not suggested it, he had. She silenced him with a slow shake of her head.

"I told you once that I loved you, and you told me I mustn't," she said so quietly that his heart stopped to hear her. "I should have listened. Allyn used to tell me

219

I had more common sense than was good for me; I guess for once I didn't use it.''

"Missy—"

"No, let me finish. I thought I could make you let me in, make you share with me whatever terrible thing it is that makes you keep everyone at a distance, especially when you said back in May that you could easily love me. I tried to forget that at first, but I found I couldn't. I was so sure that 'could' meant 'do.' And I was so damned sure that 'do' meant that sooner or later you'd have to break down and admit it, and to let me share whatever blackness has you in its hold. I even let Bill start coming around here to try to make you jealous so you'd admit to loving me. I'm sorry for that; it was a wicked, manipulating thing for me to have done, and it wasn't fair to you or to him. I guess I'll have to marry him now when he asks—"

"Like hell, you will!"

Missy looked up at last, her features a startled scowl. "I'm not finished!"

"Yes, you are," Flynn said firmly, taking hold of her arms. "I can't make any damned sense out of what you're trying to say anyway."

"I'm trying to tell you that you needn't feel responsible for me being in love with you, you wretched, over-bearing lummox!" Her face was red and her gray eyes flashed like moonlit silver.

"That's good. That's very good." He slid his hands down her arms until he found her fingers. "Because I'm holding you entirely responsible for the fact that I've completely lost my head over you, Missy Cannon, and the only way you'll ever have Bill Boland will be as my widow."

Missy's eyes grew wide, then quickly narrowed again. "I'll not have your pity, Flynn Muldaur, or your ridicule!'' She tried to yank away from him, but he held her fast.

''And I'll not have your pride nor your temper about this, Melissa Cannon!'' Damn, she could make his blood boil with rage and with passion, and sometimes even both at once. What a woman!

''How dare you!''

Flynn chuckled. ''Oh, you're good at that,'' he lauded her, relishing the look of fiery outrage on her pretty face. ''I especially like it when you puff up your bosom at me like some dowager pigeon, and that pretty lower lip of yours puckers itself like a drawstring sack. Makes me want to kiss it again—'' He tried to, and she surprised him by wrenching her hand free from his and slapping his face. Hard.

''What the—'' The room spun a little and he staggered back a good two feet. She sure packed a wallop.

''I don't know what game you're playing, Mr. Muldaur,'' she growled at him in a seething, feral rage. ''But I believe I've already proven that I don't need any help making a fool of myself, thank you. I do a journeyman's job of it on my own. I may not ever have been kissed before tonight, but I know something about love, perhaps even more than you. I know that kissing and passion are only a part of it. And I also know that secrets, especially ones so ugly they can't be shared with even one person, have no place in it. I think you'd better leave now. This''—she gestured with a wave at the quiet, laboring horse in the straw—''is nothing I haven't dealt with before. I can handle whatever happens with Miss Mabel all by myself until Mi gets back, and I suddenly find your company undesirable. So go.''

Flynn, stunned, could only stare at her. Was this the same woman who'd melted in his arms moments ago? The same one who'd welcomed his kiss and had kissed him back as he'd never expected? The sting on his cheek was nothing when compared to the gripping cramp in his gut. In a single breath, she told him she loved him and that she wanted nothing further to do with him. After having kissed him like that . . . What the hell was he supposed to do now?

He had no idea how much time passed before he was able to form a response for her.

"I'm not going anywhere." He managed, to his relief, to sound gruff and annoyed despite his hurt. "I guess we both sort of got carried away by one simple little kiss." His heart hammered a loud protest at that, as if it were calling him a liar; the kiss had been neither simple nor little, and it was a stretch for him to pretend otherwise. "But there's no need to compound the foolishness. I've seen foaling mares in this shape before, and I know when push comes to shove, four hands are almost always better than two. So let's both be sensible and forget all about this." In a pig's eye, he thought. "I'm sorry." He wasn't, and he thought he'd choke on the words, but he swallowed hard instead. Missy, as he'd hoped, met his gaze with a look of grudging consent.

He knelt beside her in the straw again, and he did not allow the faint scent of her to distract him from a new, bold plan.

Chapter Seventeen

"It's a breach."

Missy finally uttered the thought she'd feared to give voice to all night. The pale, eerie dawn filtering into the stable made the light from the three lanterns seem old and yellow like a daguerreotype. Two faces, Flynn's and Micah's, looked up at her from the front end of the struggling, failing mare. Micah had been talking to Miss Mabel right along in an effort to soothe her, and he didn't have much voice left. Trying to keep the mare calm, both men looked as tired and dejected as Missy felt. She was in Miss Mabel's birth canal up to her elbows and she was covered with blood, urine, mucus, and the smell of death.

An hour earlier Miss Mabel's water had broken, and the gush had been dark with blood and other fluids that presaged a failed pregnancy. Missy had hoped until that moment that Sheik's offspring might somehow hold on, but with such a presentation she knew her hope was in vain.

Micah went pale at her pronouncement.

"She's mighty weak," was his panting observation. "I don't think she'll walk for a turnin'."

Missy's heart hit bottom.

"We've lost the foal; damn it, I can't lose her, too," she said through her teeth, longing but unable to brush the sudden tears from her eyes. Of the four mares she'd purchased in Louisville, Miss Mabel had been the most promising as a dam for Sheik. Now that promise would have to wait for another time. Assuming, of course, that the mare survived this ordeal. Missy felt around the tight space inside the mare, praying for a miracle, not sure what form that miracle might take under the circumstances.

Her miracle, such as it was, was granted.

"No, she isn't breach," she muttered as she probed the dead, underdeveloped fetus with careful fingers. "She's contracted. Feels like—easy, Mabel, it's only me—feels like . . . Lord, I don't know what."

Once before, Missy had brought a contracted, premature foal into the world. It was not an event she recalled with any particular enthusiasm: the foal, near enough to term to have survived otherwise, had been malformed beyond being recognizable as an equine animal. A monster. The mare had lived, but only because Missy had literally removed the dead foal from her, piece by gruesome piece.

Missy shuddered against another powerful contraction. She felt as if her arms would break under the pressure, but the dead fetus inside scarcely budged. It was a stalemate. There was no choice left to her.

"Here, let me try." Flynn was beside her suddenly. She spared him a glance and noticed the lines of care and fatigue beneath his blue eyes. He had no gaze to spare for her, only for the travailing horse. Missy silently blessed him for that.

"I've done this before," she told him woodenly. "And I'm in here now. Miss Mabel knows me. Trusts me. It's better that I . . . do this." She could not bring herself to be more specific than that, although she had the feeling Flynn understood precisely what she intended.

"No, Missy." He was gentle but firm. "I can't allow it. You're exhausted. You're upset. There's no need for you to put yourself through any more—"

Miss Mabel contracted again with a distressed whinny. Missy felt the mare's body tighten against her aching arms and she squeezed her eyes shut.

"Flynn—"

His chest was firm against her back and he held her shoulders tightly.

"I'm with you, sweetheart," he whispered. "Hold on."

She took comfort in the strength surrounding her, very glad, suddenly, for Flynn's presence. She could not think of another person she would want near her in such an hour of crisis, not even Bill Boland, as experienced as he was. It just seemed right, somehow, for Flynn to be with her.

The contraction ebbed. Missy drew a shuddering breath. She wished the ordeal were over, but she knew it had scarcely begun. Flynn was on one knee in the straw before her, his hands on Miss Mabel's flanks. The lantern was on the wall right behind his head; it hurt her eyes to look up at him.

"Damn the mare and the foal!" he whispered harshly, his handsome features gathered in a scowl. "You're worn to a thread. Get out of there now and let me finish this!"

How lovely it would have been to yield to his command, she thought, closing her eyes. The stall reeked, her body ached with weariness, and she was covered with the fluids of a travailing animal. It was one of those rare moments when she regretted being a breeder and a trainer, when she wished she led a simple life in service or as the wife of a man who shielded her from life's harsher realities.

"Look at her, Flynn," Missy breathed, resting her cheek for a moment against Miss Mabel's wet rump. "She's small; too small for you to do any good. She's scared. She's in desperate, desperate trouble. She—she—"

"She needs you," Flynn finished for her with a heavy, resigned sigh. "All right. I'll help. Just tell me what to do."

Another fruitless contraction. Missy wanted to weep with the pain, and with the heavy burden of sorrow in her heart.

"Pray," she gasped. "For both of us."

Missy closed her eyes and prayed herself as she took hold of the unborn foal's slippery back leg. It wasn't really a foal's leg, she told herself, biting down hard on her lip. It was little more than a stump about the size of her forearm, with none of the joints one might expect in the rear limb of an equine mammal. Contracted, she told herself as she pulled it away from the hip joint. Deformed. Dead. Like the bramble she cleared away from her garden in the springtime.

The leg was soft, and gave little more resistance than rending a wing from a freshly killed chicken. Missy tried to think of that as she pulled the bloody, detached limb from the laboring mare's distended vulva. Flynn took the obscene thing from her hands and quickly shoved it in a burlap sack. She watched it disappear into the black mouth of the bag, wanting to be sick.

"Do you want me to take over?" Flynn put his hand

on her arm. Her sleeve was rolled up nearly to her shoulder and her arm was as bloody as if she'd severed her own artery. His hand was stained red as well, she noticed, gazing with fascination at the long, strong fingers at her elbow.

"No." She shook her head. "This is my job. I'll finish it."

She met his gaze just long enough to see him shake his head once and offer a sad, fleeting smile.

"You're a damn stubborn lady," he declared softly, and she was warmed by the tenderness in his voice. "Anybody ever tell you that?"

"Often enough that I believe it."

Even if he was only her friend, she could not have asked for a better one just then. Taking a deep breath of foul air, she wedged her hands together for another assault on the mare and her dead offspring. She felt Flynn's hand on her shoulder and his lips against her temple.

"I'm here," he whispered. "Let's finish this for Miss Mabel."

In his words, she found the strength to continue to defy her own nature and rip the foal, piece by small, bloody, deformed piece, from the exhausted mare. Each part quickly disappeared into Flynn's sack, and each time he had a touch and a word of comfort to speak to her.

The last thing Miss Mabel brought forth was the afterbirth, the sheltering pocket that had supported the foal for several months and had ultimately failed in its task. Missy, sick to death of blood, made herself examine the tissue to be certain nothing had been left behind. She was damned if she'd let the mare die because of a moment of carelessness after everything they'd been through together.

When it was over, the mare gave a huff and nosed

over her shoulder with a look at Missy as if to say thanks. Or thank God it's over. Then she laid her massive head down in the straw. Micah felt Miss Mabel's neck and swabbed her with a rag wrung out in warm water.

"She's breathin' easier." Micah sounded weary but relieved. "Guess the worst is past us. She'll rest a bit now, I guess, poor girl. You done grand, as usual, Miss. I'm just sorry—well, you know."

Missy knew. She propped herself up on both hands in the soiled straw and squeezed her eyes shut. She felt like crying, but she was too wrung out. She'd cry later, she guessed. Besides, she'd always found it hard to cry in front of her help.

"Get Rich or Jim in here to clean up," she said, and her voice sounded small and tight to her. "We'll move her back where she belongs as soon as she can stand it."

"I know, Miss."

"Best bury the—the foal and all, right here under the stall so the dogs and the flies don't get to it."

"Yes, ma'am."

"And Mi?"

"Ma'am?"

"Thank you."

"Get you to bed, Miss." The foreman shrugged off her gratitude with a gruff directive, the kind that only he could give her without feeling the sharp side of her tongue. "You've had a rough night and you won't be no good to Miss Mabel nor anybody else 'less you get some shut-eye. You too, Mr. Flynn. You're lookin' pretty done in right now."

"And you look like you're ready to kick up your heels at a church social," Flynn retorted. Missy could not miss the note of respect mingled with the sarcasm in her partner's weary voice. Her heart, already full of

228

grief, swelled an inch further with something approaching pride.

Mi grunted.

''I'll be all right,'' he replied, getting to his feet as if his joints no longer worked properly. ''Hell, I didn't do much more'n set here with a mop and a bucket and talk myself hoarse all night. Missy's the one did the hard part. And yourself.''

There was a ring of esteem in Micah's declaration, as well. Flynn, it seemed, had passed an initiation of sorts. To Missy's surprise, there was room in her full heart for another emotion, but she was unable to put a name to it. Mi nodded to them both and ambled out of the stall with movements as wobbly as a new colt's. The colt in the sack. The one she and Miss Mabel wouldn't have to nurture.

The pain of loss stabbed Missy unexpectedly behind her eyes.

I can't cry yet, she thought dully, even as three drops fell from her cheeks onto the soiled straw beneath her. Not until I'm alone. They mustn't see me cry. . . .

Behind her, Flynn let out a hard breath.

''Oh, God.'' His voice shook with the very same emotion she was trying to hold back. ''Are you all right?''

She wanted nothing more, despite her soiled, wet state, than to turn to Flynn Muldaur and find comfort in his arms as she cried out her grief and her frustration. She remained where she was and took a deep, steadying breath.

''I'll be fine.'' Saying it made it easier for her to believe it was so. She would be fine, eventually. Miss Mabel's dead foal would take its place in her memory of things that might have been but never were. It was a list that would keep on growing, she realized, as long as she continued to draw breath on earth. Such was life. She sighed.

"Why don't you go on out to the trough and get cleaned up?" she suggested, not trusting herself to look at Flynn just yet. "I'll wait here until Rich comes."

There followed a silence during which only the mare breathed.

"Do you think I'd leave you after that?" Flynn's baritone was quiet with amazement.

Her tears edged perilously close to the surface again but she fought them back. She said nothing.

"Here."

Flynn's strong hand, callused and stained with blood, appeared before her eyes. She was afraid to take it lest his touch reduce her to tears, but she doubted she possessed either the will or the strength to rise from the floor on her own. She touched only his fingers, but he closed his hand firmly about hers and helped her to her feet. She realized, eyeing his blood-soaked shirtfront, that he was much taller than she. She wondered why she'd never noticed that before.

"I couldn't have done it without you, you know." She risked a glance at him.

"I know." His grin was as pale as his face. Nevertheless, it bolstered her. She looked at Miss Mabel lying in the straw.

"I suppose there's always next year."

"I suppose."

She stretched an ache from her shoulder that had just made its presence known.

"Let's get cleaned up and see if Lucy has the coffee started," Flynn suggested, still holding her hand. "I don't know about you, but I could sure use a cup right about now."

Lucy. The backache. The doctor.

The baby!

Missy yanked her hand from Flynn's and stumbled to

the stall door in her haste. She collided with Rich, who was on his way in.

"Whoa, Miss!" He steadied her with his hands on her arms and he met her gaze with a look of sleepy concern. "Slow down; you're in no state to be runnin'—"

"The baby," she breathed, impatient with both Rich's unhurried manner and her own weary clumsiness. "Lucy's baby. Did she have it? Is she—"

"Oh, lordy, yes!" Rich laughed as the light of understanding shone in his slow brown eyes. "She had her a fine boy, just a little while ago. He's up there to the house now, a'screamin' and a'squallin'—"

"And Lucy?" Missy breathed. "She's all right, too?"

A grin continued to crease Rich's plain homespun face.

"You bet she's fine," he crowed. "Micah wouldn't have it no other way."

A hot and cold shiver swept through Missy, and she felt she had to see that live, squalling baby right away or she would burst. She didn't realize she'd voiced the wish until Rich shook her gently.

"I think you'd best get cleaned up first, Miss," he intoned, his smile fading. "I don't expect the doc nor Lucy herself would want you near them or that baby, what with you bein' covered in horse blood and all."

Missy looked down at her clothing. She'd known she was living evidence of the tragedy that had taken place in the stable. She could smell it and feel it all around her, drying to her and her clothing like a grotesque, unyielding second skin. Tearing the dead foal from Miss Mabel's loins had left her unfit to hold Lucy Battle's newborn son in her arms, and he was the only good thing to have come out of the awful night just passed.

God had finally succeeded in laying a burden upon her that she was simply unable to bear.

The Missy Cannon who broke down in Flynn's arms

in the stable was not the same woman who'd fainted on him at Filson's in Louisville. She wasn't anywhere near the burden he expected when he picked her up. Either she'd shed some weight from worry or he'd gotten stronger through months of rigorous use of his muscles. Flynn suspected it was a little of both.

"I'm all right," she murmured, sobbing softly into his neck. "Put me down; you'll hurt yourself."

Always thinking of someone else's welfare. The knot that slipped in his breast made her easier to bear rather than harder.

"Be still, woman," he chided her, pressing a kiss into her damp, straggled hair. "I'm running things right now." *And about time too,* his conscience taunted him.

There was an older man Flynn did not recognize washing up in the kitchen. Probably the doctor, he thought, shoving the door wide with his hip. He noted the stricken look on the fellow's face and deduced it must be due to the way he and Missy looked.

"Rough night." He grunted a brief explanation as he set Missy down on a chair. "Guess Mi told you. I'm Flynn Muldaur, Missy's partner. You must be the doc. Pleased to meet you." He extended his hand, surprised that he still remembered a semblance of social graces after the endless ordeal in the stable.

The older man mumbled something in reply including his name, which Flynn caught as Hollins.

"I'd appreciate your looking Missy over to make sure she isn't hurt," Flynn continued. "That damned mare was pretty rough on her. She said she was fine, but you know Missy, I'm sure. I wouldn't be surprised if her arm was broken, or maybe some ribs. Miss Mabel kicked her pretty good a couple of times. I'd have liked to kick her back."

Damn that animal, and damn everything that had brought Missy to this pass, including himself! Flynn bit down hard on his tongue to stop himself from saying anything more. He was tired too, he realized, and not thinking the way he should. But he needed to put his anger aside, or put it to some constructive purpose. Missy needed him. And by God or by hell, he'd not fail her.

Hollins tested Missy's limp arms. Flynn was pleased to see he was gentle about it. He suspected there weren't many sawbones in Rapid City, and he didn't want to be the cause of this one's untimely demise.

"Stay with her a minute, Doc," he said, after Hollins assured him that there were no signs of injury to her. "I'll be right back."

Flynn's mind flooded with a list of Missy's, and the C-Bar-C's, immediate needs as he headed back out into the yard to summon Mi. There was no shortage of tasks to be undertaken. Foremost was a bath, for him and her. A close second was help of a domestic sort.

Third was sleep. Flynn figured if he was lucky, he'd be able to take care of the first two before the third one took care of him.

Chapter Eighteen

Missy tried to get up from the chair where Flynn had set her, but a gentle hand pressed her back into it.

"No, you don't," a familiar, low voice, full of warmth and humor, chided her. "Everything's taken care of around here for now except you. I scrubbed up a bit, and now you're going to get a nice, warm bath."

A bath sounded heavenly, she had to admit. But she had work to do. People who depended on her. "Gideon," she murmured. "Lucy. The baby—"

"Never you mind." Flynn was firm. "Doc set them all up fine before he left. Gideon's out fetching some more water for this sorry basin you call a tub and Lucy's resting comfortably as a queen, nursing her cub. He's a fine boy. When you're cleaned up and rested some, I'll let you see him. She named him Jedediah Flynn Micah. Can you beat that?"

There was a singsong quality to Flynn's honey baritone that Missy found comforting. It helped dull the heartache of that lost foal. She opened her eyes at last and found her partner crouched by her chair, scrutinizing her as if he were afraid she'd try to flee if he turned his back. The notion that he wanted to keep her near, even as filthy as she was, made her feel pampered. Cherished. She liked it.

The kitchen was comfortably warm and steamy and it smelled of fresh coffee. Missy guessed Flynn had made it. As if he'd read her mind, he held a mug out to her.

"Drink this," he urged. "It's not as good as Lucy's, but it won't kill you."

It wouldn't kill her, but neither would it win any prizes. Nevertheless, it tasted wonderful to her. Bitter and sweet at the same time, just the way she liked it.

Just like Flynn himself.

"It's good."

"You're a pretty liar." He touched the end of her nose.

"I'm a sight."

"You are," he agreed with a tired but endearing grin.

"You ought to get some sleep." Missy noticed for the first time that Flynn, while he was washed up and wearing a fresh blue cotton shirt that matched his eyes, still sported a day's growth of fair stubble on his jaw and a look of profound weariness behind his smile.

"Pot's calling the kettle black," he teased her with an amused snort. "I got one or two things to do before I hit the sack, and the most important thing right now is to see to you."

"Me?" Missy tried to sound gay. "I'll be fine." She attempted to get up again, but the combination of aches in her body and Flynn's strong, firm hand pressing her back completely overwhelmed her resolve.

"You will if I have anything to say about it. Now sit still, or I swear I'll tie you to that chair with Lucy's apron strings. You're not going anywhere until I've washed you up, fed you some breakfast, and I'm ready to carry you up to bed.''

He wasn't teasing anymore. Missy tried several times to swallow a sudden thickness in her throat, without success. Since she could not reply, she was obliged to look away from his now serious countenance.

"Think this'll be enough, Flynn?" Gideon came into the kitchen from the yard, bent over by the weight of the tin bucket that sloshed water on the pine floor.

"Set it there on the stove to warm," Flynn answered him over his shoulder. "I'll be using that to rinse her hair. It ought to be warm enough by the time I need it, because she's going to soak a bit. Right, Miss?''

Soak in a tub? With Flynn right there, washing her hair? Shock and excitement battled for position in her thoughts. Flynn winked at her. The expression did nothing to lessen her apprehension.

"Stay here and talk to her while I fetch her some clean clothes for when she's done," Flynn instructed Gideon. "And don't let her move."

Missy was vaguely annoyed that he spoke around her as if she were not even there, or as if she were incapable of understanding him. Gideon nodded, pleased, it seemed to Missy, to have been granted a proprietary office over her, for once. The boy drew a chair close to her, turned it backward, and straddled it so he faced her. He spread his arms across its back and rested his chin on his piled hands. It was evident that he intended to take his custody quite seriously.

"Flynn said you had a rough night," he began, looking at her in that steady, penetrating way he had, as if his soul were far older than his body and mind. "I'm glad it wasn't Glory."

Missy understood his feelings. Still, she felt compelled to remind him, "Glory isn't the only horse in the world, you know."

Gideon shrugged. "She is for me. Did Flynn tell you about Lucy's baby?"

Flynn, it seemed, was the font of all knowledge here at the C-Bar-C as far as Gideon was concerned. Missy found herself grinning at the boy.

"Rich did. He knew about it before Flynn." She didn't know why that was important to her. Certainly Gideon didn't seem to care. He gave a careless shrug of one bony but broadening shoulder, as he was wont to do.

"Flynn sent Mi to town to try and hire somebody to come out here and feed us until Lucy's up and about." He changed the subject as he studied a frayed patch on the knee of his overalls. "Ladies are sure funny about babies."

"What do you mean?" Missy was used to Gideon's sage observations, but she never tired of listening to them. Gideon made a face.

"They're only a messin', squallin' lot of work," he remarked. "And it seems they come into the world in a mighty hard way. But that don't stop women from takin' to them like ducks to water. It just don't make sense to me."

Missy smiled. Put that way, it didn't make much sense to her either.

"I don't know whether that means we get smarter, or that we just don't care anymore about how dumb we are," she offered, laying her head back and closing her eyes. "I guess the older we get, the less we try to make sense of things and we just go ahead and try to live with them."

"Oh. You mean like you and Flynn?"

"What have Flynn and I got to do with this?"

He could steer a subject into treacherous waters

quicker than a drunken sea captain.

"Well, the two of you finally quit tryin' to figure out who was mad at who for what and just started workin' together," Gideon commented, shooting her a shrewd look. "Does that make you smart or dumb?"

"Make yourself scarce, Gid." Flynn announced his return with authority and deposited his bundle on the kitchen table, eliminating the necessity of an answer. "There's cold biscuits and sausage for breakfast in Lucy's hamper over there. Take that and the coffeepot out to the bunkhouse for the fellas. You stick close to Rich today; I'm going to be plenty busy here until Mi gets back with some help."

"Guess that means we ain't goin' fishin' today."

"Guess you're right."

"But you will take me, though."

Flynn sent Gideon a glare that Missy could not comprehend. "Git."

"Three times this week, like you promised?"

"Gideon!" Flynn bellowed a resonant warning that shook the pots hanging over the stove.

Gideon got, grabbing the hamper and the coffeepot as he did. The kitchen door swung shut behind him with a bang. Missy couldn't hold her laughter back any longer.

"Was that his price for coming on that drive with Bill and me yesterday?" Lord, was it only yesterday? It seemed a lifetime had passed since then.

Flynn eyed her sideways, acidly. "Get your leg up here so I can take these boots off you."

"I see. He wrangle anything else from you?"

"Got me to agree to do his chores for a week, too," Flynn grumbled, looking only a little embarrassed as he yanked a boot from her foot.

"Remind me never to let you negotiate with the shopkeepers in Rapid City," she teased him. "Heck, if you'd agreed to do my chores, I'd have just told Bill 'No, thank you very much!' "

Taking her other boot in hand, Flynn made a face at her. "Now you tell me!' "

Missy grinned until she noticed the garments Flynn had set on the table nearby consisted merely of a pair of drawers and her nightgown. A quick, titillatingly vivid image assailed her; that of Flynn tying the little satin ribbon at her throat. Heat fanned her face and she looked away.

"I—I'm feeling much better now," she stammered as he tossed the other boot aside. "You can just leave everything here and—and I'll take care of myself."

To her surprise, Flynn said nothing. His silence made her increasingly uneasy. After what seemed an eternity, he crouched before her, his long, jean-covered legs folding elegantly beneath him.

"Look at me, Missy."

She had no choice but to obey. She searched his shining, sapphire eyes and found only a tenderness in them that made her glad she had.

"I've watched you take care of everyone—man, woman, child, and animal—on this place," he told her with quiet seriousness. "I would consider it a very great honor if you would let me take care of you now, for a change."

He made no mention, she noticed, that he could be trusted to remain a gentleman. As weary and aching and altogether miserable as she was, Missy was surprised to find that her heart was still capable of turning a few somersaults. He did not wait for an answer before straightening and helping her to her feet.

Missy stood barefoot and watched as Flynn bolted the door and closed the shutters to the kitchen. It made the room darker, but there was sufficient sunlight through the louvered slats to conduct a bath. She tried to undo the buttons of her shirt, but her hands were stiffened from their night's work, and the blood and other fluids had partially dried, causing the garment to harden like set mortar. She let out a small cry of frustration.

"Here, let me."

Flynn, she was surprised to notice, had no easy time of solving her buttons either, and he uttered more than one sound of annoyance as he performed the task.

"Damned small things," he muttered.

"Have you undressed many women?"

She found she could not resist the question, as flirtatious as she knew it sounded. Flynn had teased her with very similar words once long ago when she'd undressed Gideon. She'd never forgotten it, and it felt good to pay him back in kind, even at the expense of her own deeper embarrassment.

He glanced up at her. Were his stubbled cheeks actually reddening in chagrin? The notion was surprisingly gratifying.

"Can you lift up your arms?" he asked, after completing only four buttons, down to her bosom. "It'd be much easier to just lift this thing over your head."

Missy tried, but her shoulders protested and her sides ached as if she'd been poled in the ribs. She stifled a whimper and shook her head.

"No, I'm afraid I can't," she breathed as the pain receded again.

"It's all right. . . . Damn it." He yanked the lapel of her shirt with enough force to send the remaining buttons pinging all over the kitchen floor, but not enough to cause her any hurt.

"I'm sorry about the shirt, but I guess it was ruined anyway," he said with gruff matter-of-factness. "I'll buy you a new one when we get into town."

He peeled it gently from her arms and cast it aside. Missy hugged her bared arms to her breast. She hadn't worn a corset, a fact she'd forgotten until just that moment. The results of her night's work had soaked through to her shift, and that, she realized, suddenly weak with apprehension, would have to come off, too.

Flynn was sure he'd lost his mind, but there he was with his hand on the belt that cinched Missy's waist in those absurdly baggy men's trousers. Her shift was soiled, but not too badly. He'd known Missy wasn't wearing a corset; he could tell the moment he'd put his arms around her in the stable the night before. But there was a world of difference between heavy flannel and thin batiste, and it would have taken a far greater man— or a lesser one—than he to ignore the bounty God had seen fit to grant Missy Cannon.

God had been neither stingy nor unimaginative.

Flynn's tastes in women had altered from youth to manhood. Where he'd once favored petite nymphs, he now found himself intrigued by a robust, alabaster Diana. He recalled the lessons of mythology learned in his youth about the young hunter who had happened upon the goddess at her toilette, and how she had, in her fury, turned him into a stag and set her hounds upon him. He was glad that Missy was merely a flesh-and-blood woman incapable of exacting such a chilling retribution, for he knew he was staring at her like a spellbound buck.

The full roundness of her generous bosom gave intriguing shape to a garment whose only purpose, as far as Flynn could see, was to drive him mad. Even in the dim light he was able to discern the darker outline of her nipples well enough to see that they were temptingly erect. . . .

He was ogling well past the point of rudeness. He forced his gaze to another spot and found a perfect round, white shoulder unmarred by the stain of dried blood. He found himself wanting to worship the pure, unblemished spot with a kiss. It was only inches away;

it would take nothing at all to accomplish. Then he would tear away that veil of batiste. . . .

"I'd best do this myself." Missy's wobbly voice yanked him from his dangerous reverie. "Turn around."

He remembered she was talking about the trousers. To his own surprise, he obeyed. He was going to see her naked in that tub: he knew it. He was sure she did, too. Yet she'd asked him to look away while she took off her trousers, and he had. And he didn't even feel foolish about doing so. Just relieved.

He blew out a breath. He hooked his thumbs in his belt, then yanked them out and let his arms dangle by his sides instead. He stole a backward look, and saw Missy Cannon's shapely bare foot step out of the collapsed shift on the floor.

Sweet heaven!

"I'm getting in the tub." Several splashing sounds confirmed her diffident statement. Flynn couldn't move. He guessed that was because half of him wanted to tear from the room and the other half wanted to turn around and join Missy in that absurdly small tub.

He heard her draw a shuddering breath.

"Too hot?"

"No. It's just right."

Lord help him.

"It feels wonderful," she went on, sounding a little more relaxed. "I didn't realize how much I hurt until just this minute."

Neither did I, he thought, clenching his hands.

"Flynn?"

"What?" It came out like a bark.

"Do you have my soap?"

Soap, Muldaur, he reminded himself. You wash with it. Remember?

"Where is it?"

"In the cupboard."

It was a cake of fancy French milled stuff, the like of which he hadn't expected of a sturdy, no-nonsense woman like Missy. But it smelled of roses, just as her skin usually did. And it was soft. . . .

"Flynn?"

He jumped. "What?"

"Did you find it?"

"Right here." He blinked hard once and clenched his teeth before he turned around.

Missy was bunched up in the small tub so all he could see of her was her smooth, white back and shoulders. You can't help her if you're only thinking about yourself, Flynn scolded himself. She trusts you now, by some miracle. Don't betray that trust you've worked so hard for.

He willed his feet to move forward even as he arranged an aloof, businesslike expression on his face. He placed the soap on her shoulder and she jerked at his touch. She was obviously as tense as he.

"It's all right, Missy." His voice felt odd. Grating. "I've already said I wouldn't . . . do anything."

Not that you don't want to, his conscience jibed.

"I know," she replied, gathering her arms still closer about herself. "But I—I just can't. . . . It isn't that I don't believe you, Flynn. Or that I don't trust you. It's just that—that—"

"I understand."

He did. He squeezed his eyes shut. He'd tried to force himself into her life in a weak moment, and she wasn't ready for him. Maybe she never would be. It was a rejection. A tender one, to be sure, but a rejection nonetheless. And maybe that was for the best. Feeling as if he'd just been kicked by a mule, he turned away from her.

"I'll set myself in a chair back here, facing the door.

That way we can talk, and I'll still be here if you need me.''

"Thank you, Flynn." Her sigh was rich with relief, and he could almost see her shoulders relax as she uttered it. "You're a dear, good friend."

Flynn couldn't think of much to say to her after that. He felt as if he'd failed her, and himself, somehow. He counted himself lucky to be numbered among Missy's friends, but at the same time he knew he would not be satisfied with that forever. Probably not even for the next nine months.

Missy soaked in the tub for nearly half an hour, thoroughly disgusted with herself. Flynn had tried valiantly to be helpful, to be a friend to her when she most needed one, and she'd politely told him No, thank you, when every part of her had wanted instead to say yes. She was glad, as she bathed herself, that she ached so fiercely in her back, arms, shoulders, and places far more intimate than those: it seemed a fitting punishment for having rejected the kindness God had placed in her path in the unexpected form of Flynn Muldaur.

And she had hurt Flynn by her rejection, too. She felt it. She heard it in his sorrowful reply, and in the condemning silence that followed. And she bitterly regretted it.

There was only one answer for it.

"Flynn, I'm going to need some help with my hair, after all." It was no effort on Missy's part to sound apologetic, but it was a struggle to keep her heart from pounding, and a losing one at that.

Missy feared that he'd fallen asleep, for he did not reply.

"Flynn?"

"I heard you." The words were gruff, as if he were losing his voice.

She heard the sound of the chair scraping a short distance along the floor as he stood up, then the steady, solid thud of his boots as he negotiated the soft pine floor. She overcame an urge to hide herself from his gaze and instead sat upright in the tub with her hands knotted and pressed modestly over the vee of her legs. It would have been futile to try to cover her breasts; there was simply too much of them, and she had no wish to look even more foolish in his eyes than she felt. She had to show him she trusted him. Completely.

She wished she trusted herself as much.

He was very good at massaging the soap into her scalp. His hands were strong and gentle, and he took his time, as if there were no task in the world he relished more than that. She very soon found herself easing back in the tub as the tension fled her neck and shoulders, giving way to a fluid tranquillity. It seemed to take forever, yet when he was through it felt like but an instant. As he poured fresh, warm water over her head, she felt dizzy with a queer, nameless disappointment.

"There," Flynn pronounced, a notch above a gravelly whisper. "All finished."

"Will you help me out?"

He nodded, his lips parted as if to speak, his silent gaze fixed on hers.

Missy surprised herself by feeling not at all self-conscious as she stepped naked from the bath and into the towel Flynn held for her. It felt, in fact, like the most natural thing in the world, even when Flynn, under the guise of wrapping her in the big towel, allowed his arms to fall down around her like the soft folds of material.

His handsome features rapt with an emotion she dared not name, Flynn took a corner of the towel and blotted the beads of water from her cheeks, forehead, and chin with great care. Lastly he brushed it across her lips. His gaze lingered there and heated for half a heartbeat before he touched her mouth with his own.

Overcome by his desire, Flynn did not hear the commotion in the house until it was too late. The door to the kitchen, the one from the rest of the house that he'd neglected to lock, exploded open like Armageddon and in strode Bill Boland, Micah Watts, and an older, matronly looking lady whom Flynn did not recognize. He immediately stepped in front of Missy to shield her from view, but the shock on Bill's and Micah's faces as well as the disapproval on the old lady's made him realize that he was too late. Behind him, Missy gasped.

"Mrs. Bonner! Bill! What are you—"

"I should have guessed it!" Bill Boland trampled Missy's weak inquiry into the floor. He looked like a thunderbolt of rage. The rancher took three bold strides into the room, which brought him within two paces of Flynn. Flynn steeled himself for a blow and to retaliate, holding Missy behind him with a firm hand.

"You always come busting into people's kitchens without an invite, Boland?"

"I didn't think I needed an invite into Missy's kitchen, but I guess I was wrong," the older man snarled, his stare cold and sharp as a January blizzard wind.

Missy tried again. "Bill, this isn't what you—"

"You be still!" He jabbed an ugly, accusing finger in her direction. "I know what I see. You played me for a fool, Missy Cannon, but the song is over. I believed it back in the spring when Mi told us Muldaur was just your business partner, but I have to believe my own eyes more. You ruined this woman, Muldaur, assuming there was aught there to ruin in the first place. Now you'd damned well better be marrying her, or I'll see to it you're drummed out of town like the snake you are!"

Flynn felt his own bile rise at the scathing insult to Missy's honor.

"Missy isn't at fault here, Boland, and I won't have

246

you or anyone else thinking she is!''

''She's a whore, and you're a son of a whore!'' A vein bulged in Boland's neck and his eyes were as bugged as a frog's. Muldaur brought his fists up before his face in the boxing stance he'd learned in Secret Service.

'' 'Scuse me, but this way ain't gonna lead to naught but trouble.'' Mi was diffident but firm as he placed a restraining hand on Flynn's balled fists. The foreman stepped between him and Boland with a resolution that Flynn could not help but admire. Nevertheless, he had an ax to grind with Boland.

''Get out of the way, Mi.''

''I can't do that, Mr. Flynn, and you won't ask me to if you care for Missy.''

He did care for her, damn it, and Mi knew it. Against his will and better judgment, Flynn lowered his fists.

''Now, I have a high regard for you, Mr. Boland,'' Mi intoned in his thoughtful drawl, turning to the rancher. ''But I can't stand here and let you call Missy no names. Nor Mr. Flynn, neither. I went out to your place this mornin' to fetch us some help. You might've just sent Mrs. Bonner here. You didn't have to come yourself—''

''But I did come, Mi, much to my regret!'' Boland retorted, and for the first time Flynn heard a note of injury in Bill's voice.

''Yeah, you did, and you seen what you seen,'' Mi nodded, putting both hands up in front of him. ''I ain't sayin' it's right, or wrong, or nothin'. I'm just sayin' it don't change the fact that I come to you on Missy's part 'cos you're a sight closer than town and I figgered you'd take it ill if I'da gone somewheres else first. Anyways, we need some help until we can get somebody more permanent and you offered your own housekeeper right enough as a neighbor. You didn't need to come with her, but you did, and ain't nobody can help that. Whatever's happened here, it don't make it right for a gentleman to come in and tear the place up. And I know you're a gentleman. Missy's had enough bloodshed on the place today.''

Mi turned to Flynn, and for the first time Flynn saw something close to reproach in the foreman's eyes. It smarted, to his surprise, and he could not sustain the gaze.

"Mr. Flynn, you know how we feel about Missy here. And you know we'd take it ill if we thought anyone'd used her badly. Now, I ain't sayin' you done that, because I don't know it for a fact.'' He sent a long look Missy's way as if trying to determine for himself. "But I expect you're gentleman enough, from what I know, to make up whatever harm you done the best way you can. 'Cos if you ain't, you'll have to answer to me, Rich, and the others. But one thing's certain: Havin' it out here with Mr. Boland in the kitchen whilst Missy and Miz Bonner stand here and with Lucy and that new baby in the next room can't be the best anybody could expect of you. Either of you.''

Flynn was ashamed that it had taken the foreman to remind him of his obligation as a gentleman, and amazed that Micah had such common-sense eloquence about him. He opened his mouth to tell the man as much but was interrupted by Boland's housekeeper.

"Them's probably the smartest words you ever spoke in your life, Micah Watts,'' the old lady declared, giving Flynn a long, narrow look that made him far more uncomfortable than any Bill had yet conferred. "And fit as you are, Bill Boland, I guess this here fella's still young enough to boot your behind from here to next Sunday, even though he ain't no spring rooster hisself. Ain't you already made a big enough fool of yourself at

the C-Bar-C without puttin' a slam-bang finish to the
job?''

Flynn marveled that anyone would speak to Bill Boland thus and live to tell about it, but old women, he
knew, often enjoyed such an advantage over men. The
rancher merely glowered at her, then turned a slightly
deeper shade of scarlet.

''This isn't over by a sight, Muldaur,'' he said in a
low, feral tone. ''I mean to see you do right by Missy
if you've ruined her, and I'll marry her myself tomorrow
to get her away from here if you haven't. You think you
can walk on in here and make free with a decent
woman—''

''I beg your pardon.'' Missy's voice was strong and
clear as a brass bugle trumpeting reveille, and Flynn was
startled into facing her. She stood draped in her towel
like Lady Liberty, the big statue in New York Harbor,
and she had a long, regal look for everyone in the room.

''This is my kitchen.'' She pronounced each word
with great care. ''And my house. What I do here, and
with whom I do it, is of concern to no one but myself.
I am not answerable to you, Bill Boland, or to Flynn, or
anyone. And I deeply resent that the two of you are
treating me as if I'm a piece of furniture being argued
over by a gaggle of greedy heirs. I want you all to leave.
No, on second thought, I'll leave. Then you can feel free
to posture and snarl at one another all you like, even
break things here in the kitchen if you think it'll serve
any purpose. Just remember before you come to any
conclusions that I, and I alone, will be the one who
decides what happens to me.''

Missy hiked the towel farther up on her shoulder, revealing a bit more of her shapely calves than was good
for her. With a last, significant look at each of them, she
swept from the room, barefoot, head high, back erect,

249

and closed the door with a bang behind her.

Bill Boland's housekeeper was the first to speak after a full minute. "She don't have a lot of sense, but she's got spunk. I give her that."

Chapter Nineteen

What a lovely, blessed mess, Missy thought, facedown on her bed. Well, Flynn had wanted to distract her from thinking about the tragedy with Miss Mabel's foal, and she guessed he'd succeeded. All too well, in fact. For now all she was able to think about was the fact that no fewer than three people had seen her and Flynn together under very compromising circumstances, and at least two of those three people were not reliable when it came to keeping their mouths shut.

Damn.

It was furiously hot in her bedroom. The July wind wasn't much help and there was still dust flying about. Bill had ridden off hard for home just a few minutes earlier, and the fine, filmy dirt his horse kicked up had filled the room. Missy couldn't say for certain, watching the rancher from her window, but she guessed by his breakneck pace that he and Flynn had not parted ami-

251

cably in the kitchen. Micah had taken the buckboard to town right afterward. That left the alarmingly perceptive and forthright Mrs. Bonner in her kitchen, and Flynn who knew where.

Just as well. She didn't want to see them, any of them. Not even Lucy's baby. She wanted to go to sleep and forget about them, forget the entire mortifying incident, and wake up to find that none of it had happened. . . .

She rolled onto her back and stared up at the ceiling. It had happened, she realized with a throbbing ache in her breast. There could be no denying it or pretending otherwise. And even if the party downstairs had reached an agreement to keep the matter private, Missy knew that such a scandal would spread like a pestilence until her good name was as sullied as last week's linens.

She closed her eyes and swore she could hear herself sweat. Any benefits of the sensuously wonderful warm bath, and the subsequent sweet interlude in Flynn's arms, had long been overshadowed by the tense drama that followed it. What madness had overwhelmed her to make her think that bathing in Flynn Muldaur's presence might be harmless?

Even if they had not been interrupted in such an untimely manner, the result would have been calamitous, she knew. With one kiss, she had been ready to give Flynn everything, perhaps a good deal more than he wanted. She'd have gladly given him the ranch, her heart, and her virtue when he'd taken her in his arms that way. She had, for one sweet, reckless moment, abandoned every precept she'd ever held dear, every shred of coolheaded common sense she'd ever been praised for, and allowed herself to be blindly, blissfully in love with a man.

With Flynn Muldaur.

She closed her eyes, but found his fond, slow smile haunting her. She opened them again. This was a catastrophe the like of which she could never have calculated or predicted: she was in love with him, utterly and irrevocably. And she had allowed that love, combined with her weakened state, to lead her to an act of sheer folly.

How Allyn would laugh at me, she thought gloomily, rolling onto her stomach again. And how I would love to have her here so I could tell her everything!

She was flip-flopping so much in the hot room that she was beginning to feel like a lamb being roasted on a spit over a bed of hot coals. She considered removing her nightgown but decided it was just such impulsiveness that had gotten her into this fix to begin with.

The door opened. A new draft of warm air accompanied it. She sat up in alarm.

"I thought you'd be asleep." Flynn stood at the door, half in and half out of the room. There was no hint of a smile on his face, nor of the tenderness he'd so freely shown her in the kitchen before they'd been interrupted.

"Don't you believe in knocking?" She sounded petulant, she knew, but she didn't care. If he laughed at her, she would throw a pillow at him, or possibly even her lamp.

"What's good for the goose is good for the gander," he told her with a shrug and a fleeting hint of a grin as he closed the door behind him. "Remember?"

She did remember, and she silently damned him for remembering, too.

"That was different," she grumbled, turning on her side so she did not have to look at him. "This is my bedroom and I have a right to my privacy. Go away. I'm trying to sleep."

"No, you aren't," he argued in a quiet voice, leaning against the closed door. "If you were, you'd be asleep already. You've been up here for over an hour and you're still wide awake. I bet I can guess why, too."

"You arrogant, presumptuous—"

With annoying ease, he caught the pillow she flung at him. He approached the bed and handed it back to her wearing a most serious expression on his face.

"Missy, you realize we have to talk."

She groaned as she lay back against her pillows.

"I don't want to talk. I want to sleep."

"I know, but I don't think you'll be able to until we settle this. Do you?"

"There's nothing to settle." She squeezed her eyes tightly shut, determined not to look at him. "We made a foolish mistake that's going to cost both of us whatever reputations we once enjoyed, although it certainly won't affect you as much as it will me. The Bible makes very plain that the wages of sin are death. While I doubt either of us will die from shame, it's liable to be a very, very long time before people hereabouts forget this. I suppose I'll lose the goodwill of my neighbors—Lord knows I've already lost Bill's—but I expect I'll survive nevertheless."

"It isn't as simple as that, and you know it."

He sounded so calm and detached that she wanted to kill him.

"Yes it is," she argued stubbornly. "Now go away. Leave me be."

"You sound just like Gideon." There was no mistaking the derision in his voice. "Grow up, Missy. There are adult consequences for what we did, and you know it."

"We didn't do anything," she felt compelled to remind him as she met his gaze at last.

She remembered the look on his face. The last time she'd seen it, they'd been in her study, and he'd struck a deal with her to buy out his share of the ranch.

"It's best if we marry." His words were flat.

"I think not." Her heart raced, belying the coolness of her veto.

"That's your trouble: you're not thinking. You're either being stubborn about this, or you're just plain deliberately ignoring the facts."

"Oh?" She tried to be blasé. "And just what are the facts, Mr. Muldaur? That you've decided it would be more convenient after all to have me as a wife rather than merely a business partner? Perhaps"—It was an awful thought, and it just materialized in her brain—"perhaps you planned the whole scenario in an effort to force me into marrying you."

His face went slack.

"I *what*?"

"You heard me."

"I asked you to marry me last night before any of this happened, if you'll recall!"

"And what does that prove?" She hoped she sounded indifferent.

"Damn it, it proves that I care about you!"

"That's not how I interpret it."

"Oh? Then perhaps you'd like to interpret this."

In a single, efficient movement, he sat down on the edge of her bed and braced himself against the headboard behind her with one hand. He brought his face near enough for Missy to see the anger, the hurt, and the determination in his ice blue eyes, and she knew what he meant to do.

She shrank against the headboard, but she was trapped, both by his nearness and the rush of emotions she'd tried to bury.

"No, Flynn—"

It was a pathetic, futile effort on her part. She knew it. He seemed to know it, too. He kept her prisoner with one hand on the headboard, but with his other hand he

255

cupped her cheek, teasing her earlobe with the tips of his fingers.

"Remember?" he said in a mesmerizing whisper.

"Yes," she breathed, just before his lips took hers.

He tasted like morning coffee, sweet and hot. He tasted clean. He tasted like the promise of love, and the coaxing of his mouth made her want to fulfill it with every part of her. He worked his silent entreaty with a mastery Missy could not resist and she found herself answering him with the same wordless enthusiasm.

Her hands found his lapels, then followed the trail to his throat. One of the buttons there gave way, and his low growl tickled the tips of her fingers even as it sent a hot, fluid ripple right down to the joining of her legs.

The hand that held the headboard found its way to her shoulder and guided her as the insistence of his mouth pressed her down against her pillows. His kiss grew stronger, harder by degrees, more demanding yet more yielding, as if for everything he took from her, he gave double of himself back.

"Fl—"

"Shhhh," he commanded her, breaking away from her lips just long enough to let the sound out.

He was no longer sitting on the bed, she realized dimly. He was lying on it. Beside her. With her. On top of her. The heavier material of his shirt abraded her breasts through the soft lawn of her nightgown and made her nipples stand tender and erect.

He teased her with his tongue, diving in, retreating, playful one moment, urgent the next. Missy followed his lead, wanting to learn, learning to want. It felt so right having him there with her, beside her. Right and yet wrong. Not enough somehow. Too much. But she knew if she allowed it to go on, the line would blur even further and she would not be capable of asking him to stop. She did not want him to stop, even now.

She turned her head aside, breaking the moment. He held her face in his hand and nibbled at her ear.

"Sweet God, Missy, if you don't marry me, I'll have to do something desperate." His hoarse whisper sounded so urgent that she believed him, although why it should make her feel like giggling, she had no idea. She was in terrible, terrible trouble; it was no laughing matter that she'd lost her heart to a man like Flynn Muldaur. She might as well have lost her mind. And if his hand moved down any farther, she was certain she would.

"We . . . we need to talk." Was that her voice? It shook like a frightened child's.

"Don't want to talk." His mouth was over hers again, threatening to send her into sweet oblivion.

"Flynn." She pushed him away, then was aware of a keen disappointment when he obliged by retreating to the edge of the bed. His hair was rumpled, his face was flushed, and he was panting as if he'd run a distance. And he was eyeing her with a steadiness she found disconcerting.

"What is it, Missy?"

How could he sound so impassive after what they'd experienced? What *she'd* experienced? She found she could not remain so near to him and not want to touch him in some way, so she eased to the other side of the bed and got out of it. She was warm, but she reached for her wrapper anyway and escaped to the window. Having put some distance between them, she felt secure enough to look at him again. He was propped up on one elbow and his legs were crossed at the ankle. His dusty boots were soiling her comforter, but that did not seem worth mentioning. His sensuous mouth was turned down in an expression that was half a pout, half a sneer. She did not know whether she loved him or hated him in that moment, but she made herself maintain his gaze.

"Do you love me, Flynn?"

She held her wrapper tightly about herself, all the way up to her throat. That way she could choke herself if he said no.

"Would you believe me if I said I did?"

"That's not an answer."

"I know."

"You're not being fair to me, damn it!" Missy wanted to strike him, but she knew she could not trust herself to get that close to him. Distance provided at least the illusion of safety.

Looking down at his hands, Flynn let out a sigh.

"I want to marry you, Missy," he said in a quiet voice. "Not because I feel like I have to or I should, and not because I think it's the best thing for either of us. In fact, I'm damned sure it isn't."

"Then why should I marry you?" She prayed he would not get up from the bed and come to her; her heart needed far less encouragement to accept him than her head required to reject him.

He looked up at her again. His eyes were unshielded this time, and their look went straight to her soul like a silver arrow.

"Because you care for me," he replied simply. "And I care for you. And I think we're both smart enough to know that, with as little chance as there is for a lifetime or even a minute of happiness on this earth, we're still the best chance each of us has."

It was hardly a loverlike proposal. Missy's eyelids suddenly felt like lead.

"You have secrets." She thought it, but the words escaped from her lips.

"And I always will," he told her solemnly. "As long as there's someone who might be hurt by my revealing them."

Missy tried to digest that, but it was a pretty big belly-ful.

"I value honesty," she murmured.

"I know you do," he said. "It's one of the many things I admire about you. All I can say is that I won't ever lie to you. I may refuse to answer you sometimes, but I won't ever deliberately mislead you."

"Will you answer one question?"

"If I can."

Cautious as a cat. Missy wondered if she could live with such canniness and fool herself into calling it honesty.

"Joshua—Joshua Manners, that is—told me that you were responsible for the deaths of two men in an undercover assignment in New Orleans. Were you?"

Flynn drew in and blew out a hard breath. He looked up at the ceiling and chewed on his lower lip.

"You don't think Manners lies, do you?"

"That isn't an answer, Flynn, and you know it," Missy rebuked him, her stomach knotting. "You just finished saying you'd never deliberately mislead me. If you'd rather not answer, say so. Don't bandy words with me. It's the same thing as lying."

Flynn looked down at his hands again, and his shoulders sank an inch.

"Well, I'd rather not answer that one, but there's no legitimate reason why I can't. So I have to say yes, Missy. I was responsible. So were a few other people, but that doesn't excuse my part in it. All I can say in my defense is that it wasn't supposed to happen that way, and that one of the things I do with the money I make is to send part of it to the widows and families of those men. It doesn't begin to compensate them for their loss, I know, but it's something I can do, anyway."

"What happens to the rest of the money?" she could not help asking, although she suspected she would not get an answer. "You're supposed to have made and lost several fortunes, which is no small accomplishment for a relatively young man such as yourself.''

"Young?" he echoed with a small, bitter laugh, glancing at her. "I'm thirty-seven years old, Missy. Not young by any yardstick. And I haven't been young since I was twenty-one.''

"Do you mean to evade my question?" she asked when he offered nothing more.

His handsome features went smooth and cold as stone, and he stared at nothing somewhere between them. "Yes."

"Does it go to that woman in Louisville? Antoinette Deauville?" She couldn't stop herself.

Flynn rolled to his feet beside the bed in a clean motion.

"This isn't going to work after all, I guess," he muttered, rebuttoning his collar. "And God, I really hoped it would. We could be good together, Missy. But we could also end up hating each other, and I don't want that. I guess I'm just not strong enough for this kind of a relationship. I thought I was. I'm sorry."

He headed for the door.

"Flynn, wait." The words leapt from her throat.

He stopped but did not turn around.

Missy didn't want a marriage of convenience or of civility any more than she wanted one of deceit, but she realized that if she allowed Flynn to walk out of her room, she was watching any chance she had for happiness go with him. She felt something die inside her, and she wondered if it was merely her pride.

"If I expect honesty from you, then I think it only fair that I give my full measure in return," she said to his back, glad that he had not turned to face her. "Almost from the moment we met, I've hoped that you could love me, and we might be married, even after I learned about the ranch deed, and what I know of your past. I've told myself time and again that I'm a fool, that a man like you would never give me a second thought. After all, I'm not rich, accomplished, or even pretty—''

"Missy, you don't have to—"

"No, let me finish," she pleaded, although her chest had begun to ache with the confession. "This isn't easy for me, God knows. Let me finish, Flynn."

He said nothing. She took his silence for assent.

"There you were in Louisville," she went on quietly. "Looking at me the way no other man had ever looked at me before: like a woman. Like a—a desirable woman. Just when I'd decided it would never happen to me, there you were. I know now that it was little more than a schoolgirl crush on my part at first, although God knows at twenty-seven I'm hardly a child. But now that I've known you, lived with you, worked by your side for these three months, I realize that the feeling is different. Deeper. You were a pleasant daydream for me in Louisville, but it's the reality of you that I fell in love with: the way you raced into town behind Bill Boland the day I came back. How you took Lucy in. How patient you are with Gideon, and the way you sometimes tease me to the point of madness.

"I lived at the C-Bar-C for ten years before you came, Flynn Muldaur, and the fact is I can't remember what it was like here before you came four months ago. I'm dreadfully afraid of finding out what it will be like if—when you leave. I think the only thing I can't live with is knowing that I'm the one who's driven you away."

Missy felt empty, as if she were a pitcher that had poured herself out onto barren ground. She had no idea how much time passed after her last word faded to silence. It might have been a moment or a lifetime. She'd told Flynn everything, virtually stripped herself naked before him. Why didn't she feel better? Why didn't he say something, or at least have the grace to leave without looking back?

It took him three slow steps to turn around in place. Missy forced herself to look into his oceanic eyes. She saw a bewildering combination of gladness and profound sorrow in his naked gaze.

"It would take a far harder man than myself to walk away from you, Missy Cannon," he said in half a voice. "And one hell of a lot less in love."

It had never felt so right to be in his arms.

"What do you suppose Gideon will say to this?" she murmured to his shirtfront, snuggling closer.

Flynn kissed the top of her head and squeezed her shoulder.

"I think he's been hoping for it," he replied, and she could hear the smile in his gentle baritone. "He asks me some of the damnedest questions."

"Me, too." Missy sighed, realizing that if she never had any more of Flynn than what she had at that moment, it would be more than enough.

"I have an idea. Suppose we tell him you're going to marry Bill after all?"

"Oh, Flynn, it's cruel to tease him that way."

"Of course it is. That's why I want to do it. You don't know what that little imp put me through just to tag along with you and Bill on that surrey ride yesterday."

"You said he'd bargained for you to do his chores. What else?"

"Never you mind what else," he told her grumpily. "It was a gentleman's agreement."

Missy felt a twinge in her stomach that she tried to ignore. She could not prevent herself from wondering, as Flynn held her close, if it was a gentleman's agreement that kept him from revealing his secrets to her, or perhaps something far worse.

Chapter Twenty

Allyn
> *Marrying Flynn Muldaur on Thursday Stop Sorry*
> *you will not be here Stop Sorry have not answered*
> *last three letters Stop Will write soon Stop Hope*
> *you Joshua Albertine and baby Joshua are well*
> *Stop Dont worry I am fine Stop Have not lost mind*
> *Stop*

Missy reread the message several times, especially the closing line, while Dick Wyman waited with his knobby hands flat on the counter.

"I close up at four, Miss."

Wyman's remark was more of a teasing prod than an informative statement: it was only noon, Missy knew. She guessed part of her hesitation was due to the fact that the telegraph message would make Dick Wyman the first person in Rapid City to know about her and Flynn's upcoming marriage a scant two days away. Dick wasn't a hound for gossip like some people she knew, but this kind of news was a tinderbox waiting to be struck. She and Flynn would be lucky to make it out of town with the supplies before they were inundated by curious acquaintances and their well-meaning but invasive interrogations.

"... thirty-eight, thirty-nine, forty. Forty words, Dick," she told the telegraph operator. "To Annapolis, Maryland. How much?"

Wyman squinted at her.

"Ain't you goin' to let me read it? It'll be a mite tough to send it, 'less I can."

She held the clipboard and paper in her hand.

"You'll see it soon enough," she told him, hoping she sounded severe even though she felt more than a little foolish. "How much?"

He consulted his book.

"Three dollars and fifteen cents. Forty words, huh? Must be pretty important. You don't usually send Miz Allyn above fifteen at a stretch."

Missy knew Wyman was just making conversation but she felt a scowl distort her features nonetheless. She fumbled in the pocket of her riding skirt for the money, still holding the clipboard with the message in one hand.

"Oh, by the way, I hear congratulations are in order."

"What?"

Wyman thumbed his striped suspenders with a smug look.

"I heared you and that Muldaur feller is gettin' married after all."

Missy nearly dropped the clipboard. "Where did— How could you have—" Further words deserted her. Wyman looked abashed.

"Oh, maybe I misspoke," he said quickly. "Bill Boland

was to town yesterday, and he said that—I mean—''

It was Wyman's turn to stammer himself into silence, and Missy looked at him sharply.

"What did Bill say?" she inquired, trying to keep a sharp edge out of her voice, not at all sure she succeeded in doing so. "And who did he say it to?"

"I—I guess I misspoke." Wyman industriously shuffled the few bills in his money box. "Don't pay me no mind, Missy. You gonna send that thing?"

Missy debated tearing the thing up unsent, but decided it was more important that she tell Allyn and Joshua her news rather than attempt to fight a blaze that had already consumed half the town. She took some acid satisfaction from the fact that Wyman seemed unable to meet her gaze as she set her coins on the counter.

"Yes," she said in a tone far cooler than she felt. "Here." She thrust the clipboard at him. "And thank you for your good wishes, Mr. Wyman. Good day."

She would have paid an extra dollar to see the expression on Wyman's face as he read the message, but she thought a swift exit the most fitting end to the exchange.

Flynn pulled the loaded buckboard up outside just as she left the office. His brown hat shielded his eyes from the midday sun. He grinned at her, although she perceived the expression to be somewhat forced.

"You sent your message?"

She nodded. Her neck felt as stiff as six starched collars.

Flynn jumped down from the driver's seat and took her elbow gently. If she weren't so furious, she realized, she would probably have enjoyed his courtesy.

"What's the matter?" He seemed to notice her tension as soon as he touched her.

"Nothing. Where's Gideon?"

"I gave him a quarter and left him at the store; told

him I'd stop back for him after I fetched you," he reported, scrutinizing her. "What's wrong, Missy?"

"Never mind. Let's go home."

"I thought you wanted to stop at the dressmaker's shop."

Missy gritted her teeth and prayed for patience.

"I do. I did. I mean, I've changed my mind. I want to go home."

"Changed your mind, hell," Flynn pronounced succinctly, releasing her arm to hook his thumbs in his belt. He eyed a passerby who seemed a shade too interested in their discussion and the fellow hurried off, averting his gaze. "What happened between the store and here, Missy? Did somebody say something to you?"

He was giving her a queer look that she might have called anxious if she didn't know Flynn better. There was darned little that jarred Flynn Muldaur's composure. She met his gaze until he broke away and glanced up the street in a very telling manner.

"You heard something, too, I take it?"

This time he looked down, and he did it just long enough to confirm her suspicion.

"Let's go get Gideon."

That he did not want to answer her made her more uneasy than she had already been.

The noise, the crowd, and the cloud of dust outside of the general store did nothing to alleviate those feelings.

Flynn pulled the heavy-laden wagon to a slow, rolling halt.

"What the—"

He didn't finish his question, but there was no need. It was obvious that there was an altercation going on. There were two boys wrestling in the dirt of the street, and they'd already attracted quite a crowd. Missy, standing in the wagon, could not see the combatants clearly but she had a sinking feeling that she knew at least one of them. Flynn vaulted from the wagon and plowed his way through the hollering spectators. Obviously he'd come to the same conclusion as her, only a little sooner.

The bystanders cleared a path and watched Flynn collar both boys. Gideon was a good head shorter than his opponent, but he struggled mightily against Flynn's restraint despite the ugly swelling of his cheek near his eye. The other fellow, whom Missy vaguely recognized as Tobias Horton, the son of a nodding acquaintance from church, was unmarked, but his shirtsleeve was torn at the shoulder and he appeared to be tiring from the contest.

"Lemme go, Flynn! I'm gonna make him eat dirt for what he said about Missy!" Gideon's outburst was passionate, but Missy was certain only she could hear the hurt it masked.

"Stop it. Stop it! Both of you!" Flynn lifted both boys by the backs of their shirts and shook them like rag dolls until their arms flapped at their sides. He held tight to Gideon while he addressed Tobias.

"Go on back to your folks, wherever they are," he ordered with a stern look.

"I guess they're in hell!" Gideon was like a fierce wild animal.

"Guttersnipe!" the other boy jibed.

"That's enough!" Flynn roared. Both boys, and the spectators, who were mostly other children, fell silent. "Gideon, don't open your mouth again. You're in enough trouble. And as for you"—he directed a long, piercing look at Gideon's tormentor—"I expect your ma and pa won't be too pleased to hear you were fighting in the street. You'd best be on your way." He let Tobias go and, with a sullen, backward look at Gideon, the bigger boy shuffled off, hands in his pockets.

Flynn let go of Gideon as well, but he did so too

trustingly and too soon. Gideon was after Tobias in a wink, landing on his back like an angry beetle, sending the bigger boy face first into the dust. Gideon pressed both hands against the back of his adversary's head, seemingly grinding Tobias's face into the street. The boys watching whistled and cheered.

"Gideon!"

Flynn gripped Gideon's arms just below his shoulders and wrenched him away again, lifting him in the air and setting him down some feet away. His victim was slow to get up, and his face, thanks to blending of sweat and dirt, was brown with mud. Flynn held on to Gideon this time, but Gideon showed no intention of escaping again. Apparently he had achieved his goal and was content. Missy was mortified.

"Sideshow's over," Flynn announced to those gathered, still holding Gideon by one arm. "There's nothing else to see. Go along home."

Flynn was panting, although Missy knew it was not from the exertion. His blue eyes glimmered like uncut sapphires and there was a tension in his jaw that spoke volumes. Gideon was in for at least a scolding, at worst a tanning. Flynn had paddled Gideon once before a few weeks earlier for worrying the cows. He'd been fair, but firm. Six strokes on the backside with the rug beater. No doubt Gideon's pride had been hurt more than anything, but the boy hadn't spoken to either of them for a day and a half afterward. Neither had he worried the cows again.

"Get in the wagon." Flynn was curt.

"I whupped him, Flynn," Gideon crowed, oblivious, it seemed, to the swelling, varicolored bruise on his cheek and to Flynn's humor. "I whupped him good! 'Dja see?"

"Get in the wagon."

"He started it! He called Missy a—"

"Gideon!"

Flynn's bellow drew the attention of several ladies emerging from the store. Missy quickly sat down in the wagon and looked straight ahead, her face doing a slow, steady burn. Gideon clambered into the back of the wagon and wisely did not speak again.

"We'll talk about this when we get home," Flynn promised him in a low tone that made Missy glad he wasn't speaking to her. "Gentlemen settle their differences in more civilized ways. And they never, ever sucker-punch people."

"What's a sucker punch?" Gideon sounded subdued, as if the gravity of his offense had finally occurred to him.

"Hitting someone when they're not looking." Flynn climbed to his seat and picked up the reins. "It's like shooting a man in the back. You don't do it, unless you want a reputation as a coward."

Missy did not look at Flynn as he clucked to the ponies, but she sensed that he was deliberately avoiding her. She was more relieved than offended. The air was so tense between them that it seemed to crackle and hiss, although it might only have been the heat.

"Well, you'd'a done what I did, if somebody said what he said," Gideon defended himself in a mutter.

"What did he say?" Missy did not really want to know, she realized, but something made her ask.

"Gideon, you've got to learn that it doesn't matter what people say!" Flynn overrode her question, and Missy had the feeling he'd done so on purpose. "As long as a man can make you mad enough to hit him because of something he says, that man has power over you as sure as if he held a gun to your head. That makes you weak, not strong. Strong is knowing you can beat the tar out of somebody but not doing it. Strong is using your head instead of your fists. Strong is—"

"Hey, Muldaur!"

Missy looked up and was surprised to see Bill Boland standing like a stone monolith in the street, blocking their path. He did not look at her. He was staring straight at Flynn, not moving, obliging Flynn to pull the buckboard to a halt. Missy saw Flynn's grip tighten on the reins, and her stomach clenched. Looking about, she saw perhaps two dozen pedestrians about the long, wide street. Some of them had apparently already noticed the confrontation.

Missy placed a hand on Flynn's arm and murmured his name. The muscles of his forearm tightened beneath the sleeve of his blue chambray shirt.

"What do you want, Boland?" Flynn's reply was quiet but equal to the challenge in the older man's address.

"Wanna talk to you."

Missy realized at once that Bill was drunk, or at least several drinks beyond what was good for him. He never drank to excess, that she knew, and she grew alarmed for him. And for Flynn. Drunk or sober, Bill Boland was a formidable challenger.

"I thought you and Bill had settled everything yesterday," Missy said under her breath, not taking her gaze from the rancher who blocked their way.

Flynn muttered something unintelligible.

She leaned closer. "What?"

Flynn's lips barely moved. "I told him he'd better be ready to fight if he crossed my path again."

Although it was hot as hell's kitchens in the midafternoon sun, Missy froze.

"Well, Muldaur?" Bill's taunt was raw and overloud, and his expansive chest rose and fell like the bellows of a blacksmith's forge. "I didn't just cross your path. I'm damned well in it. Now what do you aim to do about it?"

Missy gripped Flynn's arm.

270

"Flynn, don't." She scarcely breathed the words.

"Go 'head, Flynn," Gideon, in the back, urged, an unmistakable note of excitement in his young voice. "You can whup him, I bet. He ain't nothin' but a big old tree."

"Hush, Gideon!" Missy was aware of the note of panic in her voice, but she could no more prevent it than she could fly. "Flynn, you stay put. If we keep real still, he might just go away!"

That was stupid. That kind of logic worked for stinging bees, she knew, but Bill Boland more closely resembled a wild boar.

Boland hooked his thumbs in his belt, a pose that made him look much younger and much more menacing than previously. Missy's mouth went dry.

"Well, Muldaur?" The rasp became a lazy taunt. Several men came through the creaking bat-wing doors of the saloon, their slow-eyed gazes fixed on Flynn. Missy wondered, detached, how many wagers had been placed behind those doors.

Flynn shifted in his seat, wrenching Missy's attention back to him. His gaze was steeled to the granite figure of Bill Boland, and his jaw was set like cement.

"No guts," Boland pronounced. A smile slithered across his lips and disappeared like a snake under a rock.

"I got a woman and a child here in this wagon, Boland," Flynn said through his teeth, and Missy saw a lick of red creep up from the open collar of his shirt. "What do you expect me to do?"

"I ain't no—"

Missy silenced Gideon with a look.

"I expect you to act like a man," Bill drawled, curling his lip in a sneer. "But I guess that's expecting too much from you."

Missy climbed quickly from the wagon. Something

271

had to be done, and she guessed she was the only one who could do it.

"Missy!" Flynn muttered in warning. She ignored him in favor of approaching Bill warily, as if he were a wild animal cornered at a quilting bee.

"Bill, this is senseless," she heard herself say in a quiet voice that sounded worlds more composed than she felt. "Everything's settled between us. If you have something to say—"

"You let Missy here fight your battles, Muldaur?" Bill did not even look at her as he asked his question loud enough for it to echo down the street. "She deserves more from a man than that, even if she is a—"

"Don't say it, Boland." Flynn's growl was directed at Bill this time, just as his gaze was. Both were ominous.

"Why not? Who's to stop me?"

Missy swallowed a rock. She reached toward Bill with a tentative hand.

"Bill, you mustn't—"

His left arm became a whip that caught her on the shoulder and sent her staggering backward several steps. She felt dizzy from the force of the glancing blow, but her vision cleared quickly enough for her to see Flynn leap from the seat of the wagon and fall upon Bill Boland like an avalanche.

The men toppled to the ground. All Flynn knew of Bill Boland as a sparring opponent was that he was big, and at least a decade older than himself. Flynn hadn't used his fists in longer than he cared to remember and, as Bill landed a leaden blow in Flynn's unprotected side, he remembered why he'd always preferred other methods of settling disputes.

He regained his breath after a few quick, stabbing intakes of air that told of bruised ribs, and he used the momentum of the punch to roll himself on top of Boland. Boland's face was contorted in rage; his breath reeked of whiskey.

"You son of a bitch!" he rasped at Flynn, his blue eyes glazed and savage. "I'm gonna kill you!"

As if to back up his threat, Boland wrenched away one of his arms which Flynn had pinned during the roll. Before Flynn could contain it again, Boland had pressed his open palm against Flynn's face, covering his mouth, crushing his nose, fairly puncturing his eyes with big, ramrod fingers.

His eyes burning, Flynn let go and fell back. Boland was strong as a team of oxen. But he was also drunk and therefore, perhaps, slow enough that Flynn might have half a second to recover and regroup.

Boland gave him that half-second, but no more. Flynn doubted, as Boland's bulk landed on him like a full load of bricks, that it had been enough.

His eyes still smarting and tearing, Flynn struck at the undefined shape above him. The shape struck back, and Flynn saw sparks in his head like a fireworks display. He couldn't breathe, and some part of him realized it was because Bill was straddling his chest, preventing him from taking in air. He was going to lose consciousness, he realized, feeling, besides badly pummeled, like a complete idiot. Not five minutes had passed since he'd lain Gideon out for fighting in the street like a hooligan, and now here he was eating dirt.

He hoped he'd at least given Boland a black eye or a bloody nose. He hated to think he was going to be the only one with marks to show from this disgraceful exhibition: Gideon would never let him live it down, nor would the rest of the people of Rapid City. But a second later, not even that mattered anymore.

Missy felt maddeningly helpless, a feeling she detested, watching Bill use Flynn's face as a punching bag. To interfere was to suggest to the spectators, by now half the town, that Flynn was incapable of taking care of himself. Not to interfere was inhuman.

She stepped forward, not sure what she intended, but certain that she was going to do something to halt the brutality. In an instant someone brushed by her like a stiff breeze. She was vaguely aware that it was Sheriff Garlock moving toward the combatants in something approaching haste, an unusual occurrence for him. Something else had a firm grip on her arm and prevented her from following him.

"I wouldn't, Miss Cannon," said a deep, oddly familiar voice at her ear.

Chapter Twenty-one

Flynn felt as if his whole body were being subjected to some macabre form of torture involving heat, noise, and motion that made him feel sick to his stomach when it wasn't making his head pound in pain. But since the throbbing in his head was pretty much constant, the seasickness remained a mere undercurrent to his discomfort. Small consolation, he thought, waiting for another blow from Bill Boland's fist.

The blow never came.

Curious, he tried to open his eyes but managed only one. He guessed the other was swollen shut. To his surprise it was Missy's outline, not Boland's, above him, eclipsing the late-day sun. He felt around the tender inside of his mouth with his tongue, the only part of him that didn't hurt, for loose or missing teeth. He found none. Small favor, he reflected wryly.

"Missy." He tried his voice. It came out like the croak of a parched frog.

There was a cool dampness against his forehead that would probably have felt heavenly were it not for the stinging bruise it aggravated.

"Shh," he heard, and he was not immediately sure whether it was Missy urging him to be still or a party of people whispering in the next room.

Next room? Where the hell was he?

"You're in the wagon. It's all over." Missy seemed to anticipate his questions, bless her. He was in the wagon, and she was with him. The softness under his head must be her lap. He tasted blood in his mouth, but he smelled the faint aroma of roses clinging to Missy's muslin skirt. The wagon, or heaven? He decided there wasn't enough of a difference to worry about.

But the wagon was moving.

Who the hell was driving it?

He tried to turn his head. Gentle fingers arrested his chin, thwarting his attempt.

"We're almost home." Missy was talking again, and her voice was as soothing as a zephyr. "You've taken a bad beating, and we're going to get you into bed."

Who was going to get him into bed? Did Missy think she and Gideon could accomplish that feat alone? He would have laughed, but the breath he drew into his lungs for that purpose burned his side as if he'd been branded. He remembered suddenly that Bill had struck Missy, too.

"You . . ." He paused to try to moisten his swollen lips, and tasted iron. "All right?"

Was that her lips he felt on his forehead, warm and gentle?

"Look at you." There was forced amusement cloaking the anxiousness in her words, and doing a mighty poor job of it. A drop of moisture fell on his brow. He hadn't known it was raining.

"Lying here half dead and thinking about me," she went on, sounding very far away.

Wait a minute. Wait just a blamed minute.

"Half dead, hell," he managed to mutter, and he summoned all of his strength to try to sit up.

It wasn't enough. She took hold of his shoulders and pulled him back down where he'd been. He was surprised that it took so little to persuade him.

He heard another voice then, one he knew. In fact, it sounded something like his own. He strained hard but could not make out the words. Was he delirious, besides? Now there was an embarrassing notion. . . .

". . . wouldn't say mud if he had a mouthful of it," the voice declared. Flynn felt his mouth. It hadn't moved. ". . . as bad as when we were kids. He hasn't changed much, I see."

Seamus!

Missy's reply was a polite murmur that Flynn could not decipher, except to hear the shy aloofness of its tone. He heard another voice, blunt, sharp as a blade, tangy as a fresh-dug onion. Gideon. The fact that Seamus and Missy both laughed after whatever Gideon said did little to ease Flynn's disquiet.

That Seamus was here at all was no great cause for celebration, for that matter. Flynn had a greater incentive than ever to sit up and fight for consciousness. What the hell was his brother doing here? Flynn tried to think, but there was a damned free-for-all going on in his head. Seamus was here in Rapid City. Something was wrong, or would be very soon.

The ride back to the C-Bar-C seemed to Missy to take an eternity. Although she was dismayed that Flynn had engaged in a brawl with Bill and was injured, she was glad to be in the back of the wagon with him rather than sitting up front beside his charming and handsome older brother. Seamus had his fair share of the family charisma, she was forced to admit, but she nevertheless found the older Muldaur mysteriously intimidating.

She thought at first that it was because he was a congressman, but she quickly dismissed that notion: Joshua Manners was a congressman as well, and she harbored no such conviction about Allyn's congenial husband. Listening to Seamus Muldaur's seemingly innocuous, if incessant, banter as he drove the wagon, she realized it was because she sensed a hidden purpose behind his every remark, every simple question, an objective at which she could only speculate.

It was a subtle interrogation. He made her feel as if she were being examined under a glass and found wanting, even though it was very obvious that he did not mean for her to know that he was testing her in some way, holding her up against some invisible standard for some unknown end. She was glad when Gideon undertook to regale the elder Muldaur with anecdotes of ranch life from his 12-year-old perspective: for once the boy's garrulousness had a constructive, even agreeable, purpose.

She gave herself a mental shake: she was being foolish. Flynn had not spoken often of his brother, but never had he done so with any rancor, nor with any indication that their relationship was anything but amiable. It was her own suspicious nature as well as, no doubt, her natural shyness around men, that caused her to foster these baseless misgivings. She would tell Flynn about them as soon as he was strong enough, she decided. And he would probably laugh at her in that affectionate way of his. At least she hoped so.

By the time Seamus pulled the wagon to a halt before the front porch at the C-Bar-C, Flynn was trying, despite Missy's urgent pleas, to sit up. He looked like a badly butchered side of beef, although his eyes—well, the one eye she could see—was astonishingly alert. She jumped down from the wagon without help even as Seamus came around behind it. She did not want him to touch her, for some reason she could not analyze.

"Well, my valiant brother." Seamus's jocularity did not quite ring true to Missy as he positioned himself at the foot of the wagon, arms outstretched in fraternal greeting. "You weren't in much shape to offer a civilized welcome when I saw you in town, but you're looking better already. How little things have changed since the old days: you getting into scrapes, me getting you out of them!"

Missy suspected, eyeing the speaker, that the situation he described was more often than not the reverse, although that was perhaps because of her old contradiction of feelings toward Flynn himself: part angel, part devil. And she had never been certain, until recently, which part she was treating with.

"That sheriff was a trifle reluctant to let us take you along, you know," Seamus continued, reaching for the hand Flynn was using to grip the side of the wagon. "He was all for keeping you there in town in one of his cells along with that brute you were tussling with, but I convinced him that wouldn't be wise, seeing as you two had such, ah, contentious feelings toward one another. He agreed that his jail would be a lot more peaceful if there was some distance between you, and I was able to persuade him that the ranch would be sufficient for that purpose."

Seamus talked on, obviously every bit Gideon's equal in the area of prattle. Missy wanted to tell Seamus to shut up, but she bit down on her lip. The man was Flynn's brother; she had no desire to embarrass Flynn or herself by treating the congressman rudely, even if he was behaving more like a blustering campaigner than a concerned sibling. Instead of making a comment, she looked at Flynn again.

He was glaring at his brother with palpable enmity.

"I think it's best if we get Flynn up to his room as quickly as possible," she ventured, averting her gaze in hopes that Seamus had not noticed his brother's obvious rancor. She guessed the brothers would have out whatever dispute lay between them, but she hoped they would do so in private where she need not be a party to an ugly scene. If Flynn's malevolent stare was any indication, the dispute was a considerable one.

She found herself wondering if it had anything to do with Madeleine Deauville.

"Please help me get him upstairs," she murmured quickly. "Gideon, go fetch Mi and send him for the doct—"

"No doctor." Flynn's statement was firm and clear, as if he'd completely recovered. Missy turned to him in surprise to see him raise himself to a crouch on the floor of the buckboard and gingerly make ready to climb over the side. Seamus hurried to his brother's side but Missy got there first, causing the elder Muldaur to keep a distance.

"Flynn, this is not the time to be noble or stubborn," she told him in a low voice, fixing her gaze to his. "You're hurt, maybe more than you know."

"I trust you to take care of me."

"But I'm no doctor!" she pleaded.

Flynn said nothing more. He clenched his stomach muscles and grimaced as he swung his leg slowly over the side. He seemed not to want Seamus to be aware of the pain he was in, and Missy knew better than to believe that it was because of any false sense of pride or shame. Ignoring Seamus, whose gaze she felt upon her like soiled linen, she turned to Gideon again, who was uncharacteristically silent.

"All right, no doctor," she said, half to Flynn and half to Gideon, leaving no part at all for Seamus. "Just go inside and tell Mrs. Fedderoff—"

"Mrs. Fedderman," Gideon corrected, referring to the temporary housekeeper Mi had hired away from one of the Rapid City hotels late yesterday.

"—Mrs. Fedderman to set an extra place for supper and to make up the couch in the study for Mr. Muldaur until more appropriate accommodations may be arranged."

Gideon started off at a sprint, but was halted again by Seamus's rejoinder.

"Oh, there won't be any need for that, Miss Cannon—may I call you Missy, since we're to be related?—I'm staying in town at the hotel."

That must mean that he'd been in town before today. Did she imagine it, or did Flynn, still poised on the wagon, shoot a look of rage at his brother? Even if it was a product of her imagination, she felt a cold claw grip her stomach.

"Gideon, you go on and do as you're told." Flynn's voice was calm, at odds with the look Missy thought she saw on his battered features. Gideon went. Flynn watched as he raced into the house; then he turned to Missy again. "Let Seamus help me down and take me upstairs. If I'm going to fall down, I'd rather land on him than on you. It would hurt him a hell of a lot less. Maybe even knock some good sense into him."

Seamus laughed, although Missy suspected the jest was more for her benefit than his. She did not feel like laughing, even a little. She lowered her gaze in consent, anxious to be quit of Seamus Muldaur's company.

She stepped back and allowed Seamus access to his brother's side.

"I'll fetch my doctoring things and be up directly," she murmured, wanting to touch Flynn's hand, yet feeling awkward and self-conscious before their audience.

Flynn let out a small grunt as he landed, with Seamus's assistance, on his feet before her. He swayed a little but brushed aside his brother's further gesture of support.

"Come here." He growled the words to Missy, but they were more an invitation than a command. She found herself in his arms and she forgot to feel embarrassed.

"Give me a few minutes to find out what he's doing here," he whispered in her ear, then gave her lobe a lick. Her body shuddered with delight and her cheeks heated. Did he truly want her close, or had he merely wanted an excuse to whisper that instruction? She found it did not matter to her. She held him another moment, carefully, mindful of his bruises. When she finally let him go, she was warmed all over again to see that he was trying to smile at her.

"You look a sight," she told him, touching his mud- and blood-caked brow.

"I know," he replied, his voice soft from tenderness rather than frailty. "And I'm in for it with Gideon. Try to explain it to him for me, would you?"

"How can I do that when I don't understand it myself?"

By rights, Missy knew she should be angry at Flynn for having violated the very tenet they'd both tried to impress upon Gideon, but she could feel nothing but tenderness and desire. He'd done what he'd done out of love for her. Misguidedly, perhaps. Certainly unwisely; his bruises were proof of that. But she could not doubt his reasons for doing so.

Seamus be damned. She stood on tiptoe, intending to kiss Flynn's throat, but he dropped his head at the last moment and took her lips with his, long enough to remind her that, for better or for worse, her heart belonged to him.

"How long have you been in town?"

Flynn lacked both the energy and the patience to exchange niceties with his brother as the latter helped him slowly up the stairs. It was best, he figured, that he learn as much about Seamus's motives as he could before either he passed out from pain or Missy came to his room to see to his various hurts. Whatever Seamus's reasons, Flynn wanted to shield Missy from as much as possible.

"We don't have to talk about that now." Seamus grunted as he hoisted Flynn up another step, his shoulder wedged into Flynn's armpit. "Damn, I think you've put on twenty or thirty pounds since I last saw you. Pickings must be pretty good out here in—"

"We talk right now, or we don't talk." Flynn cut him off, gritting his teeth as he took another step. "Missy doesn't know anything about our . . . arrangement, and I mean for it to stay that way. Damn it!" A bolt of pain went into his rib cage as if an arrow had been shot through him.

"Well, that makes sense, even if nothing else does," Seamus said under his breath. "What do you intend, marrying the woman?"

A white-hot flare ignited in Flynn's breast that had nothing whatever to do with his aches and bruises.

"Missy," he said deliberately, pausing in his ascent to glare at Seamus. "Her name is Miss Cannon. You'll address her as Miss Cannon until she gives you leave to do otherwise. Understood? She's worth a hundred of the kind of women you associate with. And I recall asking you a question. Since you're in my house, you'll answer mine first. How long have you been here, and what the hell do you mean to do?"

Seamus, Flynn knew, was many things, few of them honorable, but he had never outright lied to him, as far as he knew. He stared at his brother out of his one good eye and watched Seamus grimace, look away, then, finally, meet his gaze again with great reluctance.

"You're a bastard, Flynn; do you know that?" It was an admission of defeat, delivered with a ragged sigh.

"A bastard who's saved your hide more than once, and no doubt will again." Flynn was curt. "Let's have it, Seamus. All of it."

"Let's get you to your room first. You're dead on your feet."

Flynn wanted to argue with his brother's assessment but good sense overruled his pride. He made it to the room he shared with Gideon and was grateful to sink at last onto the welcoming comfort of his bed. There was treachery in that comfort, though. He sensed it even as he smelled the out-of-doors in the fibers of the freshly aired linens. It invited him, even seduced him, to give up his consciousness once and for all to the blessed oblivion of healing sleep.

Flynn squeezed his eyes shut, then opened them wide; one of them obeyed his command. The other remained welded to his eyelid. Still, one eye was enough for him to see Seamus above him, wearing an assessing look that renewed Flynn's annoyance.

"This is as comfortable as I'm going to get, if it was really my comfort you were worried about," Flynn told his brother dryly. "Talk."

Seamus looked as if he'd rather plow a field without a mule. At least he was dressed for it, Flynn reflected, noting his brother's uncharacteristic couture.

"It's Madeleine," Seamus began.

"I figured."

"And Antoinette."

"Uh-huh."

"They heard about the C-Bar-C, and they've done some checking."

Flynn's face hurt, and he realized it was because his back teeth were clenched. Madeleine by herself was an inconvenience, Antoinette a nuisance. Together they were an affliction no less devastating than the Ten Plagues of Egypt, especially if they sensed a windfall. And their senses, combined, were as keen as a hungry grizzly's.

"Go on." Flynn didn't trust Seamus enough to reveal his dismay.

"You have anything to drink around here?" Seamus looked about. "I'm parched."

"It'll wait. You were saying?"

Seamus regarded him again, then shrugged with a lowering of his gaze. "They think you're being stingy with them. Madeleine has this idea that the ranch is a potential gold mine just waiting for proper management. Believe it or not, I actually think she fancies running the place herself."

Flynn would have laughed had he not feared for his already aching ribs.

"That is hard to believe," he declared. "I never thought Madeleine would be interested in making money any way that was legitimate. Is she interested in buying out the remainder of my share? Because if she is, I have to tell you the price has just gone up."

"Damn it, this is serious, Flynn!" Seamus stormed, looking like a thunderhead. "She's been writing to me in Ohio, badgering me to come out here and see for myself. I couldn't come before now, because—well, because Congress was in session, and I—"

He paused long enough to arouse Flynn's suspicions, which was not long at all.

"What, Seamus?" He wondered which had caused the throbbing in his head—Bill's left hook, or Seamus's uncanny ability to get himself into trouble. Probably a combination of the two.

"I got married in the spring, Flynn," Seamus said at last, staring at the bedpost. "A nice girl from a fine old Ohio family. A name. Money. Everything I've always wanted. Everything I deserve. Madeleine found out, and now she wants to bleed me, too."

"Damn you, Seamus!" Flynn turned his face aside. He did not want to hear more. "If I wasn't lying here like a corpse already, I'd—You could have had the decency to warn me about it, or at least to let me know when it happened! Where is this wife of yours now? In Rapid City?"

"No, she's home in Cleveland. She has no idea I've come here. She thinks I went back to Washington to wrap up some congressional business before the next session. I'm traveling under an alias."

"God, Seamus!" Flynn's fury overwhelmed his aches. "You lied to her? Your own wife? How many of your damned fires do I have to put out? How many times—"

"Don't get sanctimonious with me!" Seamus snarled his warning and accompanied it with a glare. "You had every bit as much to do with Madeleine as I did—"

"Not by half," Flynn cut in, equal to his brother's ire. "And I didn't have quite as much to lose as you did, even then. Now it appears you have even more to lose. What about me, Seamus? Haven't I given up enough? Don't I deserve a little happiness, now that I've found it in this most unlikely of places? I've spent the last dozen years cleaning up after you. Do you think I'm going to spend the rest of my life following you around with a bucket and a shovel, cleaning up your muck, while you do nothing but continue to send more my way? No, Seamus. No more. The Deauvilles will have to be satisfied with what tribute I send them, or you'll have to deal with them yourself. You and your wife, with her fine old name and fine old money.''

Seamus's look was reproachful. ''We agreed,'' he intoned.

''We agreed,'' Flynn repeated, unmoved except to anger, ''twelve years ago, back when your life seemed a sight more important to both of us than my own, that your career must not be jeopardized. It's different now. My life means something, not just to me, but to . . . to other people, as well. There are things now that are very important to me. And I'm not willing to sacrifice them. I'm not going to be the scapegoat anymore. Madeleine's or yours.''

''Damn it, Flynn, Antoinette could just as easily be your brat!'' Seamus's accusation was a quiet, ugly hiss. Flynn closed his eyes.

''But she isn't, and we both know it.''

''Does your—Does Miss Cannon know it, too?''

Flynn did not bother to look at him. ''If you're thinking you can blackmail me by threatening to tell Missy everything, I suggest you think again. I haven't been completely honest with her, but that's only because up until now I've been protecting your skin. Missy's best friend, as you may know, is Allyn Cameron Manners, the wife of a fellow congressman of yours. Of the two of us, I'd say you still stand to lose the most by telling poisoned tales. Get out now, Seamus. Go back to town. Back to Ohio. You've wasted your time and mine. I'm tired, and you have nothing more to say to me.''

''Yes, I have.''

The quiet danger in Seamus's voice made Flynn open his eyes again. Seamus was gazing at him intently.

''I didn't want to have to tell you this,'' he said slowly, nodding as he slid his fingers into his hip pockets. ''But you've left me with no choice.''

Seamus drew in a deep breath. Flynn waited.

"I left my name in Cleveland along with my wife," Seamus said. "But I haven't exactly come to Rapid City alone."

Part Four

Alea Iacta Est

Chapter Twenty-two

Gideon clambered up the steps behind Missy, toting the bucket of warm water. It wasn't very heavy, but it was clumsy, and try as he might, he couldn't avoid spilling some of it over the sides, leaving small puddles on the steps as well as making sloshing noises. Missy didn't say anything about either; normally she'd have scolded him in that soft way of hers that made him feel as if she were more hurt than angered by his carelessness.

Truth was, she hadn't said much of anything since they'd got back from town, and nothing at all about his fight with Tobias. That made him feel sort of bad inside, somehow. Funny, but he wished she would holler or scold, as he expected. But all she'd done was wash that sore spot on his cheek—he guessed Tobias was near as good a fighter as Bill Boland, although he'd never admit as much out loud, and especially not to Flynn—and painted that tender place below his eye with some stinging salve from one of her brown bottles. Gideon guessed, following Missy down the second-floor hall, that Flynn was going to feel as if he'd been attacked by a whole swarm of angry bees before Missy was through with him.

He shifted the bucket again, spilling more of the warm water, this time on the hall runner. Maybe, he mused, Missy made that stuff sting on purpose so it would teach the lesson better than mere scolding. If that was the case, Flynn was in for a serious education.

Missy waited outside the closed door to the room he shared with Flynn. Gideon waited with her. He thought she was going to knock, but she just stood there, very still. He wondered why until he realized he could hear everything Flynn and his brother were saying just as clearly as if he were in the same room with them.

"... said she was going to come here to see you whether I came with her or not. Knowing Madeleine, I figured it was better if I came along." That was Seamus's voice, although at first he sounded so much like Flynn it was hard for Gideon to be sure.

"Ain'cha gonna knock?" He kept his voice quiet; he didn't know why.

"Shh."

"... must know I don't mean to go through with this." That was Flynn, but Gideon missed hearing who should know, and what he was supposed to go through with.

"She says she's waited for you long enough." Seamus sounded like a headmaster Gideon remembered from his long-past days at an orphanage in Louisville: stern, scolding, mean. Gideon shuddered in spite of himself. "Maybe Missy would believe—"

"She's not a fool, Seamus." Flynn's retort was hard.

"Too bad." Seamus sounded regretful. "It'd be easier for everyone, including her, if she was."

"Go back to town." Flynn's weary reply reminded Gideon of how the man sounded after answering a spate of his questions on a fishing outing. "Tell Madeleine to be patient for a day or two. Until she hears from me. I can't have her coming out here now. I have to think. Missy will need to be told . . . something. This couldn't have happened at a worse time."

"Is there ever a good time for Madeleine Deauville?" Seamus chuckled as if he'd made a joke that didn't taste quite right in his mouth. "I think you've just given me an idea of how to make everybody happy. Well, nearly everybody. Leave it to me, Flynn. I've been letting you manage this mess from the beginning; maybe it's time I took a turn at it."

Footsteps approached on the other side of the door.

"Seamus, if you—"

"For God's sake, don't worry, Flynn!" Gideon didn't know about Flynn, but something in Seamus's voice, something tight and not quite natural, inspired a worried chill in his own breast. "I'm Harvard educated. I'm not an idiot."

"No, you're not an idiot," Flynn affirmed, as if he meant to imply that Seamus might be something much worse. "But don't think you can—"

"Get some rest, Flynn." Seamus sounded firm, like Missy when she'd tell him he needed a bath. "You need it. I'm going back to town; I'll call on you tomorrow."

Gideon remembered a time in Louisville a couple of years back when he'd watched a fire wagon speed down the street before him toward a smoking building, its bells clanging and its horses with wild looks in their eyes. People had fled before it in terror, for it was obvious those horses would have stopped for nothing. He'd felt rooted by the sight, himself. He remembered wondering if he'd have been able to get out of its way, had he been standing in the middle of the street.

293

He looked up at Missy. She glanced at him as if he'd willed her to, as if she'd just remembered he was there. She was pale as chalk dust. Looking at her, Gideon felt funny inside, as if he were a secret that got told by mistake. He looked at the water in his bucket and wondered if it was still warm.

The door opened. Gideon didn't know whether Missy or Seamus had opened it, but he didn't guess it much mattered. He couldn't look at either of them. Something was going wrong, very wrong, and he felt powerless to make it right.

"Excuse me, Mr. Muldaur, but I must ask you to leave now, unless you know something about nursing."

How the hell could Missy sound so calm, facing that snake in the grass? Gideon wondered, amazed.

Some time passed before Seamus answered; Gideon didn't know how much, except it seemed like a lot. Like when Missy asked him if he'd been smoking out behind the barn again and he didn't want to say yes and knew he couldn't say no. Like the real words got lost somewhere between them.

"No, I confess to knowing little about tending to the wounded," Flynn's brother answered at last, sounding like a slick snake-oil salesman. "I'll leave him to you. If you would be so kind as to loan me a horse to get back to town, I promise to return it tomorrow when I pay a call to see how the, uh, patient is doing."

Gideon shivered, though not from any chill that he could detect in the stuffy room. Seamus Muldaur was sounding less and less like his brother. Sort of like the difference between an empty barrel and a full one.

"Gideon, please put the bucket down beside the bed. Then go downstairs with Mr. Muldaur—"

"Seamus."

"Seamus"—Missy drew the name out as if it was something nasty she'd found in the butter crock—"and get Mi to saddle him a mount to take him back to town."

She hadn't said "one of my best mares," Gideon noted with some satisfaction. He turned to do her bidding.

"Hey, Gid?" Flynn's voice, the full barrel, stopped him. Gideon faced the man, although it pained him to see Flynn so beat up, and to know that Bill Boland had done it to him.

Flynn gave him a swollen, cut-lip grin. "See why it's no good to pick a fight with somebody?"

Gideon managed a grin in return, even though part of him felt like bawling like a baby.

"Especially if the other guy's bigger, meaner, and drunker," he managed to retort.

Flynn's grin became a grimace. It wasn't a far stretch.

"I thought you might've helped me out there when Boland had me pinned. I mean, you could've knocked him over the head or something."

Gideon guessed Flynn was only half joking.

"Somebody once told me never to sucker-punch nobody," he remarked, wishing that he'd disobeyed just once more. "Come to think of it, it was the same fella who told me that strong was using your head instead of your fists. Sound like anybody you know?"

"Get the hell out of here," Flynn growled affectionately with a wave of his dirty hand. "And take my brother with you."

"Come on, son."

Gideon felt a hand on his shoulder and he fought an urge to shudder. The gesture reminded him, sharply, of the few times when he'd been on the street back in Louisville and some policeman had gripped him the same way. And the fact that Seamus Muldaur had called him *son* when he'd denied better folks the privilege rankled him so he wanted to kick the man in the shin. Or someplace even more painful.

Gideon didn't say anything. He remembered what Flynn had told him about power and words. He'd get even with Seamus Muldaur in some other way, he decided, leading the man from the room in silence. For starters, he'd talk Micah into giving Muldaur a knothead like Jezebel, or a puddin' foot like Reliable to get him back into town, maybe by Tuesday next.

Flynn was smart, all right, Gideon decided, even if he didn't follow his own good advice: there were sure better ways of getting revenge on people you didn't like than putting yourself in the way of getting beat up.

Missy felt as if her heart had been cut out with a rusty blade, tossed in the dust, and stampeded. She could not bring herself to look at Flynn as she approached the bed with her doctoring chest under her arm. It was quiet in the room with just the two of them there. Quiet as death. She placed the chest on the nightstand feeling as if the floor had given way beneath her, hoping that nothing in her movements betrayed her devastation.

I don't mean to go through with this. . . .

She hadn't heard the first part of the conversation between Flynn and his brother, but it didn't take any imagination at all to deduce what it was Flynn didn't mean to go through with. Especially when the name of another woman was mentioned.

"You're angry, aren't you?"

Flynn sounded like a chastened schoolboy. Missy allowed herself a tiny, broken sigh of relief that he'd completely misread her reaction.

"No." She opened the chest and pretended to hunt for something. She did not trust herself to meet Flynn's gaze without crying. The noise of tiny, half-filled bottles clinking against one another was an eerie but fitting accompaniment to her agitation.

"How much of our argument did you hear?"

Flynn's weary question startled her.

"What?"

Flynn took in and let out a short breath, as if it were all his lungs would allow him. Still she fought the urge to look at him.

"We weren't making any secret of what we were talking about," he allowed, as if he regretted it. "You must have heard something that—well, that stunned you, at least. We'd best have it out in the open. I'll be as honest with you as I can."

The word *honest* struck her like a poisoned shaft. The clinking noise had stopped; she realized she was no longer rooting through the chest. *When did you mean to tell me that the wedding was not going to take place?* she wanted to ask him. *Were you going to wait until we stood before the justice? Or did you mean to show me up and publicly humiliate me, as well?* She pressed her mouth shut to prevent such questions from coming forth. Just because her heart had behaved foolishly that was no reason why her pride should compound the error.

"I heard nothing." She squeaked out the lie. "Eavesdropping is as dishonest as stealing. Or lying."

"And just as hazardous for one's peace of mind," Flynn commented dryly. "Look at me, Missy."

She did not.

"Is it that you can't bear to see my face looking like a smashed pumpkin, or is there some other reason?"

It's because I despise you, she wanted to say with a stare that would freeze his black soul. But that was more of a falsehood than she was prepared to tell. She straightened her back and held on to the edges of the chest as she formed her response.

"You do look terrible," she said to the chest.

"But that's not why you won't look at me."

"Perhaps you know the answer to that better than I."

"Damn it, Miss—Ow! Son of a—"

He'd tried to sit up, but he fell back on the bed with a stiff grimace. Missy wished with all that was left of her heart that she could feel glad that he'd hurt himself, but she could not. She shoved aside her own anguish in favor of investigating the source of his.

"Lie still," she ordered him swiftly, undoing the buttons of his soiled, bloodied bib shirt. "Where does it hurt? Here?" She slid her hand inside his open lapel. His bare chest was hot and firm beneath her fingers, except for the soft thatch of hair that ran down the middle. She wondered if that hair was honey gold, like the curls on his head.

"No," he grunted. Grasping her wrist, he guided her hand down along the lower left side of his ribs. He took in a gasp as her fingers found the spot. "Right there," he breathed. "But I don't think they're broken. I've had broken ribs before, and as bad as this feels, they felt a hell of a lot worse. Besides"—she felt his other arm slide up her back, and his free hand kneaded her shoulder—"it's starting to feel a whole lot better."

"Don't, Flynn." She wrenched away from him, pulling her hand from his shirt and retreating to the bucket Gideon had left by the bed. She fumbled for one of the washcloths soaking in the bucket. She was shaking. It had been a mistake to touch Flynn that way, a mistake to touch him at all. Her face felt hot with shame and desire. She wanted to die, but not before killing him.

"What did I do now?" he growled.

"You *b-bastard*!" Missy wrung the word out like the washcloth she dropped back in the bucket. She backed away from the bed on unsteady legs, willing herself not to stumble or faint.

"Missy . . ." With effort and another awful grimace of pain, Flynn propped himself up on his elbow. "I can't pretend to know what's gotten into you, but I sure wish you'd tell me. I hurt too bad to play guessing games. I swear to God I won't touch you again. Just—I'd be obliged if you'll just come over here and patch me up like you promised.''

Like I promised! Missy steamed inwardly, glaring at him as she clenched her fists in the folds of her skirt. *I'd like to patch you up, all right! I'd like to measure you for your burying suit, that's what I'd like to do! And after I finish with you, I'll measure myself!*

Allyn, Missy recalled, had always said she wore her emotions like a fancy new gown. She could hardly be surprised that she couldn't keep to herself what she'd overheard Flynn and his brother discussing. She felt as if she'd go up in flames if she even tried to. They were alone in the room anyway. She'd already made a fool of herself in Flynn's company on occasions too numerous to recall; she guessed one last time wouldn't make any difference.

For this would, indeed, be the last time.

''I heard some of your conversation with that flimflam brother of yours,'' she told him, pushing her sleeves up her arms as she steeled her gaze to his. ''I didn't have to listen too hard; the two of you were shouting loud enough to be heard halfway to Rapid City. Someone named Madeleine is with him. Apparently she means a great deal to you, or she thinks she does. I can almost pity her. Then you said something about not meaning to go through with it—''

''And you naturally thought I was talking about the wedding.'' Flynn squeezed his eyes shut and fell back on the bed again. ''Tell me, Missy, did you see bogeymen in the dark when you were a child?''

''I don't see what my childhood has to do with this!''

''Nothing, except that you're so damned willing to believe the worst about everything and everybody, especially me. Do you trust me, and my love, so little?''

She was silent, but the answer hung in the air between them anyway.

Flynn lay still with his eyes closed as Missy bathed his injuries. He welcomed each new hurt and sting, for they helped him ignore the ache in his gut, where Missy had lanced him with her suspicion.

But, damn it, hadn't he deserved her distrust, in some measure? He'd never been entirely honest with her, and she knew it. Was it any wonder that she suspected him of an ulterior motive where her heart was concerned?

The touch of the clean washcloth was cool against his bruised cheek. He knew the gentleness of the hand that wielded it. He suspected she probably wanted to strangle him with his pillow—no doubt an easy feat, in his current state—and it was all he could do to stop himself from catching her wrist and pressing a kiss against her palm.

She left the cool cloth against his swollen eye and dressed his bruised knuckles. It was heaven to be clean of grit and blood, but he found that he needed to be clean of one more thing, besides.

"Ask me, Miss," he breathed, catching a trace of her rose water in the air between them. "Ask me anything. I'll tell you now. It's more important to me that you know the truth than it is for me to protect anybody. You deserve that from me. You deserve that, and a hell of a lot more. Just don't freeze up on me. Please."

She was no longer touching him. He opened his good eye and found her sitting there on the edge of the bed, where she'd been all the while, staring at him. There was no smile in her opalescent gray eyes, and her small, full mouth was drawn up in a pout that was at once childlike and ancient. She blinked, and another tear escaped from the corner of her eye. She brushed it away with the back of her wrist and she looked down, sad and thoughtful.

"I can't," she whispered, wrapping a clean, soft gauze bandage about his hand. "Not now. Anyway, you shouldn't be talking. You need to rest. You need—"

"I need *you* damn it." The hell with it. He had nothing to lose. He pulled his half-wrapped hand out from under hers and caught her fingers, willing her to look at him.

His will must have been as weak as the rest of him, for she slipped her hand from his, not with any ferocity, but with a firm dignity that made him feel even worse than before.

"Missy—"

"I have to think, Flynn." She stood up. Flynn felt a chilly blast of air despite the oppressive July heat. "There are too many questions, and I suspect not even you have all of the answers. You believe you want to talk it all out, but right now that knock you took on the head is doing your thinking for you. You need to rest. I'm going to leave. I'll send Mrs. Fedderman up with some broth for you a little later."

"Would you . . ." God, his chest hurt, and he suspected that it was from more than a couple of bruised ribs. "Would you bring it up yourself?"

When she looked away, he knew what her reply would be. He felt a weight descend on him that made breathing more difficult still.

"I don't think so," she murmured, gathering up her supplies. "I have to—I mean, I'll be quite busy." She sent him one glance as if it were all she could spare. "I'm sorry."

With a brief nod, she left the room.

"So am I," Flynn murmured to the closed door.

301

Chapter Twenty-three

Seamus Muldaur called at two o'clock the following afternoon, Wednesday, by which time Missy had decided on a course of action. She doubted it was a particularly wise course; certainly Allyn would have advised her against it, even though Missy knew it was precisely the sort of thing Allyn herself would have done under the circumstances. Allyn, however, would have done it in her most beautiful and elegant attire, that being Allyn's particular—and most effective—variety of armor.

Missy chose instead her working clothes: boots and a boot skirt in a practical shade of muddy brown, a coffee-and-cream gingham shirtwaist, and a shawl collar vest, topped off with her own brown Stetson hat with its thin, braided leather stampede string. Her dark hair was forced into a knot at the base of her neck, but one or two brave corkscrew strands had escaped, she knew, to guard her cheeks.

Missy greeted the elder Muldaur with a forced smile that she could only hope masked her true feelings for the man. Seamus, though, to her relief, appeared to be preoccupied, or at least more interested in seeing his brother than in exchanging anything more than polite greetings with her. Perhaps he'd already sensed her enmity the day before. If so, she'd waste no time on self-reproach.

"And how fares my brother today? Better?" Seamus inquired as he planted one sleek, highly polished boot upon the stair.

Missy stared at him realizing, with some chagrin, that she did not know, having not seen the patient awake since late the previous afternoon. She had peeked in during the night, when both Flynn and Gideon had been fast asleep, just to ascertain that Flynn was in no particular discomfort.

"I'll leave you to determine that for yourself, Mr. Muldaur," she murmured, studying the large gold signet ring on Seamus's left hand, which was gripping the banister.

"Call me Seamus, please," he corrected her with a thin smile, indicating that he perceived her dislike of him. "And may I call you Missy?"

"Yes," she allowed, not daring to meet his gaze as she did. She'd sooner see him in hell, and she suspected her eyes would have proclaimed as much. With a ceremonious nod of dismissal, Seamus started up the stairs.

"Oh, Mr.—Seamus?" Missy remembered her own mission at the last possible moment.

Flynn's handsome brother paused, wearing a look of polite inquiry.

"Mrs. Fedderman expects you to stay for supper today," she told him, practicing a congenial tone that sounded, to her delight, quite natural. "And so do I, although I have some ranch business that might detain me. I do hope you'll stay?" That was sincere enough. It would not do at all, she knew, to have Seamus Muldaur interfere with her plans for the afternoon, and as long as he remained here at the C-Bar-C with Flynn, he would be safely occupied.

"I don't see why not," he conceded with an inquisitive inclination of his head. "Perhaps my brother will be fit enough by then to join us at the table. No doubt you two will want to discuss your marriage plans. I understand the wedding is to be tomorrow?"

Thursday. Missy had wanted to forget. She would have preferred that Seamus not be there to witness any scene between herself and Flynn, particularly if her mission in town proved enlightening, but perhaps she was worrying prematurely. Whatever the outcome of her afternoon, she doubted in any case that Flynn would be sufficiently recovered for their planned nuptials on the morrow.

What an absurd circus her tranquil, well-ordered life had become since February! She was in the midst of an audible sigh before she could stop herself.

"We shall see," she murmured at the end of it. "Good afternoon." She started for the door, hoping not to have need to look upon Seamus again for a long while.

"Missy?"

He sounded very much like Flynn saying her name, yet at the same time quite different. Enough of both to cause her to shudder.

"Yes?"

"I brought your horse back." He sounded confused. "He's tied up outside, behind my rig. I'd thought you raised champion thoroughbreds. Forgive me, but the animal I rode to town yesterday was slow, stupid, and just plain mean.''

Gideon! That imp! Missy prevented herself from laughing, but just barely.

"Horses are just like people in many ways," she told Seamus with a civil look she was sure Allyn would have approved of. "Even the best of them must occasionally be permitted a bad day."

She left the house without another word.

The day was overcast, but Missy doubted it would rain. Dakota was dry, and never more so than in July. Still, a thunderstorm, even a rare tornado, might whip up on occasion without a calling card. Not likely on a gloomy day such as this, though. Such violent aberrations usually came from seemingly serene skies as cloudless and blue as Flynn Muldaur's eyes.

"Goin' to town?"

Gideon's alarmingly astute question cracked like a whip as she mounted her mare. She recovered from her surprise at once, finding him on the porch with her eyes as she settled into her saddle.

"As a matter of fact, I am," she told him. The bruise on his cheek from yesterday's skirmish was already fading, she was happy to see. Youth recovered more quickly than age, she realized. In all matters.

Gideon was getting taller, too, she noticed as he slouched beside a pillar. None of them knew exactly how old Gideon was, not even Gideon himself, but there could be no question that whatever his numerical age, he was on the verge of becoming a man.

"Want a little company?"

A sweet man. Her heart warmed.

"No, thank you." She refused him a trifle reluctantly and did not sustain his steady, dark-eyed gaze. "I don't mean to be long. There are a few things I forgot yesterday in all of the excitement, and some things Lucy asked me to pick up for the baby. Speaking of which, aren't you supposed to be out back waxing that cradle Micah just finished?''

''Mi said I was too ham-handed,'' he dismissed, sauntering toward her with his hands jammed in the back pockets of his overalls.

''Well, then perhaps you'd better watch him do it so you'll know how next time.''

''Why? Are there goin' to be any more babies around here?''

His question was utterly guileless, but Missy blushed all the same.

''Not as I know of,'' she muttered, shortening her rein.

''Shoot, you and Flynn might have one next year,'' he observed, standing by the mare's left shoulder. ''That is, if you still aim to marry him tomorrow.''

Missy stared at the boy. Gideon was stroking her mare's muzzle as fondly as if the animal were Glory herself. He was trying very hard to seem grown-up and matter-of-fact, Missy realized, but the flicker in his unsmiling eyes gave him away.

''Whatever Flynn and I decide regarding tomorrow does not affect your place here with me, Gideon,'' she told him, wanting to touch him, feeling as if she didn't dare. ''You needn't worry on that score. Ever.''

''I ain't worried,'' he grumbled, fiddling with the mare's bridle. ''And even if I was, it wouldn't be about that, exactly.''

''Well what, then, exactly?''

Gideon stole a look at her from under a stray lock of sable hair. She made a mental note of the fact that he needed to have his hair cut.

''I heard the same things you did yesterday, outside the room.''

A knot tightened in Missy's breast. Of course he had.

306

How could she have been so foolish, and so preoccupied, as to ignore that fact?

She looked away.

"Eavesdropping is a bad habit," she murmured, unable to muster much conviction. She was, after all, as guilty of the misdemeanor as he.

"What are you gonna do, Miss?" Gideon ignored her halfhearted reprimand. "You still gonna marry him?"

"Do you think I should?"

Asking his opinion enabled her to delay voicing her own, which was fine with her, because just now she was miserably uncertain of what her true feelings were. Gideon was entitled to an opinion, of course, and she was certain he had one—Gideon always seemed to have an opinion about everything—but Missy was under no obligation to abide by it, whatever it might be. That the boy did not reply right away intrigued her, and she looked at him again. His expression was thoughtful and wise beyond his years.

"I don't know, Miss. I truly don't." He looked down at his hands, examining the black crescents under his fingernails. "I like Flynn, sure enough. Even though he did let hisself get beat up pretty bad yesterday."

On my account, Missy thought with a renewed pang of guilt. She wished, suddenly, that she had gone in to see Flynn last night, or this morning, while he was awake. It had been nearly 24 hours, and she missed him.

". . . don't you?"

Gideon had asked her a question, and she hadn't heard him. Her cheeks heated.

"I'm sorry; what was that, Gideon?"

Gideon gave a little smirk, an expression Missy found to be not at all comforting.

"Never mind; I guess I know the answer after all. You're sure you don't want me ridin' into town with you? I might be a help, you know. Like that time in

Louisville when Flynn came to call. Remember?''

Missy did. She stared at Gideon with the uneasy sense that he knew precisely what she intended to do in Rapid City this afternoon. She tried to shake the feeling, but it stuck to her like a voracious tick.

"No, thank you." She made an attempt to smile, but she knew it fell short. "I can't be sure Tobias Horton won't be in town too, and I can't risk you coming up against him twice in the same week. You only have one good eye left."

Gideon's grin was more successful than her own.

"I guess you're the only one of us ain't been in a fight yet this week," he observed. "You aim to remedy that today?"

Missy considered him. To her chagrin, she realized she had not yet thought about the variety of outcomes of her mission. She was not a violent person in the physical sense, but she was forced to conclude that fisticuffs were a possibility she hadn't considered. True, Gideon's presence, if he accompanied her, would temper any inclination she might have in that direction, but it would also hamper a frank exchange of words, and Missy intended to be as direct as ever she had been in her life. Pursuing her aims alone, she decided, was the lesser of two evils.

"I have no intention of fighting with anyone about anything," she said, trying to sound decorous but stopping short of wagging a finger at him. "And I hope you're not suggesting that you'd be the person to prevent me from doing so, even if I did have such a thing in mind. I don't suppose you've ever heard the expression 'Physician, heal thyself'?"

He frowned and shook his head.

"Never mind. Let's speak no more about it. Flynn's brother is here, as you probably already know—"

"I took Reliable around to the barn," Gideon interrupted with an innocent look that did not for one instant deceive Missy. "Maybe I'll just go on up and set with them a while."

"You're not to eavesdrop on them."

"No, ma'am."

"Promise me, Gideon."

"Aw, bleedin' Jee—" Gideon scrunched his face up like a cast-off wrapper from a mail-order package. "I mean, all right. Then will you promise me something, too?"

Missy guessed he'd added his codicil to preempt her scolding about his swearing, so, thinking he meant to extort nothing more than a sweet from the general store from her, she nodded her consent.

"Promise me you won't get into any trouble yourself."

Oh, hell. She didn't mean to, of course, but trouble, lately, had a way of finding her even when she wasn't looking for it. And today, like it or not, she knew she was definitely looking for it. Damn Gideon for wording his request in such a way that there was no dissembling! She found herself frowning at the pommel of her saddle.

"All right."

"You promise?"

"I said all right, didn't I? If that was good enough for me, it had darned well better be good enough for you, young man. I'll not have my word called into question!"

His farewell grin could only be called smug.

There were two hotels in town and a third one, thanks to the new railroad spur line, on the way to being finished. Assessing each of the three establishments on Rapid City's main street, Missy decided that Seamus Muldaur would have chosen the newest and largest of these, not to mention the one that was completed. He

309

did not seem a man to suffer inconveniences if comfort was an alternative. And whoever this Madeleine might be, Missy was sure she was of the same ilk.

The desk clerk was a man she'd never seen before, which was a boon Missy had not expected. Having lived in the area for the past ten years, she found herself in the unenviable position of recognizing, and being recognized by, nearly every person she passed on the street.

"May I be of service, madam?"

He looked and talked like a fancy easterner, just naturally chilly and disapproving. Missy was intimidated by his formal manner, and the name she dragged from her memory did not immediately come forth.

"M-Madeleine," she stammered after a time, forcing herself to meet the man's stern gaze. "Deauville. Miss . . . us." She was not sure which, if either, title the mysterious woman owned, or might have employed. Or even if she had registered by that name at all.

"Ah, yes." The clerk's disapproving mien was transformed, to Missy's amazement, into a mask of rapture, which quickly blended to pity. "They are not receiving callers at this time."

Missy was intrigued by the clerk's employment of the plural *they,* but she looked down at her hands, hoping to conceal that fact from him.

"But I have come a great distance." She felt only a little guilty about the lie; it wasn't more than five miles from the C-Bar-C. Quite a walk, true, but not at all arduous with a good horse. "Perhaps if you let them know they have a visitor?"

The clerk shook his head with a gentle indulgence Missy found infuriating. "I'm afraid not, madam. They were most specific as to whom they would accept as callers. And"—he eyed her up and down, his blank expression sufficient censure of her attire—"the brief list includes no females. I am very sorry."

Missy understood his feeling precisely; she was sorry enough herself to wring the man's scrawny, stiff-collared neck. To have come all this distance, physically and emotionally, to be turned away!

"You're quite sure? If you'd only tell them—"

"Quite sure, madam. Now if there is nothing else, I am very busy."

Missy sniffed. He hadn't been doing anything when she walked in, and she was sure he only flipped through the slim register now to try to get her to leave. She was determined not to be gotten rid of so easily, but she remembered her promise to Gideon. She turned to depart, but had a last-minute inspiration.

"May I at least leave them a note to let them know I've called?"

The clerk arched an eyebrow. "You have no calling card?"

This is Rapid City, not New York, you pompous horse's ass, she wanted to retort. Instead, she approximated a demure smile, like those she'd seen Allyn demonstrate in similar situations.

"I'm afraid that, in my haste, I left them at home," she lamented. "If I might beg a piece of paper and the use of your pen?"

The clerk appeared to begrudge her both, but he could hardly refuse. With a shaking hand, she scribbled a brief missive and hastily folded it, not caring about the resulting smear of wet ink. It wouldn't matter, anyway. She handed the message to the clerk, trying very hard to maintain her guileless smile, then watched as he turned away from her to slip it into the room box.

Number 12.

She felt a thrill of triumph. Without hesitation, she toppled the open bottle of ink on the desk. It spilled over the register with a rich spray of jet-black liquid and rolled off and onto the floor.

311

"Oh, my, I'm dreadfully sorry!" she exclaimed as the clerk faced her again. His brow creased with annoyance as he regarded the result of her "accident."

"Not at all, madam," he groaned, as if he meant anything but. He disappeared behind the counter.

It was the advantage she had been waiting for. Oddly breathless, shaking with guilty terror, Missy raced up the stairs.

Her boots made a thunderous racket. Her legs felt like lead. She was certain someone was going to stop her. The very interdiction against her activity made her feel wicked and alive, excited and terrified. She had never done anything quite like this, anything so expressly forbidden, before. Missy Cannon was someone who performed according to the rules, according to expectation. Never on caprice. And certainly never without sanction.

It was quite an extraordinary feeling. No wonder some people did it with such frequency.

"Stop! You can't . . ." The clerk's shouted admonition from below rang empty in her ears and chased her feet faster up the staircase.

In moments she stood in the hall before the door that proclaimed *Number 12* in polished brass numerals. She balled her fist to knock, then dropped her hand to her side. Having gotten this far, she had no intention of allowing herself to be turned away, not even by the inhabitants of the room. And as she was certain that the clerk downstairs would not simply shrug and allow her to make an ass of him, she knew she had only one course of action open to her.

Chapter Twenty-four

Missy had heard very little French in her life, but she was able to recognize the language in the chaos of sound that assailed her as she hastily admitted herself, uninvited, to number 12. She did not comprehend it, of course, but there could be no mistaking the meaning behind it. Her back flat against the door, Missy stared in mute wonder first at one woman, then the second, as they bore down on her from opposite sides of the room like voracious twin birds of prey on a lone brown mouse.

Neither woman was old, she realized, feeling oddly detached and calm, but one was clearly the elder of the two, and certainly several years Missy's senior. Neither was properly dressed, either. They were clad only in brightly colored silk wrappers and mules.

Another woman entered the room from what appeared to be a dressing area. Dressed in gray, she was, besides being a stark contrast to the colorful predators flanking her, obviously a menial, probably a lady's maid. The two women turned to the newcomer and issued another stream of vituperative gibberish that might have been the squawking of indignant falcons. The maid cowered before them, giving Missy an opportunity to study them further.

The elder woman, she noticed at once, was possessed of a full yet slender figure, poorly concealed by her scarlet wrapper. The softness of her form revealed that she had not yet donned her corset; Missy could only guess at what enhancements the garment would lend to an already superb shape. Her hair was curled but not yet dressed, and was a lovely hue that was neither red nor blond, but a seemingly endless spectrum of shades in between. Missy found herself wondering if the color was natural, for the woman's eyebrows appeared to be nothing more remarkable than a plain light brown. The powdered skin of her shoulders and bosom—what Missy could see of it—was so white that she might have been a corpse.

Missy finally recognized the younger woman as Antoinette Deauville, who had been introduced to her in Louisville as Flynn's niece. *Brat* . . . That had been Seamus's word for her. Missy was not surprised that she had not identified the young woman at once; this afternoon, undressed, unmade, Antoinette looked less the dazzling goddess she had seemed on that night and more what she in reality apparently was: a schoolgirl just out of pinafores. A lovely child, but a child nonetheless.

"*Ecoute!*" Antoinette exclaimed, glaring at the older woman. The sound seemed to explode from the front of her face. Another stream of unintelligible words then, ending with "*Veet! Veet!*"

Magically, the woman, whom Missy deduced to be the mysterious Madeleine, gave her one last imperious glare and disappeared with the maid into the dressing room. The door closed behind them with a dramatic bang. Antoinette turned to Missy again and drew herself up as if she wore the most regal attire, shaking her own sunset golden curls from her slight, round shoulders, shattering Missy's brittle poise.

"Miss Cannon." Perfect, unaccented English now came forth from the pouting pink mouth. The voice belied its owner's appearance; it was by no means girlish or uncertain. Missy stared at the woman before her, who pushed her loose sleeves up her white arms before she crossed them at her breast. Antoinette needed no armor of the sort that she herself relied upon, Missy realized, or of the variety that the older woman had no doubt withdrawn to procure. Antoinette's devastating youth and lethally fresh beauty were both armor and weapon enough, and it was very apparent that she intended to use them. She indicated the brocade settee with a long glance, then aimed her hard, sapphire eyes—Muldaur eyes—in Missy's direction again.

"My—my companion and I were not expecting you, but since you have"—she seemed to search for a word, but her artifice was not so practiced as to make Missy believe the term she sought had not been waiting on her tongue all along—"invited yourself into our parlor, please be seated."

Missy eyed the settee. She longed to sit, for she feared her quaking legs would not support her much longer, but she remained standing. She was not really sure why. She guessed it was because she did not want to allow Antoinette to lead the interview, and standing gave her something of an advantage as she was taller than the girl.

"No, thank you," Missy heard her own voice say, and she was both surprised and pleased at the calm—even bold—sound of it. Encouraged, she plunged on. "I suppose you know why I've come.''

At least, Missy hoped she did. Faced with a regal, beautiful, and distressingly self-possessed young woman, Missy herself was having a hard time remembering her motivation.

A smirk fell upon Antoinette's lovely, porcelain-doll features.

''Perhaps you should tell me.''

From a predatory bird to the purr of a cat. It was an extraordinary transition, enough to cause Missy to falter in her intention until she saw Antoinette's glance flicker briefly toward the closed door behind which the older woman and the maid had retreated. Antoinette, she realized, was playing for time until the older woman—her mother, the infamous Madeleine Deauville, Missy was now certain of it—returned. Hope kindled within Missy: Antoinette was obviously not the threat she had first perceived her to be.

Reality quickly doused the spark: what Antoinette lacked, Madeleine probably more than compensated for. And Madeleine, no doubt, was hurrying to dress herself in her shield and breastplate to come forth and do battle. What woman wouldn't, over a man like Flynn Muldaur? Missy felt herself redden, and she hoped Antoinette did not notice.

''Who are you?'' Missy asked quietly, glad of the oak door supporting her back. ''And who is the woman in the dressing room?''

Antoinette smiled, revealing dazzling teeth. Missy swore she could feel their sharpness tearing into her flesh.

''I am Antoinette Deauville,'' she replied, sounding both haughty and amused. ''We met in Louisville. Can you have forgotten?''

The vanity in her reply was sufficiently maddening to make Missy want to pull out her perfect gold curls and fling them in her face. She clenched her hands instead.

"I believe you ensured that no one could forget you, Miss Deauville," she said through her own teeth, which were fine but, she knew, nowhere near as stunning as the younger woman's. "I meant, who are you to Flynn? To Seamus? And why have you come here now?"

Missy had always thought laughter, particularly that of young people, to be among the most pleasing and musical sounds in the world, but Antoinette's vocal merriment was chilling. Missy longed to cover her ears.

"Why do you think we have come?"

"You—and your mother—have some hold over Flynn and his brother," Missy said, before she had any intention of replying. "I want to know what it is. I have heard . . . things. You are Seamus's daughter; that much I know. That means nothing to me. I don't care about Seamus. I don't even like him. But—"

"But you do like Flynn, I think," Antoinette interrupted with a slow, unpleasant smile. "Very much. Suppose I were to tell you that I am not Seamus's daughter, but Flynn's?"

Missy recoiled inwardly. Impossible, she told herself, rallying, remembering the story Joshua had told her so very long ago.

"But you aren't." She sounded more certain than she felt; for that she offered a scant prayer of thanks.

Antoinette raised one amused eyebrow. "And how can you be sure that I am not? My mother has said that there have been times when even she could not be certain."

The fact that the girl could so blithely hurl in Missy's face that her mother had known both men appalled Missy; she guessed that was Antoinette's intention. She felt revolted, but the sensation was not directed at Flynn or, amazingly, his brother.

"I am certain," Missy told her, realizing that it was

the truth, "that no child of Flynn's, however corrupted by its mother, could behave the way you do."

"You believe that because you want to believe it," the girl sneered. "Women who are foolish enough to fall in love with a man find it very easy to deceive themselves as to his character."

That was true enough, Missy knew, to her own dismay. She'd seen it happen before, although not to herself. Until now, that is. She blinked hard and tried to keep her breathing slow and even.

"And people—women—with no character of their own have an easy time finding fault with the character of others," she replied, shoving aside her disloyal doubts. She had to believe in Flynn now, or else everything she'd done in the past few minutes, even in the past few months, was a sham.

Antoinette shrugged. It was an exquisite expression of youthful disdain.

"Believe what you will," she said, sounding bored. "It still does not explain why you have come here to us. Unless it is because Flynn himself has made mention of my mother in an affectionate way, and you wish to protect the interests of your heart?"

"Flynn has never mentioned either you or your mother by name, and certainly not with what you might call affection."

"Then you have come here to satisfy your own jealousy."

Antoinette seemed to be growing larger with each passing moment, and Missy felt as if she herself were shrinking. She placed her hands flat against the oak door behind her, and a cold finger of sweat traced her spine. Rather than try to deny Antoinette's words, which sounded like a hanging judge's proclamation, Missy decided to take another path altogether.

"My ranch is at stake," she breathed, feeling dizzy

with the heat, the stuffiness, and the rich, heavy scent of Antoinette's perfume in the room. "The C-Bar-C. My home. My livelihood. What you—what you are doing to Flynn and to Seamus in some way affects that."

"An odd calling," Antoinette observed, inclining her head. "For a woman, I mean. There are certainly far easier and far more lucrative pursuits. Although," she added, looking Missy up and down as a breeder might an inferior mare, "perhaps not so unusual after all for one of your, ah, temperament."

Her meaning was not lost on Missy, but Missy was too intent on her mission to allow the insult to rile her. She drew in a deep, steady breath and leveled as hard a gaze as she could at the insolent snipe.

"A vocation which fosters strength of character as well as strength of quite a different sort," Missy agreed, pronouncing each word with careful deliberation. "I was called upon only recently to deliver a foal in pieces to save the life of the mare. Nor was that the first time I have been obliged to dismember a creature with my bare hands. I also once killed a man who would have brought great harm to someone I love."

Missy could not deny that she enjoyed Antoinette's resultant shudder, nor that she felt a bitter thrill of triumph at last as the girl looked at her askance.

"My daughter is regrettably impressionable. In that regard she is much like her father. I, however, suffer no such affliction. Killing a man is, to me, no significant accomplishment. I myself have done so, and felt his blood warm my fingers. However, keeping a man in the palm of your hand—how shall I say . . . dancing to your music?—is by far a more satisfying achievement."

The new voice was lightly accented. Carefully modulated. Faintly amused. Missy abandoned her scrutiny of Antoinette in favor of the older woman, who had returned to the room with a vengeance.

319

Madeleine Deauville wore a gown of midnight blue taffeta in a cut Missy had never seen on anyone in Rapid City or, indeed, anywhere else that she could recall. Missy herself was skilled with a needle, but she could only stare as a starving person would gape at a sumptuous meal at the cunning embroidery and elaborate lapis beadwork on the bodice and draped hem of the gown. Not even Allyn owned a gown as spectacular as this. It was indeed a most impressive armor.

"It is a Worth creation, Mlle Cannon." Madeleine commanded the small room with her regal gait and spread herself upon the settee without once releasing Missy from her gaze. "That undoubtedly means nothing to you, but I assure you that in matters of fashion, Worth has no equal."

Missy, staring, could not speak. She knew of Worth; what woman did not? His creations were known to be spectacular and unique, priceless and accordingly expensive, works of art better suited, to Missy's mind, to a well-guarded museum display rather than as practical garments for any but the most elegantly ostentatious social affairs. The creature reclining on the settee was wearing a single article of clothing that represented three months' earnings for the C-Bar-C, very likely more. *I need five thousand dollars,* Flynn had said in May. . . .

Five thousand dollars in the form of a Worth gown lounged on the settee before her. Worn, it seemed to Missy, for no better reason than to make her feel insignificant.

In matters of gall, apparently Madame Madeleine Deauville had no equal.

Missy clenched her fists and took two steps away from the door. Her strength and the good sense with which she was long credited returned. Madeleine Deauville and her daughter were all show and no substance. Worth gowns and expensive accessories might dress up a sow's ear, she realized, but underneath it all was still a sow's ear.

Madeleine was a daughter of a whore, and a whore herself, and very likely worse, if Joshua's tale had been true. She had a wicked web of some sort spun about Seamus and Flynn who, for all Missy knew, deserved all or part of their misfortune for having consorted with her sort to begin with.

Missy hesitated. Had Flynn's transgression been so great as to earn him a lifetime of purgatory in this woman's clutches? Missy could not bring herself to believe it. From what she had learned of Flynn in the past months, it seemed more likely to her that his role in the sordid business was to protect his brother in some way. How like him that would be!

Missy regarded both women, one after the other, and realized that the pair no longer intimidated her. She felt a resurgence of love for Flynn, and a wish to be back with him to tell him so. The only fear she experienced was the dread that she might lose her temper sufficiently to rearrange the Gallic noses Madeleine and her daughter looked down.

"You're leeches," she muttered, sickened. "Blood-suckers. Both of you. You prey on an innocent man who—"

"Innocent?" Madeleine laughed, not seeming to mind Missy's harsh characterization at all. "Hardly that. The Muldaur brothers are many things, cherie, but innocent is not a word anyone who truly knows them would use to describe them. Oh, Seamus might pretend otherwise, but Flynn"—she pronounced the name as if it rhymed with *spleen*—"would never deny it. Of the two of them, he is the more honest. But that is like saying mud is more clean than dirt."

Madeleine opened a matching ostrich-plume fan with an efficient snap and extended her arm along the arched back of the settee like a lazy snake. Missy observed her, hoping to keep her feelings of revulsion carefully hidden from view. It was better, she decided, for the women before her to believe her to be cowed by their superior physical beauty and elegance than to realize that she felt nothing but loathing for them. Loathing and possibly, if she dredged deeply enough for it, a trace of Christian pity.

"It is often hard to determine how dirty another individual is when one is covered with filth," she could not resist commenting.

"How dare you—"

"Silence!" Madeleine shot her daughter a lethal look that effectively stilled the young woman's indignant outburst. "You must forgive my daughter, Mlle Cannon. She is quite young, and has not yet learned the value of keeping one's emotions in check. I am really quite at a loss as to why you have come here, if you mean only to exchange insults and to debate everything I tell you about your Flynn. You should ask yourself what reason I have to lie to you about any of it. I stand to gain or lose nothing by his marriage to you."

She was lying; Missy felt it.

"Then why have you come to Rapid City?" she challenged.

Madeleine blinked, and her blue eyes remained half-closed as if better to assess Missy.

"My reasons are my own, and do not concern you in the least."

Missy doubted that, but she said nothing. She was determined to oblige Madeleine to continue to speak until she said something that sounded truthful. Missy hoped she would recognize the truth, but surrounded as she was by pretense and pageantry, she was not at all sure that she would. The older woman betrayed a moment of discomfort by averting her gaze and changing her position on the settee.

"Flynn is lucky to have found a woman so willing to overlook his many faults," she remarked. "Either that, or you are far more foolish than you appear to be. In any case, your position in Flynn Muldaur's life is of no concern to me or to my daughter."

"Except as to how you are to continue receiving tribute from him," Missy mused aloud, watching her adversary. "Tell me, did you come here intending to marry him yourself?"

Madeleine laughed in a melodious alto, wearing a look that betokened pity rather than astonishment. She was indeed practiced in this art, Missy thought, with no small, grudging admiration. Far more so than she herself could ever hope to be.

"Whatever would I gain from such a folly?" Madeleine inquired as her laughter faded into a bad memory. "I am accustomed to circumstances far more elegant than this mean establishment can offer." She waved her hand and looked about the room, one of the finest Missy could imagine in Rapid City, with a scornful look. "How can you seriously suggest that I or my daughter might be content in so rustic a place?"

Missy considered her. Rapid City was rustic, true, but marriage to Flynn, Missy knew, would not necessarily mean that Madeleine would be confined to this corner of South Dakota. She was certain Madeleine knew it, too. Thoroughbred racing was concentrated in major cities where society had money to squander, and it was obviously money Madeleine craved, not Flynn himself or even the C-Bar-C. But the ranch, or even part-ownership in it, if she were Flynn's wife, could provide Madeleine and her daughter entry into the expensive inner circles in places like New York, Saratoga, and elsewhere. Madeleine's mother, Missy recalled, had been a key figure in the smuggling affair that had led ultimately to Flynn's disgrace. In all likelihood, Madeleine had learned a great deal from the woman who had borne her.

Missy's arms and legs were stiffening from tension and from remaining still for so very long, but she did not dare to move yet for fear she might do some sort of violence.

"I haven't worked out your reasons yet," Missy admitted. "But I will. Meanwhile, you—and your daughter—would be well advised to stay away from Flynn and the C-Bar-C. Trespassers are shot on sight." That was an empty threat, Missy knew. She suspected Madeleine Deauville knew it, too, for the woman offered a whimsical, unpleasant smile.

"I have no need to visit your ranch. And I will stay away from Flynn, cherie," Madeleine assured her in an amused drawl. "But how will you make certain that Flynn stays away from me?"

Missy found a smile of her own meandering across her lips as if it were a scowl that had lost its way. She knew precisely how she would make certain of it. And on the morrow, Flynn, Madeleine, Seamus, and the rest of Rapid City would know it, too.

Chapter Twenty-five

Flynn rolled over to get out of bed and promptly impaled himself on a hot metal spike. He sucked in a breath, inhaling with it several ripe oaths, and allowed his head to fall back against his pillow.

"Don't try to move, Flynn." Missy's voice was soothing. "I know it hurts. Time. You need time."

Flynn squeezed his eyes closed and remembered Seamus. And Madeleine. Time was one thing he did not have.

"Missy . . ." He tried his own voice, but it came out as a groan. He felt even worse this morning than he had yesterday, or the day before, or—just how long had he lain here, anyway?

"Shh. Don't try to speak."

He obeyed, because he felt as if he'd pass out if he didn't. Besides, her voice was the sweetest balm he'd yet had. Gingerly he eased onto his back again and al-

lowed himself, by degrees, to relax into the succor of
the bed. In a minute, he felt strong enough to open his
eyes. Missy was there in a small chair drawn up beside
his bed, pale and careworn. He'd never seen anything
look quite so good. The troubling images of Seamus and
Madeleine evaporated to an inconsequential mist.

"What day is it?" he tried again after the pulsing ache
in his side ebbed. He'd be all right, he guessed, if he
didn't have to move. Or speak above a whisper.

"It's Thursday," was the answer he got, along with
a sweet, if weary, smile. "Thursday morning."

Morning again. He should have figured. The inside of
his mouth felt like the fur on his jaw and his bladder
was so full he thought he'd burst.

"Help me up."

"But you—"

"Damn it, I'm not about to disgrace myself in this
bed! Help me up! Please." That declaration had cost
him, but he grimaced and bore it, regretting only that
he'd cussed at her.

She blushed. "Suppose I just bring you a mason jar?"

"Missy," he growled, "I'm not some damn cripple.
I got up last night for supper, which you'd have known
if you'd been here yourself."

"That's probably why you feel so poorly this morning," she mused, rising. "Here."

Flynn surprised himself by relying heavily on her support to ease up and sit on the edge of the bed. The ache
was still there, but it was more like a reminder of his
injuries than a revisitation thereof.

"You slept in your clothes, I see." There was no disapproval in Missy's tone that he could detect, merely
mild amusement as she brushed the lint of the ticking
from his shirtsleeves.

Gingerly Flynn got to his feet. The room spun, but he
closed his eyes until the dizziness passed.

"Good thing for you, I guess," he managed to tease her right back, and his reward was another charming blush. Just as he was wondering how he was going to negotiate the distance to the chamber pot without stumbling, Missy hurried to retrieve the item from its place beneath the washstand. When she placed it on the floor before him, she seemed unable to look at him.

"I'll just go over here and make up Gideon's bed," she murmured, hastily turning her back. "He's already downstairs eating breakfast. Tell me when you're through."

"I expect you'll know when I'm through," Flynn remarked wryly.

She did. She covered the pot and carefully carried it to the door. Flynn, watching her, wondered if she'd still be blushing when she was a little old lady. He found himself hoping he'd be around to find out.

"Missy."

She turned to him. Her eyes were amethyst this morning, and clear as glass. They made him feel stronger and smarter than he knew he was.

"Put that thing down," he said gruffly. "And come over here."

He had to think. He needed to think. But he knew he needed to feel her in his arms, to know she wasn't angry with him, more than he needed anything else at the moment. If she denied him, he knew he would not have the strength to contest her. Maintaining her curious gaze, he prayed she wouldn't refuse him. She did, however, hesitate.

"I know I'm a sight," he said. "And I expect I smell like a flophouse. But I need to . . ."

He paused. Staring at her, he realized he did, indeed, need to hold her. But he wanted it even more. He swallowed the profusion of alien emotions that suddenly rose in him and decided to give them all one name: love. He was amazed by how easily it went down.

She was pretty and fresh before him, and he did not even want to touch the starched white lawn of her shirt-waist lest he soil it. He rubbed the flat of his hands against the hip pockets of his jeans, then tentatively felt the indentation of her waist with his fingertips. She came to him gently, as if she feared to hurt him. She smelled like a fresh nosegay. She fit perfectly with him, her head beneath his chin, her face pressed lightly to his neck and collarbone. The fullness of her figure was a reminder, if he needed one, that she was a woman.

"Are you still mad at me?" He realized that one thing mattered to him more than anything else.

"I was never mad at you," she murmured against his shirt. "Are you . . . do you still want to marry me?"

He deliberately shut out the specters of Seamus and Madeleine. "I was afraid you'd changed your mind," he replied, allowing himself a small sigh. "Of course I want to marry you. Although I guess I won't be making it down any aisles today. I doubt I could even climb into a buggy. I'm sorry."

The sweet softness of her shining dark hair beneath his nose made him sorrier still.

"Flynn."

Did she tense in his arms, or did he just imagine it?

"Mmm?"

It didn't matter to him, as long as she didn't move just yet.

"Um, the reason I missed supper last night with you and Seamus is because I had to go into town."

"Oh?"

"Then on my way back, I stopped by the church to talk to Rev. Whitmire. You won't have to walk down the aisle, or even climb into any buggy, because he's coming out here to marry us this afternoon. Sheriff Garlock will bring the license. Lucy and Micah can be witnesses. That is, if you're sure you still want to . . . ?''

She held fast to his lapels as she put the half-question to his shirt buttons. He wanted to answer her right away, but he stopped himself. When they were children, Seamus had once dared him to throw a rock through a neighbor's window, a persnickety old maiden lady who kept cats. He'd done it sure enough, but he remembered running straight home afterward, where he'd about hugged their foster mother to death. He hadn't thought about it at the time, but he recalled the incident as an adult and realized he'd needed to make sure he was still loved before the angry neighbor came to call with the disturbing news.

"Whose window did you throw a rock through?"

She pushed away from him and met his gaze with confusion.

"What?"

He wanted to laugh but he dared only a small chuckle, for the good of his ribs and for the sake of his relationship with Missy.

"Never mind. It just means I don't know whether to be flattered or frightened by this impetuosity. I think, for the sake of my health, I'll choose the former. But I need a shave and a bath for sure, and it's going to take me extra long to do both, in my condition."

In my condition. Lord, it was going to be his wedding night! And he was scarcely able to move without hurting himself!

"What is it, Flynn?" she murmured, tugging his shirt with urgency. "Are you in pain?"

He did not know what spirit had moved Missy to expedite their vows, but he was not about to suggest a delay, or to give her any reason to do so.

"Not just yet." He rubbed his stubbled jaw, attempting to hide a wry grimace. But I'm planning to be, he added to himself.

"Would you—would you like your brother to be here as a witness? We could send Rich to town to fetch him." Her tone made it clear that she was only offering out of respect for his wishes, whatever they might be.

I think you've just given me an idea of how to make everybody happy.

Flynn restrained a shudder at the memory of Seamus's cryptic remark.

"No," he replied, holding her closer despite the twinge in his ribs. "In fact, I think I'd prefer it if he weren't here."

He didn't ask. If he did, you would have told him.

" 'Though I speak with the tongues of men and of angels, and have not love, I am become as sounding brass, or a tinkling cymbal.' "

Missy scarcely heard Rev. Whitmire's solemn, resonant assertion for the guilty clamor in her conscience. Flynn stood beside her in the archway of the parlor, his crooked elbow making a sheltering nest for her hand, which was cold and trembling despite the July heat. Flynn smelled of the cedar closet where his suit had been stored, of soap, and of the clean, civilized, masculine scent of bay rum. He glanced down at her; she noticed it from the corner of her eye, but she could not bring herself to return his favor.

" '. . . and though I have all faith, so that I could remove mountains, and have not love, I am nothing.' " The Rev. Whitmire had a deep, lovely voice like the pealing of distant, sonorous, Southern churchbells. The sound of it never failed to move Missy. She tried to concentrate on First Corinthians.

" 'And though I bestow all my goods to feed the poor, and though I give my body to be burned, and have not love, it profiteth me nothing.' "

Give up my body to be burned . . . Missy burned

whenever she thought of being with Flynn, of having his skin next to hers. And the devil take whatever profit there was in the C-Bar-C or, for that matter, in a life for her that did not include Flynn Muldaur. She blushed, doubting that the apostle Paul had any such corporeal meanings in mind when penning his epistle in prison.

" 'Love suffereth long and is kind. . . . ' " That was true. Flynn was never anything but kind. And as far as suffering, weren't his bruises from his fight with Bill Boland proof enough of that? " 'Love envieth not; love vaunteth not itself, is not puffed up. . . . ' "

Vanity had never been one of her sins, Missy knew. Allyn had often told her she could do with a little more of it. And as far as envy went, well, she'd conquered her envy of Madeleine Deauville and her daughter, an accomplishment of which she would be proud, if it didn't lead to the very vanity St. Paul cautioned against. . . .

" 'Love doth not behave itself unseemly, seeketh not her own, is not easily provoked, thinketh no evil. . . . ' "

Well, as far as that went, she had some explaining to do to the Almighty, for Seamus Muldaur and the women had provoked her past endurance. Besides, she was certainly guilty of evil thoughts in Seamus's direction, as well as in Madeleine's and Antoinette's. But she was only human, not a saint like Paul. God might overlook it.

" 'Love rejoiceth not in iniquity, but rejoiceth in truth. . . . ' "

Her throat stopped up and her breast ached at that assertion. She had not been wholly truthful with Flynn, and St. Paul seemed to know it. Paul was not an apostle who let one off easily. He must have been a brutal taskmaster in his time, she thought miserably. If she were a Corinthian, she would have loved nothing better than to see him martyred. To make matters worse, Flynn patted her hand, the one tucked into the crook of his arm. The tender, protective gesture made her want to cry.

" 'Love beareth all things, believeth all things, hopeth all things, endureth all things. . . . ' "

She had been too willing, overhearing Flynn and his brother two days before, to believe the worst of her betrothed, the man she was supposed to love. Even yesterday at the hotel, with Madeleine and her daughter, she had doubted and questioned, the result of which was her hastening of these very nuptials. . . .

" 'Love never faileth. . . . ' "

But her love had failed. Or she had failed it; she could not be sure which. She doubted it mattered. What mattered was that she was taking a man, Flynn Muldaur, in a matrimony founded on deception and distrust. It was an action which shamed her before God. She should have run from the room, but the knowledge that to do so was to shame herself instead before Rev. Whitmire, Sheriff Garlock, Lucy, Micah, Gideon, and Flynn himself proved too great a wage for her. And the wages of sin, as everyone knew, were death. Would God ever forgive such a sacrilege as she was about to commit? Could she ever forgive herself, on Flynn's behalf as well as God's?

"Who gives this woman in holy matrimony?"

The room was a silent condemnation: she had forgotten to prepare for that feature of the ceremony. Her mouth would not move. Flynn started to speak but, seeming to realize that he could hardly give and receive her in the same ritual, fell awkwardly silent again. Micah Watts shuffled his feet. Eldon Garlock cleared his throat with a self-conscious rumble.

"I do."

It was young Gideon who spoke, with more than a little defiance. Missy could not bring herself to face the small assembly to watch his approach, but she did not have to wait long to see him. He stepped in front of her, right up to Rev. Whitmire, solemn and dignified, his arms by his sides and his shoulders straight. Despite overalls that scarcely reached his ankles, he looked more like a man than a child, but enough of both to make Missy's heart ache with love and pride.

Rev. Whitmire's bushy gray eyebrows met. He moved his mouth once as if he meant to speak, possibly to deny Gideon his right, but he paused, glancing first at Missy, then Flynn. His brows parted again like the Red Sea. His gray-streaked beard parted, too, in a grin.

"Well, I think that's fitting, as it was you as got these people together," the minister said slowly.

Gideon's shoulders relaxed, and when he looked up at her—truth to tell, he didn't need to look very far—his grin was irritating. Proprietary. And utterly endearing. She slipped her hand from the supporting crook of Flynn's elbow and, before she could inventory a host of reasons why she shouldn't, she hugged Gideon and kissed him beside his ear.

He did not stiffen or try to break away from her, she realized in amazement. On the contrary: she felt his hands on her elbows in a tentative return of her affection that brought a renewed swelling to the back of her throat. It was a small thing, unremarkable to those present, except perhaps for Flynn. But it comforted Missy in a way she had not expected. It was as clear a sign as she needed that God understood why she'd acted as she had with regard to Flynn, even forgave her for it. A tear of relief threatened her poise and the corner of her eye, but she blinked it away.

And if she'd had any doubt about God's hand in the proceedings, Flynn's subsequent sniffle removed it.

Gideon stayed by her side as Rev. Whitmire went on with his part. Missy intermingled her own prayerful thoughts with his words. Marriages had been founded on weaker premises—even Allyn's had begun as a union of convenience, intended as temporary—but, feeling the warmth of Flynn's arm cradling her hand, Missy knew she would not be content giving anything less than her whole heart to the endeavor.

"I, Daniel Flynn Muldaur, take thee, Melissa Judith Cannon. . . . ''

Daniel? Missy stole a look at Flynn, but he was looking at Rev. Whitmire with a most pale and serious countenance. Daniel. A nice name, to be sure, but why had he never told her about it before? The thought piqued her. Another of his secrets, she mused, grinding her teeth. The foundation of the marriage began to look weaker again.

"I, Melissa Judith Cannon, take thee, *Daniel* Flynn Muldaur. . . . ''

She could not resist placing a caustic emphasis on his real first name. She felt his gaze on her. She purposely ignored it. Gideon snickered but fell silent as she nudged him with her elbow.

"If there be any man present who knows any reason why these two should not be joined in holy matrimony, let him speak now or forever hold his peace."

No man spoke, but the sound of a door closing caused Missy to turn her head. Flynn turned too, and Gideon.

There at the back of the parlor stood Seamus Muldaur, leaning against the doorjamb like Old Scratch himself.

"Don't let me hold up the proceedings." His eyebrow was raised. His tone was amused. "Apparently I've missed most of the ceremony, but at least I've come in time to see my brother kiss the bride. Please go on."

Missy was rattled. She guessed Flynn was, too, for his sandy brow creased and remained so. When Rev. Whitmire finished his office, Flynn's kiss missed her lips in favor of another glance to the rear of the room.

"Let me be the first to congratulate the bride."

Seamus sauntered through the small assembly to the

fore wearing, along with his usual fine suit, a congenial smile that harbored no trace of ill will or irony and was all the more dangerous for it. Either he was genuinely pleased, or he was an accomplished actor. Frowning, Missy suspected the latter. Her instinct was to pull away from his touch.

He's your brother-in-law, she reminded herself.

That made his kiss on the cheek easier to bear, but only a little. She still felt violated afterward.

"And Flynn," Seamus pronounced, extending his hand to his brother. "Congratulations. I wish you both every happiness, although I must admit I'm hurt that you obviously intended to exclude me from this momentous family occasion. It was only by purest luck that I happened to visit this afternoon. Why, I haven't even a gift for you."

His gaze strayed to Missy in a way that made her most uncomfortable. She had no doubt that Seamus knew of her mission to town yesterday, thanks to Madeleine and her daughter. Her cheeks warmed as she wondered if he would mention it to Flynn, and what Flynn might make of it if he did. She suspected Seamus knew her thorough embarrassment, and that he relished it. She wanted to escape.

"I'll help Mrs. Fedderman," she murmured to Flynn—her husband—without looking at him. "I think she has some refreshments prepared. Excuse me." She started to pull away from him.

"Stay here. She and Lucy can manage," Flynn scolded tenderly, holding her hand prisoner with his own. "It's your wedding day."

"I believe, dear brother, your bride was trying with as much grace as possible to allow you and me a moment to speak alone. You are not usually so insensitive to such things. It must be due to that beating you took the other day. Indeed, I'm surprised to find the sheriff here, unless it's because he means to cart you off to jail now for having brawled in a public place?''

Rev. Whitmire, Micah, Lucy, and even Eldon Garlock seemed to take Congressman Muldaur's words as a jest, for they laughed. Flynn, however, did not laugh. Nor did Missy. She guessed Seamus knew that she found his remarks neither amusing nor tactful. She further supposed that he had not intended for them to be. She tried to smile and wished she could form a breezy, cutting retort that would not seem too rude, but she could not.

''There's nothing you have to say to me that can't be said before my wife,'' Flynn replied evenly. His tone was pleasant, but his words were a warning. Missy wondered whether Seamus had enough sense to heed it.

Seamus's grin curled downward but did not diminish.

''Marriage has emboldened you already,'' he remarked to Flynn with a slow nod. ''But you make me out to be a monster. You'll frighten your young bride with such words. Or is that your intention?''

The muscle beneath Flynn's sleeve tensed. Missy tightened her fingers around it, all too aware of the spectators in the room whose smiles had faded to stares of undisguised curiosity at Seamus's odd and faintly sinister address. The already tenuous happiness she'd felt was evaporating further with every passing moment spent in Seamus's company.

''A toast to the newlyweds!'' Rev. Whitmire's gentle, booming exclamation drew Missy's attention to the fact that Mrs. Fedderman had returned with a tray of punch glasses that were eagerly taken up by those in attendance. Missy blessed the man for dispelling the ominous mood that had clouded the room since Seamus's arrival.

''The Muldaurs would prefer whiskey,'' Flynn's brother commented with a wink at the groom. ''But in deference to you, Reverend, we'll make do with punch for now, won't we, Flynn? To the bride and groom.''

Missy thought he was going to say something else—
she feared he was—but instead he hoisted his glass high,
then drained it with an expansive gulp. The others followed suit.

Not taking her stare from her new brother-in-law,
Missy took a cautious sip of the beverage herself. It
tasted bitter.

Chapter Twenty-six

Seamus was drunk. Or else he was feigning drunkenness; Flynn could not be sure which. Certainly it was not out of the question to believe that Seamus was playing a crowd for his own obscure purposes; he'd been known to do it before. But Seamus had always been quietly cruel and articulate when drunk, whereas his exhibition before the wedding guests was of the more gregarious and slurred variety. The only advantage Flynn could see to Seamus's pretending to be intoxicated here—on three brandies!—was that his brother would then be able to say or do anything without fear of offending anyone beyond the moment, then quickly earning forgiveness. People tended to excuse drunks with an indulgence they would never extend to a responsible man.

And Seamus was a responsible man.

Hell, he's been responsible for ruining your life, up

until now, Flynn allowed, fighting a wry grin as he regarded his brother. That was not entirely true, Flynn knew. Still it would have been nice, just once, to hear Seamus thank him for his many sacrifices on Seamus's behalf. Seamus, though, being Seamus, had merely taken it all as if it were his due.

Seamus regaled the minister and the sheriff with another of his tales from the floor of the House, his long arms performing a graceful, if exaggerated, dance of dramatic interpretation.

"... so I told my esteemed colleague, the distinguished congressman from Illinois ..."

Flynn shut him out again, nosing his own glass of brandy, his first, still half-full, as he leaned his elbow on the mantel. The last time he'd heard that particular fantasy, the congressman in question had been from Kentucky. Not for the first time, Flynn wondered what percentage of Seamus's anecdotes had long ago crossed the boundary between fact and invention. He wondered if Seamus himself knew anymore.

A gentle tug on his sleeve pulled him away from Seamus's tired tale and into Missy's animated eyes.

"Eldon has pulled out his pocket watch at least three times," she murmured in a voice as soft as the summer evening. "It's getting late, and you should be resting."

As if he were an invalid. Well, he was, he realized, grimacing as a stab of pain reminded him. He mustered a smile for her tender concern and for her diplomacy. She wanted Seamus gone, it was plain. He abandoned his brandy glass on the mantelpiece in favor of caressing her cheek.

"I'll kick Seamus out," he whispered, stealing another glance at his brother and the increasingly restive audience about him. "And I think I'll ask Rich to drive him back to town. He might be too drunk to find the way himself."

339

Missy's look said what he knew she would never have allowed her lips to utter: would that be such a loss to the world or, more especially, to their little corner of it?

"*Might* be?" Her echo was evidence of her skepticism.

Flynn didn't want to burden his new bride with speculation about his brother's true condition, so he said nothing. Missy, he knew, worried sufficiently without his giving her just cause.

"Where's Gideon?"

"You know where he is." Flynn's reply was a gentle reprimand as he closed the bedroom door. Their bedroom door. "I guess you saw us from the window. He thinks it's quite a treat to be staying in the bunkhouse with the hands tonight. I doubt we'll ever get him back into his own room after this, unless he decides he misses the soft life." He chuckled.

Missy felt warmed by the tranquil sound, despite her nervousness. "Then—then we're alone."

"Yes. Except for Lucy, Jed, and Mrs. Fedderman downstairs, that is," he answered, tongue in cheek. "Why are you sitting up here in the dark?"

He didn't add *fully dressed*, but Missy, tense in the rocking chair by the window, nevertheless heard the postscript. Her hands, already clenched together so tightly that they were stiff and aching, squeezed harder still.

"I was—I was waiting for you."

She heard the creak of the floorboards and the thud of his boots on the rag rug in the dark room as he approached. "Well, I'm here now."

Hushed as a night breeze, and just as soothing to her heated brow. Had she ever even dreamed of loving a man the way she loved Flynn? No, it had not been the sensible thing to do, and she'd always been practical.

She wished she had spent more time dreaming about it, though, about what a man's love was and what it meant. If she had, she would not be so apprehensive now. So uncertain of herself, and of him.

"You're quiet," he observed, resting his hands on her shoulders as he stood behind her chair.

But her shoulders and the rest of her cried out with want at his touch. She was surprised that he could not hear it, or feel it through his long, strong, sensitive fingers. *Love me, Flynn,* it said. *Please.*

"I'm—I was thinking."

"About what?" His fingers began a gentle massage, seductive in its artful artlessness.

About Madeleine Deauville, she thought. About the underhanded thing I did to make sure you were mine, and that nobody's claim was greater.

"Your shoulders are so tense!" His midnight-blue baritone was quiet with amazement and his massage deepened. "Relax, sweetheart. It's over. Everyone's gone. It's just us now."

Just us. Just you and me, and a hundred secrets in between.

Flynn's hands were gone, and Missy felt cold, despite the heat of the summer day lingering in the room. She wanted to call him back, but she stifled her request. The result was a whimper clogging her throat.

"I'm just lighting a lamp," he assured her in answer to her unspoken query. There was no hint of amusement in his remark, thank heaven. Still, she felt foolish. She shrank deeper into the caned seat and kept her elbows tight at her sides.

"No, don't, Flynn."

I don't want you to see the guilt in my eyes.

The ensuing silence told her he was considering her request.

"All right." She felt the agreeable weight of his hands

Carole Howey

on her shoulders again. Agreeable, yet somehow reminding her of the burden she had taken upon herself . . .

"You're restless," Flynn observed. "Why don't you get up and—"

"I'm not ready to go to bed yet," she blurted.

"I was going to suggest you let me sit down there, and you could sit on my lap."

There was only a trace of gentle amusement in Flynn's voice. Missy suspected he could not have prevented it. She felt so damnably, idiotically naive! Her face heated.

"I'll—I'll hurt you." Missy choked back a lot of pride to say it, but she was damned if she'd be the cause of any more wrong to Flynn than she already had been.

He tapped lightly on her left shoulder and urged her to her feet with only his fingertips.

"The day I can't hold my wife on my lap," he intoned, in a light, teasing tone for which she silently blessed him, "is the day I hope to leave this world for the next."

Missy longed to give him a playful response, but she was feeling far from frolicsome and could think of none. He eased his long, lean frame into the chair stiffly and with a slight grimace. Doubt renewed, she looked at him.

"Well, come on." He embellished his already attractive invitation with a tender smile, a beckoning wave, and two pats of his lap. "I won't bite. I promise."

Missy could not long sustain the heat of his cobalt eyes; nor could she deny that she wanted, more than anything, to feel him around her in a comforting embrace, even if that embrace would surely lead to other things. Especially if it led to other things.

She tried to will herself lighter as she gingerly settled herself onto his lap. She meant to keep a distance between them, as much to protect his sore ribs as to punish herself, but the chair had other ideas. It rocked back with their combined weight and she was pressed against him, her shoulder to his breast. He let out a soft grunt of surprise.

"Oh, I've hurt you!"

Missy tried to get up, but his strong arms held her fast against him.

"No, you haven't," he denied on a breath that tickled her ear. "I just wasn't prepared for it. I'm fine. Just sit still. Sit here. With me."

His invitation was the most seductive one she'd ever received. She snuggled closer to him. He felt so good; so warm and so strong. He smelled faintly of fresh tobacco, and the scent of the single shot of brandy he'd consumed still tinged his breath.

He smelled like heaven. Like a man. She closed her eyes as a sigh took her breath away.

"Unnh."

There was no mistaking the discomfort in that sound. Stricken, Missy pushed away from him.

"No, sweetheart," he growled, pulling her close again with unarguable authority. "Stay here." He punctuated his request with a kiss behind her ear that inspired a fluid warmth along her spine like heated sugar syrup running straight down into her loins. "Right here." He nipped her earlobe, then licked it to ease the thrilling pinch that resulted. "With me." His kiss traveled along her neck and over the soft ridge of her chin. "Now."

Now.

His shoulder supported her head, as her own neck seemed incapable of such exertion. His mouth tried hers ever so slightly, lips brushing lips, and her jaw relaxed as if he'd drugged her with a single, simple taste. Her mouth welcomed his, and she delighted in his breathless groan of delight. Or was that pain again? She fidgeted.

"No," he murmured, then sent the tip of his tongue on a slow, torturous mission along her lower lip. "It's good.'' He paused for breath. ''So good. Be still. Be very still. . . . ''

It was good. Her left hand snaked its way about his neck until she found the thick hair that curled over his shirt. Soft as a baby's. She could play in it forever. She would, now that she had the right. She wanted to touch his neck, but the shirt hindered her attempt, despite the absence of a real collar.

''Here.''

Flynn worked the button at his throat, his lips poised a breath away from hers. His eyes were smoky sapphires. They warmed her.

''Touch me,'' he invited her, brushing the corner of his mouth against her lips. ''And let me touch you. God, I want to, Missy. I've wanted to for as long as I can remember.''

A silly giggle escaped her lips.

''When I was covered with muck in Glory's stall in Louisville?''

He laughed once, breathlessly, taking her chin in his fingers.

''Seeing as how you seem to spend half your life up to your elbows in one mess or another, I can't imagine that would surprise you so much.''

''It doesn't, I guess,'' she surprised herself by confessing. ''It's just that I would never have taken you for a man who likes to wrestle pigs.''

''Missy, what a comparison!'' He sounded appalled. ''I'd take you to task for insulting my wife like that, but seeing as you are my wife, that makes it a bit awkward, to say the least.''

Missy felt her face heat. Madeleine or her daughter might have made such a remark about her, she knew. She concentrated on the appealing cleft of Flynn's throat.

''It's only an expression,'' she told him, wishing she

hadn't uttered it. She'd just begun to feel easy with him, and words from her own mouth were causing her to stiffen up again with dark thoughts of Madeleine and her own dishonesty.

"You're damned hard to tease, Mrs. Muldaur," he scolded her with a gentle shake of her shoulders. "You're always so serious, especially about yourself. I see I have a lot of hard work ahead of me, mellowing you."

Missy managed a grin, and she was glad of the darkness in the room that hid her blush.

"I'll try not to be too slow to learn," she ventured, drawing her finger downward from the tip of his fine nose over his lips.

His mouth widened slightly in a rapt grin that pulled her even closer than his embrace.

"Oh, take as long as you like," he allowed generously, covering her touring finger with his hand in a gentle but possessive grasp. "I've found over the years that the sweetest lessons take the longest time to teach."

The Missy of six months before, she realized, nestling closer to his neck, would have run in terror at such a suggestion from a man. Flynn had already taught her much in that time, though, and she found herself eager to learn even more.

There was a sharp hiss of breath, ending in a hoarse groan.

Missy leapt up from Flynn's lap so quickly that she nearly fell backward. Flynn's head was back, his eyes were closed, and his handsome features were taut with pain.

"I'm sorry, oh, I'm so sorry, Flynn," she wailed, kneeling beside the rocker in haste. "I *have* hurt you. Oh, damn. I—"

"No, no." Flynn's attempted smile fell short of convincing her. "You didn't. I'm fine. Fi—" His repetition was cut short by a wince. "Damn it."

"That does it." Missy stood up. "To bed," she ordered him. "At once. You're obviously in no condition for—for much of anything but rest." She felt a queer mingling of relief and disappointment at the postponement of her wedding night, but she could not deny that she also felt perfectly at ease dictating a prescription for Flynn's recovery.

"I don't aim to make a practice of being bedridden, nor of allowing my wife to boss me around," Flynn growled at her from his chair, and although there was a twinkle in his eye as he said it, she knew he wasn't more than half joking. She met his teasing look boldly.

"There's an expression cowboys use," she told him with a shade of tartness, taking hold of his hands. " 'Don't squat with your spurs on.' It's good advice."

"I know another expression," he drawled, getting to his feet with her help. " 'It doesn't take too many inches to make a wife a ruler.' "

But he allowed her to lead him to the bed.

"I feel like a damned old man," he growled, stepping slowly. "Next thing you know, you'll be serving me up curdled milk with a spoon."

"If you don't take care of yourself, I just might," she scolded him as she lit the small bedside lamp. "Now hold still while I get your buttons."

Flynn tried not to think about the fact that Missy was undressing him there in the bedroom, but as her gentle fingers undid the buttons of his shirt from the throat down with ease, it became increasingly difficult to think of anything else. She went on talking to him in a singsong way, the way she might have addressed Gideon, but Flynn did not hear the words. His ears were too full of the hammering of his pulse. The clean scent of her hair was like roses blooming in the next yard over.

But there were no roses in Dakota, he knew. There was only Missy.

She was no longer speaking. She wasn't unfastening his buttons anymore either, but he had no idea how long ago she'd stopped that. It might have been moments or hours. She'd run out of shirt, in any case, and he felt her short, fast breaths tease the hair on his bared chest.

His trousers were unbearably tight. He realized, closing his eyes, that broken ribs or no broken ribs, there were some other parts of him that were going to feel a whole lot worse this night before they felt better.

"You're not finished," he observed, his voice lower and quieter than it had any business being.

She stole a glance at him. It was just long enough for him to see the maidenly hesitation in her amethyst eyes.

"Can't you . . ." Her hand moved toward the buttons of his trousers, but retreated again quickly. "You can do that yourself."

He caught it. "Help me."

"Flynn—"

"Please, Missy." It came out as a breathless croak. He wondered if she would interpret his plea as a sign of pain. She'd be right, but the pain was farther south of where it had been earlier.

"I—I'm afraid."

He knew what the admission cost her, and he loved her all the more for it.

"I know. Don't be, sweetheart. It's all right. It's just us here now."

"But I'll hurt you."

I'll hurt you, too, he thought, but could not bring himself to say. Besides, Missy was not ignorant, even if she was inexperienced. In answer, he placed his hand on hers and guided it to his waist.

He watched her swallow. Then, with one false movement, she placed her fingers at the topmost button. Their tips pressed lightly against his abdomen, inspiring a renewed shiver of want within him. His mouth went dry and he clenched his hands, praying for control.

"Flynn, I can't." The anguish in Missy's cry as she turned away from him was more than silly virgin reticence. And it had something to do with his brother. He sensed it. Damn him, what had Seamus said to her? Flynn took hold of Missy's shoulders, wanting to kill his brother.

"What is it, Miss?" he coaxed in her ear. "What's wrong?"

Missy said something he could not make out.

"What?"

"I've misled you." A whisper.

"What? How?" What the devil was she talking about?

"Antoinette," she breathed, her shoulders sagging in his grasp. "And Madeleine. I went to see them in town yesterday."

Flynn's stomach turned to a jagged chunk of ice. He longed to speak, but he knew he would say far too much if he did. He remained silent, waiting for Missy to say something, dreading what he might hear.

"What did you do afterward?"

"I meant to confront them," she explained, sounding sturdier. "Madeleine and Antoinette, that is. I meant to discover from them exactly what hold they had over you. But when I finally saw them, I found I didn't really want to know. And that it wasn't important to me after all. What was important was that I loved you, and that I would do—do anything to keep you. Even deceive you. I arranged for the wedding to be held here today because I was afraid of them, and of their power over you. I felt that if I waited until you were healed, it might be . . . too late."

Her last words died, and her head drooped like a wilting flower. Flynn, numb, slipped one hand into hers.

"Missy," he began, but he had nowhere to go, so he fell silent again.

"I accused you of deceiving me," she said after an empty moment, withdrawing her hand from his. "Yet I tricked you in the most unspeakable manner by marrying you under these circumstances. I can't ask your forgiveness, for I can't even forgive myself. But I am sorry, Flynn. Truly. Tomorrow I'll go to Rev. Whitmire and Sheriff Garlock and ask them both to draw up an annulment. That way, if you really want to, then you can . . ."

Her words choked off as if there were hands closing about her throat. *You can go to Madeleine* was what she was going to say; he had no doubt of it.

His hands were cold, and he realized it was because Missy was walking away from him.

Chapter Twenty-seven

If he laughed, the resulting pain in his ribs would be the least of his problems. Nevertheless, it was a struggle not to.

"You can't know how glad I am," he said as she reached the door, "to discover that my wife isn't above a little cunning, especially in the matter of keeping her man."

"I deserve every word of cruel sarcasm you can think of," she replied in a subdued voice. "Only I wish you wouldn't—"

"Sarcasm? Sar—Missy, come back here. Please."

"But I—"

"I can't make it across the room again; I'm too tired, and my side hurts like a son of a bitch. Come here."

She gave him a piteous, sidelong look that forced a gentle chuckle from his chest. The look became a scowl.

"No, don't," he pleaded, trying to temper his grin.

"God, I'll laugh, and I'll probably kill myself doing it. Do you know, I don't think I realized until just this minute that you love me? You really, truly love me?"

"Do you mean to say you would not think me capable of love unless I were also capable of—of—"

"Deceit?" he finished for her, his side stinging with his sigh of relief. "But that's just it, Missy, don't you see? You're not capable of it. Oh, you're quite capable of performing an act of chicanery or two, thank God, but as for keeping it to yourself, well, isn't your 'confession' to me here tonight proof enough for you of your honesty? And how could I help but be flattered that you'd go to such lengths, confronting what you saw as your competition—although believe me, Madeleine never fascinated me the way you do!—to keep me for yourself?"

The cloud over Missy's brow fled and a wan, hopeful smile took its place.

"Then—then you forgive me?"

"Come here, sweetheart."

Because she was not a fool, and because she loved him so deeply that she felt it all the way down to her toes, Missy went to him. She wanted to laugh. She wanted to cry. She wanted to beat her fists against his chest for his laughing at her. She wanted to kill him, but she didn't want to hurt him, and that paradox troubled her not at all, especially when he kissed her soundly.

"Now help me finish what you started," Flynn said in a breathless chuckle, guiding her hands to his trousers again. "If I'm going to die tonight, I intend to die a happy man."

Missy giggled.

"Never stop teasing me, Flynn," she commanded him, finding his lips with her own as she awkwardly undid his buttons. "I think I love that best about you."

"Who's teasing?"

Undressing for Flynn was as natural to Missy as if they'd been wed for half their lives. He relaxed against the piled pillows of her bed watching her, magnificent and utterly serene in his nakedness, except for one rebellious part of him that was not, thank heaven, in the least unperturbed. Normally fastidious about the care of her nicer garments, Missy allowed one layer after the next to fall to the floor, neglected. At last, wearing only her shift, she began to crawl into the bed.

"This, too," he whispered, plucking at the soft, wrinkled batiste with two fingers.

She blushed. "All right."

She pulled the filmy garment over her head and cast it aside, exposing herself to his heavy-lidded gaze.

"Sweet lord," he intoned as she eased beside him at last. "Melissa Judith, if you ever utter a contrary word about your figure in my hearing, I swear I'll strip you naked right then and there and make love to you on the floor, no matter who's watching! You're not cold, are you?"

"In this heat?" Missy was referring to the warmth of the room, but the deeper meaning of her remark occurred to her a bit late, and she felt herself blush again as Flynn's impish grin widened. He reached out with a gentle hand and cupped her breast, allowing his thumb to stroke the tender, erect nipple. She shivered with want.

"You're either cold or interested," he drawled, slowing his caress to a torturous tempo. "So I guess if it's not the former I can assume it to be the latter?"

"You can always assume I'm 'interested' in you, *Daniel* Flynn," she murmured, undulating at his touch, feeling like the cat that ate the canary and didn't get caught. He made a face that didn't suggest a hint of pain and his hand traveled down along her side.

"I never use that name, and the truth is I'd all but forgotten it, or I'd have told you before," he said, lean-

ing in to her until his chest was pressed full against her.
"God, you feel so good."

Indeed, Missy did feel good. Remarkable, in fact.
Flynn's nearness and the activity of his hand inspired a
host of sensations quite unlike anything she'd ever felt
before. She experienced a shimmer of terror as his fingers found the thatch of hair at the joining of her legs,
but it was a wondrous terror, brief and luminous, quickly
giving way to avid curiosity and . . . delight.

Missy lay very still, concentrating on the utterly for-
eign, utterly wonderful response in her loins to Flynn's
gentle but ardent strokes. She felt as if part of her had
been sleeping all of her life, and that Flynn Muldaur was
only now awakening it, introducing her to its presence
and the pleasures it offered. Her legs relaxed—indeed,
her entire body—and she found herself rubbing and
thrusting against his blessedly persistent touch, increasingly aware of a deeper need, a greater, secret joy awaiting her, awaiting them both.

"Take it," Flynn encouraged her with a hot whisper
in her ear. "It's for you, sweetheart, just for you. It's
good, isn't it?" She could not answer. "I want it to be
good, so good. . . . "

Missy did not know whether it was the gentle titilla-
tion of his hot breath in her ear, the heat of his long
body pressed against hers, or the unrelenting throb of
his fingers against her most private, womanly parts, but
in the long, lovely moment of completion it did not matter. It was probably all of them, and she prayed, on a
shuddering sigh, that she would have many, many more
chances to try to discover the secret of this unparalleled
phenomenon with Flynn.

The most shocking discovery of all, though, was to
realize that even that bliss was not enough.

"I want to make love to you," Flynn told her in a
gasp, lying flat on his back. "Oh, how I want to, but

these damned ribs—I can hardly breathe now.''

She would have had to be blind to miss the fact that Flynn was, indeed, fully prepared to enter her. She rolled onto her side and slid her bare leg over his until her thigh pressed lightly against his heat.

"Lie still," she murmured, kissing his shoulder. "We can do this. I think I know a way. . . . " Nature, she knew from her years of breeding and training horses, always found a way, especially when there was a will. Flynn's will was obvious. Her own, thanks to his skillful ministrations, was indomitable.

Flynn was not certain what Missy meant to do as she got to her knees on the sagging mattress, but when she straddled his loins as if she were about to settle into a saddle, her intention became clear. He didn't need to feel her moist heat inviting the tip of his manhood. He didn't need it, but oh, how he wanted it!

She positioned herself above him.

"Sweet . . ." he uttered.

Slowly, slowly she impaled herself on him.

". . . holy . . ."

She closed her eyes and bit her lip with a wince as he breached her barrier.

". . . blue bleeding . . ."

Her jaw relaxed with a high, wordless cry as she settled her loins against his, and he was fully inside her.

". . . Mother of God!"

That was a new one, and it surprised him. He figured he must have been saving it just for her. It reminded him, uncomfortably, of something else he'd been saving for her.

"Ohhh . . ."

She moved. Dear God, she moved, and it was nearly over before it began. He felt like a boy of 17 with his first woman, and it required every shred of concentration he possessed to hold himself in.

"Flynn, it's so . . . good," she rasped as she came down on him again, her amazement ringing like a sweet silver bell in his ear.

He was compelled to agree. It was good. Too good. He lay perfectly still and tried not to think of the glorious spectacle of womanhood above him and around him, drawing him in, taking him in a deliciously wanton manner. He found it impossible to think of anything else.

Her movement became harder. More urgent. It started a tiny, dull pain in his side, and he blessed that pain, concentrating only on that as Missy continued to torture other parts of him with her increasingly unrestrained want.

That worked for about a minute. His loins, too long unused, would not be denied their full measure of satisfaction, pain or no. He was about to lose his control in a most appallingly wonderful manner, and he was very close to not caring in the least for anything but his own gratification when he heard a low groan of bliss start in the depths of Missy's taut throat. Laying his hands on her smooth, white thighs, Flynn paid silent homage to a variety of saints as he broke the mighty chains of his restraint at last and spilled forth into her with a teeming rush.

If he'd doubted it in the past, this one act more than any other convinced him of the truth of it: Man must surely have been created in God's image, for man did, indeed, need to rely upon divine resources at certain occasions of his life.

If he was very, very lucky, that is. And if he meant to enjoy the sounds of a satisfied woman by his side.

Pride made him ask what sense told him was completely unnecessary.

"Are you all right, sweetheart?"

"Mmmm." The breathless quality of her reply persuaded him that she was more than all right, and it made that tiny pain in his side worth every twinge. Hell, it even made him think of courting danger and inviting the twinge again.

"Flynn?"

"What?" He kissed her brow.

"I love you."

Maybe he'd start attending church with Missy and Gideon on Sundays.

"I love you, too, sweetheart."

Missy fished for the light coverlet and pulled it up around them. She nestled closer to Flynn again, laying her head on his shoulder, careful not to disturb his side. She felt lithe and fluid and entirely transformed. She was Flynn's now, and he was hers. Neither of them was alone anymore. Perhaps that was the difference.

"Missy?"

"What?"

"I want to put a water closet in the house next year."

Missy giggled. "Whatever made you think of that just now? Ohh . . ."

"No, not that," he quipped with a single, snorting laugh. "I don't know. I guess I was thinking about the day you came back to the C-Bar-C. I was fixing the roof of the privy, and Bill Boland rode up to criticize my work. I told him I meant to put in a water closet next year, and he looked at me as if he doubted I'd be around until the first frost. He was an ornery son of a bitch, even then. But I guess I ought to be grateful to him."

"For breaking your ribs and rearranging your face?" She dared to tease him. It felt deliciously wicked.

He pulled a lock of her hair with a wry grimace. "No, for rearranging my head. I think he's more than a little responsible for me falling in love with you, you know."

"Oh? Perhaps we should invite him for supper sometime to thank him."

This time Flynn smacked her fanny beneath the covers and she let out a yelp.

"Not *that* grateful," he amended, rubbing his jaw with his free hand. "Unless you want to invite Madeleine, as well."

"Hmph. Now, *there's* a match."

"Mmm," he agreed. "A match made in hell."

Missy allowed herself to enjoy Flynn's nearness in the agreeable silence that followed while he traced lazy trails along her arm with his fingertips. She felt closer to him than she'd ever felt to another human being. Close enough to ask him one more question.

"What was—is—Madeleine, Flynn?" she ventured, fingering his collarbone. "Aside from being Antoinette's mother, what is her true position in your life?"

It was altogether possible, she knew, that Flynn would refuse to answer her. If he did, she would have to resign herself to continued ignorance, for she could not give him up. She prayed he wouldn't deny her, though, for she found that, having gotten so close to him at last, she needed to be privy to even his darkest secrets. And where Madeleine Deauville was concerned, she had the awful feeling that those secrets were dark indeed.

Flynn drew in a breath that caused his side to tighten, then let it out. His caress ceased, but he kept his hand on her arm.

"I wanted to tell you two days ago, but you didn't want to hear it."

There was no reproach in his voice, but Missy felt ashamed nevertheless.

"I was wrong," she admitted with a hard swallow. "I should have let you speak. I was—I just didn't have the heart to listen then. And now I don't have the heart not to. I—I gave it away, you see."

Flynn pressed his cheek against her forehead, and Missy knew she was forgiven. The knowledge made her feel lighter than one of Mrs. Fedderman's biscuits.

"Well, you already know Madeleine is Antoinette's mother." Flynn's voice was breathless, yet heavy. With the weight of past sins? she wondered.

"And Seamus is her father?" Missy had been certain of it before, but faced with the unvarnished truth, she was assailed by sudden dread.

"Yes, Seamus is her father. Although you may as well know that had our positions been reversed, it could just as easily have been the other way around. Madeleine has—had—a certain allure that we—both Seamus and I—found irresistible when we were younger. Looking back, I find that I can't explain it to myself except that she may have been the first woman to look at us and see men rather than money. Or at least I thought so when I was eighteen."

Years seemed to peel away from Flynn's baritone, leaving the energy of youth in his voice. Missy did not move.

"I know now, of course, that it was part of her training. And I learned the lesson far sooner than Seamus. Or he learned it and didn't care; I don't know which. I fell out of Madeleine's web after a short time, but Seamus remained despite my warnings, even after he began his political career."

Flynn shifted his pose but seemed to try to keep his back rigid. Missy suspected that he was still in pain.

"I saw Madeleine very little after I joined the Secret Service. I knew what she was, and I had an inkling about the depth and variety of illegal activities she and her mother were running out of their establishment, but I didn't want to be a party to her downfall, so I stayed away. I urged Seamus to do the same, but Seamus . . ." Flynn shook his head with a sad little laugh. "Seamus goes his own way. Always. And apparently he wanted to go straight to hell, because that's where it eventually led him.''

Missy allowed a long while to pass before she posed her next hushed question.

"The smuggling ring that Joshua Manners told me about: Seamus was involved with it?"

"Yes."

Another interminable silence.

"Were you?" She had to ask.

He sighed.

"No," he told her. "But it didn't matter. By the time I realized Seamus was, it was too late for me to head off the investigation. I doubt I even could have: I wasn't in charge. I was only a subordinate. I followed orders. I didn't make them. Seamus was a bright young politician with staggering debts behind him from his campaigning; that was how he justified himself. I was furious when I found out that he was embroiled with Madeleine in . . .

Missy waited. It was pain that made Flynn pause; she knew it. But she suspected it was a pain that had nothing to do with his injuries.

"They were white slavers, Missy." His whisper grated. "They entrapped young women and exported them like so much cattle to a life so horrible you can't even imagine it. It made me sick even before I knew Seamus was involved. Then afterward . . ."

Flynn dragged the back of his hand across his mouth as if to rid himself of some foul taste. Missy saw him blink hard as he stared at the ceiling. His throat bobbed.

"Seamus had a brilliant career ahead of him. I was the black sheep, of no consequence to anyone but myself. He cried. He said he was sorry, that he knew he had made an awful mistake. He pleaded with me to get him out of the mess with his reputation intact. Part of me wanted to see him burn, but . . . he's my brother,

Missy. We'd only ever had each other.''

Flynn cleared his throat and squeezed the bridge of his nose. Missy felt the swell of tears behind her eyes.

"It seemed logical that I should take the blame to shield him." He sounded detached, void of anything but coolheaded logic. "I deliberately blinded myself to the fact that Seamus didn't deserve my sacrifice. By the time I admitted it to myself, the deed was done. If I wanted to make any sense out of my life at all from that day on, I had no choice but to keep pouring my life's blood into the pretense and hope that Seamus would one day prove worthy of my sacrifices. After all, once I'd chosen to go against the law and my own ethics to save Seamus's reputation, I gave up my chance of a career with the Secret Service, or with any other reputable business.''

He asked no pity, offered no apology. He merely stated fact. Missy found herself respecting his sense of family loyalty even while deploring his misguided judgment. He had erred out of love, not out of meanness or avarice. She loved him all the more for it.

"And what now, Flynn?" she asked softly, stroking his lightly stubbled cheek. "Madeleine and Seamus came here to protect their interests. They apparently expect you to continue doing what you've done in the past: sending her money to keep her quiet about Antoinette and—and the other business. It will certainly ruin Seamus if it comes out. The C-Bar-C can make us a fine living, but you know it can't support Madeleine's excesses for very long.''

Flynn crooked one arm behind his head and stared at the ceiling.

"I can't worry about Seamus or Madeleine anymore," he said with a hardness that made Missy think he was mentally addressing at least one of the two people he mentioned. "My life means something to me now, and I've been carrying them and their ugliness on my back long enough. It's time for Seamus to grow up, to find his own way out of the mess he's made, if he can. I'm bowing out of his problems. And Madeleine's.''

Missy considered his declaration.

"Will they let you?"

"They won't have a choice."

It was a naive assumption, but Missy suspected Flynn knew that. She sensed his remark was more bluff than substance, like a fearful child whistling in the dark. Aware of a desire to take that child in her arms, or at least to light his way, she nestled her cheek against his shoulder.

"Whatever comes of it, I'm with you," she whispered, dreading what she might be promising him, knowing she would not have it otherwise. "You know that, don't you?"

His caress resumed, and she saw a grin tug at his mouth but not his eyes.

"I know, sweetheart. And I love you for it. But let's not talk of that tonight," he wound up in a gentle, cajoling tone, his fingers finding hers and locking with them. "I have other things on my mind."

Missy was not fooled by his honeyed attempt, as delicious as it was, to change the subject: he meant to shield her from whatever ugliness resulted with Madeleine, Antoinette, and Seamus; she felt it. It was going to take extra prudence on her part to watch him and make sure he attempted nothing on his own, particularly in his weakened state. It had taken her years to find the love he gave so freely; she was not about to allow Seamus or Madeleine or anyone, not even Flynn himself, however unwitting, to jeopardize it.

"You're hurt, remember?" Missy tried her best not to reveal her dark thoughts to him.

"Mmm." He nuzzled her throat. "I'm trying to forget. Help me?"

With his lips working their cunning magic, Missy quickly realized it would be difficult for her to remember as much as her own name. They were together, though alone. There was no need for her to fear Madeleine and Seamus or their treacherous designs for now. There was no need for her to fear anything tonight but the loss of her sense and her sanity as Flynn began to make love to her again in the sweet, quiet refuge of their room.

To Missy's surprise, Flynn rolled on top of her.

"Your ribs!" she cried, searching his intense features for signs of distress.

"My ribs be damned," he growled, taking her in with a long, heated look. "I want you, Mrs. Muldaur. Now be quiet and kiss me."

Missy tried very hard to be mindful of his injuries, but his teasing and coaxing was too much to bear and she let herself go with a primitive ecstasy she would never have guessed she possessed, rocking and thrusting, dancing supine to Flynn's sweet music. Voices joined the music as she climaxed, sweet, childlike voices crying out in joy, echoing her triumph.

Joy. Then wonder.

Then terror.

Flynn was very still above her. She knew he was listening, too. She opened her eyes and saw the room alight in a pale, flickering glow for which the small lamp on the nightstand alone could not be responsible.

She heard the voices again. They were real. They were outside, and they were not at all childlike.

There was a pounding on their door.

"Mr. Flynn!" It was Micah on the other side. "Miss! The stable's on fire! Come quick!"

Chapter Twenty-eight

A dry month. No wind, thank God, or the rest of the buildings, including the house, would be in danger as well. But there are animals in the stable, including the two remaining mares in foal, and they have to be gotten out before we can even begin to fight the blaze. And the pump is sluggish this time of year. . . .

All these thoughts ran through Missy's mind as fast as light through a prism as she sat up in bed, leaving no space for terror until the very last. *Lives will be lost before the end of this night. Human as well as animal.*

Flynn was on his feet, bent over like a willow tree. He fought his way into his clothing, swearing lustily. Missy, unable to move, watched him misbutton his pants.

"I'd tell you to stay here, but I know better." Hopping, he shot her a jaundiced look as he shoved his bare feet into his boots. "Just stay away from the stable; take care of the animals we bring out. Or pump water. Whatever you do, don't go near the fire!''

He cupped her face in his big, splayed hand and pressed a hard kiss to her mouth, as if that were the only thing he'd need to sustain him through the crisis. She heard him limping and cursing down the hallway before she even made it out of the bed.

She stumbled to her armoire on legs weak from lovemaking. She threw on a shirt, trousers, and her work shoes and was outside minutes after Flynn, but he had already blended into the fury of activity surrounding the very promising bonfire that was the C-Bar-C stable.

The crackle and hiss of the blaze nearly drowned out the hoarse, anxious shouts of the men and the clamor of the terrified horses inside. The hungry cries of the infant Jedediah Flynn Micah, left alone safe in the house, could be heard in between them, a plaintive, innocent obligato to the grotesque symphony. The baby's mother, with Mrs. Fedderman's energetic assistance, pumped water into the trough to fight the blaze, seemingly oblivious to her son's entreaty. Both women wore identical expressions of grim horror, their eyes fixed on the stable as they applied themselves to their task. The limitless energy of terror surged through Missy at the desperate panorama before her.

Missy did not remember being burned out of her home as an infant near the war's end, but the stories her father told her as a child had left a formidable impression. The South smelled of smoke, he'd told her many times, with a bleak, faraway look in his gray eyes. One could walk for miles and see nothing more than an inch or two of burnt stubble sticking up out of the ground, animal carcasses and the maddening, incessant buzzing of flies. There were no flies tonight—not even mosquitoes, thanks to the smoke—but the memory of her father's stories came to life before her on her own ranch, and she trembled with dread. How had this happened? What would happen next?

There was only a sliver of a moon, and the screen of black, acrid smoke rising from the blaze was already obscuring whatever insignificant light it might have offered. The only illumination to the hideous scene came from the burning stable itself, where the glow of flames flickered in the windows and in the seams of the walls. It was by that light that Missy saw the silhouettes of Flynn, Micah, Rich, and the others, darting like foolhardy moths to the bright flame when common sense should have warned them to stay away. The stench was sickening.

"Here!" Rich, coughing, black-faced from soot, emerged from the veil of smoke. He trotted up to Missy leading a horse by the bridle. When she took the lead from him, he yanked his kerchief from the restive animal's eyes and turned without pause, heading back toward the growing inferno. She wanted to urge him to be careful, but by the time the words came together in her brain, he was gone again into the fiery mouth of the stable.

Missy scanned the animal whose lead she held. It was Flynn's favorite mare, she realized, a dapple gray. The animal was unhurt, as far as Missy's cursory inspection could tell, but she was coughing and snorting from the smoke. Missy pulled the confused, terrified mare toward the far pen, where half a dozen other rescued horses milled nervously in the darkness.

Were her valued brood mares among them, Sheik's two remaining dams, Glory and Artemis? Surely Micah would have seen to them first, unless it was already too late. . . . Missy shuddered. She could not even consider that possibility. She surveyed the pen. It was too dark to see for sure, but she did not think the mares were present. Besides, if Glory were here, she was certain that

Gideon would be as well, tending the mare diligently.

Gideon!

Trying to stay her renewed panic, Missy counted heads in the chaos. Lucy and Mrs. Fedderman remained at the pump, twin machines. Jim was lugging buckets full of water to douse the smoking walls; Missy, surveying the flaming stable, could not help thinking his valiant efforts puny and hopeless. She counted one, two, three tall, lean silhouettes dark against the hot orange flames, either leading animals out or braving the intense heat to go back inside: Flynn, Micah, and Rich.

But no shorter, wiry scarecrow of animation that would be the boy who had adopted Glory as his own.

"Where's Gideon?" She asked the question of herself, but the whisper in her throat told her she'd voiced it.

"I haven't seen him," Lucy reported, her voice sharp with strain. "You don't think he . . ." She trailed off.

Dread filling her, Missy realized where the boy had gone.

She shoved Jim away from the trough.

"Missy, what the—"

She ignored the man's splintered protest and stepped into the water, boots and all. The disturbed surface reflected the bright flames shooting from the loft door, white-gold against the glimmering blackness.

She crouched down and soaked herself as if she were undergoing a hasty baptism. The water was cold. It brought her back to herself and it made her clothing cling to her like a cumbersome second skin. It would not protect her against the suffocating smoke, but at least it offered some defense against burns.

"Give me your kerchief, Jim! Quick!"

Gideon was in the stable. There was no time to lose. She snatched the proffered article away from the man and soaked that as well before she climbed out of the trough. Jim glanced at the stable, then back at her.

"You ain't goin' in there!" Jim declared, grabbing her arm. "Flynn told me not to let you, no matter wh—"

Missy wrenched her arm away from Jim's desperate, viselike hold and would have punched him besides but for her own realization that she couldn't spare even one able-bodied hand if she wanted to save every horse and human life possible.

"Gideon's missing," she told the distressed man tersely. "He's probably in there with Glory. I'm going after him." She broke away and ran toward the heat of the burning stable. "Tell Flynn you tried to stop me!" she shouted over her shoulder.

The inferno was worst near the front door, as if the fire nursed a calculated, malicious desire to prevent those inside from escaping. The heat pressed Missy even as she fought her way down the corridor, and her clothing steamed. The smell of smoke was thicker inside and it stung her eyes until she was blinded by tears.

This was a mistake. She wanted to turn back, to suck in a fresh draft of night air.

To live.

But how could she leave Gideon here in hell to be burned to death for the sake of Glory?

She gagged and bent over double. Another horse brushed by on her right, knocking her sideways. Whoever was leading it probably could not see her, she realized as she rolled on the floor. Through the smoke and brightness, she could scarcely see, herself.

How would she find her way out again?

She pressed her panic down and took a tentative breath; there was more air near the floor, but even so it was not totally free of the noxious, deadly smoke. She lay still for a moment swallowing a few breaths. She tried to get her bearings.

Glory and Artemis were stabled near the rear doors,

she knew. If she'd thought about it, she'd have gone around, but it was too late now. She was inside, and time was precious. She crawled along the dirt floor hoping not to be trampled, but there was less likelihood of that now: it sounded as if most of the horses were gone.

Why hadn't they gotten Glory and Artemis out?

Something was wrong, Missy realized, crawling her way back. First of all, the fire itself: how had it started? There had been no trace of heat lightning, and now that she was inside, she could see that the fire burned in patches rather than being centered in any one place. Besides making the blaze more difficult to fight, it was exceedingly odd. The hands, she knew, were careful to the point of obsession about smoking anywhere near the buildings, except, of course, for the bunkhouse. And Gideon hadn't been seen smoking in days.

Perhaps he'd been waiting for the right time, when everyone's attention was on other matters. Perhaps now he was trying to perform some desperate act of heroism beyond the means of a 12-year-old boy to try to atone for his carelessness.

Please, God, Missy prayed, dragging herself further along the dirt floor, below the cloud of smoke. I forgive him anything. Only please let him be all right!

Behind her, a burning beam crashed where her legs had been a moment earlier. That way out was blocked, she realized, scrambling further. No matter; she'd be closer to the back entrance once she gained Glory's stall. She could only hope it was not also obstructed. A burning stable was a fitting pyre for her, she guessed, but she had no intention of surrendering to death before her time.

The smoke and flames seemed less intense as she approached the rear stalls, as though the fire had not thought that avenue worth exploring yet. Encouraged, Missy got to her feet, keeping her head low. The sounds of men and horses had diminished. Now there was only the crackling and steady hiss of the flames.

"Gideon!"

She tried to shout, but her throat was scorched and she managed only a croak. Pointless in any event, she figured: if Gideon were in there, there was no question that he was with Glory. If he were not, she was merely wasting her strength.

Flynn will come in after you.

That realization prompted her into action: the longer she was in the burning building, the greater the possibility that Flynn would discover what she'd done, and that he would risk his life by following her. And the longer the stable burned, the greater the danger of the roof collapsing on all of them. At a stumbling run, she gained the next to last stall, the one where Glory was kept. The door was open. Missy looked inside.

It was dark, there being no open flame there yet, but she could see that Glory was gone. There was no sign of Gideon either. Tails of pale gray smoke rose from the piles of fresh hay on the floor, piles threaded with gleaming orange. The stall was about to become part of the conflagration, but apparently neither Gideon nor the mare were in any danger from it. Missy was unsure whether she was relieved, terrified, or annoyed. She would not feel completely easy, though, until she saw the boy for herself, safe outside.

Another timber crashed nearby as she turned to make her escape, sending a spray of sparks toward her. She brought her arm up to shield her eyes, but too late: the burn was quick and intense and she dropped to her knees, blinded, too overcome to cry out.

She tried to calm herself. A moment, she thought, rubbing her fists into her burning, tearing eyes. This will pass. It must. I will see again. She was only a few feet from the door, but there were flames licking at that exit already, she knew. Unless she could see, she might just as easily head the wrong way and crawl right back into the heart of the fire.

She took a breath, hoping to steady herself, but instead of the cleaner air she expected, she got a noseful of the unmistakable odor of kerosene.

As the import of this discovery sank in, she heard the door creak and felt a cool draft on her burning cheeks.

"Damn it!" It was Flynn's voice.

No, it wasn't.

Seamus?

But he had left, tipsy, after the wedding party had broken up! He did not sound tipsy now. He sounded angry. She opened her eyes. They protested with a stinging, tearing flood.

"Get in there, you four-legged bitch!"

It was Seamus, sure enough. He was black-faced and scowling, but not at Missy. Indeed, he seemed not even to realize that she was there. He was leading a skittish Glory not out of but into the stable, and the pregnant mare, despite being blindfolded, was protesting strenuously. Glory was the recipient of his harsh words and bizarre treatment. He applied a switch to her flank and she skittered into her stall to avoid it.

"Seamus, what—"

Missy broke off. There was a reason why Seamus Muldaur was there, leading Glory back into an inferno rather than out of it, and it was not to help them. Any of them.

"Damn it," she heard him mutter again.

Annoyance. She was inconveniencing him, she guessed. He meant for Glory to perish in the flames that he'd undoubtedly started, although it was anyone's guess as to why. If only she could see properly!

"Where's Gideon?" she demanded, sitting up. The boy could not be far with Glory nearby, she thought, feeling a spark of hope. Unless Seamus had already found him and done something unspeakable . . . She staggered to her feet, blotting her stinging eyes with her sleeve. "Where's Gideon, Seamus? I don't know why you've done this, but you've been found out. You'd best just give it up, before . . ."

She trailed off. She wished she could see the congressman's face, for it might help her know what he was thinking. His silence was not reassuring.

"He's in there," Flynn's brother said at last, and she made out a vague gesture toward Glory's smoking stall. "With the horse."

Missy squinted at him, but her eyes stung and watered anew and she saw him no more clearly than before.

"No, he isn't," she argued, trying to maintain a steady tone despite her dread. "I looked already."

His shrug was big enough for her to see. "Look again."

She gritted her teeth and tried to glare. "Damn it, Seamus, this is no time for games!"

"That's where I left him." He was indifferent. "Over there."

Beyond Glory was a pile of hay in a corner, not smoldering yet, thank heaven. Glory, restive and snorting in the smoke, seemed to be standing guard over it. Missy felt her way along the wall, dropped to her knees, and pushed the hay aside. Gideon was there, all right, in a heap like so much used bedding. He did not move when she prodded, then rolled him onto his back.

"Gideon!" She shook him. She wished she could see! As it was, all she had was her hands to try to determine how badly the boy was injured, or indeed if he was still alive. She pressed her ear to his chest. "Gideon!"

There was a heartbeat. The boy stirred. Missy's relief was tempered by urgency.

"Take Glory out of here," she ordered Seamus, hooking Gideon's limp right arm across her shoulder. "I'll get Gideon."

"I think not." Seamus's refusal was crisp.

"Damn it, Seamus, it's not up to you!" Missy lashed out fiercely. "Hurry, there isn't much time. I'm bringing Gideon out now, and you'd best get out of my way!"

Gideon moaned. The sound was nearly drowned out by Seamus's ugly, hollow laugh. "You can't even see which way to turn," he taunted her. "You'll never make it out of here without my help."

He was right, she realized with a shudder. Even if she could lift Gideon, and that seemed ever more unlikely, she doubted she could see to get them both out safely. "Then help us, damn it!"

"He don't mean for us to get out." Gideon coughed weakly and tried to sit up. "I found him in here spreadin' kerosene around when I came in to say good night to Glory. I tried to get the drop on him, but he was too quick for me."

His young voice was raw with regret. Just like the boy, she thought with a rush of tenderness: to take on a man's job and expect to prevail. She hugged him to her, brushing his lank hair with her fingers.

"I know. But never mind that now," Missy soothed, with a quick kiss on his brow, hoping to impart reassurance that she was far from feeling. "We have to get you out of here, and I can't see. My eyes . . . Can you stand?"

"I fell. I think my leg's broke. I—"

The rest of Gideon's reply was lost in the sound of the stall door slamming shut behind them.

"I didn't mean for either of you to die," Seamus, his voice a rasp, said on the other side of it. "But I can't let you live as witnesses. I spent quite a bit of money insuring this place against fire, and it doesn't figure into my plans to end my days in disgrace and ruin." Missy heard the bolt drop into place.

She and Gideon were locked in with Glory. There was the window, but it was high up and rather small. Gideon might have made it if he were unhurt, but he couldn't possibly get out with a broken leg. And she could not leave him behind, even if she could see to escape herself. She held her mounting panic in check by force of will alone.

"You're mad, or else you're a fool. How could you have insured the C-Bar-C?" she challenged Seamus. "Application for insurance has to be filed by the owners." She recited the words like a Bible lesson; she knew her business. Besides, she needed to keep his attention fixed on her, to play for time while she tried to think of a plan for escape. "An affidavit must be signed. Flynn and I never—"

A blade of acrid smoke stabbed deep in Missy's breast and a fit of coughing took her. Glory snorted and pawed the straw. Gideon's hands took hold of her shoulders as she sank down, seeking whatever remaining air might be found on the floor. To her left, a small flame sprouted from the straw. Gideon clumsily beat it out with his sleeve.

"Madeleine and I played a masquerade before we came here." Seamus's voice was muffled—by a kerchief, she guessed—but she could nevertheless hear the crowing note of pride in it. "On our way here, we posed as you and Flynn and we purchased the policy in Pierre, along with a rider on the brood mares. I wouldn't have used it at all, except that Flynn was so damned unreasonable about everything."

"You're lying," she pronounced, unable to conceal her disdain. "A selfish, amoral opportunist like yourself never has any compunction about his action. You sicken me." She coughed again and gained no relief.

"Really, I'm not the monster you make me out to be.

I have nothing personal against you, or Gideon, or even my brother, when it comes to it,'' Seamus argued genially. He sounded farther away; he was probably making for the rear door. "But Flynn made it clear to me the other day that this time it was him or me. And I damned well can't let it be me. I have too much to lose now: a wife, a position. Power. Money. Friends. Twelve years ago it was different.''

"What was different, Seamus?" A new voice cut through the thickening smoke like a diamond through glass. "Were you less greedy? Less selfish? Or was I merely more of a fool?''

Missy's heart found new hope. "Flynn!''

"Damn, Flynn, not you, too!" Seamus sounded disheartened. Missy prayed he would give up this madness at last. She hugged Gideon closer to her and breathed a quick prayer.

"Let her out of there, Seamus. Missy, are you all right? Is Gideon with you?''

Missy recognized Flynn's tone: he had not an ounce of charity left in him. Or more probably, given his weakened, injured state, not an ounce of strength. What if Seamus refused?

"I can't see," she called in answer. "And Gideon's leg is broken." There was no need to tell him that Glory was in there with them; no doubt he could see the top of her head, and surely he could hear the mare's nervous snorting and nickering.

"Let them out," Flynn ordered his brother again.

Gideon fidgeted in Missy's embrace as she held her breath waiting for Seamus's answer. "I got my pocket-knife here, Miss," he whispered. "If you help me, I can make it to the door and try to work the bolt myself.''

The street urchin Gideon, she was sure, was schooled in such tasks as opening locks designed to keep intruders out. If Flynn could distract Seamus long enough, they might be able to effect their own escape and Glory's, and assist Flynn in the process.

"Damn it, Flynn, why couldn't you have stayed outside?"

There was real anguish in Seamus's question. Missy supposed he had not counted on having to kill his brother, as well. She listened hard as she grabbed Gideon under each of his arms and dragged him across the stall. She felt maddeningly weak and clumsy, but soon Gideon was propped up by the door. She could see nothing but the dark shape of him against the ambient glow from the encroaching fire.

"Let them out, Seamus," Flynn repeated, sounding harder still. "I don't want to kill you, but by God I will if I have to."

Seamus responded with a small, doubtful laugh.

"You're all bluff, little brother," he said with gentle, chilling malice. "Look at you. You can scarcely stand from that beating you took the other day, yet you threaten me with death. Me, your only brother. How do you mean to accomplish the murder? With words and a hard look? I don't die so easily, you'll find."

"Look around you, Seamus." Flynn tried again. "This place is going to go any second, and if we don't suffocate first we'll all be burned to death." Missy prayed that Seamus could not hear the desperation she heard in Flynn's reasoning. "And for what? So Madeleine can buy another Worth gown? I thought you had more sense than that."

Missy heard the quiet scrape of Gideon's knife sliding about in the crack of the door.

"I have no intention of dying," the congressman replied softly.

"If you think I'm going to let you just walk out of here, you're dead wrong."

"Come on, Miss!" Gideon called her in an excited

whisper. "I've got it! Grab Glory's lead. Let's get out of here!"

How? Missy wondered, batting the air in an effort to locate Glory's dangling lead. She snagged it at last and crawled toward the shape that was Gideon, crouched in the corner by the door.

There was a crash against the outside of the stall door, followed by the sound of the latch dropping into place again. Gideon swore softly and pried his knife into the crevice again. The door rattled several times more; Missy knew the men were scuffling in the corridor.

"Hurry, Gid!" she urged. Seamus knew of Flynn's injuries; he would know where his opponent was weakest. Flynn had provided a distraction while Gideon worked the lock; now they had to provide Flynn with relief. Quickly.

The latch gave again. Missy shoved Glory's lead into Gideon's hand and leaned into the door with all her weight. It yielded with much greater ease than she expected and she stumbled to her knees as it got away from her. But it was open. There was no barrier between them and safety.

Except for their own infirmities.

Two shadows fell before her, grunting and rolling in the straw. Missy blinked and made out Flynn and his brother. Neither man was throwing any punches, she realized. It was likely Flynn could not, so he seemed to be trying to keep Seamus pinned so that he couldn't either. Desperate, Missy felt around for something to strike Seamus with.

"Go, Missy!" Flynn wheezed. "Take Gideon and— get out!"

The figures rolled again and Missy saw one more make a quick jab at the other's midsection. The ensuing groan was Flynn's. He lay still in the carpet of smoldering straw.

"Damn it, Flynn." Seamus was bitter as he got to his feet. "This is your fault, you know."

Missy knew he was addressing her, but whatever he had to say did not matter. She crawled to the immobile form on the floor that was Flynn and lifted his head to cradle it in her lap.

"Flynn," she murmured, patting his sooty, beard-roughened cheek. "Please wake up! Please!"

"Pray that he doesn't," she heard Seamus pant behind her. "The end'll be much easier for him, then."

Missy's head hurt. The smoke, she thought numbly, had finally poisoned her past endurance. She couldn't see Flynn; she could only feel his cheek and the weight of his head, unmoving, in her lap. She would not leave him now, even if she could. She could say something to Seamus, she realized through the growing darkness gathering in her brain. Curse him. But it no longer mattered to her. She drowsed, and she was in another stable, another time, a stable that was not on fire but rather was cold and dreary, a stable where she had first met Gideon and Flynn. . . .

"Glory!" Gideon's frantic voice reached her ears. "Hie! Hie!"

Now I'm going to feel the pain of a separated shoulder, Missy mused sleepily. And I'm going to fall to the dirty straw in my best dress.

But she was already on her knees. And her shoulder, she realized, dazed, did not hurt her in the least.

Chapter Twenty-nine

Another beam crashed to the ground somewhere near the heart of the stable and overhead the roof creaked. Flynn opened his eyes as if God himself had exhorted him to do so.

His side was on fire like the stable, but his two legs worked, he knew. He had to get them out of there.

"Missy," he croaked through parched lips. "Help me up. Missy!"

She was bowed over him. She shook her head weakly and coughed. "Flynn," she murmured. Her eyes opened, but they teared and seemed to focus on nothing. She squeezed them tightly shut again.

"Come on, sweetheart," he urged her. "Help me get up. The roof's about to give way."

That stirred her to action. Enduring more bayonet lances of pain, Flynn made it to his feet and helped Missy to hers, holding on to both of her hands.

"Gideon," she rasped. "And Glory."

Flynn looked. There was Gideon on the floor, holding the end of Glory's long lead. Seamus was on the floor, too, prone, as still as death. Flynn couldn't tell for certain, but it looked as if blood was issuing from his brother's left ear.

"Glory took care of him," Gideon reported, wearing a cold, ancient gleam in his young, dark eyes. "I know you told me never to sucker-punch nobody, but I don't guess we had a choice. Even so, I ain't sorry. Bastard broke my leg." Gideon sent a long glare at Seamus.

"I'm going to take Missy outside, Gid," Flynn said softly. "I'll be right back for you and Glory. Okay?"

The boy nodded, game as a trooper.

The stable looked even worse from the outside. The entire structure was aflame like a giant torch. It was a testament to the building's integrity, or more likely a miracle, that it was still standing. It couldn't last much longer, that was sure. Flynn led Missy a few yards away and made her sit down on the ground.

"Don't you budge," he warned her, hoping she meant to listen this time. "No matter what. I'm going back for the others."

Half trotting, half stumbling, he made for the doorway, making some rash bargains with the Almighty as he did so. Gideon was almost unconscious by the time he got to him; Seamus seemed not to have moved at all. Flynn wondered, detached, if he was dead. No time to speculate or even to check. Gritting his teeth, he hoisted Gideon across his shoulder. Damn, but the boy was a load! He might look skinny, but Flynn guessed it was all muscle and sinew.

"Glory," Gideon muttered.

Flynn realized the boy still had the mare's lead in his grip. Glory seemed strangely calm, as if she sensed that, despite their danger, she was going to be all right.

379

The burning roof groaned a warning.

"I think a few less biscuits with your breakfast, if you mean for me to do this again." Flynn tried to sound jovial, but Gideon didn't answer. "Come on, girl."

The mare came along as docilely as a pet, but Flynn could not pause to wonder at that miracle. It had more than a little to do with Gideon himself, he guessed. There was a bond between the boy and the mare; he'd known that, but he'd never seen it more clearly exhibited than right now in the midst of this unholy conflagration. She seemed to want to go with him, not to escape from the fire and smoke, but to make certain that Gideon came to no further harm.

Flynn set Gideon down by Missy, who was sitting up and staring blankly. The brilliance from the blaze made them both look like golden statues.

"Hold on to that lead, boy," Flynn advised, breathing hard. "I'm going back for Seamus."

"Flynn . . ." Missy's plea trailed off, and her chin dropped an inch.

"I'll be all right." He tried to sound reassuring. "I made a deal with God a little while ago."

As he turned, there was a loud cry of objection from the stable and, with a mighty, terrible roar, the entire roof collapsed inward, sending a column of sparks, smoke, and ash heavenward. God had exacted payment for his mercy. Flynn dropped to his knees, compelled by the sight. He said a brief, silent prayer for his brother's soul and could not help wondering if Seamus would have done the same for him.

"Flynn? Flynn, what's happened?" Missy's voice was charred.

"He's—it's too late." He scarcely breathed the words. His chest throbbed with a pain that had nothing whatever to do with the smoke he'd inhaled, or his injuries.

"Bleeding saints," Gideon, on the ground somewhere behind him, intoned reverently. "The whole thing just . . . went down. I never seen nothin' like it, Miss."

Neither had Flynn. A sob caught in his throat that was part regret, but mostly relief.

"I'm sorry, Flynn."

She was, he knew. He felt a rush of tenderness that was in no way painful swell his breast. She genuinely was. He wished he could be. Instead of answering her, he lay down beside her and looked up at the night sky. The light breeze was blowing the other way; there was little smoke from the burning stable to obscure the stars. He found her fingers and laced them with his.

"The stars are fine tonight," he told her.

"I—I can't see them." A simple statement. No hint of despair.

He drew her hand up to his parched, cracked lips and brushed a kiss across her knuckles.

"You will, Mrs. Muldaur." He knew it was true, just as he knew his love for her, and hers for him, was as steady and unfailing as those stars above their heads. "Oh, you will."

Missy's hand cupped his jaw, and she propped herself up until he could see not stars above him but her own sweet face, streaked with soot and tears.

"I believe you, Daniel Flynn Muldaur," she murmured, and her face drew nearer to his.

"Aw, you two oughtn't act all mushy like that in front of me," Gideon growled in the darkness, discomfited more, Flynn guessed, by their tender scene than by the broken leg that presently crippled the boy.

Missy, unheeding, tasted Flynn's mouth. He wanted to hold her to him forever.

"It's part of what it is to be a man," she said to Gideon, but her lips otherwise concentrated on Flynn. "And you couldn't learn the lesson from a better one."

Flynn knew better than to contradict her.

Part Five

Nihil
Desperandum

Epilogue

Missy drew the blanket more tightly about her shoulders and Flynn's. He was asleep beside her in the straw. He snored. He didn't believe her when she told him, so she'd stopped arguing with him and contended herself to nudge him whenever he did. Not in the ribs; they were still tender, she knew, and slow to recover from the repeated bruising they'd taken last summer.

The summer seemed so long ago.

There had been a time when Missy, blind, had wondered if she would ever see the beauty of a Dakota snowfall again, but the stark, crystalline splendor of this latest blizzard had long since been overshadowed by tragedy. The mare Artemis had labored to bring forth a dead foal late last night while the wind sang a requiem. The bereft dam now stood on the other side of the wall,

385

neighing mournfully. Nearly five months gone with child herself, Missy recognized and respected the sound of a mother in despair.

To make matters worse, Glory now travailed before them in the birthing stall, brave but fitful, having some difficulty Missy was loath to label.

It had been a pure miracle that Glory hadn't lost the foal in the aftermath of her terrible fright in the fire, Missy knew. That had been one cause for rejoicing amid the dark days that followed. Another, of course, had been the fact that no one save for Seamus had been lost in the blaze, not even a single horse.

Flynn's injuries had been exacerbated and he was still recovering. Missy's sight had been slow to return, but return it had, thank God. Gideon's slow and sadly incomplete recovery had been cause for great concern; the doctor was of the opinion that the boy would carry a limp with him for the rest of his days. Then there was the memorial service for Seamus, during which she and Flynn, both still badly injured themselves, had been obliged to lie, telling the world that he'd died trying to save them.

Except for finding Flynn, it had not been a good year. Missy laid her head against his breast and listened to his soft snore.

Finding Flynn, she realized, snuggling closer to him, made everything else bearable.

Glory neighed softly, twitched, then lay still again. Missy stayed where she was but scanned the mare sharply. If there was to be any change, she guessed, it would be rapid. She would have to take the foal. She had to be ready.

"Is she all right?"

Gideon sat up beside his horse. His blanket covered them both. His dark eyes were puffed and glassy; Missy doubted he'd slept either.

"I don't know, Gid." She sighed. Flynn's child kicked in her belly as if to mock her ignorance. "I'm afraid she may be bleeding inside."

Gideon frowned. "What's that mean?" he asked, stifling a yawn.

It means she might die.

Missy avoided his gaze, ransacking her weary brain for a more encouraging response to give Glory's devoted equerry. Just as she despaired of finding one, Flynn stirred beside her, fumbling for his pocket watch.

"Almost two." His baritone was gruff with sleep. "She's been at it for nearly three hours. Any change?"

Three hours was two hours too long. Artemis had foaled in 40 minutes.

"She needs our help." Missy started to rise.

"Oh, no, you don't." Flynn pulled her back to him with a gentle but firm hand. "I'm not about to risk you getting kicked, in your condition. You ought to know better than to think I would. Gid, go fetch Micah. Tell him it's time."

Missy could only watch as Flynn, Micah, and Gideon worked over the mare for what seemed an interminable time, yet was actually perhaps half an hour. At the end of it a big colt, as chocolate brown as Sheik himself, lay in the straw beside his mother as Gideon, enthralled, toweled him dry.

"Look at him, Miss!" Gideon was flushed with excitement and wide awake, despite the late hour and his lack of sleep. "Ain't he fine? Gol, he's a big'n, too, ain't he? And strong. Look how he wants to try and stand already!"

Missy was delighted by the colt, who looked utterly healthy in all respects, but one glance at Flynn's and Micah's grim faces tempered her joy. Flynn cast a hooded look her way.

"Something's not right," he reported tersely. "I'm going to check her again."

He slipped his fingers, then his hands and arms, into Glory's swollen birth passage, his gaze fixed on nothing, his lower lip pinched in his teeth.

"My God!"

"What?" Missy edged closer.

"Get away!" he ordered her sharply. "You saw her kick me a while ago! There's—you're not going to believe this, but there's another foal in here."

Twins! Gideon hooted with glee, but Micah, wiser, frowned. Missy did not know whether to be overjoyed or terrified, but she suspected the latter to be the more prudent sentiment. Twins were uncommon in horses, especially in thoroughbreds. Delivery was nearly always fatally stressful even on the most fit of mares, and Glory had labored excessively long already. If the twins went to term, usually one of them was born dead. Sometimes they both died shortly after birth. The colt looked robust, though; he even seemed to enjoy Gideon's rapturous attentions.

Missy gritted her teeth: she could tolerate another stillbirth if the one colt survived. If by some miracle of heaven Glory survived, it would make the night nearly perfect. She didn't dare hope for the healthy passage of the colt's younger sibling.

"It's coming!" Flynn's voice shook.

Missy's heart pounded, and she felt warm with excitement despite the chill in the stable.

Glory fishtailed, knocking Flynn sideways. He muttered an oath and righted himself. Gideon left the colt wrapped in his sheltering towel and scrambled over to Glory's head.

"Easy, girl," he intoned, stroking her sweating, steaming muzzle. "Flynn ain't gonna hurt you."

"Don't lie to her, Gideon," Flynn advised him half

humorously, positioning his hands once again. "Missy taught you better than that."

Gideon managed a grin, but Missy could see his heart wasn't in it. His eyes were too full of worry for his mare, even when he glanced over at the newborn colt. He talked to Glory all the while, and the mare settled down again, undoubtedly soothed by the familiar, beloved voice.

Flynn grunted; Missy guessed he'd gotten hold of the second foal's legs again.

"Hold her, Mi," he breathed. "This one isn't going to budge without a fight. Missy, maybe you'd best leave."

Missy caught Flynn's worried gaze. She knew he was remembering that awful summer night when she'd removed an aborted foal piece by piece. He was trying to spare her, and she loved him for it.

"I'm staying," she told him quietly, pressing her hand against the life within herself. "Whatever nature has to show me, I've seen. I'm staying for you and for Gid. And Glory."

She looked at Gideon and saw a flush of gratitude in his young face before pride made him look away from her. He sniffled, and she averted her gaze out of respect for his privacy.

Gently, inexorably, Flynn worked with Glory's next contraction to pull the foal's forelegs and head into the light. Missy held her breath. Gideon's voice quavered, but he did not interrupt his monologue to Glory.

"One more," Flynn muttered, sweat beading on his brow. "Come on. Just one more." He was talking to the horse or to God; Missy did not know which. In either case, one of them obliged and the foal, a small but perfect chestnut filly, popped out, entirely bathed in blood and fluid.

And she appeared to be alive.

389

With a cry, Missy crawled forward as Flynn gently placed the tiny foal before her in fresh straw. Micah produced a towel and, with one big, careful finger, cleared the animal's mouth. It didn't take but a few wipes to dry off this one, small as she was, but Missy did not like the amount of blood she saw. She looked up to question Flynn, but the bleak expression in his tired eyes stayed her inquiry.

"She's ruptured her uterus," he said under his breath with a wary glance at Gideon, who was still stroking and talking to his mare. "It . . ." He stopped. He shook his head, his eyes filled with unshed tears.

Missy's own eyes misted. She did not need for him to say more. Glory had fought bravely to bring her children, hers and Sheik's, into the world, and now she was going to rest. There was nothing to be done but wait.

But meanwhile the children needed looking after. Charged with a new mission, Missy found the will to get up.

"Go wash up Artemis, Micah," she told the foreman. "She has milk she doesn't know what to do with; I have two foals that do."

She never doubted that the grieving mare would foster Glory's foals. She could not afford to think it. The foals would die without that first milk, and Missy was damned if she would let that happen.

"What do you mean?" Gideon was indignant. "They're Glory's babies. Don't be giving them to Artemis! What'll Glory think?"

Glory will be dead before these two even make it to their feet, she wanted to tell him. I have to think of the foals.

"Get Rich to help you take them in to Artemis." She ignored Gideon and addressed Micah, who had gotten as far as the door of the stall on his first assignment.

390

"We've got to try to get them to bond with her. It's their best chance."

"*Missy!*"

Gideon was on his feet before her. How had she missed the fact that in the past few months he'd grown nearly as tall as she was, and that his voice was now more like a man's than a boy's? She was able to meet his gaze for only an instant.

"She can't do it, Gideon." She could not bring herself to tell him more than that.

Gideon grabbed her sleeve.

"But they're hers," he insisted, and the cry of a child emerged from the throat of a man. "You can't just—"

"I don't want to," she told him, taking hold of his shoulders because she knew he would wrench away from the hug she wanted to give him instead. "But I must. We have to think of the babies now, and what's best for them. Can you understand that?"

"But Glory . . . She's just tired out from everything," he argued, not moving from her grasp. "She's—she isn't going to—"

Glory gave a pained whinny and convulsed once again. Missy watched Flynn lay gentle hands on her. A fresh puddle of blood reddened the straw. When Missy met Gideon's gaze again, she started to tell him the awful truth, but found that she could only shake her head.

He must have read the answer in her expression, for he released her sleeve and left his mouth hanging open in shock.

"No," he intoned in disbelief, sinking to his knees. "She's not—Missy, she's not going to—"

Die. Missy heard the word, even though Gideon did not say it. She'd have done just about anything, she realized, feeling his pain even more than her own, to make it otherwise, but there it was. No longer able to stop herself, she pulled Gideon close and wept into his tousled hair.

His strong, wiry body went limp in the solace she offered for only the merest of seconds before she felt it stiffen again, and she was not surprised when the boy took two solid steps back from her.

Missy saw it then. She would have missed it if she had so much as blinked at Gideon, but she didn't, and she actually saw the shield go up before his shining, sable eyes, and his pronounced jaw set itself. She'd remember that night forever, she realized, watching Gideon go back to his tender care of the dying mare, silent but otherwise as nurturing as ever. A child was dying before her eyes, even as a mare was. Both were painful. Both were tragedies. But one tragedy resulted in a man; the other, two foals.

That was the thing about tragedies, she'd discovered. There was usually a blessing or two hiding in them somewhere, if one took the trouble to look. She prayed that Gideon would come to understand that himself one day.

Glory passed quietly. Flynn and Missy left Gideon alone with her when it was over.

"Been a long night," Flynn remarked with a sigh. "You all right?"

He looked haggard, washing the night's work from himself in a bucket outside the stall, but not so weary that he didn't have a fond look for her.

She nodded, warmed by his gaze, even in the cold stable. "Think I'll sleep late, though." She looked deep inside herself hoping to find a smile, but she only managed half of one.

"He'll be all right, Missy." Flynn put his hand on her arm.

"I know."

"And so will the foals."

"Let's have another look at them."

Flynn slipped his arm about her waist and she allowed him to lead her to the stall they'd readied for Glory and her new foal. It was Artemis in there, though, contentedly nursing Glory's two eager but mismatched foals, with Micah acting as arbitrator. Glory's tragedy had become Artemis's blessing. Missy smiled even as a tear eked its way from the corner of her eye. The foals would thrive. She was certain of it. And Gideon, when he'd mourned Glory enough, would foster the foals just as he had the mare.

"Sheik's legacy," she murmured, laying her head against Flynn's shoulder as she counted her own blessings.

SWEET CHANCE

CAROLE HOWEY

Bestselling Author Of *Sheik's Promise*

Paris Delany is out to make his fortune, and he figures cattle ranching is as good a way as any. But the former Texas Ranger hasn't even set foot in Chance, Wyoming, before his partner becomes smitten with the local schoolmarm. Determined to discourage the match, he enlists the help of a sharp-tongued widow—and finds himself her reluctant suitor.

Pretty, reserved, and thoroughly independent, Cressida Harding has loved and lost one husband, and that is enough for her. She doesn't need a man to stand up for her rights or protect her from harm, even if dumb luck has brought virile Paris Delany to her doorstep. But the longer he is in town, the more Cress finds herself savoring the joys of sweet chance.

_3733-5 $4.99 US/$5.99 CAN

Dorchester Publishing Co., Inc.
65 Commerce Road
Stamford, CT 06902

Please add $1.75 for shipping and handling for the first book and $.50 for each book thereafter. NY, NYC, PA and CT residents, please add appropriate sales tax. No cash, stamps, or C.O.D.s. All orders shipped within 6 weeks via postal service book rate. Canadian orders require $2.00 extra postage and must be paid in U.S. dollars through a U.S. banking facility.

Name _____

Address _____

City _____ State _____ Zip _____

I have enclosed $_____ in payment for the checked book(s).
Payment <u>must</u> accompany all orders.☐ Please send a free catalog.

Sheik's Promise

CAROLE HOWEY

Bestselling Author Of *Sweet Chance*

Allyn Cameron has never been accused of being a Southern belle. Whether running her own saloon or competing in the Rapids City steeplechase, the brazen beauty knows the thrill of victory and banks on winning. No man will take anything she possesses—not her business, not her horse, and especially not her virtue—without the fight of his life.

An expert on horseflesh and women, Joshua Manners desires only the best in both. Sent to buy Allyn's one-of-a-kind colt, he makes it his mission to tame the thoroughbred's owner. But his efforts to win Allyn for his personal stable fail miserably when she ropes, corrals, and brands him with her scorching passion.

_51938-0 $4.99 US/$5.99 CAN

Dorchester Publishing Co., Inc.
65 Commerce Road
Stamford, CT 06902

Please add $1.75 for shipping and handling for the first book and $.50 for each book thereafter. NY, NYC, PA and CT residents, please add appropriate sales tax. No cash, stamps, or C.O.D.s. All orders shipped within 6 weeks via postal service book rate. Canadian orders require $2.00 extra postage and must be paid in U.S. dollars through a U.S. banking facility.

Name _____

Address _____

City _____ State _____ Zip _____

I have enclosed $_____ in payment for the checked book(s).
Payment <u>must</u> accompany all orders.☐ Please send a free catalog.

Touched By Moonlight

CAROLE HOWEY

Bestselling Author Of *Sweet Chance*

Terence Gavilan can turn a sleepy little turn-of-the-century village into a booming seaside resort overnight. But the real passion of his life is searching for Emma Hunt, the mysterious and elusive creator of the tantalizing romances he admires. When he finds her, he plans to prove that real life can be so much more exciting than fiction.

To the proper folk of Braedon's Beach, Philipa Braedon is the prim daughter of their community's founding father. Yet secretly, she enjoys swimming naked in the ocean and writing steamy novels. Philipa has no intention of revealing her double life to anyone, especially not to a man as arrogant and overbearing as Terence Gavilan. But she doesn't count on being touched by moonlight and ending up happier than any of her heroines.

___3824-2 $5.50 US/$7.50 CAN

Dorchester Publishing Co., Inc.
65 Commerce Road
Stamford, CT 06902

Please add $1.75 for shipping and handling for the first book and $.50 for each book thereafter. NY, NYC, PA and CT residents, please add appropriate sales tax. No cash, stamps, or C.O.D.s. All orders shipped within 6 weeks via postal service book rate. Canadian orders require $2.00 extra postage and must be paid in U.S. dollars through a U.S. banking facility.

Name_____
Address_____
City _____ State_____Zip_____
I have enclosed $_____in payment for the checked book(s).
Payment <u>must</u> accompany all orders.☐ Please send a free catalog.

THE SAVAGE SERIES

CASSIE EDWARDS

Winner Of The *Romantic Times* Reviewers' Choice Award For Best Indian Series

Savage Secrets. Searching the wilds of the Wyoming Territory for her outlaw brother, Rebecca Veach is captured by the one man who fulfills her heart's desire. And although Blazing Eagle wants Becky from the moment he takes her captive, hidden memories of a long-ago tragedy tear him away from the golden-haired vixen. Strong-willed virgin and Cheyenne chieftain, Becky and Blazing Eagle share a passion that burns hotter than the prairie sun—until savage secrets from their past threaten to destroy them and the love they share.

_3823-4 $5.99 US/$7.99 CAN

Savage Pride. She is a fiery hellcat who can shoot like a man, a ravishing temptress with the courage to search the wilderness for her missing brother. But Malvina is only a woman with a woman's needs and desires. And from the moment the mighty Choctaw warrior Red Wing sweeps her up on his charging stallion, she is torn between family duty and heavenly pleasure.

_3732-7 $5.99 US/$6.99 CAN

Dorchester Publishing Co., Inc.
65 Commerce Road
Stamford, CT 06902

Please add $1.75 for shipping and handling for the first book and $.50 for each book thereafter. NY, NYC, PA and CT residents, please add appropriate sales tax. No cash, stamps, or C.O.D.s. All orders shipped within 6 weeks via postal service book rate. Canadian orders require $2.00 extra postage and must be paid in U.S. dollars through a U.S. banking facility.

Name _____
Address _____
City _____ State _____ Zip _____
I have enclosed $_____ in payment for the checked book(s).
Payment <u>must</u> accompany all orders.☐ Please send a free catalog.

Futuristic Romance

Nancy Cane

"Nancy Cane has proven herself a master of the genre!"
—*Rendezvous*

Starlight Child. From the moment Mara boards his starship, Deke Sage knows she is going to be trouble. He refuses to open himself, body and soul, to the raven-haired temptress until he realizes that without Mara's extrasensory powers he'll never defeat his enemies—or savor the sweet delight of her love.

__52019-2 $4.99 US/$5.99 CAN

Moonlight Rhapsody. Like the sirens of old, Ilyssa can cast a spell with her voice, but she will lose the power forever if she succumbs to a lover's touch. Forced to use her gift for merciless enemies, she will do anything to be free. Yet does she dare trust Lord Rolf Cam'brii to help her when his mere presence arouses her beyond reason and threatens to leave her defenseless?

__51987-9 $4.99 US/$5.99 CAN

Dorchester Publishing Co., Inc.
65 Commerce Road
Stamford, CT 06902

Please add $1.75 for shipping and handling for the first book and $.50 for each book thereafter. NY, NYC, PA and CT residents, please add appropriate sales tax. No cash, stamps, or C.O.D.s. All orders shipped within 6 weeks via postal service book rate. Canadian orders require $2.00 extra postage and must be paid in U.S. dollars through a U.S. banking facility.

Name_____

Address_____

City _____ State _____ Zip _____

I have enclosed $_____in payment for the checked book(s). Payment must accompany all orders.☐ Please send a free catalog.